FROSTBITE

THE HUNTER CHRONICLES
BOOK ONE

CLAIRE MARTA

FROSTBITE

ACKNOWLEDGEMENTS

I would like to thank Michelle my amazing editor for helping me make my dream of publishing come true. You truly are the best!

Tracy and Jamie thank you for your support, as you both joined me on the crazy ride to get your own books published. I love you guys and I am so happy to have you both as friends.

Thanks to Kate for knowledge as a seasoned author and encouragement.

Everyone in the Newbies group for all the positivity! Sending much love to you all.

Rachel and Michael, thank you for doing an amazing job on my book cover. Your talent shines through and I love it.

And last, Alessandro for his patience and support. I know I have been driving you crazy since deciding to get my work published.

CHAPTER 1

"JASMINE WHATEVER YOU DO, they can't know we work for Scotland Yard."

Twitch spoke in a low purr into her ear. So barely audible, she was pretty sure anyone who might be listening in on them would miss his words.

Jasmine swore low and long. She knew this could mean nothing good and it did not help her anxiety levels either. A sense of panic had already been gnawing at her gut for the last several hours. She was feeling pretty terrified, too.

They were huddled in a far corner, away from the door, their bodies inches apart. Jasmine glanced around the windowless, white-walled room again. A narrow bed was stuffed in one corner—the only piece furniture. A stark, bright light shone above their heads. A thick, metal door locked from the outside barred their way.

Their kidnappers had made sure there was nothing to use as a weapon. No way to get out. They were so screwed.

Jasmine turned back to her co-worker with apprehension. "What the fuck is going on, Twitch?"

He did not look well. Tall and slender, he was dressed all in black as usual, but his skin was unusually pale. The faded burn marks on his forehead and neck stood out more than normal. His mop of wild cinnamon curls was knotted around his shoulders.

Jasmine had the sudden urge to find a brush and work out the knots. Instead she curled her fingers into her palms. She doubted he would like her fussing over him. Twitch did not always like to be touched. She was actually surprised he stood so close.

So instead she sighed.

This was not how she had envisioned her Friday night going. Especially three days before Christmas.

One minute she had been driving the techno mage home from a celebration of a case well done. The next they had been rammed off the road.

The screech of brakes and rendering of metal was still blurred horrifically in her mind. Her fear had been almost blinding. There had been a brief moment she thought her pounding heart was going to explode from her chest. Her head still ached from where it had slammed into the steering wheel with force. The blow had been so hard she had seen stars. She was actually surprised she didn't have a concussion.

How they had survived the crash at all, she didn't know. It was a fucking miracle.

Being held at gunpoint when you were still dazed from a near-death experience was not fun. She was pretty sure shock had been swift to settle in. Even less fun when you were crammed inside a dark cargo container for hours on end.

Panic and nausea had been her constant companions. Jasmine hadn't had a clue where they were being taken, or by whom. The men who had grabbed them had been big and professional-looking. And they had never spoken a word.

Being an only child and with her parents both dead, there was no one to miss her absence.

Twitch had been sedated the whole journey, and had only been awake for ten minutes. Jasmine had spent the whole trip clinging to his unconscious form in darkness. Those hours, she had spent shaking and praying this was all one huge mistake.

So far this weekend sucked.

Jasmine winced when gentle fingers touched her forehead. She knew there was a huge, nasty bump there. It was throbbing and painful. She could have done with a painkiller, but doubted she could be given one by their jailers.

Waving away the concern on Twitch's face, she stared at him expectantly.

He hummed, his peridot green eyes wary. "Do you remember how Mark told you how we met?"

Mark was their boss. Detective Mark Cummings, head of their team in the SNC. It was a branch of Scotland Yard that dealt with supernatural cases. He was a fair man, but took no shit from his team members. The department had become public knowledge after vampires had announced their existence over a year ago. Literally overnight the world had been introduced to their existence, and suddenly they were everywhere.

There had not been as much worldwide shock as Jasmine had expected, though. Apparently the world's governments had known for centuries about their existence. No big shock there, really—not with everything else they kept quiet. And Jasmine knew now there was so much more.

She had only been on the team for two months, and so far her tasks had been run of the mill for a rookie. Well, as run of the mill as it could be when you were a sensitive.

Jasmine frowned. "Yes. He said you had gotten yourself into trouble with a supernatural black market. He saved you from some horrible people and you went to work for him."

That was all their boss had said. He was always tight-lipped about his team member's pasts, which was something Jasmine was grateful for. No one liked their secrets given out freely, Jasmine included.

An unhappy smile twisted the techno mage's lips. "These are those fuckers."

So Twitch's past had come back to bite him on the arse. Nice.

Her look turned disbelieving. "How can you be sure?"

Twitch ran a hand through his hair in agitation. When his fingers became entangled in a knot he huffed, "I recognised them when they rammed us off the road."

Jasmine swore again. This could not be fucking happening.

She watched for a moment as he roughly freed his fingers without yanking out his hair. The guy really needed a haircut.

"Can't you use some magic to get us out of here? Don't you have a gadget or something?" She glanced towards the closed door.

Twitch was a techno mage. He had the ability to fuse magic and technology. Normally he was found sitting in his lab, tables strewn with motherboards, computer chips, and a selection of musty, ancient tomes. Paranoid and a recluse, he barely left his lair. Last night had been the exception. It had been drinks down at the pub with his colleagues after they had solved a rash of body-snatching. At least she now knew why he didn't like to go out.

Twitch shook his head. "The room has wards to stop me using my magic and they stripped me of all my tech. I need a piece of technology for my magic to work anyway."

Jasmine swore for the fourth time.

All she had was the ability to sense supernaturals. Physically she could do nothing to get them out of there. Sometimes, only being a sensitive sucked.

She smoothed down the ruby red, satiny material of her dress with slightly shaking hands. It came to her knees, the bodice crisscrossing across her breasts. A long-sleeved, black, woollen cardigan covered her arms. Pretty, but not really practical. She had worn it especially for that evening's celebrations. If she had known she was going to get kidnapped, she would have stuck with jeans. Her feet were also killing her in black high heels. Why the hell hadn't she changed into her trainers in the car?

"Marcel Coupe isn't stupid," Twitch said. "He knows what I'm capable of and that's why he wants me." Twitch's lips flattened into a white line. "He's an arms dealer with big fucking plans."

Jasmine didn't like the sound of that. Not one bit. "What do you mean by plans?"

"You've seen what I can do with magic and technology," Twitch said and then sighed. "Imagine that in the wrong hands—weapons of mass destruction, Jazzy."

If her friend was right, they were in deep shit. The things the techno mage could do when he put his mind to it was amazing. And more than a little scary.

The only upside to this situation was that their boss, Mark, would notice their absence quickly. Twitch was the team's surveillance guy. His purr was like the voice of an angel, whispering in your ear when you had an earpiece in. The silence would start alarm bells ringing. Would they be able to trace them though? That was the problem. Jasmine had no clue where they were.

Twitch's gaze skimmed over her for a moment. "I don't suppose you're still wearing your . . ."

Before he could finish the sentence the door was thrust open.

Two goons stood in the doorway. Both men were walls of muscle with big, beefy arms. Their glares were meant to intimidate. And they did.

Jasmine stared at them nervously. It looked likely they were finally about to find out exactly what this Marcel character wanted, but suddenly she was not sure she really wanted to know.

Gesturing towards them, one guard said something curt in what sounded like French. Were they somewhere in France?

"Stay close and let me do the talking," Twitch purred in her ear as he passed her by.

Biting her lip, she released one long, tense sigh. Unease uncoiled in her stomach. Why did she have a sudden sinking feeling this was all going to go terribly wrong?

Technically, Twitch was in charge, as he had been on the team longer. She knew Mark would want her to follow what the mage said. It looked like she would have to go along with it. Eyes on Twitch's back, she followed him out silently.

The two guards flanked them as they were directed along a sterile-looking corridor. The walls were white, no pictures or paintings hung on them. Everything just seemed so bare and stark. It was like it had been stripped of anything the prisoners might have found useful. Anything the techno mage might have found useful. This arms dealer really knew what he was dealing with by the look of it. He knew Twitch.

Twitch's eyes roamed the area. They settled on doors for a second, as if he was taking a mental inventory. Was he looking for a way out, she wondered.

They reached the end of the hallway and one of the guards pushed open a door. With a sharp gesture of his hand he ordered them inside. They didn't bother to argue.

This room was luxurious with two white leather sofas. A red carpet covered the floor. Three half-empty wine glasses sat on a low coffee table with two trays of what looked like finger foods that lay untouched. It had more life to it than anywhere else she had seen so far.

Glancing towards the dark panoramic view from the large window, she caught sight of the glittering lights of a city. So they were in France, possibly in a major city. At least that got them somewhere.

"Ah Twitch, good of you to finally join us."

Jerking her eyes down, she regarded the three men sprawled on the sofas. The smug tone had come from a little fat man. His face reminded her of a toad. It was round and spotty with a self-satisfied expression. His beady eyes twinkled with amusement.

This had to be Marcel Coupe, the French arms dealer that Twitch had mentioned. Jasmine would not have called him threatening-looking. She knew, though, looks could be deceiving.

When her senses began to tingle, she knew they were in so much more trouble. The supernatural kind.

CHAPTER 2

ERIC RAN HIS GAZE OVER the male as he entered the room. He was tall and thin, the set of his youthful jaw defiant. His nearly lime green eyes glittered with hostility through a tangle of long, reddish brown curls.

So this was the techno mage, the mind behind some of the most devastating pieces of magical tech that had been on the black market over a year ago. The one his prey had hunted for over a year now. This was the Frenchman's obsession.

Marcel, it seemed, would have his hands full with this one. It was obvious by the male's body language he was not happy. Perhaps he would not be so eager to help the arms dealer after all.

This would make Eric's job a lot easier. He suppressed a pleased smile. It would mean one less problem to take care of.

His eyes moved to the female who had also entered the room. Her lovely jade green eyes glimmered with anger. Her heartbeat was thumping rapidly in his ears. It betrayed her fear. She had a painful-looking bruised bump on her forehead. The wounded flesh was red and angry, the blood already dried.

Who was she? The mage's sister? Girlfriend?

She was a little thing, short, no more than five feet at a guess.

Her coppery red hair was cut in a bob-like style around her slim face. Rather than make her look boyish, it was feminine and soft. The length of her neck was bared to his eyes and a tempting sight.

Eric felt his fangs begin to ache in his gums. He could well imagine sinking them into the supple peachy flesh. His eyes roved over her silken clad form. She was slender, bordering on slim. Limbs long and lean, he suddenly had an image of them wrapped around him, as he thrust himself in and out of her welcoming body.

His cock hardened instantly.

Shock hit him hard. He never got distracted when he was working. Never felt desire for anyone attached to his targets. Never allowed himself to feel anything.

It was his rule.

But it had also been a long time since he had felt such desires towards a female. He had long grown bored with meaningless hook-ups just to satisfy an itch. What he was feeling right now, though, was no itch. Want hammered through him almost violently. He felt a hunger he had never felt before.

His eyes skimmed lower to her legs. He envisioned those high heels digging into his buttocks, urging him on. A little hum of excitement vibrated in his throat.

At his age, it was always a surprise when something stirred him anew. But this was not the time for such things.

Eric kept his expression cold. He could not afford to become distracted now. The girl would have to wait.

A sense of power emanated off one of the men on the sofa. Jasmine could feel it pressing against her, tingling over her flesh. He felt dangerous. Her overactive sixth sense was ringing like church bells in her head in warning.

Darting nervously over each male, Jasmine's green eyes clashed with a pair of ice blue ones. Fixed on them like a deer in headlights, she could not look away.

They were chilling, like shards of newly formed ice. Yet they were breathtakingly beautiful—in a lethal kind of way. A shiver ran through her, as the eyes examined her slowly from head to toe. Even though the room was a comfortable temperature, goose bumps rose over her skin. Jasmine tried to remember how to breathe.

The eyes crinkled at the edges in a smile, the coldness in them thawing the more she watched. Their growing warmth sent a zing of desire down her spine. A strange kind of heat began to pool low in her abdomen.

Abruptly freed, Jasmine dropped her gaze to the red-carpeted floor. She stared at it blindly for a moment.

What the fuck had just happened? Confusion ricocheted through her.

He was not human. That was for sure. What was he?

So far, she had meet werewolves, witches, mages, and even trolls. All of them had their own unique signature to her senses. This male was something new to her, whatever he was.

An air of authority and power clung to him. The word "alpha" screamed somewhere in the back of her mind. That made him more than dangerous. It made him deadly.

Jasmine edged closer to Twitch. She doubted her friend had picked up on the creature in the room. Her senses seemed to be more acute, sharper, than her co-workers'.

"You promised us weapons, *mon ami*," the fat man said. "And we intend to make sure you fulfil this."

He dabbed at his sweaty, bald head with a silk, white handkerchief. Perspiration kept springing up, which made Jasmine wonder if he was nervous. She guessed she would be too with an alpha creature sitting so close. It was downright nerve-racking.

Twitch straightened up beside her, catching her off-guard. "I didn't promise you anything. I'm out of that business now, Marcel. I can't help you." His voice was low, but firm.

She glanced sideways in astonishment. Generally he was a very shy introvert. She had never seen him with steel in his voice. He actually sounded quite determined.

The fat man's laugh was more like a school girl's giggle. "Oh, you will."

Jasmine's eyes moved back over the three men. The fat man felt human, like his young, male, blond companion. She barely spared them a look, instead returning her attention to the non-human, who sat cross-legged on the sofa. Both his arms were relaxed along the back. His body language oozed confidence and dominance.

Jasmine examined him covertly. Maybe she could figure out what they were dealing with. She knew she had to be careful though.

Broad-shouldered, he looked like he was all hard muscle beneath his expensive, grey suit. A lean waist and hips tapered down to long, muscular legs.

He had well-defined cheekbones, an aquiline nose. His short, black, tousled hair was swept back from his forehead highlighting a devastatingly cold, handsome face, which betrayed little emotion.

His eyes were a bright cerulean blue. Their spellbinding intensity stole the breath from her lungs when she found herself caught within them. They seemed to look deep inside, right to her very soul. Dizziness swept through her. Tearing her gaze from his face, she looked away.

A smile had curved his sexy mouth. He had been aware of her scrutiny.

Jasmine felt a flutter of unexpected excitement in her stomach. She resisted the urge to bite her lip. His eyes were still on her. She could feel them sliding over her almost like a heated, physical caress.

They were being held prisoner and her body had decided to respond to the nearness of a good-looking guy. She never responded to men. Not even ones that looked this hot.

Giving herself a mental shake, she tried to get a grip of her traitorous body. This guy was a fucking baddie. Plenty of monsters—human or not—had pretty faces. She knew that from experience.

Twitch's voice snapped her from her thoughts.

"No, I mean it, Marcel," he said with anger now in his voice. "I'm done with the black market."

The fat man looked amused. His pudgy face squished up in an unattractive grin. "Oh, Twitch," he said and let out an exaggerated sigh. "Now we are going to have to punish your girlfriend for your disobedience."

Jasmine took a second to realise he meant her. Eyes widening, she stared at the arms dealer. Then she blinked in confusion, not sure she had heard him right.

Punish her? What the fuck did he mean by that? For one thing, she wasn't his girlfriend. And for another, she and pain really did not get on well.

Twitch's eyes expanded in alarm. Arm snaking out, he pulled her protectively against his side. Jasmine made a little "oomph" from the force. His tall form trembled slightly against her.

"You can't punish her," Twitch said, his voice a shaky whisper. The fingers of the arm around her shoulders clenched the material of her cardigan. He was holding her so tightly, it was almost painful.

Jasmine was not sure how he was going to get her out of this, but she trusted him so she kept her mouth shut.

"We need you in one piece," the fat man said, his white teeth flashing like a shark's. "I'm sure Pierre will know just how to treat her." His beady eyes strayed to the door.

Jasmine turned fearful eyes on the brawny man who had showed them inside.

The massive guard grinned. He rubbed one of his fists with his other hand. She had a feeling he wanted her to meet them up close and personal. It was something she would rather avoid.

He was packed with hard muscles. Obviously he spent most of his time in the gym, when he wasn't threatening people for his boss. His nose was bent like it had once been broken. His brown eyes, boring a hole into her, were hard and uncaring.

Pierre would hurt her. She could see it in the glint of his eyes. He would also take pleasure in inflicting the pain.

Jasmine swallowed hard. All the self-defence training she had learnt fled from her head. Her heart rate increased almost painfully in her chest.

"Perhaps you will allow me the pleasure." The voice was a deep baritone. It held an English accent, upper-class and cultured.

Jasmine could feel the subtle pulse of power laced in the words. They fizzed on the tip of her tongue, like bubbles from prosecco.

Suddenly with a sense of dread she knew what they faced. Only a vampire could wield the ability of persuasion so masterfully. Those were the only creatures she had heard of that possessed that gift. Not all vampires—but enough of them.

The vampire's eyes were chilling now. They were riveted on her with such intensity that she became a ball of nerves. Did he now want to hurt her, too?

Only a few minutes ago, his look had sent heat singing through her body. It was like he had flipped a switch. He had gone from sexual interest to a chilling remoteness in a matter of seconds.

"But of course, Monsieur Jeger," their host said and with a raised eyebrow, glanced at the vampire. "You may deal with the girl."

Disappointment shadowed Pierre's face. Jasmine was suddenly thankful he could not get his hands on her. She didn't want to be his punching bag. Then again, she wasn't sure she wanted to find out what the vampire had in store for her either.

She understood, though, that they wanted to make an example of her. Something to get Twitch's cooperation, something he would not forget. That just did not bode well for her.

The vampire rose from the sofa and towered over her.

Jasmine had to tilt her head up just to meet his gaze. He was at least six feet tall. His presence was menacing and she had never felt so small in her life. She knew she was a shorty, but no one had ever made her feel this tiny.

Alarm constricted her chest. Those eyes were cold and unfriendly. These were the eyes of a killer. A monster.

Oh crap, what the fuck was she going to do?

Jasmine pressed herself fearfully into Twitch's side. His arm squeezed her tighter. She wasn't sure how much longer she could keep quiet. They were, after all, threatening her well-being.

Suddenly she wished she had not been the one to offer Twitch a ride home. One of her seasoned team-mates would have coped with his situation far better than she was capable of. They would have known what to do.

"No, don't hurt her."

Jasmine's eyes shot up at her friend's words. What the fuck was he doing? He could not give them what they wanted. They both knew that.

"You agree to my terms?" Marcel asked, his eyebrows inching up.

The self-assurance on his face made her feel sick. The arms dealer was so sure he had Twitch right where he wanted him.

With a frustrated sigh, the techno mage nodded. Miserable green eyes met hers.

He was agreeing to protect her. Jasmine knew she could not let him do it. Creating weapons that could take innocent lives would destroy Twitch. She could not let herself be used as his vulnerability. Not even to save herself.

Taking a shaky breath, she swallowed down her fear.

"No, don't do it, Twitch."

His eyes flickered in confusion for a moment at her whisper. "Jasmine."

Jasmine shook her head, eyes pleading. "No, no. You can't do this even to save me. It's wrong and we both know it. We can't trust them."

It wouldn't matter what happened to her. Not if she was saving the lives of others. Not if she was stopping her friend from making a terrible mistake—a mistake he might never recover from.

Marcel probably planned to kill her anyway once he had what he wanted. Why would he keep her alive? If she was going to die, she would rather go out knowing she had done so heroically.

A hand curled firmly round her bicep. A little zing of electricity shot up her arms. It didn't hurt—more of a strange little sensation. Jasmine gasped.

Raising her head, she caught a ghost of a smile on the vampire's sensual lips. With a tug he wrenched her from Twitch's protective embrace. It wasn't painful but a show of force.

Struggling, she found her back pressed against a hard-muscled front. A pleasurable heat shot through her from the contact. Her heart was racing in her chest with fear and a disturbing sense of excitement.

"Get the fuck off me, arsehole," she snarled in shock.

"It sounds to me like this little girl needs a lesson in manners." The vampire's deep voice washed unsettlingly over her, making her shiver. Apprehension tightened her chest.

The fat man's grin turned into a leer. "I do believe you are right."

Twitch lunged to grab hold of her again, but Pierre stopped him. A swift punch to the stomach and the mage folded like a deck of cards to the floor with a pained grunt. On his hands and knees on the carpet, he gasped for breath. It looked like the guard had winded him badly.

"Leave her alone arsehole. I said I would help you." His voice was panicked when he lifted his head. Discomfort was etched across his face, as he held the place he had been hit.

"We need you to take us seriously, Twitch," the fat man said as he dabbed at his head again. "Once this is done, you will be more agreeable."

Jasmine found herself pressed harder against the male. It made her all too aware of the growing erection that was pressed against her bottom.

"Get off me," she hissed, struggling desperately to break free.

The vampire laughed. The grip on her arm was now bruising as he dragged her fighting from the room.

CHAPTER 3

STRUGGLING TO BREAK FREE, Jasmine tried to dig her heels into the floor to no avail. Nothing worked. No one was around to help her, no one to intervene, although she doubted anyone would.

Down the corridor he manoeuvred her through an open door.

Jasmine's eyes took in the sight of another sitting room, this one with armchairs around an antique table and empty of occupants.

As he yanked her arm, she squirmed, trying to loosen his hold. "I said get the fuck off me," she said through gritted teeth.

She was frightened but did not want to show it. For all she knew, he was probably one of those sick bastards who got off on other people's fear.

The hand on her bicep dropped away.

Eyes wary, she watched as he closed the door behind them with a click. A strangely ominous sound.

What would he do now? Beat her? Drink her blood? Drain her dry? She knew it was meant to send a message to Twitch. But how much of a message would it be? Her mouth went dry. Suddenly she did not feel so brave.

Leaning back against the wood, he surveyed slowly. Starting with her feet, his perusal was slow and through, travelling upwards over every inch of her until he reached her face.

The intensity of his dark, hungry look burned her to the core. Every part of her prickled with awareness at the touch of his gaze. She found it both disturbing and arousing.

Jasmine knew she was blushing from his inspection. She could feel the warmth in her cheeks. Slowly, she backed away.

She knew that kind of look. What he wanted, though, she would not willingly give. Not without a fight. He was physically stronger than her, but she had determination on her side.

"It's in your best interests to be nice to me, Kitten." His expression was amused, and his blue cerulean gaze again warmed. Gone was the coldness she had seen before. Gone was the look of a killer and a monster.

That voice of his curled pleasurably down her spine. She could barely breathe and let out a soft moan as she finally exhaled. What the hell was happening to her? She never reacted to men, at least not since her ex, Dan. How could the sound of this vamp's voice excite her so much?

"Fuck you, bloodsucker," she said in a shaky mutter. She made sure to keep a good distance between them.

Surprise flared for a millisecond in his eyes. It was snuffed out just as quickly.

"And how is it, precisely, that you know what I am?" His voice was a low menacing sound now. Any warmth in his features was wiped away at her words.

The frosty chill was back in his beautiful eyes, and though there was no hint of fangs when he spoke, Jasmine knew they were there in his mouth ready to descend.

She swallowed hard.

She realised maybe she should not have let that slip. Fear raced through her anew. He could probably snap her like a twig if he wanted to. Vampires were notoriously strong and fast.

"Stay away from me," Jasmine said as she backed up further. Eyes wild, she searched for a weapon, but there was nothing in sight. If she could break off a chair leg, maybe she could use it as a stake. How she would achieve this, though, she didn't know.

A cold gaze fastened on her. Dark and dangerous, he stalked her across the room. Yet even as scared as she was, she also felt a delicious quiver of desire deep inside. A feeling she could not understand in this situation.

She bumped into an armchair and slid it between them. She knew it was not much of a barrier, but it made her feel a little safer. It was better than nothing.

"You will enlighten me now, girl," Eric said, his voice low and stern.

While trying to steady her breathing and avoid hyperventilating, she suddenly found herself rooted to the spot. Tendrils of power were swirling around her. They kissed her flesh like a winter's breeze, frigid and bitter.

Before she could blink he was before her—so close she could smell the scent of snow and pine trees. It filled all her senses, heady and bewitching. As he leaned down, his breath whispered against her face. Jasmine shivered.

Those chilling eyes, unblinking and intense, bore into hers. They were so mesmerizing she was unable to look away. All she could do was stare back, helplessly trapped.

Jasmine's heart had gone into overdrive, thudding in her ears and accompanying the sound of her racing blood.

Her tongue poked out to lick her suddenly dry lips. Eric tracked the slight movement.

"I sense things some times," she admitted in a near whisper. "I guessed you were a vampire, as I've not met one before."

He stared at her for a moment longer, seemingly considering her words. Tension ebbed from his shoulders. The bite of his frosty power began to fade. Long, thick eyelashes lowered to hide the expression in his eyes. He was standing so close she could feel the heat radiating from his big body. Strangely, the sensation began to melt her fear away. It warmed her, pushing out the cold that had enfolded her from the lash of his vampiric powers.

Her heartbeat began to slow.

Why, she wondered, had he been upset that she knew what he was? Surely his friend Marcel knew he was a vamp? Or maybe it was a secret? Was he hiding this fact?

Before she could think on it any more, Jasmine found herself pressed back against a wall. Her soft breasts were crushed against his hard chest. The length of the vampire was pinned to her front. A gasp escaped from her lips. What the hell was he doing?

"D-don't t-touch me," she murmured.

Jasmine tensed up and tried to squirm away, but he had her trapped. Her arms bound to her sides by his. The movement, though, had made her very aware of the unfamiliar, pleasurable weight of his male body.

"It is not advisable to tease me," Eric said into her ear. His breath warmed her cheek.

Inching forwards, he rested his cheek to hers. It was a strange gesture—unexpected, intimate.

A thunderbolt of pleasure struck through her. Her nipples abruptly hardened while moisture flooded her lacy panties.

Jasmine was stunned at how fast she had gone from fear to full arousal. Her body, which had felt nothing for so long, was now betraying her. How could this be happening?

The vampire inhaled deeply. It was a very animalistic act, as if he were scenting her.

"I know your boyfriend works for Scotland Yard." The words were a husky whisper against her ear. "I would recommend he obeys Marcel's commands if he does not want to get you killed."

Jasmine squeaked when her earlobe was sucked into a hot mouth. He suckled on it gently before releasing it with a little tug. The tip of his tongue then delicately traced the shell of her ear.

"How do you know that?" Her voice was breathy. She wasn't sure what was happening to her, but she had no control over it.

The vampire's hands began to roam over her satin-covered hips. The caresses caused a flood of alien sensations between her legs. Jasmine drew in a sharp breath.

"I know many things, Kitten." He began to nibble gently on her neck. "Things others do not."

Her insides clenched with pleasure. Biting her lip, she tried to focus on what he had said. Her mind, though, was falling into an enjoyable, vampire-induced haze. She fought the urge to tilt her head to give him better access. This vamp was a bad guy. She had to remember that. It was fucking hard, though, when every little touch was arousing her beyond belief.

She had never been so turned on in her life. Ever.

Her dress was being inched higher by big, warm palms brushing her upper thighs.

Jasmine tried to stifle another moan. It felt way too good. She could feel herself getting even wetter by the second. No one had touched her like this before. Her body was throbbing with an anticipation she couldn't understand. Her hands, now free, moved up to his chest. Clenching the material of his suit jacket, she held on tight. What would it feel like skin to skin?

She bit her lip at the wayward thought. A slither of common sense though wiggled to the forefront of her mind. Just like that, it doused the blinding desire that had swept over her.

What the fuck was she doing? Pushing against his pecs to free herself, she found he was immovable.

A deep chuckle vibrated against her neck. "Do not fight me, Jasmine." He said her name slowly and deeply, as if savouring it in his mouth and letting it linger on the tip of his tongue.

Jasmine felt herself melt against him, but her mind hung onto clarity.

If she fought back would be hurt her? Did she want to fight back? The question popped into her mind before she could stop it.

Then reality slapped her in the face. He was going to want sex. He would never just settle for touching. Just like that her body went cold.

She could feel the sizeable bulge of his erection pressed against her stomach. He was so wrapped up in wanting to touch her. His hands seemed to be everywhere at once. The vamp hadn't noticed how tense she had become.

For her part, bad memories were scratching at the back of her skull. Other hands that had once touched her, held her down, hurt her. Jasmine shoved them down. Having a panic attack now was not an option. She had to keep thinking straight.

Maybe she could somehow work this to her advantage, she thought. There had to be a way to get Twitch and herself out of there. She would not have sex with the vampire, whatever he thought otherwise.

Letting her body relax, she rubbed herself against him. She didn't have a clue what she was doing, but this kind of thing seemed to work in films.

As he drew his head back to look at her, Jasmine gave him a tempting smile. Her body practically hummed from his attention again. She could play along for now. This was just a bit of foreplay. They would not be heading for the main event. She would make sure of that.

Surprise lit Eric's cold eyes for a moment.

She ran her hands up his sides slowly in a caress. The hard, well-defined muscles beneath his shirt bunched and coiled. Higher, she explored the expanse of his broad back. He was all male, every last inch of him.

A smile curved the vampire's mouth. He seemed pleased with her compliance. His hands abruptly cupped her backside, and the next moment Jasmine was being carried.

Panic and uncertainty flashed in her gaze. Where the fuck was he taking her?

A soft, pillowed surface greeted her bottom. She found herself sitting in a comfortable armchair. Panic pushed her heartbeat up another notch. She could feel her heart pounding against her ribcage like a trapped bird.

Maybe this had not been such a good idea. Do not fall apart, she told herself repeatedly.

Those blue eyes of his gave nothing away. Calming waves radiated from him, as if he were trying to soothe her. She knew he must be able to smell her fear.

"Close your eyes." His voice was huskier now. Persuasion trickled in his words, thick and heavy. They lulled her like an intoxicating drug, demanding she obey.

The vampire towered above her, his steely stare intense and almost hypnotic.

Jasmine felt her eyelids grow weighted as they drifted shut. With her eyes closed, the rest of her senses became a little sharper, more alive.

The material of the chair was soft beneath her. The room was warm enough that she didn't feel cold in her thin dress. Snow and pine were the scents that surrounded her. They filled her lungs with each breath she took. She could also sense the force of his power. It pulsed in the air around her, a tightly leashed energy. Her awareness of the vampire somewhere in the room made her heart pound faster and faster.

"Listen to me now, Jasmine, to my voice." He was very close. She jumped at the sound. The breath from his words caressed her cheek. "Let any worry slip from your body, your mind, you are safe."

The deep, velvety baritone flowed through her like rich hot chocolate. Command vibrated in his every word. She was helpless, unable to not submit. She sank back into the embrace of the chair as her body relaxed. His words poured smoothly into her mind, blowing away her cares and worries, and her heart slowed to a more normal rate.

A hand closed over her shoulder and gave it a reassuring squeeze-firm and strong, soothing.

Sighing, Jasmine leaned further into the chair and rested her head against the back. A sense of well-being was spreading through her with a dreamy languor. Everything suddenly felt surreal.

"That's it, my lovely. Let all of it go," the deep voice insisted softly.

The hand pulled down the cardigan she was wearing and began to massage her bare shoulders, his fingers flexing and relaxing while gently kneading. So skilful. So delightful.

A shiver of pleasure darted from his touch and ran down her body and into her belly. Another hand rested on her other shoulder, mimicking the movements of the first.

Jasmine could not contain the moan that left her lips. This vampire was so good with his hands. In one way his touch was relaxing, in another arousing. She could not stop the shivers of excitement quaking through her. Strange warmth began to spread through her belly.

Another jolt of bliss arrowed its way down, this time to the centre between her legs. Gripping the arms of the chair, she pushed her thighs together. A dull ache had begun to throb between them. She could feel the dampness between her legs, now coating her inner thighs. Rubbing them together, she couldn't seem to alleviate the sensations.

Strong, firm fingers were playing with one of the strap ties of the dress. Jasmine could feel it being pulled back and forth against her skin. It was teasing and slow, seductive. She felt it brush over the curve of her shoulder and down her arm with infinite care as he unlaced it.

Now she was exposed. Immediately she felt her nipple pucker and become taut as it was uncovered to the air.

Panic skittered down her spine. Jasmine's eyelashes fluttered slightly against her cheeks. They were so heavy though they wouldn't open. Raising her arms, she moved to cover herself with her eyes still closed.

"No," the vamp said in a gruff command. "Do not hide yourself from me. Lay back. Relax."

That voice wrapped itself around her again. She had no way to resist its deep, velvety order. The sense of panic that had swept over her melted away, and with a sigh she gave herself up to it.

Lowering her arms back down, she let them sit on the armrests once more.

A finger traced its way down her neck, over her shoulder, and across the curve of her naked breast. Jasmine could not help but arch a little when she felt it circle her excited nipple. Another moan slipped from her throat. Her breathing began to grow shallow. She heard movement and then her shaking legs were being gently parted. At the touch of his large hands they opened willingly in surrender.

A male groan vibrated through the strapping body that had wedged itself between her thighs. Eric was still fully dressed.

Jasmine could feel the rough material of his trouser-clad hips rubbing against the bare flesh of her quivering inner thighs. She arched her back further just as the clothed heat of a male chest pressed against her front. It warmed her through the thinness of the silk. Again, it was a strangely pleasurable feeling.

She could smell a hint of soap and the vampire's own unique scent. It was like pine trees in a snow-covered forest. She drew it in deeply, enjoying how it filled her lungs, intoxicating and rich.

Something warm and wet touched the peak of her nipple, and then a hot hungry mouth sucked it into its depths. Jasmine gasped as heat engulfed her, burning over her and heightening every touch, every stroke. His tongue swirled around her straining flesh.

Hands moving restlessly, Jasmine blindly felt her way up his broad shoulders. She wanted to touch him. Moving higher, she caressed his chiselled cheekbones before tangling her fingers in his silky hair.

No thought to push him away entered her head. The only thing that mattered was having more of what he was doing to her.

Groaning loudly, she pushed her chest more firmly against his lips. He was suckling greedily. His other hand toyed with her other breast beneath its silken barrier. She began to feel dizzy with need—for what she didn't know.

The lick of his tongue suddenly lathered the curve of her breast. She whimpered at the loss of his mouth on her aching nipple.

And then a pain sharp and fast pierced her flesh. It lasted only seconds before sweet ecstasy rushed in to replace the sting. The sensation was blinding.

Moaning long and low, Jasmine arched her back up into his face. Each pull of his mouth as he fed from her body sent another wave of pleasure crashing through her. Clutching his hair, she began to pant, a slave to the sensations rocketing through her. Tension was growing low in her belly. Jasmine could feel it building as every delightful feeling centred in that one place.

A hand slid slowly down her rib cage. The silkiness of her dress teased her skin with the movement.

The vampire made a hum of pleasure, which vibrated deliciously against her breast. She mewled softly in response. Jasmine's breathing grew faster with excitement. Her mind was swamped with every new sensation. She could feel her body tightening further.

A massive palm glided up her trembling thigh and gently stroked her skin, slowly edging higher. The fingers of his other hand, still playing with her covered breast, tweaked the nipple hard.

With a startled cry Jasmine's hips bucked and jerked. Ecstasy she had never experienced before exploded through her. Bliss swelled, roaring through every fibre of her being, shooting her upwards into a state of rapture. With her breath fast and irregular, her dazed mind took a while to float back down into her body. When it did she felt boneless.

The vampire still knelt between her legs. His tongue delicately caressed her breast. Like a cat, he lapped at the puncture marks he had left. All the while, one hand continued to fondle her nipple while the other teased the thin lacy barrier guarding her womanhood.

Jasmine tensed.

Eric's fingers grazed the black panties. The heat from her little cunt almost scorched him with its touch. He wanted to touch it, taste it, and most of all bury his aching cock within its hot, moist depths.

Jasmine's flesh was now flushed with a pleasing glow from her release.

Even now the taste of her sweet blood tingled pleasingly on his tongue. He licked his lips. Her little pants and moans had burnt his lust for her higher. Need was blazing through him.

What he wanted to do now was taste the rest of her, every inch. Eric knew he could do it. It would be easy to bend her to his will and take all of her without a second thought. He wanted to fuck her senseless.

The fact was he could not do that here.

The look in her eyes had stopped him. Although they were still heavy with fulfilment, the wary fear still remained. Too many ears and eyes could also be watching. Forgetting himself in the middle of a job had never happened to him before. He had fed and so easily could have been caught doing so if someone had walked in.

Eric knew he was being foolish. He had never been this close to having his control shattered. It was alarming and exciting, a sense of things being subtly altered, out of control. He was not sure he liked it. It shook him, how easily he had been swayed from his task. It was most unprofessional.

When the French man's henchman had looked at her, though, Eric knew he had to intervene. The male's intent had been clear. He would have hurt her. This was something Eric found he could not allow.

The little female's eyes were heavy with a stunned, dazed shock. Tension was creeping back into her body, as the languid lethargy began to ebb.

Eric realised this was a good thing. He needed to drag things back on track. She had called him a vampire.

He had heard of rare mortals being able to sense supernatural beings but never had he met one. This, he acknowledged, could be a complication. It made sense that she was the techno mage's girlfriend.

With excessive care and almost against his will, Eric pulled his hands away from her delectable body. She was truly stunning when aroused. He had never seen anything more magnificent. Sitting back on his heels, he watched as she pulled up the strap of her dress to cover herself, still seeming to be in a daze.

He swallowed down the sounds of protest in his throat. This was for the best. At least he had proved to her that she did not have to fear his bite. He had also brought her pleasure, something which pleased him greatly, although again he was not sure why. The look when she had orgasmed had suggested she had not experienced one before. This niggled at him.

Could she be a virgin? She had trembled enough to alert him of inexperience. But if this was true, how was she the mage's girlfriend? Had they yet to be intimate? These questions were puzzling. His gaze softened on her innocently confused face.

FROSTBITE

Sitting up straighter, she wrapped her arms protectively around her chest. Shoulders hunched defensively, she lowered her head.

Confusion snaked through Eric. She wouldn't meet his eyes— again not a good sign.

He gracefully pushed up onto his feet and observed Jasmine. What was she thinking, he wondered? Had she not enjoyed what he had done?

"Is your lesson over?" Her voice was quietly angry.

Eric froze.

Ah yes, he was playing the part of a villain. Once more he had forgotten himself. Did she think he had pleasured her as punishment? Used his powers to dominate her?

The thing was the temptation had been too great. He knew very well he could have fed from her neck, but those delicate breasts had looked so inviting. They were perfect. The need to taste her blood had been searing through him from the moment he had set eyes on her. So he had sampled her. Even at this moment, he savoured what he had taken. Now perhaps he could focus on his assignment instead.

Again, though, he had broken protocol. What was this girl doing to him?

"Yes," he finally answered her, keeping his voice void of emotion. "I think we are done here."

Eric took in her face, which was much paler than when he had brought her into the room. Her tiny hands were shaking again. Had he taken too much from her? Concern darkened his eyes. Her slenderness was perhaps from lack of eating properly. Was she on some kind of silly fad diet?

After sliding to her feet she swayed for a moment. Body tense, he stood poised to catch her if she fainted. As she straightened up without assistance, she tossed him a withering look. He caught a flash of green, defiant fire. Eric bit back a smile. She had not lost her spark, which pleased him.

But now it was time to get back to the game.

CHAPTER 4

JASMINE FELT SHAKY and a little light-headed as she was led back to the cell. Experiencing her first ever orgasm had left her confused with a strange sense of lethargy. It had been fucking mind-blowing, especially when he had bitten her. The bite still tingled pleasurably.

Now she knew what all the fuss was about over a vampire's bite—why so many people offered themselves as blood donors. It was a bigger business than prostitution nowadays.

The walk back gave her time to regain her equilibrium. This vampire knew who Twitch worked for. Did that mean Marcel knew, too? She had a feeling the arms dealer did not know his buddy was a vamp. Why, she wondered, was this a secret?

"Jasmine, are you OK?" Twitch practically raced across the room when he saw her. His face was stricken, his green eyes searching her for signs of abuse.

She could tell he was worried sick. He had probably spent all that time beating himself up about it.

Taking her by the arm gently, he led her towards the bed. She was grateful for the assistance. Her limbs felt heavy and she couldn't stop trembling.

Jasmine sank down onto the mattress with a shaky sigh. She could not tell him what happened. She did not want him blaming himself more than he already was.

"What happened?" he muttered anxiously.

"It was nothing for you to worry about." She assured him with a weak smile. "Really I'm fine. He didn't hurt me."

Twitch frowned as if not convinced. "You're telling me that guy did nothing to you?"

She nodded. "Yup."

A glimpse of cerulean blue eyes flashed through Jasmine's tired mind. A shiver that had nothing to do with the cold ran through her. She'd only had one boyfriend in all her twenty two years of life: Dan. And only one sexual experience, if that's what you could call it.

Nothing had prepared her for what she had experienced at the hands of the vampire. She had never imagined it could feel that way. His bite. His touch. It had been shocking at how enjoyable it had been. The way he had caressed her, arousing her body from its state of limbo. A sense of shame welled up inside her. She couldn't let herself remember how good he had made her feel.

He was a bad guy—an arms dealer whose weapons killed millions of people. The only reason he had done it was to prove a point, and that was to show she was helpless against what he wanted. She had actually been surprised he hadn't taken things further. Not that she had wanted it to, she assured herself quickly.

Only one good thing had come from the event.

Fumbling in her cardigan pocket, she fished out a slim phone. Jasmine had managed to nab it when she had been fondling his sides. The fact he had not noticed was a miracle, though that did not mean he wouldn't notice soon.

"What can you do with this?" she said, handing it to Twitch.

Twitch stared down at the mobile phone in astonishment. He took it from her outstretched palm and slipped off its back. Nimble, long fingers began to fiddle with the device.

She was glad he did not ask how she had gotten it.

Reaching down to his knee, he unzipped a hidden compartment. A moment later he had a tiny screwdriver in his hand.

Jasmine blinked in confusion. No visible zippers were anywhere on his clothes. Where had that pocket come from, and more importantly how about the screwdriver? There had been nothing bulky to show it had even been there. It was impossible.

"Are you still wearing your watch?" Twitch muttered, still playing with the phone. His green eyes never wavered from his work. The dishevelled locks of his long hair partly hid his face.

Tugging up the sleeve of her cardigan, Jasmine bared the watch. No one had taken it from her. Luckily it also didn't seem to have been damaged in the crash. In fact, she had forgotten she was wearing it.

He did not even look up, yet somehow was aware it was there. "Give it to me."

It was something Twitch had created himself. Although it now looked like a harmless mechanical wristwatch, it was filled with wires. A press of a knob on its side and the screen became a sleek touch screen.

Jasmine unclipped it and dropped it into his extended palm.

Holding it up under the light, he began to twiddle with it, taking it apart. Soon there were dozens of tiny wires strewn across his lap. They were a rainbow of colours.

Lips moving with soundless words, power began to leap from his hands. His fingertips were glowing with florescent blue light. It danced and crackled over the wires like lightning. The hairs on her arms rose from the electricity in the air.

Jasmine could feel the brush of his magic as it washed across her skin. A rush of power hit her senses. Electric. Charged.

"I thought you said this place was warded and you couldn't use your magic?" she questioned with a frown.

Twitch gave her a guilty sideways glance. "I didn't know how closely they were listening. Right now we're alone."

Surprised inched up her eyebrows. "How do you know that?"

"I can feel it." His agile fingers were rearranging and manipulating wires between both devices now. "Technology has a hum I'm attuned to. It makes it easier for me to know when it's being used."

Jasmine guessed that made sense. Twitch was used to working with both mediums. He would have become accustomed to them on another level.

"So that's how you know no one is listening to us right now."

A smile spread across his face. "Yes."

She still felt a bit dizzy and suddenly wished there was something to eat. No doubt her blood sugar was low from where the vamp had fed. Had he enjoyed her taste, she wondered?

"We are going to need a distraction for the guard," Twitch said, bringing her thoughts back to the present.

Jasmine glanced towards the closed door. "What do you have in mind?"

Twitch seemed to have finished what he was doing. The wires were now shimmering with magic. Carefully he tucked them back inside the devices. Both now looked exactly as they had before.

"Pretend you're unconscious so we can lure him in?"

She nodded. "I guess that might work."

After handing her back the watch, he slipped the screwdriver back into his hidden pocket. The modified mobile phone, he kept in his hand.

"You were shaky and pale when you came back, so it should be believable." His look was sharply questioning. He did seem to want to know what had happened after all.

Jasmine sighed inwardly. She realised that Twitch was going to have to know about the vampire. He would need to know all the facts if they intended getting out of the building alive. A vamp could be a huge complication.

"The dark-haired man who took me from the room," Jasmine whispered softly. "He's a vamp."

Twitch's eyes sprung wide in surprise. They then darted up to her neck. "What the hell did he do to you?"

She shifted uncomfortably on the bed for a moment. Jasmine was not about to explain why there were no fang marks there. She was also not going to tell him where they actually were. It was embarrassing enough already. She could feel the throb of the bite against the satin of her dress. It felt like there was a brand on her breast.

"He knows who you work for," she continued in a hushed tone, ignoring his question. "He didn't seem to know about me though."

Twitch's lips pressed together in the only sign that he was annoyed she had not answered his question.

"If Marcel knew, you wouldn't be sitting here with me now."

He had a point. If they had known who she was when they snatched them, they would have left her with a bullet in her brain. Jasmine was certain of that.

Jasmine nodded. "I think the vamp's keeping secrets."

Twitch mulled over her discovery silently for a moment. "If we're lucky, he won't sense us when we get out."

Vampires had heightened senses, more acute than a human, but that also came with a disadvantage.

She glanced at her watch. "It's thirty minutes to sunrise. He should be at his lair by now ready to sleep. We shouldn't have that problem."

Vampires were nocturnal. They had a major aversion to sunlight, one that left them in a pile of dust if they were dumb enough to venture out in the day. Jasmine knew that the sun rose at 8:40 as she was usually up at the same time most winter mornings.

As she strapped the watch back on, she noticed it felt different. She had grown used to the magic that imbued it but now it prickled against her skin. It wasn't uncomfortable; rather it just made her fully aware of the device around her wrist.

Twitch glanced nervously towards the door. "How long can you hold your breath for?"

Jasmine blinked in confusion. She did not answer him straight away. It had to be a joke or a trick question. Meeting the gleam in his peridot eyes, she realised he was serious. She sighed. No joke then.

"I don't know. It's not something I have ever timed. Why?"

Twitch shrugged. "It will be more convincing if he thinks you've stopped breathing. They need you alive to keep threatening me."

Jasmine rolled her eyes. That would probably be a little over dramatic for what they needed. "I'm not holding my breath until I bloody well pass out. Laying on the bed will have to do."

He was palming the mobile phone tensely. "OK, but you have to make it look good."

"Twitch, just get on with it, will you?" Jasmine said under her breath. She was starting to lose her patience. A headache was thumping through her skull, probably because of tiredness and lack of food. Two things she was not getting any time soon.

He stood up, allowing her to scoot fully onto the bed. Jasmine sprawled across the mattress, her limbs akimbo. She knew this position would probably look more convincing.

Eyes fluttering shut, she pretended to be unconscious. It was easy enough to do as fatigue had worn her down.

When a hand tugged up the skirt of her dress, she gasped. Her eyes snapped open and she gave her friend an astounded look. "What the fuck are you doing?"

A red flush had crept into Twitch's pale cheeks. He was standing awkwardly beside the bed.

"It's more enticing if he sees a bit of thigh," Twitch purred softly, not meeting her look. "Both the guards were eyeing you. He might be tempted to give you mouth to mouth."

Jasmine really did not need that visualised in her head. Would it be Pierre outside?

"God, I hope not," she muttered, fighting down the urge to pull the material back down. "Just hurry up, will you?"

Twitch scuttled over to the door. Banging on it loudly, he started shouting out in French.

She only had a moment to be impressed that he spoke the language. Her knowledge of French was non-existent.

Seconds later, there was the sound of the bolt being drawn back. Then a voice was answering her friend. She tried not to tense up.

Jasmine peeked through the veil of her thick lashes. The guard loomed in the doorway. It was not Pierre, but the other big goon. Relief poured through her.

Twitch was pointing at her, playing the role of a frantic, concerned friend. Then he began tugging wildly on his hair. He was going for full-on drama and manic gestures. She doubted the mage could pretend to panic normally. Twitch was unique, in his own weird kind of way.

The mobile phone he had been holding was nowhere to be seen.

The guard gestured for him to back up near the bed and stand against the wall. Without a second thought, the mage obeyed.

Jasmine made sure to close her eyes properly. If the guard realised their plan, it would land them in a whole lot more shit. They had to make sure this worked. She had to look believable.

A heavy breath blew over her cheek. She could feel the large man's face inches from her own. Jasmine stamped down the urge to recoil.

He said something harsh in French. A hand touched her arm. She took a chance and peeped through her thick eyelashes. The man's face was tightened with annoyance. As he raised his hand, she realised he was preparing to slap her. What the fuck?

With almost feline grace, Twitch was suddenly behind him. His green eyes were fixed with intent.

He jammed one end of the mobile into the big man's neck. The guy didn't even have time to make a noise. A sinister crackle and pop filled the air. Then his eyes rolled back up in his head. As the whole weight of his body landed heavily on top of Jasmine, the air left her lungs in an oomph. She found herself pinned.

Trying not to panic, Jasmine struggled and thrashed. She was being crushed and struggled to breathe.

"Get . . . him . . . off . . . me," she managed to hiss.

"Hold on, Jazzy," Twitch called to her before going over to heave the unconscious guard off her.

She sat up and while panting from the exertion scrambled off the bed. A full body shudder rolled through her. Just the feel of him on top of her had made her skin crawl. Panic was still trying to take hold. Taking a deep breath, she tried to relax.

"You OK?" Twitch asked with concern.

She nodded, straightening her clothes. "Yes, let's just get the hell out of here."

The quicker they left, the better chance they would not be discovered. Later she could deal with the bottled up memories and emotions clawing to get out. She had no time to fall apart now.

Twitch took her hand and gave it a squeeze before leading her to the door. It was friendly, reassuring, and just what she needed. He really did seem to be in a touchy-feely mood today. Maybe it was fearing for their lives that was doing it.

Cautiously he poked his head out. When he seemed certain all was clear, he stepped out with her in tow.

Jasmine did not even bother to look back at the guard. He had been breathing when they had rolled him off. That was good enough for her. They guy worked for an arms dealer. She would not waste any sympathy on him.

Twitch seemed as jumpy as a cat on burning coals. Every so often, she could feel the jerky movements of his muscles through his hand. They both kept silent, both fearing their luck wouldn't hold if they made a noise.

He seemed to know where he was going, so Jasmine followed, no questions asked. If he could get them out of the building, she was more than happy to follow him anywhere.

They paused by a door. A green exit sign flashed above it. Testing it gingerly with his hand, he discovered it unlocked. He stilled for only a moment, then practically dived through the door and yanked her inside a brightly lit stairwell. Were they in some kind of office building? This had to be Marcel's place of work.

Twitch had let go of her arm and was crouched on some steps. His head was swivelling up and down as he checked for people. He reminded her of a meerkat looking for predators.

There didn't seem to be anyone about. He focused his shrewd green eyes on the ceiling and then above the door. Checking for cameras, she realised, but for whatever reason, there were none she could see on this floor.

A silence stretched around them.

"We have to get downstairs and out," Twitch whispered after a second and glanced her way as he beckoned with a finger. Silently as they could, they crept down the stairwell.

"How are we going to get out of the building?" Jasmine whispered.

It was one thing to get all the way down without being spotted, but she very much doubted they could just stroll out of the main doors. The arms dealer would have been careful to make sure that never happened.

Twitch placed a finger to his lips to silence her. Eyes flashing downwards, he alerted her to a camera. It was directly above a door on the next landing. If they made a move down, they would be spotted.

He placed his hand flat against the wall and closed his eyes.

Jasmine felt the flurry of magic as it leapt up at his command. His lips moved silently while weaving his spell. A crackle of electricity leapt and spread like tiny bony fingers across the wall. They raced, dancing like neon streaking flashes. When they hit the camera, nothing happened. Then the little red light turned blue.

Twitch's face relaxed. He pushed the hair that had fallen into his eyes away and started down the stairs.

Jasmine hesitated, not sure what he had done exactly. He seemed happy with the results though, so it must have worked. She took his offered hand and followed him on the descent.

"All the cameras on the stairs are now on a loop," he said as they turned a corner in the stairwell. "Getting out has been sorted already with your watch and the phone you gave me."

She frowned and her hand absently rubbed the watch on her wrist. "What do you mean?"

"A magical hologram," Twitch explained patiently. "It settles over our features. Anyone looking at us will see that instead of our actual faces. But doesn't last long. Maybe ten minutes at the most. Possibly less. It's unstable so we need to move fast."

Why did she not like the use of the word 'unstable'? What exactly did that mean? Unease swirled through her.

They had stealthily made it down four flights of stairs. Not much longer and she knew they would hit the bottom.

"Unstable?" she queried uneasily. They could not afford for anything to go wrong.

"It means it might suddenly stop working or there's a risk it might explode." He sent her an apologetic smile. "It's the best I could do with what I had and with the limited time."

She stared at him in disbelief. What the fuck did he mean by 'explode'? But she knew it was their only hope. His gadgets had never failed them in the past so she pushed aside her worry and doubts and nodded.

"So we need to use it sparingly?"

Reaching back, Twitch gave her arm a reassuring squeeze. "Exactly."

"Why are you so touchy feely all of a sudden?"

Surprised flashed in his eyes. He shrugged. "I thought it would help calm you down."

Jasmine frowned in confusion. "But I thought you didn't like being touched."

He seemed so casual about it. Two months of knowing him and she had never seen him touch anyone. It was something he just did not do.

A smile touched his lips. "I do in the right circumstances— being kidnapped and held at gunpoint is up there on my list of times. There's nothing wrong with it."

"I thought you had aphenphosmphobia or something," she admitted awkwardly as they turned another corner.

She had googled the condition and everything. It had seemed important to put him at ease on her first week of work. That was before they had become firm friends. Best friends.

They were just three floors up from the bottom now. All the cameras were still showing a blue light as the spell laced through them.

"That sounds contagious," Twitch purred back softly. Laughter danced in his gaze.

Jasmine rolled her eyes. "It's the phobia of being touched or touching dumb arse."

Twitch gave a raspy chuckle. He looked damn well like he knew what she was talking about.

They both froze at the sound of a door opening above them. Eyes wide, they stared at each other. Both of them were mirroring the same look of dread and fear.

Voices filtered softly down. The echo of footsteps descending had them flattening themselves against the wall. A male and a female voice chatted away. The woman laughed. Then there was the sound of another door opening. Then silence.

Jasmine sagged with relief. She knew their luck would run out eventually and their escape would be discovered. She just hoped they were out of the building first.

Twitch looked just as relieved. A fine tremor was in his hand when he pushed his hair away from his face.

He was scared, but he was trying not to show it. They were both trying to be brave. Usually he was the guy in the van or back at base giving out helpful advice through the earpieces. He had never been a proper field agent. This was probably a little too much real life even for him.

In unison they moved a little more quickly down the steps. A pressing urgency was now beating down on them.

Finally, they reached the bottom. Jasmine was certain they would find at least one security guard. Time would tell if that was going to be a problem.

"Ready?" Twitch asked in a smooth purr. His eyes kept darting back up the stairs. She could tell he was worried they were going to get caught.

Grabbing his hand, she gave it a squeeze. Twitch met her trusting eyes. "Let's get the fuck out of here," she whispered with a nervous smile. All she could hope was that everything went as planned.

Eric frowned when he was unable to locate his mobile. It was not like him to be careless with such a device. Running a hand through his black tousled hair, he sighed.

He was also still a little preoccupied with his encounter with the girl. Her blood had been so deliciously potent. That petite body of hers had been so warm and pliant. He now regretted not taking things further. Lust shot through him and he felt his cock rise.

Damnation! This was not the time to be distracted. He needed to find that blasted phone.

Racking his brain, he tried to remember when he'd had it last. Searching the meeting room had come up with nothing. It had not slipped down any of the sofa cushions. The room where he had taken the girl had also come up empty. Yet it could not have simply disappeared. That was most unlikely.

Eric stilled.

Eyes narrowing, an astonished smile curved his lips. That coy, enticing smile she had given him. The way her hands had caressed his sides, his back. And he had never noticed! So far gone with the need to touch and taste, he had let his guard down. How easy he had made it for her. That little minx must have lifted it from him when he'd had her pinned to the wall. It was the only explanation.

Eric knew in the hands of the techno mage, even a small thing like a phone could be used with cunning. He had no doubt in his mind they would try to escape.

If they succeeded Marcel would hunt them. If they failed, the girl would feel the Frenchman's wrath. She would be the one to pay the price.

Eric sighed in annoyance. If he followed his instincts and helped them, he could well blow his cover. Years of infiltration would be wasted. His conscience, though, wouldn't let him just stand by. When, he wondered, had he suddenly grown one of those?

Maybe he could help them discreetly, he thought.

Raoul?

Yes, Eric is something wrong? The voice of his comrade in arms whispered into his mind.

Eric turned to the window and pretended to admire the view, which was of Marcel still celebrating his capture of the techno mage. His lover, Claude, was hanging on his every word. The blond man was feeding his master canapés from a tray. They were huddled together on one of the sofas, cooing to each other like a pair of lovesick pigeons.

I believe we may have a problem my friend. Eric raised his wine glass to his lips and took a sip. *The female with the mage seems to have acquired my phone. They will no doubt try to escape.*

Raoul did not responded straight away. *And how did she come into possession of this object?* Amusement was laced in his tone when he finally did.

Eric was not about to tell him of his foolishness or his lapse in judgement. He should never have let her get so close. Nothing good ever came from being blinded by lust and emotions.

He pursed his lips. *The how does not matter. It is now in her hands, and I would like you to keep an eye on the outside in case they need aid.*

You wish me to help them escape? The other vampire knew what was at stake if their mission failed. He also knew Eric did not make decisions without thinking things through thoroughly first.

Only if they manage to escape the building successfully. Marcel cannot know of our interference.

Eric felt his friend's agreement along their connection. It was all he could do to assist the dainty female. He just prayed to the gods they did nothing to foolish and that she did not get herself killed. The next move was now hers.

CHAPTER 5

TWITCH FUMBLED WITH THE mobile phone. He glided his finger across the screen and it jumped to life. A pleased smile touched his lips. Strange blue glyphs began to stream across the surface. They reflected across his face in an eerie glow.

"That's the spell beginning to work," he said rather smugly. "Touch the button on the left side of your watch to activate yours."

Obediently Jasmine pressed the button. The skin beneath the watch tightened slightly in discomfort as the spell took effect. Glyphs danced across the smooth surface of the watch.

As she raised her eyes, she was shocked to find her friend's face blurred. It was almost like a photo taken too fast. His features were a smear, unclear, as if the colours and shapes had merged. It was fucking disturbing.

Blinking, she tried to clear her vision. It took her a moment to realise there was nothing wrong with her eyes. It was him. The spell was starting to take effect. Jasmine watched in amazement as the fuzziness slowly dissipated.

Twitch no longer looked like himself. The teeth in his smile were crooked, his eyes were now brown. His face was angular with a sharp hooked nose. The only thing that had not really changed was the tangle of his cinnamon-coloured curls.

"That is just creepy," Jasmine said with a shudder.

He giggled a strange hoarse sound. "I wouldn't advise looking in a mirror. You don't look much of a catch either."

Which of course meant her hologram was now in place and was just as unattractive. She couldn't feel anything though.

Jasmine raised her hand and touched her face. Nothing felt different. She could still feel her button nose and full lips. The hologram she released through was just an image. She had not physically changed.

"Couldn't you have made them look a little more attractive?" she asked with curiosity. "You look like a demented hill-billy."

Twitch sighed. "I don't have time to make them perfect. The fact they work should be enough. I wasn't going for beauty. Just practicality." With swift movements he reached the door. "Come on, we don't have long now. The spell's active and we've got to move."

Swallowing down her nervousness, she followed his lead into the foyer. Large and spacious, the room had Christmas lights placed tastefully around some paintings on the walls. An oversized tree sat in one corner, the limbs of which were weighed down and overcrowded with decorations.

Two uniformed security guards in grey sat idly behind a reception table. No one else could be seen. A pretty nice place for an arms dealer to run his business from. It looked like any other office reception area. It felt normal, mundane.

Now that the spell was working, she fought down the urge to grab Twitch's hand and run. They had to act normally, as if they worked there. Hopefully the guards didn't know everyone in the building on sight. Probably not likely. The place seemed huge.

With confident steps, Twitch led the way. He did not look back but kept a slow enough pace for her to keep up. She could practically feel the excitement and nervousness rolling off him.

Jasmine felt jittery and clumsy, but adrenaline pushed her forwards. She had to fight to keep her breathing even and calm. Panicking was not an option.

As they passed the bank of elevators, she took a chance to glance at her reflection. Blue eyes stared back at her. Thin, pencil-drawn eyebrows rose high up on her severe-looking forehead. The thin lips of her mouth were turned down in a permanent scowl.

She tried hard not to laugh. She looked like a freaking Victorian spinster from some historical novel. With that expression, she was ready to browbeat anyone into submission. It was scary.

Had Twitch really had no control over what they would look like? She knew he had a strange sense of humour. But this? Was it leaking out with his nervousness, affecting his magic?

Catching his eye, she could see he was trying not to grin. Damn him. He had done it on purpose. She could see by the twinkle in his eyes. How the hell was this blending in? He was playing with fire and they both knew it. They couldn't afford to be caught.

The guards were busy talking and barely looked their way.

Jasmine felt her confidence grow. Not to draw suspicion, they carried on strolling slowly towards the main doors. If no one looked their way they might be safe. No one would ever forget these ugly mugs.

Then it hit her. That's exactly why the mage had done it. No one would recognize them. The descriptions anyone gave after the fact would be unbelievable. They would be ridiculous.

Twitch must have guessed that she had figured out the method to his mage madness. Catching her eye again, he winked.

Jasmine pressed her lips together, stifling a grin.

She could see people on the street just outside and cars passing by on a very busy road. They had no plan beyond getting out. Once they were some streets away, they could decide what to do next. For now she could practically taste freedom already—just within reach.

That was when their luck ran out.

A sudden ear-splitting screech, high and agonizingly painful, came out of nowhere and almost deafened her. Jasmine slapped her hands over her ears in a desperate attempt to shut the sound out, which didn't work. At one point, she thought her eardrums were going to start bleeding.

Screwing up her face, she glanced at her companion. It was then she knew everything was going to Crapville. Just his freaked-out expression said it all.

The mobile phone in Twitch's hand hissed frighteningly—a sound, she was pretty sure, it was not supposed to make. Then it exploded in a hail of blue, pulsing sparks, lighting up the foyer like a miniature fireworks display.

Twitch dropped it with a yelp. Curling his fingers into his palm, he held it against his chest. A stream of curses left his lips.

The holographic disguise dissolved from the mage's face like wax melting from a burning candle. The sight was horrific, something that would have given anyone nightmares.

Jasmine didn't know who looked more shocked, them or the two security guards. Both men had paled so much, she thought they were about to pass out. She doubted watching someone's face melt off was something they were going to forget any time soon. Maybe even ever.

The elevator pinged behind them. They glanced back at the same time. Their luck really had gone for good.

Pierre was just stepping out. Shock hit his face when he saw the techno mage. It was obvious from his reaction their escape had still gone unnoticed. They had been doing so well.

"RUN!" Twitch practically roared beside her. It was the loudest she had ever heard his voice and it was frightening.

Not waiting to see if he followed, Jasmine launched herself towards the door. Adrenaline was pumping through her at full throttle. It fuelled her flight forwards.

The two guards were coming round the table. They could only get out one at a time with the narrowness of the gap. The one in front tried to grab Jasmine as she passed. Jabbing her hand sideways, she smacked him in the chest. Somehow she caught him well. He stumbled backwards, taking his friend down too with a crash.

Wearing a grin of triumph, she kept on moving.

Twitch was quick to pass her now.

They raced towards the doors. Jasmine struggled to keep up in the heels of her shoes. They were impractical to run in, but she didn't even have time to kick them off. They didn't stop her though.

Pierre was yelling something in French at the top of his lungs. Jasmine could hear the sound of heavy footsteps giving chase. She knew the guards were after them again. They had to keep going.

They burst out through the main doors onto the street. It was already busy with people on their way to work. Without stopping, they sprinted towards the road.

The chill of the December morning cut deeply into her skin. The little dress and cardigan she was wearing gave no warmth. She shivered and wrapped her arms around her middle as she chanced a glance back. Pierre had a gun in his hand and was taking aim.

Screams erupted from passers-by. Someone on the street must have suddenly noticed the guy with the gun. The people panicked as everyone ran or ducked for cover.

Pierre met her eye. Jasmine froze mid-step. The gun was aimed at her head and she knew he was ready to take the shot. If he was a good marksman, she was sure as dead. This was it. She was about to die. Fear, rage, regret hurled through her in a split second.

Jasmine tried to move but knew it was too late. She braced herself for impact. If the shot was clean, she might not feel a thing.

But Pierre's arm suddenly jerked upwards and the bullet fired into the sky, sailing harmlessly upwards. He stared at the gun in shock. His arm was pointing straight up and did not seem to want to come down of its own accord. It was almost as if he'd lost control of his own limb.

She blinked in confusion. What the heck had just happened? Jasmine knew she had been seconds from a bullet in the head. How was she still alive?

Twitch grabbed her wrist tightly and she quickly found herself being dragged at a run down the street again. They were melding into the other pedestrians trying to get away.

"Did you do that with the gun?" Jasmine panted at Twitch.

He looked fearfully back over his shoulder. "No, it wasn't me."

They skidded around a corner and carried on pounding down the street. They couldn't stop moving, not even for a second. How long Pierre was just going to stand there was uncertain. She doubted it would be long, though.

Kicking free of her heels, she scooped them up. She was done running in them. Barefoot was a lot faster. Hell, she never wanted to wear heels again in her life.

She spotted an empty taxi waiting at a red light, and apparently so did Twitch as he pulled her along, sprinting across the road. He grabbed the handle of the back door and yanked it open. The driver didn't even glance their way.

Twitch bundled her into the car and rattled off an address. The door closed with a thud and the car began to move. Jasmine slumped in relief.

They had done it. Somehow they had managed to escape. Upon raising her chin, she found Twitch staring at her. That was all it took. They grinned at each other like a pair of idiots. Huge, shit-eating grins. They were free.

CHAPTER 6

JASMINE FELT A TINGLE DOWN her neck. All her senses were suddenly on full alert. Glancing up, she met the gaze of the taxi driver in the rear view mirror. Warm, honey-brown eyes were settled on her in interest. She could not see his face. A black scarf concealed most of it from the nose down and a black cap covered his head. All to keep out the morning chill, no doubt.

She could see short black hair poking out, though, and smooth mocha-coloured skin around his eyes. The driver seemed to be curious about them.

"Where are we going?" she asked her friend. She shivered with cold and huddled closer to his body. Now that they had stopped moving, she was feeling the chill. It was fricking freezing.

Her eyes slid to the front seat again.

The taxi driver was a supernatural. She was certain. What he was exactly, she didn't know. Many supernaturals had normal day-to-day jobs. They blended in well with the human population. It was how they lived. Hidden.

He was probably wondering who the hell they were. The woman holding her shoes, barely dressed and the tall man dressed in black with dishevelled, curly hair. They had practically dived into his taxi like the hounds of hell were after them.

She noted in the rear view mirror, the mage's spell had completely worn off. The face reflected back was happily her own.

Twitch was nursing the hand the phone had exploded in. "I have friends here in Paris. We can go to their place."

"Let me see that," Jasmine said and reached over to grasp his hand. The flesh on his palm was burnt, and she saw a quick flash of red, puckered skin and blisters before he pulled it back.

"It's nothing," he said while looking at the window. "No worse than the ones than I already have."

Jasmine's eyes flicked to the old burn marks faded on his face and neck. "So that's where you got those from."

Twitch suddenly looked uncomfortable. He lowered his head and let his long hair flop forwards to hide his face.

"It just happens if spells don't work, which doesn't happen very often at all."

Maybe not so much now, but it was obvious from his old scars it had once happened a lot. She could tell he was self-conscious about them. Was that why he kept his hair so long? So he could use it as a shield to hide? Why the hell had he carried on messing with magic if it hurt him? It had to be dangerous.

Maybe, she thought, like her, he didn't have a choice. Jasmine had found out pretty swiftly you couldn't ignore a gift. The universe wouldn't let you.

She practically hummed with pleasure when she felt warm heat start to flow in the car. She flashed the driver a smile of thanks for turning it on. He must have seen her shivering.

His honey-brown eyes returned her smile.

Twitch was still turned towards the window. He did not seem to be in a talkative mood anymore. Fine by her.

Jasmine's adrenaline rush had finally crashed. Nausea rolled through her stomach. Suddenly she was feeling exhausted. All she wanted to do was sleep, but that was far from possible yet.

The taxi was already weaving in and out of the manic Christmas traffic.

Christmas decorations and lights glittered from every window. It all looked so normal. She could hardly believe they had been prisoners not long ago.

After a while, the Arc de Triomphe appeared in the distance. Jasmine was feeling more than nervous by then. French drivers seemed to be crazy. Each lane was a free for all with seemingly no rules. Mopeds and scooters crossed their path, without even bothering to signal or look.

Every time the driver hit the brakes, Jasmine jerked forwards against her seatbelt. The taxi was constantly battling for a position in the lanes making it feel like they were rally driving. Every so often, a flow of French would leave their driver's lips. She was pretty sure they were swear words even though his voice was soft and pleasant.

All in all, Jasmine was thankful when they finally pulled up not far from the Arc de Triomphe.

Twitch unzipped a concealed pocket on the knee of his black trousers. He tugged out some notes and stuffed them into the driver's hand. Jasmine could see they were English. The driver couldn't be happy. She cringed.

The guy didn't even check the currency. He shoved the wad into his coat pocket and tipped his cap at them as Twitch thrust open the door. He hopped out and Jasmine scrambled after him, trying to keep up.

She frowned at the driver's odd behaviour then gave herself a mental shrug. She had never been to Paris before. Maybe it was normal. He probably dealt with crazy tourists all day. The taxi had driven off quickly enough.

Loathing to do so but with little choice, she slipped her heels back on. Her feet protested and she groaned. She was hoping they did not have far to walk. It was going to be torture if they did.

After the heat in the taxi, the cold air was again a shock. Jasmine shivered and hugged her body. Not matter what she did, she couldn't keep warm. Any heat she had accumulated on their ride was already sucked out of her.

Twitch did not seem to feel it and she began to envy him.

He led her along the street for a good twenty minutes. He did not talk but kept glancing around uneasily. She could sense his edginess and knew he probably wanted to get off the street. When Marcel realised they had escaped, he would soon be after them. Then they were in real trouble.

Her body was aching and she knew she was functioning on automatic now. All her energy was spent. Sooner or later, the fumes were going to give out. She wanted to be safely inside when it did.

They soon stopped in the front of a cheerful, cosy Internet café. "In here." Twitch motioned with his hand.

Jasmine followed him silently inside. At this point, she didn't care where they were so long as they were inside.

The café was bright with white walls and a big window, which flooded the room with sunlight. Posters of video games and popular sci-fi series covered the walls—a place for those who choose to lose themselves in fantasy. A nerd haven.

Only a few customers were scattered about, mainly young kids glued to whatever they were doing on their screens. Individual booths for privacy lined one wall and some tables and couches sat in one corner for physical socializing. Not that they probably did a lot of that, she thought.

A heater in one corner provided the warmth Jasmine needed to begin to thaw out once more. The shivers that had gripped her began to slow.

Twitch hurried up to the counter and started talking to the man behind it in hushed tones. He was young, in his early twenties at a guess. He was cute with dark blue eyes and strawberry-blond hair.

Jasmine could not follow what was being said as it was all in French. She hadn't really paid attention to the foreign language in school, which she now kind of regretted.

The young man turned and called out the back. A moment later another man appeared. From the resemblance, they were clearly brothers. This new one was older, though, and his blond hair slightly darker. Both looked like they spent hours hunched over their laptops. It was no wonder they knew Twitch.

"This is Ralph and Jeremy, Internet friends of mine," Twitch introduced quickly as he switched to English. "This is Jazzy— Jasmine—my girlfriend."

Jasmine noted he wanted to keep up the pretence of their relationship, so she played along. Knowing the techno mage, he was being as paranoid as ever. She couldn't blame him. She was feeling that way a little, too.

Both nerdy males looked her up and down in stunned surprise. They seemed hardly able to believe their eyes. She guessed they hadn't expected Twitch to produce a girlfriend.

"Hello." She pinned on a bright smile. "It's nice to meet you both."

"She's a babe," Jeremy exclaimed with a lopsided grin. His eyes were lit with friendly interest.

"You're Alan's girlfriend?" Ralph shook his head in his belief. "I don't believe it."

Alan, she was guessing, was the name Twitch used online. How fitting he would use an ordinary name, Jasmine thought. Online, she supposed, that's what he strived for.

"She's braless and her panties are fine, black, and lacy," Twitch purred low. His eyes did a nervous dance over the room for a moment. With one hand, he shoved some tangled cinnamon curls out of his face.

Jasmine stilled.

A short silence followed.

She tried not to let her surprise show. How the hell had he known what she was wearing under her dress?

It felt like the one time she had been at home and had to contact him. He had known exactly what she was wearing then too, as if he had eyes inside her house. It was a tad creepy. The words "potential magical cyberstalker" came to mind. If he wasn't one already.

Jasmine realised then that both guys were staring at her expectantly. She repressed the urge to growl. Of course they wanted the evidence verified. They were nerds after all.

Giving them a stony glare, she flashed them her bare shoulder.

When their eyes dropped low, she shook her head. "Don't even think about it," she snapped. "I'm not showing you my underwear. You're just going to have to take my *boyfriend's* word for it."

Twitch made a hum of agreement beside her. Giving him a sideways glance, she could see he was still looking worriedly around. Anxiety was pulsating off him, making the air almost oscillate.

"So can we use your spare room or not?" His green eyes swung back round to his friends.

Jeremy smiled and nodded. "Sure, Alan. You and Jasmine can stay as long as you like. We don't mind at all."

The guy beckoned them behind the counter. Twitch went first with her bringing up the rear. They made their way down a narrow corridor and then up some steep stairs.

"The bathroom is there," Jeremy informed them as he passed a blue wooden door. "Kitchen's downstairs and here's the room."

He turned the knob on the dark brown door and pushed it open. The room was sparsely furnished with a heavy, wooden wardrobe in one corner and a double bed in the centre.

Twitch strode quickly to the window to take in the view. A white netting in front of it to stopped anyone looking in. Finally he turned. "This is perfect, Jeremy. thank you."

The young guy nodded. "Anything to help out a friend. I just can't believe you got car-jacked in our beautiful city. It must have been awful."

He turned sympathetic eyes towards Jasmine.

"It was," she replied grimly, playing along with the story Twitch had obviously fed him. "Our first romantic getaway and this happens." With a sigh, she sauntered up beside her friend. Jasmine stared up at Twitch with an adoring smile.

Wary surprise lit his peridot green eyes.

She was feeling like a little payback was in order.

She draped her arm low around his waist and leaned against him. Now that she knew he didn't mind being touched, she wasn't about to let him get away with it.

"I'm sure he will make it up to me though. Won't you *Alan?*"

Twitch looked nervously down at her. He suddenly seemed to have gone timid and shy. His tall, slender form was tense against her.

An evil grin itched to spread across her face. It was hard, but she managed to contain it. Then, curving her hand over one of his butt cheeks, Jasmine pinched him hard.

He jerked with a little squeal. "Yes, yes Jazzy. I promise I will make up for this."

Jeremy laughed. "I can see who wears the pants in your relationship." He gave Jasmine a little wink.

Twitch had gone a little red. Just for good measure, she kept her hand on his butt. Jasmine tried not to smile.

"I don't suppose you have a phone I can borrow? I promised my Dad I would call in while we were here," she said. Their team would be wondering where the hell they were.

"Sure. There's a cordless phone in the bathroom you can use," Jeremy informed her. "Just down the hall. The blue door."

Jasmine did flash him a smile this time. "That's great. I can freshen up at the same time."

"Well if you need anything, Ralph and I will be downstairs." Jeremy retreated from the room and closed the door behind him with a click.

The moment he disappeared, Jasmine dropped her arm. She pulled off her heels. She was happy to finally be rid of them. A hum of pleasure left her lips. She wiggled her toes on the carpeted floor. Bliss.

"Do you think we're safe here?" she asked.

Twitch shook his head. He hadn't moved from the spot she had left him in.

"We won't be safe until we get out of France," he said quietly.

She dumped her shoes beside the bed. The mattress looked so tempting. It was practically calling to her. Jasmine knew, though, she didn't have time to rest. Not yet.

She sighed. "I'm going to phone Mark and let him know where we are."

Twitch had turned back to peer nervously out the window. If anyone saw him, it was going to look creepy. "OK."

Trying not to roll her eyes at his back, she slipped out of the room.

CHAPTER 7

THE FAINT SOUNDS OF THE STORE filtered up the stairs. Soft voices in French chatted away—probably the brothers excited to have a friend visit. She doubted this happened often. Having people turn up on their doorstop was probably juicy drama. They had to be wondering why they didn't have any money or luggage. The carjacking story would only stretch so far. Hopefully they would be out of here before the brothers became suspicious.

Jasmine arrived at the blue door and pushed it open. The bathroom was also blue. The tiles, rug, sink, and bath all the same shade. Masculine toiletries cluttered the shelves. You could tell a pair of bachelors lived there. There was not one single piece of femininity anywhere to be seen.

Finding a bolt on the door, she slid it into place. Out of habit she noted the items in the bathroom. Her parents had raised her watching the 80s show 'MacGyver' on DVD. He was an American secret agent who could get out of any situation using the things around him. Jasmine had been obsessed with it. Many of her childhood memories were of using things around her to escape the house. Even now this kind of thing came in useful, so she kept on doing it.

The cordless phone was sitting on the bathroom cabinet. She grabbed it, dropped the lid on the toilet, and sat down with it in her hand. She knew the number to the office by heart—the only number she could ever remember.

She tapped it in quickly and heard the ring on the other end. She hoped her boss was at his desk. Normally his butt was always firmly in his chair during working hours unless they were out on a case.

"Detective Cummings," Mark said business-like over the line.

She had never been so relieved to hear her boss's voice in her life. The guy liked to give her hell. She knew, though, he was just trying to toughen her up.

"It's Jasmine."

She could almost sense his stunned shock at the sound of her voice.

"Holy fuck, Jasmine! Where are you?"

She decided not to waste any time with pleasantries. "I'm in Paris with Twitch."

A long silence followed at the other end of the phone. She was not sure if her boss was experiencing shock again or surprise. Maybe he thought they had run off together? Maybe he was having a heart attack? She suppressed the urge to giggle nervously.

"You better start at the beginning." His voice was so grim when he finally answered that she didn't have to worry. It already sounded like he had figured out what had happened. For that she was grateful.

It took her fifteen minutes to explain the previous several hours' events. Mark had listened patiently, only butting in a few times to ask questions. Thankfully he did not have many.

"I want you and Twitch to sit tight," he finally said. "I'll get someone over there from the French police to take you somewhere safe."

His tone had become a little harsh. Jasmine knew from experience, though, it was only because he was worried about them.

"I'm worried about Twitch," she admitted softly.

"Just keep an eye on him, Jaz. This is probably bringing back some bad memories for him."

She glanced towards the bolted door. "What do you mean?"

The squeak of Mark's chair moving, like he was shifting around, sounded down the line. Then in a lower voice, he said, "He sold what he thought was harmless magical technology. People died.

He blames himself for not realising what it would be used for."
Mark sighed. "Just stay where you are, please."

"OK, we can do that," she assured him.

They had nowhere else they could go anyway. She doubted
Twitch would want to leave again until they had a guaranteed safe
house. She felt the same.

"And Jasmine?"

She knew what was coming, Mark's speech about not doing
something stupid. Why was she the one who only ever got it?

"Yes, boss?" she asked.

"Promise me you'll be careful. Marcel Coupe is a dangerous
man."

Jasmine blinked in surprise. "I promise. Both of us will."

She hung up after saying good-bye. Her boss's concerned
warmed her. It was nice to know he cared about them.

How long it would take Mark to arrange a safe house for them
was anyone's guess. For now though, they could hide out in this
spare bedroom. It was a safer place than any. She was pretty
certain no one had followed them. They could stay until the police
arrived.

Just then she noticed the first-aid kit tucked on one of the
shelves. She hauled it out and unlocked the bathroom door. As she
headed back to the bedroom, she noted it was now quiet
downstairs. The brothers must have calmed down.

Twitch sat cross-legged on the floor of the room. His long body
hunched over as he worked. The little screwdriver was in his hand.
Several tablets, mobile phones, and a laptop were strewn around
him. He looked like a little boy surrounded by his toys.

She was not sure where they had come from or how he had
gotten them so quickly. He seemed to be very focused. She realised
then, having these probably made him feel relaxed. That was a
good thing. His head was lowered and the tangle of his long,

cinnamon curls obscured Jasmine's view of his face. She was not even sure if he knew she was there.

Sinking down onto the side of the bed, she watched him.

"I got hold of Mark. At least now he knows where we are."

Twitch didn't respond. She watched as his nimble fingers danced over the insides of a tablet. They never hesitated, never ceased from their task. With a sigh she pulled open the first-aid kit. He was going to have to damn well stop long enough for her to see to his hand. She wouldn't allow it to go untended.

Rummaging around, she found a bandage. She couldn't remember if she was allowed to put cream on an electrical burn. Jasmine decided a covering would just have to do. It was better than nothing.

She stood up, moved to his side, and sat on her knees beside him. Watching his moving hands, she got ready to pounce. When his wounded hand came close, she grabbed hold of his wrist.

Twitch immediately stilled. She could feel the strong beat of his heart through his pulse point. He didn't try to move away.

"I'm going to bandage this up now," she told him quietly tugging the arm closer.

Twitch allowed her to take it. Relief flooded through her that he wasn't putting up a fight.

Jasmine carefully inspected his palm. The small deep burn was red and blistered in several places, but at least there was no blood and it wasn't weeping. She reasoned that had to be good. Not that she was an expert or anything.

She rested his hand on her knee and picked up the things she needed. As gently as she could, she covered the burnt skin with a sterile gauze bandage and quickly and efficiently secured it in place with a knot.

Twitch admired her handiwork for a moment. "Thank you, Jazzy."

"You're welcome, Twitchy." She gave him a tired smile. "You want to tell me what you're doing?"

"Marcel will not give up." His whisper was grim, his eyes hard. "I have to make sure we're prepared."

Jasmine had a feeling he was right. She doubted they would be safe until they were out of the country. Even then they might not be. The arms dealer had already found him once. Would Twitch then have to go into hiding? Would he be forced to leave the team?

She pushed down the unease these questions bought. The team without Twitch would never be the same.

"Why does this guy want you so badly?" she murmured.

Suddenly he looked very uncomfortable. A look of bitter guilt passed across his face. "People died because of things I sold on the black market. I was so fucking caught up in creating I didn't even stop to consider what they would be used for. When I finally did it was too late. I lost . . .things important to me. Marcel was one of my customers and recognised my potential to make him more money."

Jasmine hesitated, not sure if he would answer the next question. "What things did you sell?"

Twitch's shoulders became rigid with tension. It was then she sensed she had pushed him too far.

He turned his face away with a jerk. The fall of his tangled hair acted like a curtain to hide his features. "I don't want to talk about it."

"OK." She wasn't going to push. He was obviously feeling uncomfortable about the whole thing.

Her head was still aching and she wanted to rest her tired feet. She crawled back over towards the bed. Leaving him in peace seemed the best option. Tinkering calmed him.

She took a painkiller from the first-aid kit and swallowed it down.

"Why not try to get some rest, Jazzy? You looked shattered," Twitch said from behind her.

Exhaust was heavy on her shoulders. The big bed did look inviting. She hadn't slept since they had been taken. Everything had finally started taking its toll. She knew if she didn't rest now, she would be more than dead on her feet. Being at the top of her game was a must. For Twitch's sake, she would rest.

"OK," she agreed, looking back at him. "But just for a few hours. Don't let me sleep all day."

Twitch nodded. A moment later he was back busy fiddling with the electronic devices on the floor.

With a sigh, Jasmine dragged herself onto the mattress. The softness actually made her body ache more. She doubted whether she would fall asleep with everything still churning around in her head, but the moment her head hit the pillow, she was out.

Eric gazed out at the early afternoon sunlight through the tinted window. The black limousine was moving smoothly though the flow of traffic. Paris was bustling with mortals all bundled up against the wintry cold. Enfolded in the luxury of the car, they were safely away from the mayhem of Christmas shoppers on the streets. Safe from prying eyes.

Eric adored the winter. His icy powers were at their height during the coldest season of the year. This made him more powerful than at any other time. He was in his element, so to speak. A force to be reckoned with.

"You do not appear to be upset that your genius had flown the coop," he remarked, settling his gaze on the man opposite him.

Dabbing at his continuously sweaty head Marcel smiled. "He has not fluttered far."

So he was already aware of where they were hiding? Eric did not let his dismay show. He had been hoping the mage and the girl were safely tucked away. Marcel, though, he realised, would not give up. Would he have to intervene? Could he risk it again without being exposed? The more he interfered, the more his plans were forced to change. He had never had his formidable control and composure tested so much.

It was the girl's fault, of course. He had been perfectly in command of himself before he had set eyes on her. She had bewitched him somehow—he was sure of it. Perhaps she was a witch. She certainly had a siren's body. Just thinking about it made him hard all over again.

"You liked Twitch's girl, *mon ami?*" Marcel gave him a sly smile. "Perhaps I will gift her to you to sweeten our deal, hmmm?"

Eric kept his face expressionless. How careless he had been to let the arms dealer sense his interest in her. Foolish. He let a cold smile touch his lips.

"I'm sure she could entertain me for a while before I grew bored. The weapon you have promised excites me far more."

The Frenchman waved his hand dismissively. "Yes, a few nights until our business is finished. Then you can be rid of her. It will be easy enough to do. The weapon will be in your hands soon."

Claude, who was also in the car, had his face pressed against the window. He looked like an excited puppy.

"Baby, can we go and buy some macarons? You know how much I love them." His voice was soft and pleading. He turned his eyes on the fat man.

The young, blond American was handsome. His grey eyes danced as he looked at his lover.

Eric knew the boy was in his early twenties—a tourist Marcel had taken a fancy to. Now he warmed his bed. How long that would last he could not be certain. Claude was not even his real name. Marcel, as far as Eric could gather, had a habit of renaming his young pets.

The American, though, would probably never return home. He would disappear once the arms dealer grew bored of him, just like many others. And there had been many more.

A twinge of sympathy squeezed in Eric's chest. He sighed inwardly. One by one, he shut down any emotions that tried to escape his control. Feelings were a weakness he could not afford. Not now.

"Of course." Marcel smiled and patted Claude's knee.

Eric returned his gaze to the window. He would be more than happy when this was all over and this monster was finally off the streets.

CHAPTER 8

JASMINE AWOKE TO FIND herself tucked up under a thick white duvet. She blinked sleepily with confusion. Where the heck was she? This was not her bedroom.

The memories of the last hours came flooding swiftly back with jarring clarity. The car crash, the cargo container, Paris, Marcel the arms dealer, and the tall, sexy vampire. The intensity of those icy blue eyes. She felt like he had branded her with just a look. God, he had been so sexy. The way he had awakened her body. The sweet pleasure he had given her.

A groan left her lips. Why the fuck was she thinking about him now? She shouldn't be thinking about him at all.

Twitch was suddenly hovering beside her. "Jazzy, are you alright?"

"Yeah." She sat up and flung the duvet from her body. "What time is it?"

"Two p.m."

Blinking owl-like, she gave him an incredulous look. "I told you not to let me sleep so long."

His green eyes slid away from hers and then he shrugged. "You needed it."

He was right. She knew he was. Her headache was gone and she did feel a hell of a lot better. The long sleep had done her good.

Twitch shoved something into her hand. "Here."

Jasmine looked down. It looked like a piece of pink, well-chewed gum. The texture was slightly sticky but smooth. As presents went, it was just plain weird.

Flattening her palm, she eyed it. "Eew, what the hell is this? I hope you haven't chewed it before it went in my hand."

He gave an exaggerated, long-suffering sigh. "I haven't chewed it. It's a crude earwig. I'm not sure of the range, but at least we can talk if we need to. There's an incantation on it so we don't need microphones like usual."

An earwig is what they called their earpieces. The fact they didn't ever need a microphone to chat back always came in handy.

She eyed it suspiciously. "It doesn't look like your normal one. It won't explode will it?"

Usually they were smooth all over, blue, and sunflower seed-shaped. What she had in her hand looked like it could have been stuck beneath a table for a few months—after having been chewed within an inch of its life.

Twitch looked a little hurt at her question. His chin dropped a little and his dishevelled hair flopped forwards. She could see him watching her out of the corner of her eye.

She realised she might have actually offended him a little—something she never wanted to do.

"No, Jazzy, it won't explode. It's the same design I use for my others. Just not as advanced. That's why it looks like gum and is a different colour."

The guy was trying his best in the circumstances. She knew that. He could only work with what he had available and with limited time. Suddenly she felt bad.

She sent him an apologetic smile. "OK, sorry. It's great really."

Jasmine knew she was going to have to install it. It was the only way he would believe her now. Taking a deep breath, she tried not to feel too squeamish. This bit she always hated.

Tilting her head slightly, she popped it securely into her ear. She could feel it oozing slightly as it melded with her flesh. Jasmine curbed the urge to claw it out. It always felt weird and a little creepy as it settled in. Like there was a slug squirming in your ear. At least it wasn't slimy. Once it settled she would not feel it at all.

A few times, she had even forgotten to take them out after assignments. It hadn't been until Twitch had started whispering to her that she remembered they were in. It was an experience she tried to avoid. Having the mage suddenly start chatting when you were in the middle of a shower was unnerving. Even worse when you were in the middle of watching a horror film.

She knew, though, from experience, that when she wanted it out, it would just drop out without a fuss. Well she hoped it would like all the others had.

Twitch plonked himself down on the side of the bed. He looked tired. She felt suddenly guilty. He hadn't rested at all.

"Are you OK?" Jasmine asked as she crawled along to sit beside him.

He was fiddling with an electronic tablet. His slender fingers caressed the smooth screen. "Yeah, better now that I have something to do."

"So tell me more about how you know Jeremy and Ralph." Jasmine didn't really know what the techno mage had meant when he called them 'Internet friends' earlier. She wasn't into video games. Occasionally she might find something she liked to play, but she did not become obsessed with them. She didn't live and breathe it like other people could.

He glanced up at her and smirked. "We met on an RPG. We group up and kill virtual monsters, quest things like that. Chatting through typing or over mic's is fun and I find it stress relieving."

She frowned. "And you made friends that way?"

Twitch's attention was focused on the tech in his hands again. "I don't have many friends apart from you guys on the team at Scotland Yard. My online friends know me as Alan. I never planned on meeting any of them in real life. I just use them for the game play. I play to relax."

That made sense. It had to be lonely for him stuck inside all the time. Online he could escape and have fun. He could also hide his real identity. She knew that she was the only member of their team to visit his house. It was an old Victorian building, which looked like it was in a constant state of disrepair.

They had movie nights on Wednesdays. The mage had a huge, flat-screen plasma TV. It was something they had done for over a month now.

"Friendships are hard for me," He continued leaning further over the tablet he was fiddling with, not meeting her gaze. "People can fail you or not really care when they say they do," he continued in a soft purr. A hint of pain was in his words.

This was the most Twitch had ever talked about himself. Someone had hurt him in the past, obviously.

Compassion swelled in Jasmine's chest. "You and I are friends. In fact, you're my best friend."

"Yes, we are." He looked up at her then. Trust and affection shone from his green eyes. "I don't know why or how, but we just seemed to click, didn't we?"

She couldn't help but smile at that. It was true. Ten minutes after they had met, they had become firm friends. It was crazy how quickly they had bonded, connected.

Maybe it was because she didn't have many friends either.

Her mind wandered to the men downstairs. Then another thought hit her.

"How did you know what underwear I was wearing and why the hell did you tell your friends downstairs?" Jasmine prickled slightly. She still couldn't believe he had done that. What the hell had he been thinking?

Twitch suddenly looked sheepish. "It's obvious you're not wearing a bra. I could see the hard outline of your nipples when you got cold outside. Your panties . . . well . . . I got a glimpse, when you were pretending to be unconscious back at Marcel's."

"Oh." Jasmine glanced away from him, embarrassed. She was still stuck in the same clothes and would be unless they found her something else to wear.

Twitch did not seem bothered he was wearing the same stuff. Maybe that was a guy thing. She just didn't know. Her experience was limited when it came to men.

Maybe they could borrow some money from his friends. There had to be somewhere she could buy some jeans and a top. At least she would feel warmer and more comfortable.

"As for telling them," Twitch continued. "If I knew what you were wearing underneath, it makes it more convincing that we're a couple."

Jasmine frowned. "Maybe in your dirty mind, but honestly it doesn't."

Twitch chuckled. "Did you think I had been spying on you?"

Startled at Twitch's question she met his stare. "It did cross my mind," she murmured in response.

Twitch smirked. "I was a bit disappointed you didn't wear the red matching set. The one with all that frilly, sexy lace."

That was a set she had bought online from her favourite boutique. How the hell had he known that? She hadn't even worn the set yet. It was still in its bag on her dresser at home.

Stunned, Jasmine was silent for a moment. "You have been fucking spying on me again!"

He giggled. "Maybe I just found the electronic receipts from when you bought it."

She gave him a sceptical look. "And went through the lingerie website to see what they looked like?"

"In one of my bored moments, yes, and it's amusing." Twitch was playing absently with the tablet in his hands again.

"You really found the online receipt?" She still wasn't sure she believed him.

"I don't spy on you, Jazzy," he assured her. "But imagining you in that lingerie is nice. It's not like I'm ever going to get to see you in it."

No, he wouldn't. In fact she wouldn't be wearing any of it for anyone.

A knock sounded at the door before she could reply.

She pushed up onto her feet and padded to the door. She figured it was one of the brothers checking up on them. It probably seemed a little weird they hadn't left the room at all.

Twitch tensed up. His hand was hovering over the piece of technology he was holding like he was ready to strike down any threat. For all she knew it was a weapon of mass destruction. Jasmine swallowed down a bout of panic.

He would not do anything stupid. If he did, she would kick his arse. She glanced at him warily for a moment before opening the door.

Jeremy stood the other side with a tray and some clothes draped over one arm. His smile was friendly when he saw her.

"I thought you guys might be hungry," he told her pleasantly. "You've been up here for ages."

Jasmine stepped back to let him inside. "Wow, thanks, that's really kind of you. We've been catching up on some sleep."

It was an easy excuse and half-true. The bed looked rumpled enough as evidence. Not that any would be needed.

Twitch had moved back onto his position on the floor. He was busy with his screwdriver again. "Hey, Jeremy."

Jeremy grinned. "I have a free computer if you want to play online later you know."

The mage raised his head. Interest was sparkling in his eyes. "Maybe a bit later on. Thanks for the food."

Jeremy placed the tray down on the floor by the bed. "It's no problem. Ralph had to pop out but got some things from the local bakery before he went."

Two white mugs of tea and a plate of warm, freshly made croissants lay on the tray. The smell was delicious.

Jasmine's stomach rumbled loudly. She hadn't eaten in many hours and her body was demanding to be satisfied. After sleep, food was its next agenda. She inhaled the scent of French pastry.

"This looks great, I'm starving," she said, reaching for a croissant.

"I found you some clothes, too." Jeremy carefully handed her the bundle.

"Ralph's ex-girlfriend left some stuff here. She was slim like you so hopefully it all fits."

Jasmine examined the clothing. The jeans were light blue and faded and seemed to be her length. The jumper was black and made of wool. The material was a little itchy, but she was happy to live with it, especially if it meant finally getting out of the dress and being warm.

Eyes happy, she smiled at Jeremy in pure delight. "Thank you so much. I have been dying to get out of this bloody dress."

"Hey, I'm just happy I could help. Why not drink your tea and eat and then get changed?" he suggested softly. "I better get back downstairs to the customers. I can't leave the place alone for too long."

Twitch picked up one of the mugs as Jeremy left.

Instead of sitting down beside the tray, Jasmine just hovered beside it. She stared longingly at the jeans in her arms. Did she really want to wait a few more minutes? She was starting to hate this dress. Another minute and it might drive her crazy. She needed to be in something familiar, more comfortable. Then maybe she could relax.

Twitch lifted the mug to his lips then hesitated. "If you're that desperate to change, why don't you go do it now?"

He had a point. The tea and the food could wait a few more minutes. Once she was dressed more comfortably, then she could eat.

"I think I will." She grinned. "Don't eat all the croissants."

She reassembled the first-aid kit, closed it, and picked it up. She thought she heard him mutter something like 'better be quick' as she disappeared out of the bedroom.

Jasmine hurried back along the corridor and into the bathroom. As quickly as she could, she shoved the first-aid box back into its place. She did not want to leave it laying around in case someone else needed it. It was the polite thing to do.

After making sure the bolt was secure, she peeled off the dress. When it pooled at her feet, she released a sigh of relief. Never had she been so glad to be rid of a piece of clothing. With a nudge of her foot, she kicked it into a corner. Turning, she glanced at herself in the mirror.

The bruise on her forehead just above her left eye, which she hadn't really bothered to look at before, was nasty. The skin was blotchy and discoloured. Twisting her head slightly, she examined it in the mirror It could have been worse. She knew that and was thankful it wasn't.

Jasmine touched it lightly, wincing when it hurt. She grabbed some tissue paper, wetted it, and cleaned away the dried blood. It looked a little better afterwards.

Her eyes then dropped to her bare breasts. Two small puncture marks were visible on the swell of her left tit, no longer throbbing. Using a fingertip, she touched the area. Heat bolted through her. A strange tingle shot through her belly. Jasmine gasped at the unfamiliar sensations.

The image of the vamp's head against her breast played slowly over and over in her mind. Her body began to thrum with remembered pleasure. Biting her lip hard, she crammed the memories back. She leaned forwards, and grabbed onto the sink tightly. She had to forget what had happened.

Yes, it had been eye-opening. Never in her life had she responded to a man like that. Maybe she was finally moving on. Two years was a long time to heal. Maybe she was finally getting over the trauma of the past. A storm of emotions was brewing inside her. Things she wasn't sure how to cope with right now.

Then again maybe it had been the vampire himself. She knew they all had weird different powers. Had he affected her in some way? Pulled her past her fear to pleasure?

A shiver ran through her. Unfortunately, it was something she couldn't think about right now. She returned her focus to the clothes and quickly got dressed.

The jumper was a little tight and you could tell she was not wearing a bra. Her nipples were visible through the woolly fabric. Turning sideways, she stared at their taut outline.

Jasmine found this a bit annoying. Her breasts weren't big, but they still needed a little support. Maybe if she kept her arms crossed no one would notice.

The jeans, on the other hand, were a little loose around the waist. Pursing her lips, she glanced around. She could see nothing she could use as a belt. Maybe Jeremy had something she could borrow.

As she pondered whether to go down and ask him or not her senses began to jingle. It sounded like the little tinkle of bells, soft yet insistent—the feeling she got for imminent danger. Suddenly feeling jumpy, she peered out of the bathroom window.

Everything seemed quiet outside. Grey clouds hung heavily in the afternoon winter sky. Nothing looked threatening. Still, the bells kept tinkling in her head. Jasmine knew by now to trust her sixth sense. As a sensitive, she knew they were almost always never wrong.

She unbolted the door and moved back along the corridor. One of the other doors was half-open now. Stopping in front of it, she peered cautiously inside.

Another bedroom. No one was inside. A large green duvet was spread over the double bed. Rather messy as clothes were strewn across the floor and piled haphazardly on a chair.

She spotted the end of a belt peeking out from the clothes pile. After checking over her shoulder to make sure she was alone, she nipped into the room and claimed it. She figured she'd just tell Jeremy she was borrowing it. Whomever lived in the bedroom might not like her sneaking in, but it was kind of an emergency. Besides, they would have had to lend it to her anyway. It made sense to take it now.

Trying not to feel guilty, she slipped back into the spare bedroom.

Jasmine froze. "Twitch?"

He was slumped sideways over the carpet. His mop of hair was obscuring his face and he was not moving.

She dashed to his side and crouched beside him. The electronic tablet he had been playing with rested on the floor near his hand. Had he blown something up again? Had he hurt himself badly this time?

Jasmine shook him hard, but he did not respond. Smoothing the hair back from his face, she couldn't find any wounds. Frowning, she eased him gently onto the carpet and searched for a pulse. He was breathing, just unconscious. His heartbeat was steady and strong.

What the hell was going on? He didn't seem to be physically hurt. She had not heard an explosion. Maybe there was another reason he was out cold. What had happened while she was using the bathroom? Scanning the room, her eyes fell on the tray. One tea cup was still sitting untouched.

She then glanced suspiciously at the broken cup on the floor. Had he been drugged?

Suddenly she was grateful she had not drunk her own tea. Only one explanation could she come up with.

Someone must know they were here. Had one of Twitch's friends betrayed them? It was the only thing that made sense. Suddenly not sure what to do, she looked around the room. He was too heavy to carry. Maybe she should contact Mark again or the French police?

Jasmine stilled. Why hadn't the police turned up yet? Mark had told her he would get in contact with them, yet they had been here for hours. Surely someone should have turned up by now. What the fuck was going on?

The sudden sound of voices downstairs made her panic. She darted to the door and stood out in the corridor. Like a deer ready to take flight, she stood poised. Maybe she was being paranoid, but her sixth sense for danger had gone into overdrive. It was jingling away inside her skull, so loud it was almost painful. Like a hundred little tinkling bells all set off at once.

Standing by the stairs, she tried to listen to the male voices. They were talking in French. She recognized Jeremy's voice. He was obviously the little bastard who had sold them out. Did his brother know, too?

The other man speaking sounded strangely familiar. When she heard footsteps coming up the stairs, she leapt into action.

She scampered into the open door and found herself in the other bedroom again. Panic beat through her. A hiding place is what she needed. She could not let herself be found. Without a second thought, she dropped to the floor and rolled beneath the bed. Luckily there was nothing much under it—just a few boxes at the end facing the door, which she used to shield herself. She knew if she stayed completely still, no one would be able to see her. That was her plan.

Her knee poked something hard when she wiggled to get comfortable. With one hand she reached down. Smooth wood met her fingers. As carefully and quietly as she could, Jasmine pulled it upwards. Tilting her head, she discovered she had hold of a baseball bat. A pleased smile curved her lips. Her fingers curled around it. At least she had a potential weapon now.

Peeking through a crack in the boxes, she saw four pairs of legs pass by. They were heading for the spare bedroom. She stilled. Ears straining, she listened for any sound.

Jasmine recognized Pierre's voice. Now she realised who Jeremy had been talking to downstairs. He did not sound happy. Was he pissed off because she was missing? Seemed so.

"Jasmine?" she heard Jeremy's voice call. He did not sound frightened. In fact he sounded slightly annoyed. "Jasmine, where are you?"

A short silence followed. She knew they were waiting for a reply. If she was lucky they would think she had gone out. If not, she was certain they would search for her.

An angry voice was suddenly shouting. Pierre sounded like he was having a full-on rant.

A loud bang like a balloon popping filled the air and then a thud.

She froze. With a sick feeling, she realised it had been a gun shot. Had they killed Twitch?

Jasmine bit her bottom lip until she tasted blood.

No, they wanted Twitch alive. It didn't make sense for them to hurt him. In the back of her mind, she knew they wouldn't do that. Marcel had risked too much to kidnap them. He wanted the mage for weapons. Killing him now would not make sense.

That could only mean it had been Jeremy. Obviously he had not come through with his part of their bargain, or maybe they had planned to kill him all along.

She could hear low voices talking. It left at least three men. That was still too many to take on alone. Not while they had guns.

Jasmine clutched the baseball bat to her chest. Would they look for her now? She knew she was just a bargaining chip to make sure Twitch obeyed Marcel. If they couldn't find her, they would find another way to get what they wanted. She was pretty sure of that.

Jasmine stilled when she heard movement.

She watched with dread as Twitch, head slumped forwards onto his chest, was dragged past the door by two men. She couldn't see his face thanks to his damn long, messy hair. Each man had one of his arms. He still seemed to be completely knocked out.

Pierre was walking impatiently behind them. His hard, brown eyes glanced inside the room.

Every muscle in Jasmine's body tensed. Holding her breath, she dared not release it.

His eyes danced over everything. Then after a moment he moved on.

Jasmine waited until she heard them descend the stairs. Then she waited another ten minutes.

She badly wanted to go after her friend. The only thing that stopped her was the fact that they had guns and her baseball bat was no match. Also if she let herself get captured they were back at square one. They would be stuck in a cell with Marcel using her as Twitch's weakness. She couldn't let that happen. Not again.

Crawling like a lizard on her belly, she moved from beneath the bed. Stilling, she listened to the sounds of the building. Silent. Eerily so.

She rose to her feet and crept to the door. She raised the bat, ready to strike if anyone surprised her. The warning bells were still going off in her head, making her jumpy.

Biting at her raw lip, she looked at the stairs. Maybe she was being paranoid, but she wanted to be certain they were gone. Knowing her luck this was all a trap. When she was sure she still heard nothing, she moved. The door to the spare room was open.

Jeremy's body lay on the bed. His face was slack with death, his eyes glassy and empty. A growing stain of crimson was spreading on the duvet beneath him. Jasmine knew there was no point looking for a pulse. He was dead. Nothing could be done for him now.

The tablets and phones Twitch had been playing with were scattered over the floor. Some of the screens were broken. Had someone done it deliberately? She knew she had to contact Mark. He needed to know Twitch had been kidnapped again. They had to find a way to save him.

She sprinted back towards the bathroom and the cordless phone. If her boss could contact the French police like he had promised, maybe they could coordinate a rescue. Marcel could not be untouchable.

BOOM.

The world suddenly exploded around her in noise and fire. A roaring rumble deafened her ears. Heat rushed upwards searing her flesh as an explosion rocked through the building. Jasmine barely had time to scream as she was thrown backwards. Then everything went black.

CHAPTER 9

ERIC STOOD IN THE DOORWAY staring at the large luxurious bed. Jasmine lay unconscious in the middle of it, covered by blankets. The little female was lucky to be alive.

Raoul had seen the building explode. He had managed to get inside and carry her out before it was too late. Eric himself had tended to her. She had superficial burns on one forearm and shoulder. That she was not seriously hurt was a miracle.

Eric's chest tightened painfully. For some reason, the thought of her mortal life being snuffed out left a bitter taste in his mouth. This was odd, as he barely even knew the girl. Eric also knew he should not care.

He was more than certain Marcel had been behind the bomb. Even now, the techno mage was back under the arms dealer's lock and key. The Frenchman was no doubt celebrating yet again.

Did the mage even know, Eric wondered, that he had been deceived by one of his friends for money? By one of the males he so trusted? Greed was a powerful motive for betrayal.

Eric sensed Raoul's familiar and grounding presence in the other room.

I have all the information you requested, the other vampire whispered into his head.

Moving with silent ease, Eric left the girl to sleep. She would no doubt be sore and shaken when she awoke. Allowing her to rest now would do her good.

He found the other vampire in the living room of the hotel suite.

Raoul smiled as he sank down onto one of the black couches. With a sigh, he made himself comfortable.

"Her name is Jasmine Hunter. She was adopted at two years of age. Birth parents are unknown. The couple who took her in died in a traffic accident three years ago." Raoul paused for a moment, making sure he had his companion's full attention. "She works for a branch of Scotland Yard that deals with supernatural crimes called SNC. She started the job only two months ago. The unit itself has been running for the better part of sixty years. It is made up of six teams and they do not just deal with cases in England."

Eric sat at the opposite end of the sofa. "You mean to say she is a co-worker of the techno mage?"

"Yes."

Eric was not sure why this pleased him. The thought of her as the mage's girlfriend had not sat well with him. They had not acted like a couple. The fact he also suspected she was a virgin had baffled him about their relationship. She was a desirable woman. Why would you wait to have her in your bed?

Raoul was watching him carefully. "My sources say they were together in the car when Marcel's people grabbed them. They did not confirm her identity."

"That was indeed sloppy." Eric had not thought the arm's dealer would be so foolish. His lust for having the techno mage seemed to have blinded him to all else. Very careless.

"More than fortunate for the girl. Marcel would have had her killed already."

Eric made a hum of agreement. She was a loose thread, which even now the fat man would want cleaned up.

The other vampire glanced at him sideways. "I have never known you to act so impulsively, Eric."

Eric knew his friend was referring to his interference with the girl. When they were deep undercover, he never let anything meddle with their missions. He was cold, calculating, and meticulous—even ruthless at times. It was a necessity in his line of work. So why now was he jeopardizing it all for this human girl?

"It was only logical to pluck her from danger," he replied. "I am sure Scotland Yard will thank us."

It was the only rational answer. Perhaps he had even felt sympathy for her—an emotion that should have been tightly leashed like all the others he possessed. He was not known as Frostbite for nothing.

Turning his head, he fixed his eyes on the door where the young woman slept. He was still trying to understand the unsettling rush of warmth he had felt when her name had so easily left his lips.

She was also, as Raoul had pointed out, making him act impulsively. This was all so out of character for him. He liked to be in control; it was much safer and tended to ensure one lived longer. This woman, though, brought out emotions he rarely experienced so intensely. Protectiveness, lust, worry, and compassion—they were all tumbling around inside him like a raging storm.

"I think your little female might be a sensitive," Raoul said, breaking into his thoughts. "A run of the mill human would not have been able to sense what you are, even though she was mistaken."

Sensitives—humans who could sense and see supernaturals when others could not—were rare. If trained properly, their gifts could be extremely useful and unique.

Still, Jasmine had been slightly wrong though with her guess. He and Raoul were vampiria, born vampires who had never been mortal. The world did not know that two breeds of vampire existed and they liked it that way. It was a secret they intended to keep.

They were the original vampiric race—far stronger and superior. They had no problem with sunlight and were much tougher to kill. Humans-turned-vampires were weaker. They were not pure bloods. The vampiria knew they would be considered more dangerous if others knew the truth.

They didn't number as greatly as they once had as not many of the clans or nests survived. Many failed to find a compatible mate even in the ranks of the human vampires. No immortal was truly indestructible. The right strike or blow could easily end even them.

Eric rested his head back on the padding of the leather sofa.

"I believe you may be right," he murmured softly. "We cannot allow this to change our plans. She will have to be kept in the dark regarding our true purpose for now."

Raoul nodded. "So we are to continue our charade in front of her?"

Eric considered his friend's words for a moment. Keeping up their pretence seemed the most logical route. If she could be kept quiet and docile, then she would never need to know the truth. A perfect solution.

His cold gaze met the eyes of the other vampire. "I believe it is for the best for now."

CHAPTER 10

JASMINE AWOKE SLOWLY. She felt like she had been hit by a truck. Everything was aching. The skin on her left shoulder and forearm hurt. She rolled over on the comfy mattress and groaned. A moment later she realised she was naked. Her eyes snapped open. She found herself in a strange room. Confused, she frowned. Where the hell was she?

She hauled the blankets up to keep her breasts covered and sat up. Muscles aching in protest, she groaned again.

Soft lamp light illuminated her surroundings. The bedroom was huge with cream walls and burgundy furniture. A plasma television hung on the wall directly opposite the bed. She could see no personal items lying around. Two smart, comfy armchairs sat against one wall by the door. An antique writing desk and matching chair stood beside the floor to ceiling window, which led out onto a balcony.

The curtains had not been drawn and Jasmine could see the outline of the Eiffel Tower in the darkness. The city lights glittered and glimmered around it. The suite gave off a hotel vibe. A very expensive hotel at that, but what was she doing here? How she had gotten there was the most pressing question in her mind.

"Jasmine, you have finally awakened."

Deep and smooth, the voice was like thick, dark chocolate—and startlingly familiar. That crisp upper class English accent was unforgettable. Jasmine glanced its way.

The handsome, dark-haired vampire she had met at Marcel's now stood in the open doorway. Jasmine's mouth suddenly went dry.

His black hair was slightly tousled and he wore an impassive expression. Black jeans encased his long legs and a white shirt buttoned up over his broad chest. He looked sexy as hell and dangerous.

Her name falling from his lips had come out in a deep, rumbling caress—like he was savouring every syllable. An addictive sound that seemed to stir her senses, although she did not know why.

He exuded a formidable sort of energy. It seemed to swirl unseen around the room, subdued. She could feel it, potent and ready to be unleashed, brushing against her heightened senses.

What the fuck was he doing here? And where was here?

A slight thrill zinged through her and she shivered. Tugging the thick burgundy duvet up more, she kept herself completely covered. Jasmine had not forgotten what he had done to her. God knows she had tried. Experiencing your first ever orgasm was hard to forget.

Her nipples beaded in excitement. The rosy, taut peaks brushed against the material that covered them. She inhaled deeply to stop herself from moaning.

The intensity of the vampire's cerulean eyes swept slowly over her. Heat scorched through her just from that look. She felt vulnerable but strangely not as much as she thought she would.

By the glint in his eyes, he knew the effect he was having on her. How could he turn her on by just standing there?

Jasmine tried to remember how to breathe. Tearing her eyes away from him, she glanced around the room. She needed to focus. Her body might feel horny, but she needed to keep a clear mind. She suddenly realised she had let a silence stretch between them.

"Where am I?" Her voice sounded a little hoarse and she tried to clear it.

"My hotel suite." He glided closer. "You were caught in an explosion. Do you not remember?"

Frowning, she tried to recall what had happened. Twitch had been taken by Pierre. She had gone to use the phone and then there had been an explosion. Jasmine remembered the noise, the pressure, the searing heat, and momentary pain. Dropping her eyes, she found a small burn on her forearm. She had expected it to be red, angry, and blistered. Instead it looked pink and shiny, as if it had been healing for days. How long had she been here? It had to be more than a few hours.

Panic seized her. "Oh my god! Twitch! I have to find him."

"Your friend is safe." The vampire's deep voice assured her. "You know he was not in the blast, but already out of the building when it occurred."

She turned narrowed eyes on him. He would only know that if he had had something to do with it. Being in league with Marcel, they probably had planned it together. Maybe he even set the bomb. That did not explain, though, why he had gotten her out. Surely letting her die would have been better for them. So what was she doing here?

"Who are you?" she asked softly.

A ghost of a smile touched his sensual lips. "Forgive me for forgetting my manners. My name is Eric."

She had been the first thing on his mind when he had woken. The urge to set eyes on her again and soak in her presence had been overwhelming. Disconcerting, too. Eric had always been cool-headed, logical, and detached. He had never felt this way before—never this pressing need. This human girl had stirred up emotions long buried in him. Still, business came first. Then pleasure.

Moving to a chair beside the door, he picked up white fluffy robe. He could sense she was uncomfortable with her nakedness. Normally this would not bother him. She was under his protection now; it should not matter what she felt. Strangely, though, he felt the need to put her at ease.

Prowling slowly towards the bed, he held it out to her. "Here."

He could hear the swift beat of her heart. Those lovely green eyes of hers were dilated. Eric could tell she found him arousing, desirable. The scent of her arousal was an enticing aroma. One he had not forgotten. Jasmine smelled of sunshine and flowers. A natural fragrance, he had never come across before on any other being. No odour of artificialness. This smell was unique and all her own. Eric found that it stirred his blood.

He knew it would be easy for him to join her in the big bed. To feel her silken limbs entwine with his as he pleasured her with his mouth, his hands, his body. Eric knew he could take what he craved.

Even though her eyes were full of desire, the fear and distrust in them stopped him. The defiance he had seen before was now subdued. She was like a cat he had once found. Half-starved and wild, the tabby had been injured by children and limped into his garden to hide. After many nights, he finally was able to coax it from its hiding place. Even longer for the feline to consent to be petted and stroked.

Maybe it was the similar look in their eyes that did it, he was not sure. All Eric knew was he could not take advantage of the situation. No matter how much he wanted to.

Slowly as not to frighten her, he sat on the edge of the bed. He wanted her trust.

She seemed even more wary now. Those green eyes watched his every move. Eric knew that, like the feline, it would take time to erase the look in Jasmine's lovely eyes—much longer than a mere hour. He would have to convince her. Let her become used to his touch and caresses. These were things he was more than happy to do. Then her body, her pleasure would be his.

Jasmine accepted the offered robe. If he thought she would put it on in front of him, he would be sadly disappointed. She might be attracted to him, but that did not mean she would act on it. Flashing him bare skin was also out.

He was a bad guy. He either worked for Marcel or bought weapons from him. Those weapons killed and destroyed innocent lives. The vamp had probably only kept her alive because he fancied her. Maybe he planned to keep her to feed on. She tried not to think about how good it had felt when he had. Jasmine wouldn't let that happen again. No way was she becoming some vamp's pet. She would probably find herself back in a cell with Twitch soon enough.

"Come, I have taken the liberty to order breakfast for you." He rose to his feet and offered her his hand.

She stared at it warily. Did he think she was going to get up naked?

Jasmine dragged the robe behind the duvet and fed her arms into the sleeves one at a time in a slow, clumsy process as she used one hand to hold the cover up to hide her nakedness. After a few moments and a little bit of wiggling around, she was sufficiently shielded.

Eric's lips were quirked in amusement. He seemed to find her modesty funny by the expression on his face. She didn't give a fuck what he thought. If she was covered, she wasn't so vulnerable. She wondered if he had been the one to undress her. Someone must have.

Absently she glanced around for her clothes. Unfortunately there was nothing in sight. She guessed she was stuck with the robe.

"How long have I been here?" she asked as she slipped out of the bed, ignoring his hand. The plush cream carpet was soft against her bare feet. She resisted the urge to wiggle her toes.

Eric dropped his hand back to his side. He did not seem bothered that she hadn't taken it.

"Since my associate bought you here yesterday afternoon."

He was watching as she kept the robe, which concealed her from neck to ankles, tightly closed. Yanking on the belt she tied it firmly in place.

Jasmine frowned. That couldn't be right. How could the burn on her arm be so healed already? She pulled up her sleeve and stared at the burn on her forearm again. This was not fresh.

"A little of my blood on your burns encouraged them to heal more swiftly," the vampire said with a smirk as if reading her mind.

Eyes shooting up, she stared into his coldly handsome face.

"You healed me?" Her tone was disbelieving.

Eric's eyebrows inched up slightly in surprise. "But of course. I did not want you to awake in pain when it was not necessary."

This was starting to confuse the hell out of her. He actually looked slightly offended she would think such a thing. Surely pain was what he wanted. Wasn't it?

She glanced down and noticed her naked wrist. "Where's my watch?" The one item she didn't want to be parted with. Twitch had made sure it was a handy little gadget to help her get out of certain situations. Jasmine was sure she was going to need it.

"I fear it was damaged and rendered useless of the magic your friend impregnated within it," the vampire said smoothly.

His explanation sounded so sincere, she wasn't sure if he was lying or not. He had to be lying, right? Disappointment settled over her. So she would have to escape without techno mage gadgetry. That might not be so easy against a vampire's abilities.

A guarded expression graced the vampire's face now. Had he guessed what she was thinking? Shit.

He motioned politely for her to follow. Not quite sure what to make of everything, she followed him cautiously from the room.

Jasmine found herself in an elegant, bright, spacious, and airy sitting room. A wide-screen TV was on one wall. Two black leather couches faced the television with a glass coffee table between them. By a large window sat a table and chairs. The overhead lighting was soft rather than harsh.

On the table sat a plate brimming with French pastries, two cups, a teapot, a pot of coffee, and a little jug of milk. Eric gestured politely towards it. "Please, sit."

Jasmine moved closer and was surprised when he held a chair out for her. The vamp had good manners? Why was he being so nice and gentlemanly? Was this some kind of trick? She sank cautiously down into the chair. The food looked so good and her stomach had been empty for far too long. Jasmine was not sure it was wise to eat. What if he had done something to the food?

The vampire slid around the table and took the seat opposite, creating a strangely domestic scene. Not exactly like prisoner and captor.

"Why am I still alive?"

One of his dark eyebrows rose slightly. He plucked a croissant from the overflowing plate and laid it on her dish, where it taunted her. Jasmine's mouth began to water. Nervously she licked her lips and forced her gaze upwards.

"I mean, why am I here?" she asked, watching him now instead. "Why go to all the trouble of helping me? What do you want?"

"Perhaps I merely saved you for my amusement. Your blood is delicious," he confided. "Or perhaps to keep you as a bargaining chip so your friend behaves. I confess I have yet to decide."

Jasmine got the strange impression he was teasing her. She also noticed he neatly avoided answering her questions properly. She reached out and picked up the teapot. Tipping it over, she poured the hot amber-coloured liquid into a cup. After adding a little milk and a ton of sugar, she stirred it with a spoon.

Eric picked up the coffee pot and filled the other cup.

"When do I get to see Twitch again?" she asked. If she could find out where he was being held, maybe she could help him escape again. She very much doubted Marcel had him in the same building as before. That would be too easy.

Eric sat back in his chair and surveyed her thoughtfully. "If you are good, kitten, and cause me no trouble? Soon. It is completely down to you."

Kitten? Did he think she was cute and fluffy? She might be smaller than him, but that did not mean she would surrender without a fight. Even kittens had claws. Lowering her head she stared at the table top. Maybe if she gave the impression of being helpless, he would let his guard drop. She could work the explosion to her advantage.

Jasmine began to pick apart the pastry on her plate, but she didn't eat it. Her insides were knotted with tension. She needed to figure out a plan to escape his hotel suite.

The vampire was watching her through narrowed eyes.

"I can understand perhaps you are a little subdued after your ordeal yesterday, but you should eat something," he said in what sounded more like an order than a suggestion.

Ignoring him, she took a sip of tea, which helped soothe her nerves. Jasmine took another sip. The shitload of sugar in the tea was easing her hunger pangs.

"You suspected the food of being tampered with, yet you neglect the tea?" The vampire's voice was softly mocking. He clucked his tongue.

Jasmine froze. Eyes wide, she stared at the cup in horror. The liquid she had swallowed was already warming her stomach. Crap.

How could she have fallen for that trick when it was what had taken down Twitch? It was ridiculously stupid of her.

Eric chuckled, a deep, rumbling sound, which sent goosebumps over her flesh. "Fear not, kitten. There is nothing wrong with the beverage. I was merely pointing out the fact you overlooked it."

The bastard was playing with her. Pinning him with a glare, she was tempted to flip him off. She knew it wouldn't help her image of a helpless female. The fact he was right just irritated her.

Eric raised his cup and took a sip of coffee.

Jasmine watched him with a suddenly astounded expression. "I didn't know vamps could drink anything other than blood."

Eric paused for a moment and then shrugged. "I merely enjoy the taste, though it does little else for me." Gaze never wavering from her face, he drank some more.

Jasmine observed the muscles of his throat working. Her eyes wandered down to the top of his shirt, where three buttons had been left carelessly undone. A sprinkling of rough, black hair peeped out.

The irritation she had felt drained away.

Was he hairy all over his chest or was it a light covering? Jasmine could feel heat burning her cheeks at the thought. They burnt even hotter when she imaging having a look to see.

She was watching him with desire. The scent of her arousal had strengthened again, teasing Eric's senses like a heady perfume. A pretty blush on her cheeks, however, spoke of innocence.

"Are you a virgin?"

Shock lit her eyes for a moment at his abrupt question. Then he saw a flash of old pain.

"No." Her answer was sharp, clipped. A shuttered went down over her gaze, hiding her emotions. Bowing her head once more, she continued to dismantle the pastry on her plate—her movements jerky, almost savage.

Eric sensed a great tension within her now, as if his question regarding her innocence had somehow hurt her. His gaze narrowed. Like a lightning strike, a sense of clarity struck him. Someone had put the pain in her eyes. Someone had hurt her? The anxiety and fear, he had sensed, had been more than just because she believed she faced a vampire. Had something happened to her at the hands of a male? A story lay behind her reaction. One Eric was not sure he would enjoy.

"I will not harm you, Jasmine," he assured her, wanting to put her mind at ease. "All I wish is for you to remain out of trouble."

She looked at him doubtfully, wariness still in her eyes. He knew she did not believe him. Eric sighed inwardly. Nothing more could be done for now. He would see that she was comfortable and kept from danger. Then he would see about having her returned home.

"There are clothes for you in the wardrobe in the bedroom, along with undergarments and shoes. Ladies toiletries are in the en suite bathroom," he informed her.

He knew women enjoyed having their own things. Perhaps this would cheer her up. He had not meant to bring up any bad memories.

Now she frowned with confusion. "Where did they come from?"

"I had them purchased for you while you slept." Eric held back the urge to smile. She really did have the most beautifully expressive face. Would it be the same in the heat of passion?

As his thoughts wandered towards intimate pleasures, he pulled them back. He could not afford to become distracted now. The girl was out of harm's way. He and Raoul had a job to continue.

"Thank you." She lowered her lovely green eyes demurely.

Perhaps she would be no trouble at all, he mused. The girl seemed shy. The explosion had no doubt been a shock she was still recovering from. Possibly she knew the sensible thing was to do as she was told.

"You are most welcome, kitten." Eric's voice was soft as a caress.

Jasmine remained silent and kept her head down. She was still reeling from his question about her virginity. What the fuck had that been about? Had he hoped she had been untouched? Maybe a virgin's blood tasted better for all she knew. She was still learning as a rookie. The supernatural creatures that existed in the world had many differences.

Vampires tended to just feed and fuck. She also knew they were a lot faster and stronger than humans and had freaky powers they could use to defend themselves. Mark, her boss, had mentioned a few customs and beliefs they had. He had not gotten around to going in-depth yet. She knew there was a lot more to learn about bloodsuckers.

Jasmine did not even know if Eric was a rogue or belonged to a nest. Rogues were solitary and moved around a lot. Nest vampires lived in a group with a leader. They had territories they defended and a hierarchy. Not that she cared, she reminded herself. Her main task was to get away. Maybe if he thought she was not any trouble, she could find a way to escape.

It was seven a.m. Another hour and forty-four minutes and the sun would rise. Then she could try to make her escape.

"Is it alright if I go back to bed? Maybe watch some TV in there? I'm still a little tired and achy." She made sure her voice sounded shaky. She hoped he wouldn't try to join her. Jasmine had not missed the male interest that kept darkening his eyes, which was doing strange, pleasurable things to her insides. Just the thought of him climbing onto that big bed with her had her hot and bothered.

Eric smiled indulgently. Those cold, blue eyes warmed. "Of course. I have some calls to make now anyway. You may amuse yourself as you wish."

CHAPTER 11

JASMINE CHECKED THE BEDSIDE clock for the millionth time. It was an hour after sunrise. The vampire would be sleeping by now. As long as he didn't have human guards, she could make her escape. Eric wasn't stupid, though, so she doubted he had left her unwatched. She had no idea how she would deal with guards.

She had searched the room thoroughly when she first arrived back there earlier. Anything could be used as a weapon. You just needed a little imagination. The towel rack in the bathroom could not be removed. Jasmine had gone for the shower curtain rod instead. Motivation had fuelled her. Removing it had been a little tricky, but she had it now as a weapon. She had also found a can of hairspray that could come in useful.

The phone that should have been in the room was missing. Guess the vamp hadn't wanted her phoning for help. Her boss would have been her first call and that's exactly what she intended to do the moment she got her arse out of there.

For now she needed to move.

She rolled off the bed, making little sound. The clothes she had found in the wardrobe all fit her perfectly. They all still bore brand new tags. How Eric knew her size was a mystery. She had been quick to pick out a pair of jeans, trainers, a black jumper, and a short, black leather jacket. Practical and warm without restricting her movement. Good for running in, which she knew she would need.

Pressing her ear to the door, she listened intently. Silence. No voices or other sounds to indicate anyone was out there. She was going to have to take a chance. Jasmine bit on her lip. She could not make any mistakes. If she was caught, Eric would make it a hell of a lot harder next time. If, that is, she even got a next time.

She placed her hand on the knob and opened the door. The other hand held the curtain rod, and the hair spray can was stuffed in the pocket of her jacket.

The adjoining room was empty. No signs of life at all. She noted that another door, which she guessed led to another bedroom, was closed.

Was Eric sleeping in there? Were the thick, velvety curtains enough to keep out the sunlight? Vampires, she had learnt from her team, rarely stirred from their day sleep.

Randomly, she wondered if he slept naked. An image of pale muscles and hard, firm flesh flashed into her mind. Jasmine felt heat wash into her cheeks. She really needed to stop thinking about the vampire and naked body parts. Her libido, though, seemed to be out of control around him.

She tiptoed across the room. The breakfast table had been cleared already. Who had done that? She hadn't heard a maid service. Maybe it was one of the vampire's people? He worked with Marcel and he seemed to be rich, so he would have thugs working for him, too. People who would willingly do his dirty work for him.

She kept the curtain rod resting lightly on her shoulder, ready if needed. Her other hand fingered the top of the hairspray can in her pocket.

Moving cautiously, she was actually amazed when she made it to the door. She had not fallen over her own feet once. Nothing stirred inside the suite. It was actually eerily quiet. Her own breathing sounded terribly loud to her own ears.

Hand a little clammy, she turned the knob, which opened smoothly out onto the cheerful, white-walled corridor. Deserted. No guards greeted her outside. From the look of it, they were in the penthouse. That meant that this suite was the only one on that floor.

Jasmine frowned. The vamp had gone to bed and left her unguarded? Was he really so confident she could not leave? Only an idiot would be that trusting.

Something was off, but her sixth sense remained silent. What the fuck was going on?

She looked towards the lifts. They would be faster, but she would also be trapped if anyone did come after her. Jasmine knew she could not chance it.

She moved towards the door for the exit, knowing it would lead to the stairs. She pushed it open and peered cautiously inside. No one was waiting for her on the stairs.

Now she was feeling jumpy. This had to be some kind of trap. Jasmine knew she couldn't waste this one chance, though, so she began sprinting down the steps.

She made it down the first flight, at which point her inner warning system decided to jingle. A sense of power quivered in the air around her, brushing against her senses like the wind through leaves. The energy left her a tad dizzy.

When hands grasped her wrists, Jasmine squealed in fright. Struggling, she tried to yank free. She pushed her body backwards, attempting to ram back into her captor. If she could catch him by surprise, she might have a chance. But she was met with nothing but air.

Confusion bolted through her. What the fuck was going on?

Gripping the curtain rod, she jabbed it backwards. There did not seem to be anything to hit.

Suddenly she found herself airborne. In the blink of an eye, she was pinned spread-eagled high up against the wall. Jasmine realised then nothing physically had hold of her. Her captor did not seem to exist. Invisible hands held her immobile. She could feel them gripping her ankles and wrists tightly. They flexed against her flesh.

Panic washed through her. Jasmine began to thrash desperately. Twisting and turning, she tried to break free, but to no avail. By the time she stopped struggling, her chest was heaving from the exertion. The whole time she had been held firm but gently.

The force holding the hand gripping the curtain rod squeezed until she dropped it. Jasmine gasped in pain. The makeshift weapon clattered to the floor.

Wide-eyed with shock, she looked back up the steps. Eric was standing in the doorway watching, arms crossed over his big chest. How was he doing that? She felt her heart miss a beat.

Lips pressed together in a thin white line, he did not look impressed. In fact he looked something akin to very pissed off.

"Going somewhere?"

Jasmine swallowed down her dread. Had the bastard been watching her somehow the whole time? Toying with her?

"I . . . was just going for a walk," she responded weakly.

"Hmmm."

The can of hairspray was tugged from her pocket. It floated in front of her for a moment before joining the curtain rod on the floor with a thud. She stared helplessly down at her weapons.

Crap. She was so screwed.

Slowly she found herself gliding away from the wall. An invisible force drew her towards the vampire. Jasmine found she dangled helpless in the air. The unseen hands still held her arms and legs. Her body no longer felt like her own. Eric seemed to have complete control over her movements.

He positioned her so their faces were inches from each other. Icy eyes stared coldly unblinking into hers. A chill touched her skin. The temperature in the stairwell seemed to drop a few degrees.

Jasmine couldn't help but shudder even though she was wearing a jacket.

Eric sighed. "Your disobedience is tedious." His deep low baritone sent another shiver down her spine. He had her helpless and at his mercy.

Jasmine could not believe how aroused she suddenly felt. How wet. Nipples growing hard, she felt them stiffen against the material of her bra. Her eyes dipped to his sexy mouth, then back to his eyes. Jasmine licked her dry lips. God help her, she found this darkly exciting. This was so wrong.

Apart from the angry slash of his mouth, no other emotion showed on his face. What was he thinking? What did he plan to do with her now? The questions crashed around inside her head.

The force holding her abruptly let go. She fell straight into his waiting arms. They coiled around her like steel bands. As she tried to struggle, he carried her back into the suite. She was embarrassed at how easily he subdued her. Controlled her. Turned her on.

"Get the fuck off me," Jasmine hissed.

Without even stopping, he stalked back into the bedroom. The chill in the air seemed permanently attached to the vamp as it followed them as they went. Unceremoniously he dropped her, still struggling, onto the bed. Jasmine bounced on the mattress. She scrambled backwards and her back hit the headboard. Warily she watched him.

"Perhaps I should have not given you the clothes," he mused angrily. "I doubt you would try to escape naked."

The temperature dropped even further and she shivered. Why the fuck was it suddenly so cold? The windows weren't open so it wasn't a draft. Eric was standing at the end of the bed, gaze fastened on her face. Anger was crashing off him in hot, angry waves. He was seriously pissed.

"How are you awake? Vampires sleep during the day," she said in confusion.

Winter sunlight was pouring into the room from the window. He was standing, uncaring, in its light. By now he should have been a pile of ash.

Eric narrowed his eyes to blue, glittering slits. "Perhaps you were wrong and I am not a vampire."

Jasmine frowned. He had bitten her, taken her blood. What else could he be but a vampire? She didn't know of anything else that fed on plasma.

Slowly she shook her head. Suspicion narrowed her eyes. "No. I'm not wrong you're definitely a vamp."

An image of Jasmine naked, wrists handcuffed to his headboard, flashed in his mind. Her ankles would also be clamped to a spreader bar. A position that would leave her helplessly exposed to his private pleasures. Something he wanted very much. Eric felt a slither of excitement buzz through him. His anger lessened. Bringing her to mind-blowing orgasms while he played with her was something he now craved. He could also teach her a little obedience. It was something one day Eric would accomplish when he had her complete trust. For now, though, it would have to wait.

Her jade green eyes were lit with wary defiance. That cute little chin of hers was raised in challenge. The softness of her coppery red hair was a messy halo around her head. His little female was ready to fight. It had been amusing to watch her escape attempt. She had done rather well, which made him proud. The game was now over, though. He needed her to abide by his rules.

Reining in his anger helped leash his wintry powers and gain control. Letting them slip free had never been his intention. It had never happened before. Eric had not missed her shiver nor the look of wary confusion. His power ebbed. The temperature in the room rose back to normality.

"I need your compliance, Jasmine. You must obey my wishes and stay in this room," he informed her sharply. "Do not attempt to leave again."

The look she returned seemed to question his sanity. "I'm not doing anything you say, bloodsucker, and you can't keep me here against my will."

A sigh of frustration left his lips. He did not have time for this. The girl was stubborn. She had tried to lull him into believing she was manageable. A clever ploy, but it had not worked. He knew he should have already used his power of persuasion—the logical step. With anyone else, he would have already had them enthralled. Eric knew he should have placed her under his will earlier. That she should now be a slave to his words. It would be only temporary.

But it felt wrong. He could not explain why. Seeing her spirit dulled and controlled was something he had no wish to see. Eric wanted her to retain her free will in all things, including when she finally succumbed to his desires. It would make it all the sweeter.

Eric knew only one way she would calm and obey now. He would tell her a certain degree of truth.

"Would it help if I told you I am here to prevent Marcel from using your friend?" He knew telling her this would break his plans, but what other option did he have? Neither he nor Raoul could waste time babysitting her.

The defiance on her face faltered for a moment. "Why should I believe you?"

"You have little choice in the matter and if you do not, you will no doubt wind up dead," Eric mocked with a sardonic lift of his eyebrow. "And that would be such a pity."

Her eyes narrowed suspiciously. "Who are you working for then? CIA, Interpol?"

He was not about to tell her he was freelance. That he worked for any government or agency that required the certain skills he and his team possessed.

Eric kept his expression remote. "I am not at liberty to give you that information."

The little female moved nervously on the bed. "Then why should I believe you?"

"You work for Scotland Yard and have done so for two months. If I was really working with Marcel Coupe, do you not think I would have informed him of this already?" Eric slid his hands into the pockets of his jeans. "You would be dead, Jasmine. Not sitting in this hotel suite."

Uncertainty shadowed her face.

He could tell she was mulling over his words. All he could hope now was that she believed him.

"You're really here to stop the arms dealer? How do I know this isn't just bullshit?"

Eric sighed again.

"Jasmine I have not lied to you. We have been hunting him for over a year. There have been whispers of a silent partner, a Doctor Dasyurus. We know nothing about this person. There are no photos and information is limited. We do not even know if it is a male or female."

He had not planned to tell her so much. The words, though, had spilled from his mouth unhindered. Eric frowned. How did this girl have the power to twist him in knots, make him burn with lust, and bare some of his most guarded secrets? It was most disturbing.

"You want to know who this doctor is?" Her soft words dragged him from his thoughts.

"Yes," he responded a little harshly. "This doctor is turning out to be very dangerous. He or she seems to have a passion for science, but not in a way to help mankind."

Just then, Raoul abruptly appeared in the bedroom doorway.

Jasmine eyed the man at the door. He had smooth, mocha-coloured skin and short, spiky, black hair. He was handsome in an androgynous supermodel kind of way. He was tall. Not as tall as Eric, but still broad-shouldered and slim. His tight scarlet jumper accentuated the muscularity of his torso. Black jeans showed off narrow hips and long legs.

Warm, honey-brown eyes settled on her. "My name is Raoul. I have someone who wishes to speak to you online, Miss Hunter," he announced in a slightly accented voice.

Jasmine's sixth sense was already tingling. This guy was also a vampire. Power clung to him like an invisible cloak. She could feel the flow and ebb of its muted force, like gentle waves on a beach. It was a familiar feeling. She had sensed it the other day in the taxi. Had this Raoul been the driver?

Her eyes slid back to Eric. Could she really believe everything he had just told her? He wanted her compliance. Maybe he would tell her anything, just to get her to stay. How could she trust this vampire?

CHAPTER 12

A LAPTOP HAD BEEN SET up on the table in the sitting room. She padded cautiously closer and peered at the screen. A familiar face stared back at her. From his expression he did not look happy.

"Hey, Jaz, you OK?" asked Mark Cummings, her boss. He was sitting behind his desk at work. A pencil with one end badly chewed was resting behind one of his ears. Behind wire-rimmed specs, his caramel brown eyes brimmed with concern.

"Mark." She flopped down into the chair before the laptop. "Marcel's taken Twitch again... I couldn't help him. I'm sorry." Guilt thickened her throat.

Jasmine knew there was no point mentioning the vampires. No doubt Eric was an agent of some kind, as he had said. The fact they had gotten hold of her boss only confirmed it. She couldn't really doubt him now.

Mark nodded slowly. "Don't beat yourself up about it. Raoul's just filled me in on what happened. Thank God he got you out of that building in time before it collapsed. You're lucky to be alive. If they had not been working this case, you might be dead already."

So it had been the other vampire who had gotten her out. She glanced his way. Leaning against the door frame, he stood by the bedroom watching. A kind smile touched his lips. His honey brown eyes were watchful as they regarded each other. She would have to thank him for saving her life.

Sunlight was bathing his form from the large sitting room windows. Apparently he, too, was unaffected by the sun.

"Jasmine, you have to do what Mr. Méchant says. This has come down from way above our heads," Mark continued.

She looked back at the screen, confused for a moment. Who the hell was Mr. Méchant?

"That would be me," Eric murmured from the position he had taken on one of the sofas. He had his feet up on the glass coffee table, ankles crossed. Gone were the anger and the harshness. He had an air of relaxed ease about him now. Amusement was dancing in his icy blue eyes. This would make him her superior. She had a feeling he was enjoying this. He seemed to like control.

Jasmine felt a sinking sensation in her stomach. She cleared her throat. "So he's my boss while I'm here?"

"Yes," Mark responded gravely. From his expression he was not happy about it. "You have to assist him any way you can, even if that's staying put and keeping quiet." He began to twiddle with the pen on his desk. "I wanted you sent home, but as he's pointed out, Marcel Coupe might try to get hold of you again. I want you and Twitch back here in London in one piece together."

That made sense. Besides she wasn't going anywhere without Twitch. No way was she abandoning him. Wisely though, she knew not to mention that. Mark would just get pissed off.

As for the vampire, she did not have a clue what he would do.

Jasmine nodded. "Alright, Mark. I can sit in a hotel room for a few days, I guess."

She could see he wanted to say more and knew he couldn't in front of the vamps. Running his hand through his messy, short, chestnut locks was the only other sign of his agitation. He had to hate this.

"Watch your back and try not to be a pain in the arse like you usually are," was all he said in a grim, don't-do-anything-stupid tone. Then he was gone.

"I am not a pain in the arse," she muttered under her breath.

Jasmine stared at the blank screen for a moment. Was this going to get complicated? Eric was her boss. Yes, he now seemed to be a good guy, but could she really trust him? She didn't know what his agenda was.

With an audible sigh, she turned to face him. "I guess, it looks like I can trust you after all."

His eyebrows inched up slightly with amusement. He did not reply.

What the heck did he want, an apology for her mistrust? He wasn't about to get one. The vampire hadn't exactly trusted her cither.

"Why didn't you just tell me who you are when I woke up?" she asked, unable to hide her irritation. Jasmine knew they could have wasted valuable time. Twitch was a prisoner and was in need of rescuing. She didn't know why they wanted Marcel, but if they could help she would be happy. Even if that meant she had to follow the vampire's orders.

"The less who know the better." Eric replied silkily. "I had hoped to keep you in the dark until our task was complete."

She could understand their need for secrecy. They had probably risked a lot to just help her.

"Why did you contact Mark then and tell me now?"

Eric released a long sigh. "Because we cannot continually watch you and carry on with our mission. You do not seem to take orders well."

Jasmine suddenly felt defensive. She could follow orders just fine.

"That was only because I thought you were a bad guy, Eric," she pointed out, the tension in her voice palpable.

The vampire's eyes narrowed. "That does not appear to be the case from what your boss has just revealed. Did he not just call you a pain in the arse?"

"That's just because I have a tendency to question things a lot, that's all," she responded defensively.

The vampire sat for a moment watching her in silence. His face was unreadable. How he had perfected such an expression, she did not know. It gave nothing away. Not even his eyes hinted at what was going on in the mind behind them.

"Please do not hesitate to call down to room service whenever you require food," he replied suddenly in his deep, sexy baritone. "Skipping breakfast will no doubt leave you hungry."

Confusion darkened her eyes. He was changing the subject? If he did not believe her that was just fine. She didn't care. The vampire was just in charge until she got Twitch back. Then they were gone.

"Thanks," she mumbled.

Eating was low down on her things to do. She wanted to know how he had stopped her from escaping. "How did you hold me against the wall without touching me?"

Eric tilted his head to one side and watched her shrewdly. "I merely borrowed some of Raoul's power to restrain you."

Jasmine's brows drew together. She had never heard of this being possible before. "So it wasn't yours?"

"No." Eric's gaze dropped away from her face. "We are blood brothers, share blood, which allows us to borrow each other's abilities if we are close enough in range."

Turning, she faced the other vampire. He had taken a seat on the other sofa, which was closer to the coffee table. He, too, was watching her intently.

Jasmine was starting to find the attention a little uncomfortable. It was like they found her fascinating. Coldness blew against her senses. She could feel a power rising like a bitter winter breeze.

Raoul placed one long finger on the table. Ice began to creep outwards from his touch coating the surface in tiny glittering crystals. They sparkled in the sunlight.

"Ice?"

"That is one of Eric's abilities." Raoul responded quietly. "I am only demonstrating."

The moment he removed his finger from the table, the ice vanished.

Jasmine was pretty sure she had never heard of vampires being able to do such things. She was getting more questions than answers.

"You were the taxi driver yesterday, weren't you?"

Surprise showed on the dark-skinned vampire's face for a moment. "You are obscrvant. Yes, that was me."

"You also stopped Pierre from shooting me too didn't you?"

She had not forgotten how the guard's hand had jerked upwards. The bullet had gone up instead of into her body. There had been shock on Pierre's face when he had lost control of his arm.

Raoul nodded.

"We believe you may have a mole in your department," Eric said, cutting into her thoughts. His voice was brisk and all-business now, like he was uncomfortable discussing their vampiric powers.

"Your boss, Detective Cummings, hid the techno mage's identity well," Raoul said softly. "He knows our concerns and is now investigating his end."

She could barely believe his words. Jasmine could not imagine someone in her department betraying them. Everyone seemed so dedicated to the job. Would Mark really find a traitor?

"He doesn't know you're vampires, does he?"

Raoul's eyebrows inched up. "No, he does not. It is a secret we would rather have kept."

"Because you can go out in sunlight?" The words were out of her mouth before she could suck them back in. Jasmine bit at her lower lip. She really needed to curb the habit of talking before thinking first.

Amusement flared in Raoul's honey brown eyes. "Correct. In our line of work, secrets like this are important. So we would rather you kept it to yourself."

He was right. Something like that had to be a big advantage. It still didn't add up though. If every vamp could go out in sunlight, someone would have caught them doing it by now.

"We must now focus on Marcel Coupe." Leaning forwards, Eric rested his forearms on the top of his thighs and laced together his fingers. "He believes I am an avid party in a new weapon he is having perfected. He has also mentioned a demonstration."

Jasmine leaned back in her chair. "That doesn't sound good." She couldn't imagine what the demonstration would be. It would probably cause meaningless deaths.

"No, it does not." Eric continued. "I have yet to be told when and where. It is something, though, we must not allow."

Jasmine knew he had to know more than that. Whatever Marcel was selling seemed to have the vampires worried.

"What kind of weapon is it?"

Eric answered with a grim smile. "As I have said, Marcel has partnered with a doctor whom we know nothing about. He has been responsible for various new deadly toxins that have come onto the black market. The result of this was diabolical."

Toxins, which she realised, must have gained the vampire's interest. This had to mean it was deadly serious. They must have already seen the damage this Doctor Dasyurus had done with his previous results. Now they were here to stop him. Did this mean it affects vampires too?

"So you think it's some kind of toxin Marcel will be selling?"

Eric lifted one big shoulder in a shrug. "I believe it is possible, but I also have a feeling Dasyurus will branch into other areas. He or she does not strike me as someone who will be content dabbling in only one area alone."

Jasmine hesitated for a moment. "What did the other toxins do?"

Eric's gaze met hers. "I would rather not say. Not because it is a secret, but because I would prefer to spare you from nightmares."

This meant she probably really did not need to know. If it was as bad as Eric was letting on, then they had to stop this new one from being sold.

Jasmine began to nibble nervously on her lower lip. "Why are you telling me all this? I thought you wanted me to stay in the hotel."

Raoul, who had been silent up until now, answered her. "Your knowledge of the techno mage . . . your friend may come in useful."

He was still leaning back against the sofa, a picture of ease. Arms crossed over his chest.

Jasmine suddenly felt uncomfortable. "I guess that makes sense."

"Besides," Eric continued, "you will no doubt overhear our plans. At least this way you know what is at stake."

That was true. Jasmine also knew she couldn't just sit around now either. "I want to help."

Eric rose from the sofa and strode to the window. Hands clasped behind his back, he surveyed the view for a moment. He was silent for so long she thought he was ignoring her.

"You may assist Raoul with surveillance," he replied, turning back to the room.

"You still need an escort for the party tonight," Raoul pointed out quietly.

"True," Eric replied, drawing out the word. "I am not sure Jasmine is up to such a task after her ordeal with the explosion, however." He moved his gaze to her face.

"Party?" Jasmine asked, focusing on that rather than on the last part of his sentence.

Eric frowned. "A Christmas party Marcel is throwing for friends and acquaintances. It is to be held on a boat on the Seine, but I am not sure . . ."

"I feel fine and I want to do this," she insisted cutting him off with a smile. "But won't Marcel recognise me?"

The vampire was still frowning at her. His cold blue eyes coloured with what looked like concern.

"He knew I had some interest in you. Perhaps we can find a plausible excuse for your presence. It is conceivable."

Was he worried about her? Maybe he thought as she was human, she couldn't handle it. Jasmine felt a swirl of annoyance.

"I can try and contact Twitch at the same time," she responded firmly. No way was she not doing this. Feeling useful was something she needed. Jasmine knew she would go nuts just sitting on the side-lines. She was not someone who could just wait about.

From the expression on Eric's face, she had caught him off guard.

"You are in contact with the techno mage?" His tone was surprised.

Jasmine couldn't stop the small, smug smile forming on her lips. "Only if the range is close enough. He gave me a magical earpiece."

The vampires glanced at each other for a moment. Some kind of message must have somehow passed between them, she realised when she saw Raoul give a subtle nod.

Eric's gaze returned to hers. "Very well, but you will spend the day resting. You were in an explosion yesterday and I will need you vigilant and awake tonight."

CHAPTER 13

JASMINE SPENT THE REST of the day sleeping or watching television in the bedroom. She deliberately kept the door open to keep an eye on what was going on. Not that much did. The vampires were busy making phone calls or on their laptops. They seemed to forget she was there at all.

Eric entered the bedroom once in the morning. Curtain rod in hand, he prowled into the bathroom and fixed the shower. His eyes were amused when they met hers. She wondered if he was impressed with her ingenuity.

Raoul went out at some point. She didn't know where as no one had told her. They had surveillance on the arms dealer from what she had overheard, so she guessed he had gone to check that.

Around lunchtime, room service brought up a sandwich. Jasmine hadn't ordered it and guessed Eric had done it for her. He insisted she eat and drink tea. Why he was so intent on feeding her, she did not know. Still, she was very grateful for the food.

Her nervousness had passed and she was starving. After watching her devour the sandwich, he sent her back to bed. She was beginning to feel like a naughty child. She got the impression he was doing it to keep her out of the way. That suited her just fine. Her body still ached from her ordeal and she was happy to rest it.

By six p.m., though, she was getting bored. She learned quickly there was only so much satellite TV one could watch. Most of it was Christmas movies, which, of course, reminded her there were only two days left until the holiday. Where, she wondered, would she be by then? Hopefully she and Twitch would be back in London. Back home where they belonged.

Jasmine wanted to feel useful. Lounging in the luxurious bed like the Queen of Sheba felt like a waste of time. She itched to get out and stretch her legs. Having a shower, she decided, was the best idea. She was supposed to be accompanying Eric to a party after all. Not that he had mentioned it again.

Eric was waiting for her when she emerged from the shower. A little gasp left her as she found him standing in the middle of the bedroom, his hands shoved into the pockets of his jeans. The look on his face was brooding.

His gaze skimmed over her robed form. "I have already laid out on the bed in Raoul's room what you will be required to wear. I hope you do not mind. I need to change myself in here."

She was suddenly aware of how very naked she was beneath her robe. Jasmine tugged it more securely around her. Another towel was wrapped around her short wet hair. "No, no, that's fine."

"Are you sure you feel up to this?" He looked worried.

Jasmine nodded. "Yes, Eric, I'm sure."

Icy blue eyes studied her face for a moment. "Very well then."

Standing awkwardly for a moment, she stared at him. Then with a nervous smile, she padded out of the door.

The living room was empty. She guessed the other vampire was still out. Jasmine could feel Eric's scrutiny on her back as she crossed the room. Heat rippled down her spine. Her stomach clenched with excitement.

When she reached the other bedroom, she turned but the door to Eric's room had already closed.

How did he manage to do that to her? Just a glance and he had her all wet and trembling. Her experience with men was non-existent, but still she was pretty sure this was not normal. Was it because he was a vampire?

She shut the door and walked over to the bed. Eric had not been kidding. A black dress, underwear, and a pair of black high heels lay on top of the neatly made bed. Jasmine moved closer. Sheer black hold ups were also on the pile along with a black-beaded clutch purse.

Had he chosen the outfit?

Jasmine hooked the lacy black panties with her finger and held them up.

He had definitely gone for sexy. She guessed wearing sturdy cotton panties would not go with the rest of the outfit.

She eyed the little black dress. Not the kind of thing she usually wore. Hell she rarely wore dresses at all only on special occasions. Jeans and T-shirt were her usual choice of clothing—warm and practical. Tonight, though, she had no choice but to wear it.

She stripped off her robe and slipped on the expensive, lacy wisps of nothing. She glanced at the mirror against the wall. Jasmine was surprised to find she looked quite sexy.

The panties, she quickly discovered, were a thong. Low on her hips, it felt a little uncomfortable as it was something she did not normally wear. It extenuated her hips and the slight swell of her tummy. She could see the curve of her crescent moon birthmark high on her hip peeping out.

Frowning she searched for a bra but came up empty handed. It looked like she was going without. She picked up the dress and slipped it over her head. Shimmying a little helped to get it on.

Jasmine stared at herself in the mirror again. The dress was short, the hem falling above her knees. The waistline flared slightly at the hips. Three-quarter sleeves finished at her elbows, leaving the burn on her forearm visible.

A scooping neckline kept her breasts modestly covered, which was a relief. The deep-plunging back, which ended at the small of her back, made up for the good coverage of the front, however.

She felt self-conscious and a little too exposed. Now it made sense why she was bra-less.

The sheer black hold-ups caressed her skin as she eased them carefully up her legs and settled them around the tops of her thighs. Jasmine was careful not to rip them. A groan left her lips when she eyed the shoes. High black heels. She had sworn to herself she would never wear heels again. With a deep sigh she slid them on.

Heading into the bathroom, she brushed out her coppery hair. It always dried quickly being so short. Styling it into a feathery bob around her face was easily done—the exact reason she had picked that cut.

A few makeup items were scattered on the counter. Eric no doubted wanted her to put them on. Jasmine settled with some foundation and concealer to hide the bruise on her forehead as best she could, eye shadow, mascara, and lipstick. If she were going out back in her everyday life, she'd usually wear these, but normally she was happy with just a dash of lip gloss. Quick with no messing about.

How Raoul and Eric had guessed her size in everything was beyond her. Everything fit perfectly. She took a bottle of perfume off the bathroom counter and sprayed her wrists and neck. Light and flowery. Jasmine sniffed appreciatively. Had Eric chosen all this to? He seemed to have hidden talents.

Her eyes strayed to the counter of cosmetics. Could she get away with taking some sort of weapon with her to the party? They were going into enemy territory. She would be silly to go unarmed. She bit her lip. Eric probably wouldn't like it, but he wouldn't have to know. It could be her little secret.

She grabbed the lipstick she was wearing and scooped up a pair of nail scissors and a mini can of deodorant. Things a woman could carry in a purse. Things Jasmine could possibly use as weapons if needed. She hurried back into the bedroom and stuffed them into the clutch purse. Everything fit. To her relief, it didn't look to full either. Hopefully no one would notice.

Checking in the mirror, she dubbed herself ready. Nervousness fluttered inside her. Taking a deep breath, she walked from the room.

Eric stood in the doorway of the second bedroom. He was busy fiddling with his cuff-links and did not see her enter. Jasmine's steps faltered when she saw him. With female appreciation, her gaze wandered over him. The stylish black tailored tuxedo he wore was cut to precision, emphasizing the broadness of his strong shoulders and the leanness of his waist. The rich fabric of the trousers sheathed his long muscular legs, giving him a lithesome appearance. The snow white shirt beneath his suit was sharp in contrast against all the black. A narrow black bow tie dangled from his neck yet to be done up.

He had an air of confidence and danger about him. The vampire didn't just make it look good—he made it damn sexy.

Jasmine felt excitement uncurl inside her again. She found it hard to tear her gaze away from him. The guy was her temporary boss. She knew she could not be caught panting over him. It was so damn hard when he looked this hot though.

Eric looked up and caught her inspection. A sexy smile tugged at the corners of his mouth. "Will I do?"

She could tell he knew how gorgeous he looked. A woman would have to be blind not to notice. She was pretty certain there would be plenty of women noticing him tonight.

Jasmine smiled back shyly. "You look very handsome."

He chuckled, reaching up to tie his bow tie. "My first compliment from you. I feel honoured."

Eric's gaze started a slow, thorough wander from her head downwards. She felt every inch, like a heated caress against her skin. By the time he got to her waist, the coldness in his eyes had melted. Approval was shining in their depths.

Jasmine looked away. When he looked at her so intensely, it always left her breathless. The desire she had seen had practically been scorching.

"I picked well. That dress is spectacular on you. It is . . ." His silky voice trailed off.

Looking round, Jasmine found him staring at her feet. A strange, dark, hungry look took over his face.

"Eric?"

The sound of his name falling from her lips snapped his attention back up. He could not believe how sensationally stunning Jasmine looked. The black dress he had picked suited her perfectly. Just the thought of her wearing the sexy black lingerie beneath made him hard. She had on those 'fuck me now' heels too. All the blood in his body seemed to have gone south. He was having a hard time forming an intelligent thought in his head.

Her make-up was not overdone. She didn't really need it to enhance the beauty of her face. Mascara and subtle eyeshadow brought out the greenness of her large lovely eyes. Her short, red hair had been brushed into a sleek bob, which feathered pleasing around her slender cheeks. She looked like more than perfection.

He suddenly had a feeling it was going be a little difficult to concentrate this evening. The problem was he was going need his wits about him. Tonight was an important step. He took a deep breath and clamped down on his screaming libido.

Eric cleared his throat. "Raoul will be driving us."

The other vampire appeared in the doorway of the suite, as if he had been waiting for his name to be called. Knowing Raoul, he probably had.

He was wearing a smart, light grey chauffeur's uniform with a matching grey cap perched on his head. Two long woollen coats were draped over his arm.

Eric saw that everything was ready.

Raoul's honey-brown eyes took them both in. "You make a most elegant couple."

Jasmine had a pretty blush to her cheeks. "Thank you, Raoul."

Eric gallantly offered her his arm. "Ready?"

CHAPTER 14

THEY STOOD IN THE CONFINES of the lift on the way down to the lobby of the hotel. Eric, as always, hid his discomfort. He despised such contraptions. He hated the enclosed space so much that he normally took the stairs down. The fact that he could escape the elevator with ease if it should become stuck did not matter. The fear remained.

To distract himself, he examined his companion. The little female had begun to fidget with her purse. She was wrapped warmly in the long, black, woollen coat Raoul had provided. Eric knew it would keep her warm from the December evening chill. He could sense her nervousness. Her normal sparkle was subdued. He doubted it had much to do with the lift but rather with what lay ahead of them this evening.

Curving an arm around her waist, he tugged her gently into his side. She did not resist but went willingly. This pleased Eric immensely. Had she decided to stop fighting against him? The press of her body fit perfectly. He felt the slight tremble to her limbs. Definitely nervous.

Jasmine did not raise her head, but her fingers tightened around the purse she held.

"Relax, Jasmine. There is nothing for you to fret over," he whispered against her ear. "You look very beautiful and tonight all you need do is listen and stay observant."

A shiver ran through her at his words. The increase of her heartbeat pleased him. Eric knew it was with excitement. He could practically taste it in the air.

His cock stirred.

"I am a little nervous," she admitted quietly. "I can't help it."

Her subtle sweet arousal teased his senses.

The pulse point at her throat caught his eye. Blood. He could perceive it beneath her warm supple skin. Sense the movement as it pumped within her veins. Eric wanted to taste it once again. Feel the coppery potent liquid as it coursed down his throat and quenched his hunger. Would she moan with desire as she had before? Her lush little body would be awash with pleasure. He would make sure of that.

Eric felt his fangs begin to ache within his gums. Slowly he moved his gaze to the curve of her neck. He did not need to feed for at least a few days. Unlike a human vampire, his kind did not need to feed every night. He knew it was Jasmine's blood he wanted when he did, though.

She had not moved from where he had tucked her against him. The heat of her body warmed his side.

Are you hungry Eric? Do you intend to feed on her here in the lift? Raoul's teasing voice whispered through his mind. *Do you wish me to halt its progress so you may ravish her?*

Eric's attention snapped upwards and met his friends. Honey-brown eyes stared back at him with laughing amusement.

Eric knew he was not acting like himself. He had never been caught ogling a female's neck before. Even Raoul could see the girl's effect on him. He repressed a growl.

His friend had also been witness to his divulging information to her regarding their powers. Eric had never done such a thing before, never revealed their abilities to a mortal. It was most unheard of. Jasmine was worse than a truth serum. She seemed to be completely unaware of her effect on him. She was dangerous.

No. He growled back.

She is quite the little distraction is she not? She has that 'je ne sais quoi.' Raoul continued.

One of Eric's dark eyebrows rose. *I believe she will be nothing but trouble.* Straightening up, he began to draw on his icy control. A slip like this would not do. He could not afford to make a mistake tonight. Eric could not allow a distraction to ruin his plans. He could only hope he had not been wrong to let the girl come along.

Jasmine moved from his side when the door sprang open. Together they moved into the foyer and waited while Raoul went to get the car.

The foyer was gaily decorated with brightly coloured Christmas decorations, reflecting the festivities of the season elegantly. Eric barely noticed them.

Jasmine hadn't said much since they had left the suite. Eric wondered what she was contemplating. Maybe she, too, had second thoughts about this evening. Did she now regret agreeing to come? He knew there was still time for her to change her mind. It would be easy enough to leave her at the hotel. Attending the party without an escort could be easily covered if necessary.

"Jasmine, you do not have to accompany me tonight if you do not wish," he said softly.

She was standing so close. He could feel the heat from her body through her coat. He had never been so aware of how small she was before.

"Hmm . . . no, I want to, Eric." Tilting her chin up, she met his gaze with her lovely green eyes. Her smile was nervous but genuine. "I've just never been to anything like this before. I don't want to let you down."

He could not help but smile at her words. "I assure you that will be impossible."

She knew what they were there for. His plan was to let her mingle and nothing more. He would not put her in any danger.

"Do you think Twitch is OK?" Her eyes darkened with worry.

She caught him off guard for a moment, but Eric recovered quickly.

"Marcel requires him. I doubt he will have been treated shabbily." He gave her a small smile of reassurance. "You care for the techno mage?"

Did she have feelings for the young man? Perhaps a budding romance had started between them. It could, for all he knew, have just begun.

Jealousy ripped through Eric so violently he almost hissed. Tamping down the unpleasant emotion, he let none of it show on his face.

Jasmine was fiddling with her purse again. "He's my best friend as well as my co-worker. I don't want anything bad to happen to him."

A sense of relief flooded through him. "Then we shall do all in our power to bring him home safely."

He knew the words would give her false security the moment they left his mouth. No power on Earth could assure her friend's survival. Eric would do all he could to try and bring the mage out alive, though. That much was true.

Jasmine relaxed at his words. It was a subtle movement that his eyes detected—the tiny loosening of her slender shoulders and her facial muscles.

Pleasure rushed through him. She believed him. Why that felt important, he did not know.

Eric frowned, slightly dizzy at the successions of emotions he had just experienced in the space of a few minutes. It was most unsettling and he was not sure he liked it. Since meeting her, he had lost all self-control over his feelings. Normally they were ruthlessly kept leashed from centuries of discipline. His icy reserve generally was absolute. Nothing melted it.

What Eric needed was to fuck her until she was out of his system. When that was achieved, he could move on. There was no doubt in his mind he would soon be back to his old self. This lapse in control was a temporary setback.

Jasmine would be a wonderful diversion. It was just a pity they did not have time. Perhaps after this business in Paris was completed, he could take his time to satisfy this craving for her.

Raoul was suddenly beside them once again. "The car is outside, Sir."

Gently taking her elbow, Eric steered her towards the door. They settle into a natural, matched pace. He knew they looked like any other rich couple heading out to dinner. No one suspected he and Raoul were vampires. They had long ago learnt the ability to hide what they were. It came as natural as breathing.

The elegant grey Bentley was parked at the side of the road.

Jasmine's eyes ran over the vehicle appreciatively. "Nice car."

Eric tried not to smile at her words. He very much doubted her department could afford such things for any of their cases. It was one of the luxuries he had for being very well paid and freelance.

"It suits our purposes for this evening," Eric replied.

"Is it rented?"

Amusement shone in his eyes when he met her curious glance. "But of course."

Raoul was already holding the door open for her. He had fallen into his role as driver as smoothly as any other role he had played. The other vampire was the perfect actor. Back straight, he stood passively, awaiting them. He wore the bland, respectful expression of a treasured employee.

They were masters of fitting in and could easily assume any character they needed. It was what they trained for. What they lived for.

Eric was already focusing on the alias he was using. Richard Jeger, a businessman who had found a market in the Middle East for dangerous new weapons. It had taken a year to carefully build a reputation. In that time, Eric had nurtured acquaintances that would lead him to Marcel Coupe. He had done so with the utmost care. Now things were finally coming together.

Jasmine slipped gracefully into the lavish car. Eric followed her in silently and watched as Raoul closed the door. Moving to the front, Raoul slid easily behind the wheel.

"So how am I supposed to play this?"

Jasmine's softly asked question shattered the composure he had gathered.

Blinking in confusion, he met her gaze. "Play?"

Her words conjured up images of just how Eric would like to 'play' with her. Long and hard, until they were both pleasurably sated. Then he would take her some more.

She was glancing out at the night through her window. "Yes, how do you want me to act?"

Eric wiped the dark, hungry look from his face just as she turned to look at him. It would not do for her to see it. The girl was nervous enough as it was. Knowing he was lusting after her would not help.

He kept his expression remote. "Marcel believes he knows my tastes in women, so you will have to act accordingly."

Jasmine's green eyes were wary. "And that is how?"

"Submissive and obedient."

"Oh." A pretty pink blush kissed her cheeks.

Eric tried not to grin but a smirk escaped anyway. "I am sure you will be able to play the part well, Jasmine, to assist your friend. Merely look at me adoringly, I think that will suffice. Pretend I have seduced you into becoming my mistress with my charms."

He did not want Jasmine acting submissively tonight. Obedient would do. She would need to follow his orders to the letter. Eric would expect this from her.

"Is that your taste in women?"

He blinked at her abrupt question.

Picking his words, he answered her slowly. "I have known many women over my long existence. All have been different in many ways. Submissive females, I do find pleasing to an extent, but not always. Sometimes I like some fire, a challenge."

She nodded, then turned to stare out of the window again.

Eric wondered which one Jasmine would be. Would she bring fire to his bed or submissiveness? He hoped it was a little of both.

CHAPTER 15

THE MASSIVE BOAT GLITTERED in the dark on the Seine. Jasmine eyed it nervously. It had to be at least seventy five metres long. No doubt Marcel had bought it with the money from his weapon sales. He did well with his blood money, it seemed. Just thinking about it made her feel sick. In her eyes, the guy was a monster.

Coloured Christmas lights had been hung across the long deck. They shone welcomingly in the darkness. She could make out other guests walking down towards the vessel along the river.

Jasmine was still thinking over Eric's words. She wasn't surprised he liked submissive women. He was, after all, a very dominant male and probably liked having his own way all the time. Even in his bed. No wonder it annoyed him that she had not followed his orders. Jasmine could not imagine following someone else's wishes blindly. She was not built that way.

Her parents had raised her to question things, which was why her boss Mark called her a pain in the arse. She was always questioning things or voicing her opinion. Her behaviour annoyed the hell out of him, but he did not discourage it.

With Eric as her boss, would he try to stamp that out? Would he expect her to obey him without question? Jasmine shifted uneasily. She had to admit she was already having a hard time thinking of him as her superior. Every time he came close, she just got so turned on, which was both annoying and exciting.

When he had held her so close to his side in the lift, excitement had rushed through her body. She had practically melted into him. Just him whispering in her ear and she'd been wet. God help her if he ever tried to seduce her. Jasmine feared she would be putty in his hands. She was seriously going to have to work on her focus.

They had parked along a road beside the river in silence. Jasmine wasn't sure if the vampires were nervous or not. They weren't showing it if they were. If this is what they did for a living, they were definitely seasoned operatives. They had probably done things like this more times than she could count. She had to wonder what else they did. With the set of skills and powers they had, they could probably do almost anything. Be anything.

Raoul helped her politely out of the back of the car. "I shall be here waiting in case you need me," Raoul informed her quietly.

Jasmine gave him a nervous smile. She really hoped they wouldn't. If all went as planned, they would just blend in with the party. Eric had the reason she was with him covered. They should not need any back-up.

The night was chilly and she was thankful for the warmth of the long, woollen coat. The crisp air filled her lungs as she took a deep, steadying breath. Fuck, she wished she could stop being nervous. She would have given anything to be calm and collected. Maybe over time she would gain that. Her own team did undercover work from time to time, too. Not that she had taken part in any yet.

Eric was suddenly beside her. His arm wrapped around her waist, drawing her close into his warmth. Jasmine's little shiver had nothing to do with the cold. Desire poured through her. Damn vampire. Why did he have to affect her in such a way?

Eric frowned down at her. "Come, I have no wish for you to get cold. The boat will be suitably warm."

Settling her arm through his, she allowed him to escort her towards the boat.

Jasmine heard her heels clicking on the path as they moved. Other arriving guests joined them as they walked down towards the river. Excitement was heavy in the cold night air. The voices of those around them were enthusiastic and animated. She didn't know what they were saying as it was all in French, but they seemed happy. Did they really knew who Marcel was? Did they just know him as a French businessman? She doubted it would be common knowledge he was a notorious arms dealer.

The walk down towards the boat did not take long. They easily reached the boarding area, where two large intimidating men stood guard. Guests, it seemed, had to have an invitation to board the boat. Marcel probably didn't want just anyone at his party. He certainly had enemies. If any of them wanted to take him out, this evening might be a perfect opportunity. Jasmine kind of hoped someone would. At least she might get Twitch back a lot quicker.

Jasmine glanced at the vampire at her side. Eric was already slipping the invitation from his coat pocket. Catching her gaze, he gave her a wink.

"Invitations only." One of the men held out his large hand.

Dutifully, Eric placed it into the outstretched palm.

Jasmine was so focused on what he was doing that she didn't pick up on the noise straight away. A soft buzzing in her left ear abruptly morphed into a whine. She winced as it grew in pitch.

"Fuck." She pressed a hand to the offending ear.

Eric gave her a sharp cold look. "Jasmine, you cannot use such language when we are aboard the boat," he scolded lightly.

She ignored him as pain sliced though her eardrum. Jabbing a finger into her ear didn't seem to help. Pressing her lips together held back a cry of pain. Just as it became skull-splitting, it stopped.

"Jazzy, can you hear me?" Twitch's voice purred.

A grimace tightened her features as the pain subsided. The earpiece Twitch had given her was working. Sort of. She had been a little worried she might have lost it. This just proved the little sucker was still attached and working. Relief flooded through her.

Now how the fuck was she supposed to respond? If she just started talking it was going to look strange. Looking up, she found

Eric's eyes now lit with a questioning look. The guard was also watching her with a bemused expression. Great. She had an audience.

Jasmine pinned a smile on her face. "Eric, darling. I think I might have dropped my bracelet on the way down."

"Who the hell is Eric?" Twitch whispered in her ear.

She ignored him.

Eric caught on quickly. An indulgent smile touched his lips. "Are you sure you did not leave it at home?"

Jasmine batted her eyelashes at him. "Can we phone the maid and see if I left it in the bedroom?" She pouted. "I don't want to get on board until I'm sure it's safe."

She tugged at her earlobe. To anyone else, it might look like a nervous gesture. She just hoped the vamp remembered what she had said about the earpiece.

Nothing changed in his expression.

Jasmine tried not to roll her eyes. She was new at playing spy, but surely a gesture like this was universal.

Eric's hand curled around her elbow. "Of course we can." He glanced dismissively at the guard. "Excuse us for a moment."

Plucking the invitation from the man's hand, he slid it back into his pocket. Jasmine did not resist as he led the way. He guided her gracefully away from the boat. They kept walking until they were out of earshot. Stopping in the darkness, Jasmine glanced back. The lights on the boat twinkled and glittered. A steady flow of guests were still boarding. The guards did not have time to glance their way.

Eric stood with his big body shielding her. He slid his hand into his pocket, pulled out his mobile and handed it to her.

"What if someone walks up behind you?" Jasmine asked.

The blue, icy eyes watching her warmed with amusement. "They will not get a chance. I will know long before that if they move in our direction. Talk to your friend."

His vampiric senses would warn him, she realised. Sometimes it was easy to forget what he was.

Jasmine pretended to use the phone. Pressing it to her ear she talked freely. "Twitch?"

"Who the hell is Eric?" Twitch's voice was low and menacing.

She knew he was just worried about her. He probably had been going out of his mind wondering where she was. She couldn't blame him for being suspicious.

"A friend," she assured him quickly.

He sighed almost tiredly. "I have been trying for hours to reach you, but the range on this thing fucking sucks. Are you OK?"

She could hear the anxiety and concern in his tone. Some of the tension she had been holding inside melted away. He was safe for now. At least now they could communicate.

"Yeah I'm fine," she said. "I'm with that vamp I saw at Marcel's. Turns out he's one of the good guys."

She sensed his relief. "Marcel wouldn't tell me where you were. He said if I didn't do as he asked he'd hurt you."

That was not surprising. Just because Marcel had lost her didn't mean he would have stopped using her as a bargaining chip. Twitch would have had a hard time doubting his word as they had last been together. Knowing the techno mage, he wouldn't have risked it.

"Where are you? Are you on the boat?"

Twitch made a little hum of annoyance. "No, I'm locked in a basement. Why are you on a boat?"

Disappointed flowed through her. They would find Twitch one way or another even if it wasn't tonight.

"Marcel is throwing a Christmas party. I'm undercover with the vamp."

She glanced up at Eric. He was watching her closely with a cool aloofness. The predator in him was focused on her every word.

Jasmine could feel the push of his will against hers. His eyes were practically hypnotic, glinting like hard blue sapphires in the light.

He didn't like being left out of the one-sided conversation. She could sense that. That was just tough. If he couldn't hear her friend with his heightened hearing, he would just have to live with it.

"Be careful, Jazzy. Marcel is dangerous." Twitch purred softly in her ear.

He was the second person to tell her that today.

Dragging her eyes away from the vampire, she stared at a point on his chest. She didn't want to get mesmerised by those cold eyes again. They made her feel like he could unearth all her secrets.

"I am. I promise." The words came out a little shaky. "What's he got you working on?"

"He won't let me see all the specifications, but it's some kind of dispersal system. Jazzy, I'm not the only one Marcel's got working for him." Her friend's mutter was hushed and urgent. "His other inventor is building some kind of device."

Jasmine narrowed her eyes. She could sense Eric's growing interest in what was being said. He was probably good at reading facial expressions. All he needed to know was probably written all over her face. Damn nosy vampire.

"Do you know what it is?" she asked softly.

Twitch sighed. "No."

Was it something to do with a toxin? Having a dispersal system would certainly make sense. But why have Twitch work on it? Something like that didn't need spells.

"At least we know what he's got you doing."

The mage was silent for a moment. "Someone planted a bug on Marcel. I'm guessing it's the vampire." He whispered the words as if fearful of being overheard. "I have hacked into its frequency, so you can listen in if you're close enough. Don't tell the vamp."

Jasmine glanced up at Eric. He was still watching her carefully. She suddenly wasn't sure if he could hear the conversation going on in her ear or not. His cold, handsome face, blank of emotions, gave nothing away.

Twitch was being paranoid like normal, but that was fine by her. The vampires probably still had plenty of secrets of their own. Maybe it was better to keep some of theirs, too.

"Sure."

"As long as you stay within distance, I can listen in and let you know if I can hear anything through the bug," the mage assured her. "I better stop chatting before my guard checks in."

"OK, Twitch. Be careful."

"I'll keep the line open," he whispered.

She knew this meant he would be listening in. He probably found it reassuring. Twitch was good at eavesdropping. Maybe it should feel strange having some guy hearing everything she was saying, but Jasmine found it calming. She was also comforted to know he wasn't going to vanish completely. Thankfully he wasn't a heavy breather. That would have just been gross.

"Your friend is well?" Eric murmured softly.

Trying not to look nervous, she met his gaze. "Yes. Marcel's got him working on some kind of dispersal system, but he doesn't know what it's for."

One of his dark eyebrows rose slightly, but his expression remained impassive. "That is most intriguing."

Jasmine had the strangest feeling he knew what she was talking about.

"Any ideas what it might be used for?" She didn't really expect him to spill it if he did, but she had to try.

"No. None." His poker face gave nothing away, yet she somehow knew he was lying. Why wasn't he sharing with her? They had told her a lot already or maybe it wasn't really much at all. He definitely had secrets. Suddenly she did not feel guilty for having her own.

A cold breeze brushed her face. "I guess we better get to the party."

He glanced over his shoulder at the boat and then offered her his arm. "Yes, indeed. We do not want to draw to much attention to ourselves loitering outside."

Walking side by side, they strolled back towards the boarding area. More guests had arrived and they had to join a queue.

It looked like Marcel had invited every well-to-do person in Paris. The men were dressed in dashing tuxedos and the women wore elegant, fashionable dresses. The expensive jewellery they wore glittered and sparkled in the Christmas lights. They looked like small fortunes in gems.

"I should have adorned you with pretty baubles, too. Forgive me for the oversight," Eric said in apology.

She wasn't wearing any jewellery at all in fact. Not that she minded. Jasmine did not really do jewellery. The few cheap pieces she owned, she always forgot to wear.

She slid the vampire a sideways glance. "I'm not into expensive jewellery."

An amused smile touched Eric's lips. "Why I am not surprised?"

"Besides," she murmured softly, "I would have spent the whole evening worrying about losing the damn things."

Eric's deep chuckle rolled over her.

The guard was eyeing them suspiciously as they found themselves at the head of the queue once more. He had not forgotten them.

Jasmine smiled. "I forgot to even put it on after all that. Silly me," she said, holding up her bare wrist.

His expression didn't alter as he handed back the invitation. He looked almost bored. With a wave of his hand, he sent them on their way.

Jasmine felt herself relax a fraction. This wasn't so bad.

As they stepped aboard the boat, members of the crew showed them where to go. The staff who took their coats gave them a ticket so they could retrieve them again later. The main inside part of the boat was decked out with red and blue Christmas decorations glittering beautifully in the light. Guests mingled. The murmur of voices blended with the dulcet, sultry tones of a female singer and band. The music was slow and romantic—something people seemed happy to slow dance to around the makeshift dance floor.

As a waiter passed them by, Eric took two flutes of champagne. Jasmine accepted the offered glass. She was happy to have something to do with her free hand. She knew if she kept playing with her purse, the vampire might become suspicious. He did not need to know about her potential weapons. No one did but her.

They stood to one side near the windows where it was less crowded. She had yet to spot Marcel and Pierre. Dread and nervousness were churning inside her. What would they say when they saw her with Eric? What would they think? Could she really pull this off and pretend to be his new lover? His mistress?

She was too nervous to try any of the canapés the waiters were offering on their trays. Her stomach was in knots. Skipping dinner had probably been a good idea after all. Jasmine was certain that if she had food in her stomach, she would puke.

The vampire's breath suddenly warmed her cheek.

"Relax, Jasmine," he murmured in a deep low voice. "Enjoy the party. That is all you need do. I shall take care of the rest."

A confident firm hand, settled on the small of her back. Eric's palm on her bare skin scorched her. Jasmine tried not to gasp. A little thrill of pleasure tightened inside her. Her nipples hardened inside the confines of her dress. Nervousness evaporated as desire took its place. Could he feel her trembling slightly? He was so close that the smell of snow and pine enveloped her. She licked her suddenly dry lips. How the hell did he keep doing that to her? Was it some kind of vampire trick?

She raised her glass and took a gulp of the alcohol. The bubbles fizzed on her tongue before sliding down her parched throat. They left a warm glow in her stomach.

Just then, Jasmine spotted the arms dealer through the crowd. He seemed to be holding court over a group of men. They all stood avidly listening to his every word. She watched them covertly over the rim of her glass.

Who were they? Other buyers for the weapons? People who worked for him maybe?

"It is time to go to work," Eric said into her ear. He nodded at the fat man when he looked their way.

Marcel raised his hand in greeting. Excusing himself from the crowd, he moved in their direction.

Jasmine tried not to bite her lip. Acting cool and collected was what she needed to do. She noted the young blond guy at his side. He was cute and looked like he was in his twenties. His head was slightly lowered and he looked uneasy. She vaguely remembered him from her first meeting with Marcel. He had been sitting next to him on the sofa. He looked like a kid. What was he doing with an arms dealer?

The fat man's arm coiled around the young guy's waist. He tugged him in until they were walking hip to hip. Jasmine suddenly understood the blonde's role. He had to be Marcel's lover. Somehow she wasn't surprised that the fat man liked them young. He had to be in his mid-forties himself. Was he hoping to cling to his youth by taking younger boyfriends?

The mismatched couple weaved their way towards them. It took them a few minutes to arrive as guests kept stopping Marcel to say hello. He seemed to be very popular. All the while Jasmine could feel Eric beside her watching. A detached remoteness seemed to have settled over him. She could sense his icy façade slipping into place.

"*Mon ami*! I am happy you accepted my invitation." Marcel exclaimed as he reached them. Taking Eric's shoulders in his chunky hands, he pulled him close to kiss both his cheeks.

Jasmine stood quietly watching. The Frenchman did not even look her way.

"You have a charming boat, my friend," the vampire's deep baritone replied smoothly. "And I did not want to give up the opportunity to show off my latest acquisition."

The hand that was still branding her bare back nudged her forwards. Jasmine suddenly found herself the centre of attention.

Marcel's eyes widened with surprise when he saw her. "*Mon Dieu*! I did not recognise her for a moment. It is Twitch's girl?"

Eric's grin was smug and self-assured. "Do not look so shocked, my friend. As you said yourself, I have an interest in her. It was easy enough to find her and convince her it was in her best interests to warm my bed."

His tone was the right mix of arrogance and superiority. It made Jasmine want to hit him.

"I am surprised she agreed." Marcel dabbed at his sweaty forehead. He seemed to have a never-ending supply of handkerchiefs.

"It did not take long to persuade her of the benefits." Eric's hand caressed over her bottom. A possessively intimate touch. "Or show her."

Jasmine lowered her head. Heat warmed her cheeks and spread up into her hairline. She knew what Eric was implying—that they had been having sex. Even though it wasn't true, it still made her feel uncomfortable.

The hand on her bottom moved to cup her hip.

Marcel chuckled.

The urge to punch him in the face was hard to ignore. Instead she tightened her grip around her glass.

"The young lady is shy, I see. It is always the way at the beginning before it loses its sparkle." His eyes slid sideways to his companion. "This is Claude. I do not believe you were introduced last time we met."

Claude looked a little nervous. He paled at Marcel's words. Was he worried the Frenchman had tired of him? Had that been a veiled threat to his lover?

"You have quite a turnout here," Eric said, pulling Jasmine from her speculations and the group's attention from Claude.

Raising the glass flute in her hand, Jasmine took a sip of the contents.

"*Oui.* It always is when I throw a party." Marcel looked around with a proud smile curving his lips. "Come, I have some people I wish to introduce you to."

He gestured back across the room. They followed through the packed, jubilant crowd. Eric moved with a confident poise. The hand on her naked back remained in place. It was sensual, arousing. Little sparks of pleasure danced from his touch down past her belly. They left her feeling strangely needy.

Three men were waiting for them as they drew closer.

Marcel greeted them with a friendly smile. "This is Monsieur Jeger." He turned back towards Eric, as Jasmine realised this had to be the vamps alias. "Let me introduce you to Sir John, Herr Randall, and Mr. Smith."

"Good to meet you." Sir John was English. He was darker haired with a severe-looking expression. His gaze seemed to dismiss them as of no consequence.

"You have an interest in Marcel's merchandise?" Randall sounded German. He was the tallest of the males. Hair cropped and sun-bleached blond, his eyes gauged them shrewdly.

"I am keen to see what he has to offer me," Eric responded. Glancing up at him, Jasmine could tell he was sizing up each man. Did he know if they were wanted? If they were interested in weaponry, they had to be buyers. That could easily make them mercenaries or international criminals. Suddenly she felt like she might be out of her depth. This was not the kind of thing she dealt with at work. Hell, she had barely done anything in her first two months.

"Who's the lovely little lady on your arm, Monsieur Jeger?" Mr. Smith had an American twang.

An easy-going smile was spread across his lips. He looked like the oldest of the bunch. Grey was sprinkled in amongst his short, tawny-brown hair. His face was lined with age, but there was sharpness to his eyes.

The hand on her back pushed her gently forwards. "This is Jasmine."

Jasmine wished Eric would stop doing that. She hated being the centre of attention. Right now, all the men's eyes were on her.

A nervous smile fluttered across her lips. "Hello."

Mr. Smith's eyes twinkled in amusement. "Pleased to meet you, ma'am."

The other two men did not even bother to acknowledge her. Their eyes were happy to ogle her breasts and legs, though. She tried not to stiffen in response. Now Jasmine realised why Eric had picked the dress. She came in handy as a distraction. A little bit of eye candy to hang on his arm.

"We have some business to discuss, gentleman," Marcel interrupted.

At the Frenchman's words she was instantly forgotten. The eyes on her body moved swiftly away. She gave an internal sigh of relief. She wasn't sure if she should be annoyed with the vampire or not. This had to have been his plan all along.

Eric's breath whispered against her cheek. "Stay here, Jasmine, and enjoy the party. I shall not be long." His tone was warm and pleasant, but the flash of his eyes told her to stay put.

Jasmine nodded.

The hand on her back dropped away. With it went the amorous sensations she had been experiencing. Strangely, she had a moment of feeling bereft without it. She brought the glass of champagne to her lips and took a long sip. Whatever game the vampire was playing, he seemed to want to play it alone.

Jasmine watched Eric and the men retreat to the back of the boat. Shamelessly, she kept her eyes on the vampire's perfect, tight arse. The kind of backside you could bounce a dime off. In black trousers it looked amazingly good.

Claude shifted nervously beside her. Jasmine pulled herself back from ogling her temporary boss. Never in her life had she checked out a man's butt before. She rather enjoyed it.

She turned her attention to the blond man. It looked like both of the lovers had been abandoned. At least they had that in common.

Turning, she decided to take pity on the guy. "Claude, is it?"

"Actually my name's Kevin," he mumbled back, his eyes focused on his champagne. "Marcel just calls me Claude, so everyone else does, too."

A frowned marred her brow. Weird. Why would anyone rename their partner? He wasn't a pet.

"How long have you been in France?"

He sounded American. Now she was getting curious. Maybe if she asked him enough questions, she could learn something new. Eric had said nothing about that.

Claude sighed. "A couple of months, I was visiting with friend and met Marcel."

He did not seem happy. Was he now regretting that he stayed? Being close to the Frenchman, he had to know what was going on.

"Where are your friends now?" Jasmine asked.

He glanced away awkwardly. "They went home. Marcel insisted that I say awhile."

Raising his glass flute, he sipped quickly at the alcohol.

She was sure what he really meant was Marcel had made him stay. Had he threatened him? Was he a prisoner? He definitely seemed frightened. Maybe he needed help.

Jasmine lowered her voice to a murmur. "Do you want to go home?"

Claude's gaze jerked back to hers. The desperation in his eyes was unmistakable. This young American did need help. He was begging for it.

"Yes. I miss my family." The words barely disguised his plea.

Taking his arm, she gave it a reassuring squeeze. Jasmine knew she had to tell Eric. If there was a way they could help him, then they had to try.

She caught movement out of the corner of her eye. Pierre was making his way towards them through the crowd. His hard, brown eyes were fixed on them with intent. A grim expression tensed his features.

Claude visibly paled in front of her. She knew then he had seen the bulky guard, too.

Staying relaxed as possible, she smiled up at Claude. She dropped her hand from his arm.

"So you think I should definitely try macarons?" Jasmine asked casually.

Pierre's presence suddenly loomed over them. "What are you two doing?"

Faking a gasp, she gave him a startled look, hand rising to her chest. "You startled me! We were just discussing French food. Weren't we, Claude?"

He nodded, taking a gulp of his champagne. Head turned, he refused to look anywhere but her. The guy obviously didn't do subtle.

The bodyguard didn't seem to notice.

Pierre's eyes ran insolently over her. "Tell me, was it easy to give up your boyfriend to become the plaything of another man?"

Jasmine knew he was baiting her. Twitch wasn't really her boyfriend. He also didn't know who Eric really was. As far as they knew she had agreed to be his mistress, most likely for money. She knew she had to play the part. The problem was her inner bitch wanted its say.

"It wasn't that hard. Eric has a lot more to offer me." A coy smile touched her lips. "How could I refuse?"

Pierre's eyes rested greedily on the swell of her breasts for a moment. Then they dropped lower to her legs. Suddenly the dress felt too exposing and not so sexy. Jasmine resisted the urge to cross her arms over her chest.

"I see he's already paying for that sweet little arse of yours." Jealousy laced his every word. She could tell he had wanted his chance with her. Jasmine was grateful he never had. Never would.

She gave him a slightly bored expression. "That's really none of your business."

Claude was looking uncomfortable. He seemed even paler now and was avoiding her eyes.

The big man shifted closer. His arm brushed against her shoulder and Jasmine tensed. She did not like having him this close. Her skin crawled in disgust.

"Don't expect his interest to last too long, sweetheart. Once he's done with you, then you're *mine*." Pierre said the words inches from her ear. His hot breath slid across her skin.

Tilting her head up sharply, she met his eyes. A promise of pain shone in them. He really believed Eric was going to hand her over to him. She was thankful that was not about to happen. Ever.

She couldn't let him know that though.

The wary dread in her eyes was real enough. She took a step back. No matter what the vampire had said, she wasn't hanging about for more threats.

"If you'll excuse me." Jasmine made her way through the crowd. The feel of Pierre's angry eyes practically burned between her shoulder blades. Head held high, she somehow managed to keep it together.

CHAPTER 16

AFTER MINGLING FOR A WHILE, she had made sure to lose Pierre's watchful gaze. He made her uncomfortable. At least now she knew he was waiting for his opportunity to have her. Not that it was ever going to happen.

Curiosity was starting to get the better of her now. Where had Eric gone? After discarding her empty champagne flute, she collected another from a passing tray. She knew she couldn't drink much. On an empty stomach that would be asking for trouble. Already the alcohol had melted away her nervousness. Any more and she would on the way to being drunk. That would be dangerous.

Jasmine moved to the back of the boat. It was the same direction she had observed the men take. She knew Eric had told her to stay in the main area, but she did not want to give up an opportunity to snoop. Looking around a little couldn't hurt. Not in her mind anyway.

"Twitch you there?" Jasmine murmured softly.

"Of course I am, Jazzy," the techno mage responded.

Relief swept through her at the sound of his voice. She had been starting to wonder if the range on the earpiece had gone again. It was obvious it wasn't working as it should.

She was now at the end of the main room, from where all the smartly dressed waiters seemed to be coming. A steady flow of trays were still being carried out for the guests to enjoy. This had to lead towards the kitchen.

She waited until one of the servers had passed to talk again.

"I've left the party area to have a look around."

Twitch took a moment to respond. "Marcel will probably have guards. Try not to run into any of them."

She couldn't miss the concern in his voice. A smile curved her lips. It was nice having someone worry about her.

Eric had seemed happy to leave her to fend for herself. Not that it bothered her of course, she assured herself swiftly. The vampire was busy with business. She had no reason to feel a little hurt.

"I will try," she replied softly. "By the way your earwig almost deafened me earlier."

He sighed. "I told you it was a crude version."

Jasmine pulled a face. "You didn't say it was going to hurt."

If he had told her that, she might not have bothered putting it in.

A corridor that seemed to stretch along the length of the boat was before her now.

"Where's the vampire?"

Jasmine glanced into an open door. A gym. She carried on.

"He went to speak with Marcel and some other men."

She sipped her champagne. The arms dealer certainly had a fancy boat. Everything was opulent and luxurious. He obviously liked to show off his wealth.

"Didn't he tell you to stay put petal?" Twitch asked. "Are you sure we can really trust him?"

"Yes. He got hold of Mark and I have been told to follow Eric's orders. I'm just having a quick look around. It's not like he's ever going to know," she murmured back, trying to justify her actions.

Twitch was silent for a moment. She was not sure if he was happy or upset by the news. He had trust issues. After everything that had happened, she couldn't blame him.

"So what are you wearing?"

Jasmine blinked in surprised confusion at his random question. "I'm sorry, what?"

Twitch audibly sighed dramatically. "Jazzy, I'm stuck in a damn basement. I can't get electronic eyes on the boat. A mad man has me working on a diabolical weapon. Give a guy a break."

She rolled her eyes. Trust the techno mage to try to guilt trip her.

Most of the doors she was strolling slowly by were closed. And no one seemed to be around either.

"A little black dress that comes to just above my knees." Jasmine made sure to lower her voice to a seductive whisper. "It flares at the hips, scooped neck and backless, sexy as hell."

"Heels?" Twitch's voice had lowered too. It was husky with a faint hint of anticipation.

She smiled. "Of course. Black. Very high."

"Underwear?"

Jasmine's eyes widened then she laughed. "You only get the dress details, sorry."

"Damn it, woman," he grumbled crossly. "You're a tease."

"Twitch, you're a pervert," she replied back with amusement.

The guy seriously needed a girlfriend. She knew he also played this game with Gemma, the other woman on their team. Once he had even convinced her to have earpiece sex with him—basically the same as phone sex. Gemma had taken pity on him. Apparently it had been fun.

This was all before Jasmine had started on the team. It was a miracle their boss Mark had never found out. He seemed to always know everything.

"But you still love me," Twitch chuckled in her ear.

She could not keep the smile out of her voice. "I have no idea where I am going right now. There are so many cabins."

The corridor seemed to be endless. Worry had started to swamp her. What if she ran into Marcel and Eric? She had no doubt the vampire would be pissed off. Then again, what would

CLAIRE MARTA

the arms dealer say? Maybe, she realised, she should have thought this through. Getting caught was not an option.

"I feel useless," Twitch suddenly complained. "If I had Internet access, I could have a floor plan of the place for you."

Knowing the techno mage, he would have had everything in front of him. The boat plans, guest list, a way to track everyone's movements, video footage. The whole shebang. When he was up and running, he was a blessing to have around. Right now she could understand his frustration. It had to suck.

"You can't access anything?"

"I am warded with magical restraints up to my eyeballs. It's a miracle the earwig even works," he grumped.

The sudden sharp sound of voices fading in and out of her ear was disorientating. It blotted out anything else her friend was saying. Confused, Jasmine stopped to glance around. The corridor was still empty. Frowning, she looked towards the closed doors. If it was coming from a cabin, why did it sound so loud?

"What you're hearing is the bug I'm picking up," Twitch said, answering her unspoken question. "It means you're close to wherever Marcel is."

Jasmine stilled. "Why does it sound so weird?"

"I'm adjusting it now. Move along more. It should get clearer as you get closer."

She was not sure she wanted to get any closer. Eric might be able to sense her with his vampiric senses. Jasmine didn't want him to find her. It was safer if he didn't know she had ignored his orders.

She took a deep breath. "How close?"

Twitch made a little hum. "You won't be right outside the door, I promise. You will have time to escape if it's needed."

Cautiously she stepped further along the passage. If she could work out where they were, she could estimate how close she needed to be. The voices continued to buzz in and out. They were so scrambled that Jasmine couldn't make out what was being said.

148

Twitch's creation was definitely faulty. Jasmine knew, though, he would be trying to fix it. The techno mage's silence confirmed this.

She suddenly picked out the lower timbre of Eric's voice. It was distorted, but she would recognize it anywhere. A slither of desire rippled down her spine. Oh yes, it was definitely the vampire. No one else's voice had such an effect on her.

Slowly she edged further.

"The neurotoxin is ready. All Doctor Dasyurus needs is for it to be tested." Marcel's voice filled her ear.

Jasmine's heartbeat sped up with surprise. Pressing herself back into the wall, she stopped.

"Has it not been done? I thought all the required testing was completed in the lab?" Eric queried.

"Of course, and he assures me it works," the fat man replied smoothly. "He just wants to see the results over a large distance."

Jasmine did not fail to note the Frenchman had said 'He'. The doctor was a male. At a guess, the vampire had to be pleased at this bit of information. It wasn't much, but a start. They also now knew the weapon was a neurotoxin.

"When is this test scheduled?" The German Randall sounded impatient.

"I don't have all the details. You will know when I do," Marcel assured him.

Jasmine peered up and down the corridor. She would look weird just standing there if anyone walked past. She had been lucky up until now. That didn't mean it wouldn't change. A glance further along revealed a few open doors. Maybe she could hide in one of the rooms.

"I want to see results before I spend a dime on anything," Smith the American drawled.

"I agree with Smith. We do not even know what it does yet." Eric sounded like he was really pushing for information. Jasmine couldn't blame him. Not with what was at stake.

Pushing off the wall, she began to tiptoe towards the open doors.

"Marcel has always provided the goods and never lets customers down," the English guy Sir John defended.

Marcel giggled. "Oh believe me, you won't be disappointed with what it does. That I can guarantee."

Her hand tightened around her champagne flute. Jasmine felt dread engulf her. That could only mean whatever the toxin did, it was nasty.

"Is the good doctor joining us this evening?" Eric asked.

"I am afraid he was detained." Marcel's reply was apologetic. "But please, do not let that stop you from enjoying the party."

A door opened further down. Panic lanced through her. Fuck. She was going to get caught.

Jasmine scrambled into one of the cabins. Thankfully it was empty. Sliding behind the half-open door, she hid. The sound of footsteps teased her ears. Slowly they drew closer. Through a crack in the door, she watched the men pass by. Randall and Sir John were in front. They seemed eager to get back to the party. Smith the American came along at a more leisurely pace. Eric and Marcel then followed.

The vampire paused for a moment. His dark head tipped slightly to one side, but he did not stop walking. Jasmine held her breath as she stared at his back. Had he somehow sensed her? Shit. She was in serious trouble if he had.

Sinking her teeth into her bottom lip, she worried the flesh. Jasmine knew there was nothing she could do about it now. All she could hope was that he had been focused on something else. Not her.

"Tell me, has the mage been giving you any trouble?" the vampire asked casually.

Even though they were moving away, the words were crystal clear through the ear piece. Jasmine felt a twinge of foreboding.

"He is a little defiant," the Frenchman confided. "But that is to be expected. I have broken lesser men."

She heard Eric's rumbling chuckle. "You mean to keep hold of him this time?"

"*Oui*. He will become accustomed to being in my employ and then perhaps one day in my bed."

She heard a sharp inhale of breath in her ear. Twitch had obviously been eavesdropping, too.

Marcel intended to make Twitch his lover? Jasmine paled. She knew her friend was not that way inclined, but she doubted the arms dealer would care. No wonder Claude aka Kevin had been looking worried this evening. Did he know of Marcel's plans? What did that mean for him now?

"What of Claude?" Eric asked, mirroring her thoughts.

The fat man sighed. "Claude is a pretty thing, but he lacks imagination. Twitch, I think, would keep my interest for quite a while."

Jasmine did not even want to think about how. From the amount of swearing she could hear going on, neither did the techno mage. It was then she realised she could no longer hear the other voice.

The bug had to be out of range now. This was probably a good thing. She was not sure she wanted to continue hearing Eric being chummy with Marcel.

"It's OK, Twitchy. I will get you the fuck out before he does that to you," she whispered quietly.

"At least now I know what he's intending," he replied in a low purr of disgust.

Jasmine knew she didn't have a lot of time to re-join the other guests. Eric would be looking for her. If he hadn't worked out already that she had gone walkabout, he would soon. Then she would be screwed.

"Get back to the other guests, Jazzy," the techno mage suggested.

"Don't worry, I'm going."

She peeked out. The passageway was empty and there was no one in sight. Slipping out of the room, Jasmine began to make her way back.

Her champagne glass was still clutched in her hand. The alcohol she had already consumed was buzzing pleasantly through her blood. She was tempted to take a fortifying sip but resisted. No more drinking. It would be foolish to do so.

Somewhere up ahead a door clicked open. Jasmine's steps faltered. It looked like her luck had just run out. Anxiety gripped her. She prayed it wasn't Pierre. God knows what he would do to her if he found her alone. It was something she did not want to find out. Ever.

A sandy-haired guy stepped out of a cabin in front of her. He was standing with his back to her. He hadn't seen her yet. Jasmine stilled. Slowly she took a step back. She did not want to be caught back here. Even if he was one of the guests, she wanted to avoid it. If Marcel knew she was wandering around his boat, she doubted he would be happy. She also dreaded to think what Pierre would do.

Tingles began over her scalp. The signature of werewolf bristled against her senses and raced down her spine, sensual, fierce. Wild and potent. The feeling always took her breath away, as if she were aware of the beast that lived beneath their flesh.

Werewolf was the one type of shifter she sensed perfectly. One of her team back in London was a wolf. She was well acquainted with the feel of them.

The sandy-haired guy stopped. Tilting his head to the side, he sniffed the air lightly.

Jasmine bit her lip. Shit.

He had her scent. Now there was no escaping a confrontation. If she backtracked he would just follow her smell. She had no choice but to face him.

He said something in French as he turned. A low stream of words that sounded slightly threatening.

Jasmine pinned a smile on her face. "Sorry, I don't speak French."

Making sure she swayed slightly, she tottered towards him. Maybe if she played her cards right, she could get away from him quickly. All she had to act was drunk and harmless. Raising her flute she took a long swig. The champagne bubbles fizzed on her tongue. She inspected him over the rim of her glass.

His sandy-brown hair was slightly shaggy. The features of his face were rugged and sharp. Brown, unsympathetic eyes did a slow dance over her. They lightened with interest.

"You are not supposed to be back here," he told her softly. A French accent thickened his words.

Jasmine smiled widely. "I don't suppose you know where the ladies room is. I seem to have gotten a little lost." Using one hand, she gestured around exaggeratedly. This caused her to waver on her heels. "Oops." She giggled, bracing her free arm against the wall.

The wolf smiled, eyes amused. "Perhaps you have had a little too much to drink, *chérie*."

"But it's so good, isn't it? The champagne? It's just divine." Jasmine leaned back against the wall.

She was hoping he would steer her back towards the rest of the guests. If he was part of security that would be his job. She doubted she was the first drunk guest he would have had to deal with. Or the last.

Folding his arms over his chest, he rested against the opposite wall. "I am not allowed to drink when I am on duty, but maybe I can join you for one after?"

Jasmine kept the smile fixed on her face. OK, so this was not what she had been expecting. She would have to rethink her way out of this one.

Eric would probably be wondering where the hell she was. He had to know by now she had wandered off. She really was now seriously screwed. The vampire wasn't going to be happy with her. She had disobeyed. Jasmine knew this probably meant spending the rest of the time stuck in the hotel room. She very much doubted she would be allowed to help again.

The smile abruptly slid from wolf's face. His eyes were on something behind her now.

An icy breeze rushed over the back of Jasmine's neck. It was the only warning she got.

A firm arm slid around her waist. "There you are, darling. I have been searching for you everywhere."

Jasmine's heart skipped a beat.

Startled, she looked up to find Eric behind her. The blue eyes that stared down at her were glacial and hard. Not a trace of warmth showed on his features. He was pissed. Jasmine swallowed down her dread. Turning, she pressed her front to his. Hard packed muscle greeted the softness of her chest. She hadn't seen him naked, but she could tell he would be all sinewy and toned. Eric was deliciously well built.

The arm around her waist allowed her to move but remained in place.

"Oh hello, darling." She made sure her voice came out in a breathy, slightly slurred murmur. Her arms wrapped around his waist.

They still had an audience. She knew she needed to keep up the pretence of being drunk. Giggling, she nuzzled her face into the crook of his neck. His skin was wonderfully warm. The smell of snow and pine wrapped itself around her senses.

Desire rolled through Jasmine. Closing her eyes, she kept her face pressed to his skin. Oddly, she felt safe there.

The vampire's arms tightened around her.

"Forgive my girlfriend." Eric's deep voice rumbled in his chest. "It seems she is partying a little too much this evening."

A smile curved her lips. The vamp always caught on so fast. She liked that about him.

"She is not allowed back here." The wolf's voice was now hard. Was he disappointed she was taken?

Jasmine didn't answer. Letting the vampire deal with the problem seemed the best thing to do. He was, after all, in charge.

Eric's free hand slid slowly down her side. His big palm abruptly cupped her bottom. Jasmine made a little squeak of surprise.

"I shall endeavour to make sure it does not happen again," he assured the other male calmly. He squeezed one of Jasmine's cheeks possessively. Kneading gently, he massaged the flesh.

She bit back a moan of pleasure. What the hell was he doing? Suddenly she got the impression he was staking his claim. Did he know the guy was a werewolf? Maybe he was warning him off.

When the hand shifted its attention to the other arse cheek, she could not hold back the moan this time. Burying her face against his chest, she gripped his tuxedo jacket. Excitement was rocketing through her.

Jasmine trembled. She practically melted against him, unable to stop herself.

The vampire nuzzled her hair.

"Come, my lovely. Let us get back to the party," he murmured softly against her ear.

Eric hid his irritation as he led Jasmine back into the main part of the boat. She had not followed his orders. This he found infuriating. What in damnation had she been doing sneaking about the boat? He had scented her the moment he and the others had left the cabin. Jasmine had been damn lucky not to be discovered by Marcel or Pierre. He did not need them becoming suspicious of her presence. Not now. They had worked far too hard for things to be jeopardized.

The fact that his body had reacted instantly to her nearness also annoyed him. It had only taken her snuggling close to make him painfully hard. Even now he was sporting an erection of steel. And his fangs had practically been screaming for release. The slender curve of her neck had been on display. Eric had taken a moment to greedily drink the sight in. The urge to sink his fangs into her had made him almost dizzy with need.

Scenting the other male's arousal had not helped. Eric had acted instinctively laying his claim. He wanted to leave no doubt in the other man's mind she was his and his alone.

Jasmine was not his, though. Not yet anyway. Even that would be temporary. Eric did not need a female in his life. A permanent arrangement was impossible with the work he did. He did not need the complication.

It also disturbed him that it had pleased him in some measure to mark her as his own. He did not mark or claim women. They were a pleasurable distraction and nothing more. Nothing was more important than his work.

Eric suppressed a growl. Stamping down his lust, he focused on his mission. Tonight he had learnt of others in the game. Marcel, it seemed, was a wanted man. A target was on his back. No doubt a price as well.

At any other time, he would have been happy to allow one of them to have the arms dealer. However, there was more at stake than dealing with the fat man. His partner, Dasyurus, was a dangerous man. Eric could not afford to let any of his creations fall into the wrong hands.

They emerged into the main area. Eric had not spoken a word to her since leading her back. Apart from his hand on her elbow, he hadn't touched her again. This was kind of a relief. She was still trying to recover from having her bottom fondled. The vampire definitely had skilled hands. He had seemed to know right where to touch her.

Jasmine glanced at him nervously. Was he still angry with her? She had never expected him to come to her rescue. He had found her far too quickly for it to be coincidental. This could only mean he had sensed her when he had passed where she had been hiding. Crap.

Jasmine was not prepared when Eric swept her out onto the dance floor. One minute they were walking. The next she was in his arms. He curved them around her waist as he dragged her up against him. His eyes glimmered like cold sapphires.

Swaying them to the rhythm of the slow music, he moved them into the dancing crowd. They were body to body. Jasmine's eyes shot wide in surprise. The press of his erection rested against her stomach. His very large erection, she registered in a daze.

"What were you doing back there?" The words were said in an even, pleasant voice.

He was still angry with her. More than angry. Although his face was remote, she could see it in his eyes.

"Looking for the bathroom," she managed meekly.

She knew it was a lame excuse. With him so close, though, it was the best she could do. Her body had gone into overdrive. The points of her nipples were taut with excitement. A strange neediness flowed through her. Already she could feel moisture soaking her panties. How could being pressed up against him flame her desire? Jasmine kept her eyes on his face.

Irritation tightened his features. "Jasmine, do not lie to me."

She sighed shakily. "I wanted to see if I could help. Maybe learn something."

Eric pressed his face to her hair. Then his nose nuzzled the curve of her neck. His breath was warm against her skin.

"And did you?" It was the softest of murmurs.

Jasmine was having a hard time concentrating. She felt breathless and dizzy. "N-no, n-nothing."

They were still moving to the music. Their forms glided fluidly together with the slow, sultry voice of the female singers.

"I should spank you for your disobedience," he muttered angrily against her ear. "I know I would enjoy having that delectable little bottom under my palm."

Jasmine could not contain the shudder of excitement. Confusion darkened her eyes. How could he say things like that to her and how the hell could she find them so arousing? It was crazy.

Pulling back a little, he stared down into her face. Eric's frosty eyes glittered knowingly. "You would enjoy it too, would you not, kitten?"

"I-I don't know," she admitted quietly.

She had never even thought about that before. Now for some reason, she couldn't get the image of Eric slapping her naked arse out of her head.

Nervously she bit at her lower lip.

A smile touched his mouth. "Hmm . . . perhaps when we have some more time we shall find out."

Jasmine had a feeling he would do it, too. She felt her body clench with desire.

"H-how long do we have to stay?" she managed to ask. They were still in the middle of the party. Neither of them could let themselves get distracted. The bloody vampire knew that. Yet here he was teasing her.

Amusement danced across his features. "I have concluded my business, so another hour or two to be polite."

His arms loosened, allowing her to move fractionally away. No longer squished against him, the haze of desire in her mind dimmed.

"OK."

One of Eric's dark eyebrows rose enquiringly. "Are you bored already, my lovely?" he mocked softly.

Jasmine shook her head and looked away. "No." She just didn't want to be sexually tormented by Eric all night. Having to deal with all these feelings she hadn't experienced before was already overwhelming. Sexual frustration was something she did not need. She also didn't want to bump into Pierre again. With the vampire back at her side, though, it probably wouldn't happen.

"Then enjoy yourself," the vampire suggested as he twirled her around gracefully. "We shall dance and enjoy the atmosphere of the party and play our parts well."

Eric spent another hour whirling her around the dance floor. He was polite and friendly but always vigilant. They ended up chatting about the city mostly. Eric had apparently been to Paris many times before. He had even seen the Eiffel Tower being built, which she found a little amazing.

He looked like he was in his late thirties, but from what he had said, he had to be hundreds of years old. The vamp blended in so well, it was easy to forget what he was. A vampire.

Jasmine noticed, though, he made sure not to touch her seductively again. The distance between their bodies was rigidly maintained. He was an attentive partner, smoothly leading them into each dance.

Twitch had said nothing more, but she had a feeling he was still listening in on his end. She was half-tempted to tease him, but she didn't. Too many people were around. Jasmine could not take the chance.

By the time they stopped dancing, her feet were killing her. Jasmine limped from the dance floor. Now she remembered why she hated wearing heels.

The vampire's hand rest gently on her elbow. "Come. Another drink I think."

Alcohol sounded like a fabulous idea. Hopefully it would dull the pain, which was shooting up her ankles. She bit back a moan of agony. Sitting down was another good option.

With ease, Eric retrieved two flute of champagne from a passing waiter.

"My feet are killing me," she muttered, accepting the offered glass. "I hate these fu . . . fricking things." At the last minute she managed to stop herself from swearing. The vamp would probably get pissed if she cussed. He was angry enough already.

Eric glanced down at her legs. "Forgive me. I forget those must be uncomfortable when worn for so long."

"You have no idea," Jasmine responded bitingly then sipped at her champagne.

How other women could wear them all day she didn't have a clue. She was happiest in trainers. These were starting to feel like cruel and unusual torture devices.

The champagne poured smoothly down her throat. She prayed it wouldn't take long to deaden the cramps, which were twisting the soles of her feet.

The vampire chuckled. "I count myself lucky that I shall never know."

"I would have to agree with you there." Mr Smith was standing just behind them. "Those things look darn dangerous."

Jasmine glanced at him nervously. How long had the guy been standing there?

Eric did not seem surprised to see him. "I am amazed to see you this far over the pond, Smith."

The American moved closer. A pleasant smile tilted his lips, as he regarded them.

"We've had our eye on Marcel Coupe for a while now." The man slid him a meaningful look. "You're here on business, too?"

Jasmine took another sip of alcohol as she watched them. They obviously knew each other. She wondered how.

The vampire's eyes were alight with amusement. "But of course."

Smith gazed out of the crowded dance floor toward the arms dealer. He was mingling with his guests. A smug smile was on his toad-like features.

He had an unhappy looking Claude in tow, with Pierre trailing them at a distance. Randall and Sir John were both also not far. They seemed to be gravitating round the Frenchman like he was a round, little sun.

"This damn business is making me uneasy," the American muttered softly. "It was a helluva lot easier back in the old days."

Eric made a hum of agreement. "Weapons evolve. Things become more dangerous. I agree it is not as it once was."

Rubbing a hand tiredly over his face, Smith sighed. "I may just step back and let you deal with it then."

Eric's eyebrows inched up slightly in surprise. "How generous of you."

After taking a flute glass from a passing waiter, the American took a deep gulp of the contents. His eyes remained on Marcel.

"I'm getting old, Eric. I think it's time to get out while the going's good. I want to retire."

Concern darkened the vampire's eyes. "Perhaps that is the best, old friend, if you truly feel that way."

By now Jasmine had worked out that Smith had to be working for some kind of agency. The FBI or CIA seemed like the best bet.

At that point, she realised she still didn't have a clue who the vamp worked for. It was a little annoying and also frustrating. He was so damn secretive sometimes.

"I want at least one dance with this young lady, though, before I go," she heard the American saying.

Jasmine almost groaned. The cramping in her feet had dulled, but it still ached. Could she really put herself through another dance?

Amused sympathy settled over Eric's features. "I believe Jasmine is all danced out."

She glanced towards Smith. Could be an opportunity to dig for information. Could she really give that up? This guy obviously knew Eric. Jasmine wanted to know how.

She pinned a cheerful smile on her face. "Oh, I can dance one more for your friend."

The vampire showed no surprise. In fact he looked like he might have even been expecting it.

"It seems she's keen to leave you," Smith said with a chuckle.

Eric's lips quirked in amusement. "Indeed, it does."

"Maybe I just fancy a different dance partner." She flashed the vampire a quick smile. He accepted the champagne flute she shoved into his hand.

The American offered her his arm. Placing her hand on his elbow, Jasmine let him draw her back out onto the dance floor.

The moment she started moving, her feet began to throb. Gritting her teeth behind her lips, she settled into the dance.

Smith didn't dance as well as Eric. He was not as smooth and fluid in his movements. She also felt none of the red hot desire she had experienced in the vampire's arms.

"How do you know Eric?"

Smith didn't seem shocked at her question. Wary amusement glinted in his eyes. He chuckled. "Straight down to business, aren't you, little lady?"

She could feel a pair of icy eyes on her. The vampire was watching them. Goosebumps rose over her flesh with excitement. Eric could probably hear their every word, but she didn't care.

Jasmine smiled instead. "I don't believe in wasting time. You act like you know each other."

The American pulled her closer. His lips rested gentle against her ear. Anyone else watching would probably think he was whispering intimately.

"We do." His soft murmur made her shiver.

"How?"

Jasmine felt him smile. "We've worked on a few situations together over the years."

So Smith did work for a government agency.

He pulled back until he could see her face. "I see you understand my meaning."

Amusement danced in her green eyes. "More than you know. I work for the Yard in London," he whispered back.

Something flickered in the older man's eyes for a moment. Then he smiled. "I thought there was more to you than meets the eye."

He twirled her suddenly across the floor before reeling her back into his arms. Jasmine couldn't help but laugh. The movement left her feeling a little dizzy. Her feet were in constant pain now, but it was worth it.

"Are you really going to let Eric deal with this?" she asked a little breathlessly.

Smith nodded. "He's the best freelancer in the business. It's his neck on the line instead of mine for once. Plus he's a little more indestructible."

As they meandered around in a circle, Jasmine caught site of Eric. He was sipping his champagne, but those intense cerulean eyes of his were watching her with a smouldering look.

She swallowed hard. God he looked so damn sexy in that tux. His eyes burned hotter when they met hers. Something dark and hungry passed within their depths. One moment it was there; the next it was gone.

Jasmine felt her heart rate pick up with excitement. Dragging her eyes away, she looked back at her dance partner. He hadn't seemed to notice her distraction.

"You know what he is?" she whispered leaning a little closer into him.

Smith chuckled. "It took me near enough twenty years of working with him to work that out." His sharp eyes met hers. "I can see why Eric likes you."

Jasmine drew back with surprise. "You do?"

A grin spread across the American's face. "You have a little sass and I have a feeling you'll keep him on his toes."

Jasmine laughed and grinned back. She very much doubted Eric saw it that way. He probably thought she was a pain in the arse like her boss did.

The song came to an end. Gallantly, Smith took her arm and led her back across the room. The vampire stood waiting for them.

"You have yourself a little charmer there," Smith told him before stepping back. "It was nice to meet you, ma'am." He tipped his head politely in her direction.

"It was nice to meet you to, Mr. Smith," Jasmine replied with a smile. She watched as the American turned and made his way through the crowd.

"Enjoy your dance?" Eric enquired softly. He held out the half-empty glass he had been holding for her.

Curling her hand around it, she accepted it back gratefully. She needed more alcohol after all that. Her feet were balls of agony. It fucking hurt. A lot.

Jasmine winced as pain cramped through her legs. "Yes."

The vampire's deep chuckle filled her ears. "Learn anything useful?"

She sent him a sideways look. "Yes, that you're not the only one after the fat man. But you knew that already."

A ghost of a smile touched his lips. "Of course. Do you think only one government would feel unsafe? Smith isn't the only one I noticed in this crowd tonight."

"There are more?" Her eyes danced around the teeming room for a moment. The glamour and glitzy folks in front of her did not look like operatives. Then again nor did she or Eric.

"Indeed."

Pain tightened her features. She wasn't sure how much longer she could keep standing up. Eric watched as she took a welcome gulp from her glass.

"Why don't you let them deal with him then?" Jasmine asked after a moment.

He turned away from her to scan the other celebrating guests. "I fear this weapon cannot fall into human hands."

Was there something about the toxin he wasn't telling her about? It seemed a little strange he didn't want anyone else getting their hands on it. Surely anyone stopping Marcel was a good thing. She had more questions now. Ones she was not sure would get answers to.

She frowned. "Why not?"

The vampire's expression was now closed and remote. His cold, blue eyes fixed on hers. "I have said more than enough here. Come now, let us make our farewells."

With his free hand, he relieved her of the glass. As a waiter passed by with a tray he deposited both his and hers on it. Jasmine blinked in surprise.

His big, warm hand then settled on her lower back. A riot of sensations exploded through her as his skin touched hers. Jasmine bit her lip to stop herself from moaning. The feeling was electric.

A moment later he was guiding her across the room. Their host was among a circle of guests. They all seemed to be hanging on the Frenchman's every word. Laughter erupted as they reached his side.

"Marcel we have come to say our *adieus*," Eric informed him with a smooth, friendly smile.

The fat man looked up in surprise. "You are leaving so soon, *mon ami*?"

He pulled out a handkerchief and dabbed at his brow. He seemed to be sweating more than usual. Jasmine wondered if he was nervous about something.

The vampire's arm curved around her waist and tugged her close. The heat of his side seared her.

"Jasmine is getting tired and I fear I shall have to get her to bed." His voice was husky and suggestive now.

Every pair of eyes in the group turned to her. Jasmine felt her cheeks redden with embarrassment. Why the fuck did Eric have to use that as an excuse? Centre of attention again. She hated it.

Pierre was hovering, keeping Claude from trouble. The big man's eyes met hers. He flashed her a lecherous grin. She was tempted to flip him off but managed to resist.

Marcel giggled. "Of course. Then I shall not detain you."

Suddenly she found her hand in the fat man's grip. He raised it to his lips. The kiss on her skin was wet and cold. Jasmine managed to hold back the shudder of revulsion. Barely.

Claude waved at her cheerfully. His eyes were over-bright and he'd had too much to drink. At least he didn't seem too miserable now.

"I shall be in touch," Marcel told the vampire.

Eric shook the arms dealer's hand confidently. "Until then."

Muscled arm still around her waist, Jasmine found herself manoeuvred to the front of the boat. Sending the vamp an irritated glance, she sighed.

She didn't like to be dragged along. He seemed to be in a hurry now.

They reached the staff who had taken their coats, and Eric produced the ticket. The woman in charge took it without a word. They watched in silence as she ferreted about on a coat rack until she matched the numbers.

"What's your hurry?" Jasmine muttered, slipping on her coat. Getting to sit down was all she could think about now. It was just way too painful to keep upright.

"We have remained long enough," he murmured back. "I do not need to be recognized by any other agent we may run into."

Jasmine eyed him curiously. "Would they?"

Guarded, eyes slid to hers. "It is a possibility. I try never to involve myself with them. I tend not to work well with anyone other than my own team."

Yet the vampire was working with her. She wondered why. He could have easily not let her come tonight. She could have spent the evening sitting in the hotel room doing nothing. Jasmine sighed. That's probably what she would be doing now after disobeying his orders. She had royally cocked up.

Eric tucked her arm through his. In silence he led her off the big boat. They seemed to be the first to be leaving. She had a feeling everyone else would be partying until the early hours of the morning. Not that she cared. She winced as they made their way back up beside the river. She held in a moan of despair. The short distance suddenly looked daunting. Why the hell did it have to be so far?

With a squeal of surprise, she suddenly found herself in the vampire's arms. One arm under her shoulders, the other beneath her knees. He held her as if she weighed nothing. His hard, muscular chest was pressed against her side. The heat of his big body enveloped her, chasing away the winter evening chill. Jasmine shivered.

Desire surged through her. She didn't want to admit how damn good it felt to be in his arms. She peered up into his dark, brooding face.

Looking down, he met her gaze as he strode along with a confident ease.

"Your whimpers of pain are distracting," he informed her softly. "I wish you would have told me earlier how bad your feet were."

Had she been whimpering? Jasmine realised she hadn't even noticed. Embarrassment engulfed her. "Why?"

Eric shot her a look of exasperation. "I would have found you somewhere to sit."

"I didn't want to spoil your undercover work," she admitted, not meeting his eyes.

Maybe not telling him how bad it was had been a little silly. Jasmine honestly had not wanted to get in the way. Especially as she had already pissed him off.

The vampire shook his head. "So you suffered in silence."

As she opened her mouth to reply, another voice interrupted her.

"Jazzy, what's going on?" Twitch's voice purred softly in her ear.

Blinking, she realised she hadn't told him they were no longer on the boat. It was so damn easy to forget he was there. The techno mage had to know what was going on anyway. He loved to listen.

"Twitch, we're leaving the party now."

Eric's arms tightened around her momentarily. Glancing up, she found his icy blue eyes narrowed to slits. He really hated not hearing the conversation.

Jasmine felt her lips twitch. Pressing them together, she resisted the urge to grin. She found it amusing that he found it so irritating. She had to bet he had never had this problem before.

"OK," Twitch sighed, sounding tired. "The range of the earwig will probably make it stop working for a while."

Worry tugged at her insides. She didn't want to be parted from her friend again. OK, he wasn't physically with her at the moment, but being able to hear his voice was reassuring. At least this way she knew he was fine. Without any kind of connection, if anything happened she wouldn't know.

She tensed a little against Eric's chest. "Be careful, Twitchy. Good night."

"You too. Night," he whispered back.

Jasmine felt a lump form in her throat. They had to get Twitch away from Marcel. She would never be able to forgive herself if something happened to him.

With a sigh, she rested her head against the vampire's firm chest. The steady thud of his heart was reassuring against her ear. Eric had promised to get the techno mage out. Unfortunately, Jasmine knew promises sometimes could not be kept.

They weren't far from the road now. Raoul would be waiting patiently for them with the car. She suddenly remembered there was something she needed to tell Eric. Someone else needed their help. An innocent.

"Claude needs help, Eric. Marcel won't let him leave," she said, tilting her face to stare at him.

His sensual lips tightened for a moment before he responded. "I am well aware of the boy's situation."

So he knew already? Had that been before or after the party, she wondered. Jasmine wouldn't have been surprised if it had been before. Damn vamp with all his secrets. Why wouldn't he share more?

"Can we help him?"

Eric sighed wearily before meeting her eyes. "We will do all that we can, Jasmine."

By the time they reached Raoul and the car she was exhausted. She never wanted to be put down. Just the thought of standing up again made her grimace.

The other vampire was waiting to greet them with a polite smile.

"Are you alright?" he enquired with concern.

Jasmine raised her head from Eric's chest. "My feet are fucking killing me," she grumbled and then yawned.

She was never wearing heels again as long as she lived. Not even if she was paid to do it. From now on she was sticking with flat shoes.

One of Raoul's dark eyebrows cocked at her reply. With quick efficiency he had the car door open and ready.

Without a word Eric deposited her into the leathery interior of the Bentley. Resting her head back, Jasmine sighed.

Maybe now she could relax.

CHAPTER 17

ERIC JOINED THE LITTLE FEMALE in the back of the vehicle. The fact that she had hidden her distress and discomfort irked him. Had she really thought he would not care about her comfort? He was not a monster. He could have easily eased her pain. Jasmine was certainly stubborn and curious. She both annoyed and intrigued him.

She had handled herself remarkably well this evening. He was proud of her. Smith had naturally liked Jasmine. He had not seemed to be fazed by her digging questions. In fact, he looked like he had been enjoying it.

Eric repressed a smile. It had been good to see his old friend. The passing of time had been kind to him. For a mortal in his fifties, he had not lost his handsomeness. Many female eyes had admired the American. No doubt he would not leave the party alone. It would be a shame to no longer come across him when their paths occasionally crossed. This was one of the reasons Eric did not work with humans. Nor make friendships with them. Their life spans were painfully short. Even more so in the business he was in.

He could feel Jasmine's eyes on him. She was twenty-two. Like Smith, she would age and grow old. For a mortal, time was precious—minutes, hours, days, years. For him time meant very little. He was a born immortal.

A sigh left his lips. He could not afford to become attached to her. Perhaps it was time to give her a little punishment. After all, the girl had disobeyed him. Plus she had left him painfully aroused

171

most of the evening. Now it was her turn to experience a little frustration.

He was going to enjoy this immensely.

"So what are we up against?" Jasmine asked.

They had been driving in silence for a good ten minutes. Eric seemed to be lost in thought and Raoul was sticking to his role as driver.

Eric didn't bother to turn from the window as he replied. "Only time will tell."

So he wasn't going to tell her about the neurotoxin. Was that because he didn't trust her or because he thought she didn't need to know?

She pressed her lips together in annoyance. Slipping off her high heels, she groaned. She wanted to have them burnt. Her feet were still aching with cramps.

"Place your feet upon my lap," Eric said softly but firmly.

Startled at his commanding words, she stared at his face. His icy, sapphire blue eyes glittered at her enigmatically.

"I-it's OK, really."

Why was he watching her like that? She felt both excited and nervous.

"Come now, your feet are sore, are they not? Let me help," he encouraged with a sphinx-like smile. Eric suddenly looked dangerously irresistible.

Jasmine bit her lip. They were hurting a lot. Was he offering a foot rub? It was the last thing she had expected from this mysterious vampire. Just the thought of having the cramps kneaded out almost made her groaned.

Carefully she slid her feet onto his lap. His thigh was hard and firm beneath her calves. The contrast between her slender stocking legs resting on his black suit pants was striking.

Still nibbling on her lip, she watched him warily.

Slowly he glided the palms of his hands down her knees to her ankles. His eyes now were focused on her legs. Gently his fingers began to massage the sole of her right foot. She barely bit back a small sound of pained bliss. Leaning her head to the left, she rested it against the leather seat.

Soon he was kneading a little harder. His clever fingers worked away the little spasms and cramps.

"I sensed a werewolf on the boat." Jasmine was surprised how thick her voice sounded. "The sandy-haired guard you found me with."

Eric frowned but did not look up from his task. "Are you certain? I sensed nothing."

"Yes, I'm more than sure." Her reply was soft, husky now. "Wolf is something I pick up easily. One of my team is one. Wouldn't he have sensed that you're a vampire?"

A sharp jolt of pleasure hit her right between the legs. Jasmine gasped. Pressing her thighs together, she tried to ease the sensation. Just then she remembered someone telling her about pressure points on the feet that affected other parts of your body. From the look of satisfaction on Eric's face he knew about those, too. Had he done it on purpose?

When she tried to wiggle her foot away, he held it tighter. Raising his head, he pinned her with the intensity of a single look. It demanded her submission.

Jasmine suddenly found it hard to breath. The force of his will pushed against hers. Dominant, potent, forbidding her to escape. Sagging back, she left her foot where it was. She was tired and did not have the energy for a battle of wills. Not tonight.

His big hand caressed her ankle. She sensed he was pleased with her compliance.

"No. I have the ability to hide what I am from others, even supernaturals. Except, it would seem, from you. Perhaps the wolf has learnt the same trick," he mused softly, answering her question.

The kneading of his thumb on one particular spot had her gripping the leather seat as it was stimulating another area of her body. Clamping her thighs tightly once more, she tried to ride through the feeling. Shockwaves of ecstasy exploded between her legs. Jasmine whimpered, rolling her eyes shut. Chest rising and falling rapidly, she tried to catch her breath. Holy shit, how had he done that? Playing with her feet and he was pleasuring her beyond belief.

He had moved now to her other foot. The attention he had given her right was now lavishly applied to her left. A low groan escaped her lips before she could stop it. Jasmine thought she heard him chuckle.

She glanced nervously towards Raoul in front. He did not seem to have noticed. His eyes were on the road ahead.

Eric continued his manipulation of her flesh. Jasmine was almost a boneless puddle of pleasure by the time they were back at the hotel.

Scooping up the high heels, she didn't bother to put them on. The pain had been worked out of her feet. Now her soles tingled pleasantly from the vampires ministrations. Her body felt tight with need. For some reason the bliss of his foot massage had left her feeling strangely craving . . . something. She had an ache deep inside she could not explain.

Eric helped her gently from the car. Legs shaky, she used the car for support for a moment. Her eyes slid to the vampire. His face was unreadable once again. Nothing showed on his handsome face or in his cold, intense eyes.

He didn't comment when she padded bare foot back into the hotel.

By the time they hit the elevators she was steady on her feet. Neither vampire said a word as they travelled smoothly upwards.

Jasmine kept quiet. She was a little embarrassed about what had happened in the car. Raoul must have realised what was going on. He had sensitive vampiric hearing for fuck's sake.

When he met her gaze across the small space, he smiled. Heat rushed into her cheeks and she looked away. He definitely knew.

As soon as they reached the suite, the vampires switched on their laptops. All their attention was now focused on work. Raoul was checking his contacts and surveillance footage. Eric was looking at emails.

Jasmine headed into the bedroom and changed. She had decided to swallow her embarrassment. Both vampires seemed happy to ignore her and she was fine with that.

She tugged off the little black dress and left it on the bathroom floor with the purse. She found a pair of jeans and a white t-shirt and pulled them on. Much more comfortable. She also felt less vulnerable and more in control. She didn't bother with shoes. Instead she remained barefoot. It gave her feet time to recover a little more.

Now that they were back, she realised she was starving. None of the finger food at the party had touched her lips. Her stomach had been too tied up in knots for her to eat. She quickly made a call down to room service. Eric had told her to use it for whatever she wanted and she wasn't about to say no.

She had forgotten to eat too many meals lately. Breakfast she never ate anyway. Lunch was if she could remember to buy it. Most of the time it took one of her teammates waving food under her face to get her to eat at all. Dinner was usually some kind of sandwich. Mark was convinced she lived on nothing but air and copious amounts of tea. Jasmine guessed it was partly true.

"I ordered something for dinner, if that's OK," she informed them as she wandered back into the room.

"Of course, Jasmine. You must keep your strength up," Eric replied, barely looking up from his screen. "I am glad you took the initiative this time."

He sounded so brisk and business-like. As if he hadn't touched her in the car at all. Had he just been playing with her? Maybe it was a weird punishment for disobeying him at the party. He had, she recalled with some pleasure, threatened to spank her.

Jasmine bit at her lower lip. The vampire evoked confusing feelings within her. He aroused her with his words, his touch, and his looks. Never had she considered letting anyone smack her bottom. Yet here she was wondering if he still intended to do it. She wasn't sure if she liked this feeling inside her at all.

After plonking down onto the free sofa, she watched them. They were working quickly, quietly, and efficiently. There was a flow to their movements, like they had done this a hundred times before. Had they? How long had they been doing this kind of work? Years? Centuries even?

Eric glanced up from his computer screen for a moment. "Why not just ask the question that is burning on the end of that lovely tongue of yours, Jasmine?"

Taken aback, she stared at him apprehensively. "H-how did you know I wanted to ask you something?"

"Your face is very expressive," Raoul informed her, his eyes still on his laptop screen. "You would not do well at poker."

Jasmine wrinkled her nose. Had they been able to read her emotions the whole time she had been with them? Was she that predictable? She was only a rookie, she reminded herself. Gaining skills to hide his emotions like Eric had done over the years would take experience and time. She so badly wanted to acquire those skills.

A tired sigh tumbled from her lips. "I was just wondering how long you guys have been freelance operatives."

Eric's brow furrowed as he looked up at her. "Quite a while indeed," he mused quietly.

Raoul laughed softly. "Sixteen-eighteen we started here in France. Our first client was King Louis, the thirteenth."

Eric's lips curled in a fond smile of remembrance. "Ah yes. The Thirty-Year War between the Protestants and the Catholics."

Jasmine blinked a few times. "That was nearly four hundred years ago!"

Vampires were immortal. She knew that, but it was still crazy to imagine just how long these two had been around.

"It certainly was and the beginning of a most enjoyable career to date," Eric responded as he typed away.

A knock at the suite door dragged her from her shock. She jumped up quickly to answer it. A young French waiter with an easy smile was waiting with a cart. Her empty stomach gurgled at the sight.

Jasmine returned his smile. "Thank God. I'm starving." Standing back, she allowed him to wheel it into the room. When he stood looking expectantly, she wasn't sure what to do.

Raoul was suddenly beside her stuffing some notes in his hand. "*Merci.*"

The waiter grinned and left them with a little bow.

Peering up at the mocha-skinned vampire, she flashed him an awkward smile. "Shit, sorry. I don't have any money with me to tip with."

"It is quite alright, Jasmine," he assured her and gracefully moved back to his laptop.

She pushed the cart further into the room, settling it close to the little table and chairs by the window. The vamps were using the coffee table. At least eating on the table made sure she wouldn't make too much mess. Jasmine glanced at the carpet. How much would the hotel charge them if she accidentally dropped something and marked the floor? She shuddered to think of the cost.

She lifted the silver metal dome on the cart and found the Beef Burgundy she had ordered. Something she had always wanted to try. She sniffed the deep bowl of chunky pieces of braised beef and strips of bacon in red wine and beef broth. Onions mushrooms and carrots, mixed with herbs and garlic were also in the mix. The stew smelt amazing.

She grabbed the basket of rolls from the cart and carried the whole thing to the table. Hungrily, she ripped of a piece of bread and dipped it in the broth. She popped it into her mouth, groaning around it. Divine. She scooped up some meat with her fork.

Eric and Raoul did not look up from their laptops, very absorbed in what they were doing. Not that she minded. She didn't need an audience while she ate.

Jasmine chewed her food and thought about the vampires. Would they need to feed soon? Where would they get their blood from? Plenty of blood banks nowadays offered vamps their services. Most vampires still liked it straight from the source, though, and there were plenty of people who offered their blood in exchange for money. Being living blood donors was a booming business. People also liked to be bitten just for the pleasure of it. Vampires were never going to starve.

Would Eric take her blood again? Just remembering his fangs sinking into her breast had her all hot and bothered. The pleasure had been overwhelming.

She pushed the thought from her mind.

Now was not the time. Thinking about the vampire and what he could do to her body was dangerous. He had already proven that numerous times tonight. She needed to stay on track.

Twitch was the most important thing and getting Claude out, too.

Jasmine turned her gaze to the window. The twinkle lights of Paris brightened the darkness. She had always wanted to visit this city, but never had the chance. Now she was here and she had barely seen it.

She ate in silence until her stomach was pleasantly full. Getting used to eating so well was something she could not afford to do. She would soon be back on her sandwich dinner and not much else.

After placing the empty bowl and basket back on the cart, she pushed it to the door and outside to be picked up later by the hotel's staff. She turned to survey the vampires. Both still busy typing. Neither had moved from their positions since she had started eating. Whatever they were doing, they were dedicated and looked like they were there for the night.

"Is there anything I can do to help?"

Running a hand through his short, black, tousled hair, Eric looked up. "No, there is nothing. Go to bed, Jasmine."

"What about you?" She felt her cheeks heat as she asked the question. It was Eric's room. She didn't want to put him out of his bed. She could sleep on one of the sofas.

"I require little sleep at the moment." A smile touched his lips. "Go rest. You will not be disturbed."

She was happy she wasn't putting him out. After this evening, she would have willingly slept on the floor.

Biting her lip, she nodded. "OK then, thanks. Good night."

CHAPTER 18

ERIC COULD HEAR THE little female moving around in the bedroom. She had slept peacefully last night. The sound of her slow, steady heartbeat had been almost soothing in his ears. A strangely appealing feeling. One he did not care to examine. But he had been mulling over Jasmine's abilities. Eric knew that only a traumatic event could trigger a sensitive's buried gifts. What harrowing experience had caused Jasmine's to activate? Did it still haunt her? She was certainly more sensitive than he had first realised—confirmed by the fact she had picked up a werewolf when he had not.

Raoul's contact inside Marcel's organisation verified he now, indeed, had a wolf on his payroll. A wolf who had been on the boat last night. But why did Marcel even have a werewolf on staff? This could have led to complications if it had not been for the girl. She had proved her usefulness.

Perhaps with time and the correct training, Jasmine could become quite powerful, which would undoubtedly benefit her at work. Eric could help her with it.

"Eric, what is it about this girl that has you so enthralled? I have never seen you like this before," Raoul said from the corner of the room. He was busy checking early morning surveillance footage. The other vampire had not failed to notice his friend glancing towards the close bedroom door.

They had taken turns napping during the night in the other bedroom. Sleep was something they didn't need much of. Not when they were working anyway.

"I am drawn to her," Eric confided. "Since the moment I first set eyes upon her."

He did not want to admit it was getting worse, but it was. Finishing this business was pressing, but when it was out of the way, he could turn his attention to the girl. Once his cock had its fill of her young, nubile body, he would quickly move on. Jasmine would be a pleasant memory.

The other vampire was regarding him with astonishment. "She seems most resourceful. Did you know she carried a pair of nail scissors and deodorant in her purse last night?"

Eric's eyes lit with wary amusement. "Indeed, I did. I thought it better to pretend ignorance. She seemed nervous and I believe feeling armed calmed her a little."

He had been entertained to realise what she was carrying in her purse. The little female certainly had a lively imagination. He wondered what she might do next.

"It did not calm her in the back of the car on the way back," Raoul mused softly. "I distinctly heard her moan once or twice."

Eric's gaze fell away from his friend. Turning, he surveyed the sitting room with a critical eye. Then he moved to the end of one of the sofas. "I was punishing her for her disobedience on the boat. She has a habit of not following orders."

He had found it quite pleasurable himself to play with her body with such a simple touch. She was so responsive it made his lust burn hotter. Watching those big green eyes, dazed with desire, had been most satisfying, almost as much as hearing her little moans.

"It sounded like a most interesting punishment."

He knew the other vampire was finding enjoyment out of his odd behaviour. A mere mortal female had destroyed his cold exterior, which he surely found most amusing. Eric was not sure he would ever live it down, especially when it got back to the others. Raoul would never keep his mouth shut about something like this. Not with their other comrades in arms.

"Stop asking questions, my friend, and help me prepare the damn room," Eric growled in reply.

The other vampire chuckled.

Jasmine ordered some breakfast from room service and then hopped into the shower. She was happy to find a plate of brioche on the bedside table when she emerged from the bathroom.

The cream pastry was amazingly good—definitely worth all the calories just to try it. A good cup of tea had also been fortifying.

Now dressed again more comfortably in jeans and a blue jumper, she was eager to find the vamps. Did they know anything more about Twitch's situation? Had anything happened while she was sleeping? These questions were circling in her head as she left the room.

She opened the bedroom door and paused in the doorway. Eric was sitting on the floor, dressed in what looked like black yoga pants and a black top. Both were tight and showed off his thick legs and muscled chest. Jasmine bit her lip. Did his tight arse look just as good in these, too?

It had taken her a while to fall asleep last night. A strange sense of frustration had plagued her. She was pretty sure it was the sexual kind. After the way he had played with her all evening, she guessed she shouldn't have been surprised.

They had pushed the sofas further apart to make more space. The coffee table was now against a wall.

Jasmine frowned at him, not sure what he was doing. "What's going on?"

Eric smiled when he saw her, a slow charming curving of his sexy mouth. The intensity of his gaze pinned her breathlessly to the spot. How could just a look make her feel strangely needy and hot?

"Come sit over here," he said and gestured to the floor next to him.

Raoul was also in the room. The mocha-skinned vampire was lounging on a chair by the window. A book was open in his hand, his expression absorbed.

Releasing a long breath, she ignored the feelings of arousal washing through her. Probably the reaction he had on all women, she told herself crossly. He was not doing it on purpose.

Obediently, Jasmine joined Eric on the floor. He was sitting cross-legged. She mirrored his position, crossing her legs slowly, grunting a little when her body ached.

She had woken up with slightly achy feet, but they didn't feel bad as she had imagined. The vampire's massage, she knew, probably had something to do with it.

Jasmine felt her cheeks warm slightly at the memory.

"Close your eyes."

She blinked, then gave Eric an are-you-serious look? She remembered the last time he had told her that. It had been right before he had started arousing her. Right before he had bitten her.

He chuckled, blue eyes twinkling. She had the distinct feeling he knew exactly what she was thinking about.

"Jasmine, trust me. All I wish is to help you focus your gifts. Nothing more." His deep baritone was slightly gruff.

Raoul made a small hum of agreement, but did not look up from his book.

"Why?"

One eyebrow slightly raised, he sighed. "Stop asking questions and close your eyes."

Trying not to look to suspicious, Jasmine slowly lowered her eyelids. Silence filled the room for a moment, and it felt eerily quiet and still.

"I require you to concentrate on your breathing," Eric's deep voice said. He hadn't moved.

Jasmine felt a little tension seep out of her shoulders. She had not even realised she had been so tense.

"Inhale," he said and breathed in. "Exhale," he said, letting out a long breath through his mouth.

"I feel like I'm in a yoga class," Jasmine said in a near whisper. She heard both vampires laugh.

"I promise I will not bend you into any unusual positions," Eric said. Amusement and something else she couldn't identify thickened his tone. "Unless you allow me to do that, kitten."

"You need to learn to focus and centre yourself. Meditation will help this," Raoul said softly somewhere to her left.

Had he moved from his chair?

Jasmine felt the tension grip her once more. Awareness tightened uncomfortably through her skull.

The other vampire was behind her now. She was sure of it. Power pushed at her from behind like the lap of a gentle wave – not painful, just there—battering lightly against her senses.

"What's Raoul doing?" She could not keep the creeping alarm out of her voice. Being sneaked up on was something she hated. Even as a child, it had scared her.

Raoul made a noise of astonishment inches from her back, which made her jump.

Her eyes snapped open and she jerked around. Jasmine fixed him with a wary, unsure gaze.

He was kneeling right behind her. Warm, honey-brown eyes stared back into hers. His fine, dark eyebrows were raised slightly in surprise.

"Testing you're senses," Raoul replied lightly.

Jasmine scooted back to make sure both vampires were in her view.

The fact he had been suddenly behind her was unsettling. With their vampiric speed and strength, it was natural for them to move so fast. Really though, she had not needed the demonstration. It just reminded her what they were. Vampires.

"Jasmine, do not be alarmed. We mean you no harm," Eric assured her.

The look in his cold eyes was sincere. For a moment, she thought she even saw a hint of concern before it was swallowed by the ice.

"Just . . . don't sneak up on me, please," she said firmly. Playing silly games was something she was not interested in.

Raoul bobbed his head in agreement. Slowly he rose to his feet and backed away. The push of power retreated.

"It was merely our way to observe how open your gifts are," Eric explained. He had not moved from this cross-legged position. "The fact you sensed Raoul moving proves how open you are now."

She slid back to her original position. "What do you mean?"

Raoul had flopped himself back into the chair in the corner. "You should not be able to sense us."

"Because vampires can move so stealthily you mean?"

The vampire shared a strange look. Jasmine had the feeling they were having a private conversation. Was that even possible? What had she said to put those expressions on their face?

"Let us return to breathing, shall we?" Eric suddenly said with a smile.

"Shouldn't we be doing something else?"

Taking it easy for a while was great, but didn't they have an arms dealer to stop? And an evil doctor with a diabolical toxin?

"There is nothing else to do but wait," Eric informed her patiently. "Raoul's contact will inform us if anything is happening. For now we have time for this."

The vampire seemed determined to get her to do breathing exercises. How it was supposed to help her sensitivity, she didn't know. It felt rather silly.

Jasmine pulled a face beginning to fidget. "I still don't understand why we're doing this."

Eric ran a hand through his tousled, black hair. He pinned her with a patient look. "I told you, your gift is extraordinarily strong. If you were trained correctly, it would benefit you greatly."

Her ears perked up. "How?"

"No supernatural would be able to hide from your detection. Not even if they knew how to hide themselves."

Jasmine tilted her head and stared at him across the space with astonishment. Holy shit, if this were true she would be so much more valuable to her team. Her boss would appreciate her a little more. She might even become indispensable.

A smile of amusement spread across the vamp's handsome features. "I see from your expression you understand the potential for this."

Drawing the plump flesh of her lower lips between her teeth, she nibbled on it. Why was this vampire helping her? She had been nothing but trouble for him since they met. She had to ask.

"Why are you helping me, though? Won't I be a threat to supernaturals like you?"

Those cerulean blue eyes of his narrowed to gleaming, assessing slits. "I do not believe you would ever use your gifts for the wrong reasons, Jasmine, and I am willing to take the chance."

A sense of overpowering pleasure rushed through her at his words. He trusted her to use her gifts for good. How strange that this made her so dizzyingly happy.

"Now close your eyes."

With a big grin, she readily closed them.

Half an hour later Jasmine was getting bored. Meditating was not as easy as she had thought. Her mind kept wandering. She couldn't seem to find her Zen place, as Raoul called it, and let her brain switch off.

She had no idea how the vampires managed it.

Hearing movement in the room, Jasmine peeked with one eye open.

Raoul had left his spot in the corner. He had been back on his laptop for the last ten minutes, doing God knows what. The soft sound of typing had become distracting. She watched as the mocha-skinned vampire walked almost silently across the room. He reminded her of a big jungle cat on the prowl. When he reached the mini fridge, he yanked it open. Tucked inside were four plastic bags of dark red liquid.

Jasmine's other eye popped open. Gaze glued to the bag, she recognised them for what they were. Blood.

He hadn't seemed to notice he had an audience. As he was turned to the side she could see his profile. Raoul tugged out one of the bags, closed the fridge, and lifted the blood up to his mouth.

She watched in fascination as his fangs smoothly descended. They were long, sharp, and lethal. He sank them into the bag and began to suck.

"From the local blood bank," Eric informed her.

Startled, Jasmine glanced his way.

His eyes were hooded with an intense look in their depths as he watched her.

"It is not so pleasing cold, but there's no microwave in the suite to warm it. The alternative is a living donor, but we do not have time for those." His eyes slid to her neck for a moment and lingered.

Unless they used her, she thought, which she was not sure she would agree to anyway.

A shiver ran though her. Jasmine nervously licked her suddenly dry lips.

"So you just feed on cold blood?"

Eric shrugged one large shoulder. "It serves our purpose and we do not need to feed very often."

That little piece of information got her attention. "But vampires feed every day."

That seemed to snap him out of his fascination with her neck. Any emotion on Eric's face vanished in a blink of an eye. Once more he was unreadable. "We have the luxury of not having that necessity."

She had not heard of such a thing before. Eric and Raoul did seem to be very different from the vampires she had learned about. Almost like they were another breed. That was ridiculous, though. Vampires were all the same – turned humans.

As she shifted her position she yelped in pain. A cramp spasmed painfully through her crossed legs.

"Fuuuck," Jasmine ground out through gritted teeth.

Sitting for so long like this was apparently getting annoying for her body, too. She stretched out her legs on the soft carpet, groaning as they protested.

"I do not like your use of this word," Eric responded crossly. "Fucking is a pleasurable pastime and should not be used as a swear word."

Shooting him a disbelieving look, she scowled.

"I've got cramp," Jasmine replied grumpily. "What should I say then?"

In one fluid movement, he crawled across the floor to reach her side. "Perhaps you should not swear at all. It is most unladylike."

Taken aback, she didn't protest as his big, confident hands began to knead her jean-clad calves and thighs. A groan of pained relief escaped her. He really knew how to work a massage. If he ever wanted to change careers, he would earn a fortune as a masseur. Hell, she would pay anything for him to keep it up. It was fucking heaven.

"I like to swear," she answered on a contented sigh.

Raoul was watching them with interest. The blood bag in his hand was almost empty. He pulled his fangs smoothly out of the plastic and smiled.

"How about thunderation? I know Eric is also fond of using the word damnation," Raoul mused softly. "Or gadzooks! Bloody hell!"

The cramp had been worked away. Now other sensations were taking its place. Bliss rolled through her. Pressing her lips together, she held back a groan. Why did she keep letting him touch her? It only ever led to trouble.

Jasmine wanted to do nothing more than lie down and let the vamp massage the rest of her. She knew this couldn't happen.

"They all sound so Victorian," she managed to reply a little breathlessly.

Eric removed his hands from her legs and sat back on his heels.

"They are," he said with a tiger-like smile. A dark heat lit, his hungry gaze as he observed her. The kind of look that said he wanted to eat her all up.

Jasmine swallowed hard.

"How old are you anyway?" The words blurted out of her mouth before she could stop them.

It was something that had been on her mind, but she hadn't had the courage to ask. Her nervousness had her spewing out anything in her head. Embarrassment engulfed her.

Eric's eyes narrowed, his head tilted to one side. "It is rude to ask someone's age."

She flashed him a nervous smile. "I thought that was only for women."

"It applies to vampires, too," Raoul replied in an amused tone. He had a second bag of blood in his hand. Hip resting against the mini-fridge, he raised it to his mouth. Fangs still extended, he jabbed them into the plastic and began to drink. The muscles in his throat rippled as he swallowed.

Jasmine wasn't becoming squeamish about it, strangely enough. Curiosity was what she was experiencing the most.

"Why haven't you just enthralled me with your persuasion yet?"

Raoul froze mid-gulp. Honey-brown eyes moved from her to the other vampire. He looked shocked at her words.

Eric had also stilled in the process of running his hand through his hair. Features once more void of anything but coldness, he stared at her. "And how is it that you know about that?"

Jasmine suddenly felt uncomfortable. Maybe she should have kept her mouth shut. "I sensed you use it on Marcel when we first met. And, well, you also used it on me."

Eric suddenly looked uncomfortable. In one graceful movement, he rose to his feet. "I did not think it wise."

Jasmine didn't move from her position on the floor. The vampire towered over her, but she didn't feel threatened at all. What he was saying did not make sense. Her brow furrowed in confusion. "You could have made me stay without exposing what you're doing."

Eric swung around and faced away from her. Shoulders taut, he was tensing up. "It did not feel right."

Fuck. The vamp really seemed to be uncomfortable with her line of questioning. Some little imp inside her wouldn't let her drop it, however. Cracking that remoteness Eric had mastered had begun to fascinate her.

"Why?"

A nippy chill swept through the room. Power pulsed, crisp and raw, around the darkly handsome vampire. Were his icy powers connected to his emotions? They certainly seemed to spike when she got emotion out of Eric.

Jasmine suddenly realised maybe she had pushed him too far.

"Jasmine, please do not pursue this. Now if you will excuse me I have things that need attending to." Words harshly spoken, the vamp stalked from the room.

The door of the bedroom slammed so hard it rattled in its frame. Silence ensued.

Nibbling on her bottom lip, Jasmine looked towards Raoul. "What did I say?"

The dark-skinned vamp hadn't moved. The blood bag was still in his mouth as he sucked it down slowly. Eyes astonished, he pulled it from his lips with a little pop. "You really do not realise your effect on him, do you?"

Jasmine bit her lip harder. "What are you talking about?"

In one elegant movement he discarded the empty bag in the bin. "Is it not obvious that his control is not as it should be around you?"

She hadn't known these vampires long, so no, she had no idea how Eric normally acted. As far as she knew this was it.

Was Raoul implying this wasn't his normal behaviour?

"How should it be?"

Wiping his mouth with the heel of his hand, he fixed her with a wary look. "Eric feels nothing. His control over his emotions is legendary. It has earned him the reputation of being coldly calculating and merciless. It seems to have taken one little mortal female to destroy all that."

He looked pointedly at her and her mouth turned down.

Shit. Was she really messing with Eric's control that much? Why was he affected by her, if this was all true?

"Oh."

Raoul walked across the room and collected his laptop. "Oh, indeed."

CHAPTER 19

RAOUL WAS WORKING quietly on his laptop again on the sofa. His lithe, muscular form lounged gracefully against the comfortable pillows. It was like he was welded to the thing with the amount of time he spent on it. She had a feeling he and Twitch would get on well.

Another laptop sat on the table in front of her. Her boss's face abruptly filled the screen. From behind his wire-rimmed glasses, concern brimmed in his soft brown eyes.

"Hey Jaz, how's it going?" He couldn't hide the worry from his tone.

A reassuring smile curved her lips. "I heard from Twitch last night. He's OK at the moment."

Worrying about them was something she knew Mark would do well. Since joining his team that's all he seemed to do. It was comforting to know their boss had their backs. His support was unwavering.

Her eyes skimmed over Mark's boyish features. A pencil was resting behind his left ear. The end was badly mauled; he had obviously spent the last few hours gnawing on it. Such a telling, nervous habit.

"Thank God for that," Mark muttered softly.

Jasmine glanced nervously in the vampire's direction for a moment. Raoul had agreed to let her talk to her boss as long as she mentioned nothing about their mission or any details. It was incredibly hard to do, though. She was bursting to talk to someone about it all.

"I can't say anything more than that," she informed him and stole another glance at Raoul, who still seemed engrossed in his work.

Working for Scotland Yard, Mark would understand this. He was probably more than aware of how delicate this situation was and knew she couldn't say much.

A nod was his only answer. The plains of his face settled into a look of understanding.

Jasmine felt herself relax. "How's the team?"

Gemma and Fergus, her other teammates, were suddenly blocking Mark.

"Hey, sweetcakes! You OK?" The werewolf's rugged face was creased with worry. His amber eyes danced over her features.

Jasmine grinned wide. "I'm fine, mutt."

The wolf was sometimes annoying but always damn loyal to his department. She missed his dumb jokes and never-ending need for junk food. He was a true fast food junkie.

He was jostled away as her other friend and co-worker shoved the wolf aside. Fergus growled. Gemma smacked his smooth, bald head. With another low growl, the werewolf retreated, muttering to himself in annoyance.

"How's Twitch holding up?" Gemma asked, nibbling nervously on her lower lip. Her beautiful flawless face was tight with anxiety. Wild, black curls hung loosely to her shoulders.

Jasmine had never seen her look so worried. Gemma was tough. She didn't take shit from anyone, especially the males on their team. The amount of swear words that left her pretty mouth would probably shock the vamps. She made Jasmine look like a nun.

"He seems to be OK. Not freaking out or anything."

"You staying out of trouble, Jaz?" Fergus asked, shunting Gemma away from the screen. She squealed in a mixture of surprise and anger.

Jasmine bit her lip to stop herself from laughing. "I'm trying to, yes."

"What are the agents you're working with like?" Gemma's face appeared over the werewolf's muscled shoulder.

Her eyes darted to Raoul. A small smile tilted his lips. He looked amused.

"They're . . . different. Very professional and focused," she replied nervously.

They had asked her to keep the fact they were vampires a secret. It was something she wanted to do. Her team didn't need to know. It wasn't like they were ever going to meet. Once Twitch was rescued, they would be heading back to England. Where the vamps would go, she had no clue.

"What Gem means is: are they hot and have you got lucky?" Fergus's eyes slid sideways to the woman in question. A lopsided grin was on his face.

Wrinkling her nose, Gemma scowled at him. "Stop putting fucking words in my mouth, wolf."

One of his thick, muscled arms, curved around her waist. He pulled her close. "We both know that's what you meant."

"If you two have quite finished," Mark barked from somewhere behind them. "It's like running a playgroup instead of a bloody police department sometimes."

"Geez, boss, can't you see we're worried about our girl?" Fergus quibbled, glancing over his shoulder.

"As you can see, she's fine," Mark snapped back. "It's Twitch we need to worry about."

Mark's face was filling the screen again. He seemed to be glaring at something just over top of it. Jasmine guessed it was probably her co-workers as they made their retreat out of his office. When his eyes found hers, she knew they were alone. Now was the time to ask a question that had been burning on the tip of her tongue. She had to know.

"Did you find out who the mole in the department is? Who told Marcel where to find Twitch?" Her voice was low, nothing more than a mumble.

Mark shook his head. "No. We don't have any leads. Everyone's come up smelling of roses so far, but I'll keep looking."

The bedroom door swung open. Eric's gaze immediately zoomed to her as he stepped out. He looked distracted, but she didn't miss the frown.

Was he still annoyed with her?

Trying not to nibble on her lip again, she leaned towards the screen. "I gotta go."

"Message me when you have news," Mark told her with a sigh.

"Yes, boss."

A moment later the screen went dark.

She snapped the laptop shut and leaned back in her chair.

Raoul had also discarded his computer and his entire attention was fixed on the other vampire. From the look on Eric's face, Jasmine had a feeling something must have happened.

"Marcel has requested to meet this lunchtime," he announced as he strolled into the middle of the room and stopped. "Seems to be very last minute."

Jasmine didn't know if that was good or bad. If the weapon-testing was soon, that could explain the urgent meet-up.

"What do you intend to do?" Raoul asked. Interlocking his hands, he rested them behind his head. The muscles in his arms bunched and rippled with the movement.

Eric's expression was brooding. "I must attend. He may have the details of the weapons test."

"I may have a lead on where the techno mage is being held." Raoul's honey-brown eyes briefly bounced to Jasmine's. "I would like to check that out."

Eric nodded. "Very well."

"Can I go with Raoul or am I being grounded and left in the hotel?" The words were spoken low and quiet.

After the night before, she was pretty certain she would be stuck in the room watching daytime television. It wouldn't hurt to ask though. Maybe she could do surveillance on the laptop. She wasn't sure Eric would trust her on another undercover mission again. She still wanted to help any way she could.

"No, Jasmine. I would like you to attend the lunch with me." Cold eyes intent on her face, he smiled. "If Raoul confirms the location of your friend, we can making plans this evening to get him out."

Jasmine's heart leapt in her chest. Was he giving her another chance? Finding Twitch was important to her, but as Eric had pointed out, they needed a plan. Raoul was probably the best person to search for him.

But why did he want her with him if she threatened his control? Maybe it didn't happen all the time. Without anyone actually explaining it to her properly, she just didn't know.

Jasmine wasn't about to look a gift-horse in the mouth, though.

"Alright. I don't have to wear a dress again, do I?" If it was a case of heels again, she would stay put.

Amusement fluttered over Eric's features. "No, you may wear jeans if you like. That outfit will do, but bring your coat."

Nipping back into the bedroom, Jasmine grabbed the thick, long woollen coat. It had kept the wintery cold out the night before and would do for today as well. She hurried back into the living room, where she found the vampires ready to go.

Eric was now wearing a short, black leather jacket over dark blue jeans and a black polo neck. His hair was tousled like he had just rolled out of bed. How could he make every outfit look sexy? He could easily make money as a male model.

Raoul was dressed as he had been when pretending to be a cab driver. A scarf was wound around his neck and a cap on his head.

A thick, black jacket covered his torso and black jeans encased his legs ending in a worn pair of trainers.

Both vamps were ready to play their parts. She could only hope that she was ready, too.

In silence they travelled down in the lift. Neither seemed to be in a talkative mood. Jasmine knew they were probably going over what needed to be done. Getting in the right head space was always important.

Raoul disappeared out of the hotel the moment the lift doors opened. She watched him go, every movement fluid and agile as he crossed the foyer. The way both of these males moved was so beautiful.

"How are we getting there?"

Eric's eyes dropped to her face. "Raoul is taking the Bentley. I have another vehicle at my disposal."

Striding quickly, he was soon at the reception desk. After a short conversation with the woman there, he was soon back beside her. He seemed to be lost in thoughts.

Jasmine took a moment to take in the Christmassy feel of the place. She had been too nervous to appreciate it the night before. Pretty coloured decorations and a fancy Christmas tree adorned the area. Everything was elegant and tasteful, just like the hotel itself. It all felt a little surreal. So much had happened in the last few days.

A man appeared with a set of keys. Eric took them without a word and strode towards the doors.

Jasmine followed the vampire out into the street, where she was greeted by the sight of a silver Porsche. Sleek, shiny, and brand new. How the heck did they afford all this?

Eric lowered himself nimbly behind the wheel and snapped on his seat belt.

"You must get paid a lot by the countries that hire you," Jasmine commented while sliding in beside him. She reached to her side and fastened her own belt.

The vampire smiled. His hands caressed the steering wheel for a moment as he considered her words. Like any man, he seemed to have an appreciation for cars.

"Smith told you I was freelance," Turning the key, the engine purred into life—a low, deep sound that sent a thrill down her spine.

She sat back and got comfortable in the supple leather seats.

"The clothes you wear, the cars, the five-star hotel. I doubt my department would even be able to afford a room in that place." She jerked her thumb over her shoulder at the hotel.

Eric belly laughed. "I have lived for a very long time and have amassed my own fortune. I do not need the money this job provides."

With smooth experience, he pulled onto the road with ease. The traffic was moving steadily.

Jasmine frowned. "Why do it then?"

Eric reached over to turn the heater on in the vehicle. After adjusting it to his liking, he settled back. Warm air blew out from the little ducts, filling the car with comfortable warmth.

"For the thrill, my lovely. When you are immortal it is sometimes all you have when you have experienced all else."

She couldn't imagine living forever. As he wouldn't tell her how old he was, she could only guess how long it had taken him to get bored of everything.

"I think we will get snow soon," Eric said, neatly changing the subject. He glanced skyward for a moment. Thick, grey clouds hung low in the sky.

To Jasmine it looked more like it would rain. The rest of the drive they travelled in a companionable silence.

The restaurant Marcel had picked was a fancy little place near the river, not far from Notre Dame. Small and intimate. The tables were filled with other diners enjoying quiet lunches. They were led quickly to the back.

The arms dealer had secured a table in a secluded corner, away from prying eyes. An elegant flower arrangement sat in a glass vase in the middle of it. The red petals of the flowers were bright against the whiteness of the table cloth. Three places lay set with napkins and cutlery.

Marcel dabbed at his sweaty forehead as they approached, the blue silk handkerchief clutched tightly in his podgy hand.

Pierre, his watch dog, stood beside the table like a sentinel— back straight, legs slightly parted. His eyes were hard as flint as he watched them draw closer.

Jasmine managed to rein in the shudder of revulsion. Pierre gave her chills. He watched her moving with a hint of lust on his face.

A wide smile of welcome spread across the fat man's face. "Welcome." He didn't bother to stand, only gestured to the empty seats before him.

None of the other men she had met the other night were there. It seemed it was just the four of them. Eric had not mentioned it would just be them.

Glancing at the vampire, his face was unreadable. If he was surprised at all, he wasn't letting on.

Eric held out a chair for her, as he asked Marcel, "Are we early?"

"No, you are right on time," Marcel responded while signalling for a waiter.

Jasmine slipped into the chair and pulled off her coat.

Eric gracefully dropped into the seat beside her. "Marcel, I assumed the others would be here." He shrugged out of his leather jacket and hung it on the back of his chair. He took Jasmine's and draped it over a chair at a nearby empty table. The smell of snow and pine wafted around her. Jasmine fought back the urge to breathe in deeply. Now was not the time to lust after the vampire. Keeping a clear head was what she needed.

Marcel shook his head. "No, *mon ami*, I do not enjoy their company as much as yours."

"Where's Claude?" The question was out of her mouth before she could stop it.

Marcel barely spared her a glance. "He was unable to come today. Far too much to drink last night."

The waiter had appeared and was hovering. His eyes kept darting to Pierre, and Jasmine noted his hands were shaking as he took down their orders. The guy was frightened. Did he know who was sitting in the restaurant?

Too nervous to eat much she ordered a salad.

"I shall decline lunch and stick with the wine if you do not mind," Eric said. A tiny pulse of compulsion threaded his words.

Jasmine felt it and shivered.

The food came quickly. Eric and the fat man spent the time in idle chatter, mostly about the city, which she did not bother to follow.

A bottle of wine had been opened. Marcel and Eric drank it liberally. Jasmine, on the other hand, didn't even take a sip. No alcohol to cloud her thoughts, she reminded herself.

She felt Pierre's eyes burning a hole in the side of her skull. Out of the corner of her eye, she could see him watching, staring at her, unblinking. It was extremely creepy.

She picked at her salad when it arrived, barely managing a few mouthfuls.

This really didn't feel right. Even her sixth sense was now doing a tiny little jingle in her head. Not a full-blown warning yet, but she recognized the feeling. They were in for trouble.

Marcel sat forward and wiped his mouth with a napkin. His plate was clean.

"The reason for the lunch is that Doctor Dasyurus want to meet you."

One of the vampire's eyebrows rose with interest. "Does he, indeed? Why now?"

Eric wasn't letting any emotion apart from mild curiosity show, but Jasmine knew this had to excite him. This Doctor character was someone he was after. He could not give up the opportunity to meet him.

The fast man smiled slyly. "He saw you at the party last night and asked for the meeting. I do not question his motives. He is the genius after all."

"I thought you said he wasn't on the boat last night?" Jasmine questioned a little too sharply. Eric stiffened a little beside her. Damn why had she said anything? She had planned to keep her mouth shut, but things kept slipping out.

Pierre shrugged one chubby shoulder. "A small lie."

The vampire lifted his glass of wine and held in in front of him for a moment. "Will he be joining us?"

Marcel shook his head, watching as Eric drained his glass of its contents. "No. We will be joining him. There is a lab beneath this restaurant. We will be visiting him there if you are done with your wine?"

Jasmine's eyes widened slightly. A lab under this place? No wonder the staff looked edgy. This had to be a front for the arms dealer's other business.

"Yes, indeed." Eric took one long gulp of wine and placed the empty glass on the table.

The next thing she knew both men were standing and pulling on their coats. Abandoning her salad, Jasmine got to her feet.

Eric held her coat out for her and slipped it over her arms. He didn't meet her gaze, though. His eyes never left Marcel.

The restaurant had emptied out. When had that suddenly happened? The warning jingle in Jasmine's head had now become chiming church bells. Danger was imminent.

Dread welled upside her. How could she tell Eric when the fat man and his muscled goon were within earshot?

Marcel led the way towards the back of the place. Pierre shadowed their every step. Even the staff seemed to have vanished without a trace. Jasmine bit her lip. Something here was seriously wrong. She only hoped Eric could see it, too. The vamp was sharp. He had to know something was up. Maybe he just intended to play along?

The kitchen was empty, like everyone had just gotten up and left for the day. This did not make sense.

Marcel motioned to a lift in the corner. It looked like a service elevator of some kind.

Pierre jabbed the button on the wall and a moment later the doors opened. The space fit all four of them easily. They all entered in a tense silence. The atmosphere was so thick you could almost choke on it. Marcel stood close to the doors next to Eric. The bodyguard positioned himself at the back. Without a word, the fat man pressed the control panel. The lift rattled into life and began to descend.

They seemed to be going into the bowels of the restaurant. It felt like it took forever before they shuddered to a halt.

The doors slid smoothly open. Tension knotted inside Jasmine's stomach. She didn't want to get out. Whatever lay ahead of them wasn't going to be good. Why the hell had she gotten into the lift in the first place? If Eric was leaving this to the last minute he was cutting it close.

"Come. It's this way," the fat man told them with a gesture of his hand.

Marcel and Eric alighted first. When she didn't make a move, Pierre's hand shoved her in the back. Sending him a glare over her shoulder, she was met with cold hard eyes. She stepped out and looked around.

The room seemed to be a basement. Old boxes were stacked against the wall. A thick layer of dust covered them. Didn't seem to be used much. The sight in front of her though told another story.

The door before them looked like it belonged to a vault. Thick and steel, it looked recently installed. It was all solid with no windows of any kind.

Pierre moved past her towards it. She then noticed the electronic keypad to the left of the door. Without a word, the bodyguard typed a code into the keypad. With a hiss, the door began to swing open.

Jasmine shivered as a chill rushed out to meet them. It felt more like they were entering a meat locker than somewhere you kept your valuables locked up. Why would someone be down here? She took a nervous step back. The lift doors were still open and reachable if necessary.

Marcel was smirking. "The good doctor is very careful about security." He gestured towards the door. "Have a look it's ingenious."

Jasmine sensed Eric's unease. At this point the situation was screaming 'it's a trap' to her quite clearly. If it had not been clear to the vampire before, then it was now.

"We will take your word for it, Marcel," Eric replied with an easy smile.

At that moment, Jasmine realised Pierre now had a gun trained on her head. She tensed.

Shit, why hadn't she noticed quicker?

"I must insist, *mon ami*." The smirk slid off the arms dealer's face. "No, don't reply. I know about that persuasive tongue of yours."

She felt Eric's power begin to rise. Its frosty kiss caressed against her skin as it began to swirl around them. The two men shivered.

"Try anything, vampire, and the girl gets a bullet in the head." Pierre's tone was confident and smug. "You may be powerful, but I doubt even you are faster than a bullet."

Eric's power abruptly dropped away. He stood unnaturally still beside her. She had to wonder if he was now regretting let her come along. In her mind, she was pretty certain that if he had been alone, he would have dealt with both men easily.

"What's going on?" Jasmine asked, knowing full well Eric would want to know. It looked like his cover was blown. They knew he was a vampire, but how?

"You can drop the act. I know you work for Scotland Yard, Miss Hunter." Marcel's voice was cold and unfriendly. "And you, Mr. Jeger, if that is really your name, are in the employ of the French government."

Pierre nudged his gun in the direction of the open freezer. He wanted them to get in.

They edged towards it slowly. Jasmine almost stumbled over her feet, but the vampire's hand on her arm steadied her.

"It pains me that my own country has decided to turn on me like this," Marcel said with a sigh as he fished out his handkerchief. "My revenge, though, will be swift and sweet." He started to pat at his perspiring, bald head. Annoyance was written all over his face.

"You can't do this," Jasmine blurted out as they got closer to the door. Not getting inside did not look like an option. Her eyes darted back to the lift. Maybe if she could get out of the way, Eric could attack. Almost as if he had sensed her thoughts, his hand tightened on her arm. It was clear to her then. He didn't want her to do anything stupid. It looked like the freezer was happening. Fuck.

"Of course I can, *ma chérie*." the fat man scowled, as if she had insulted him. "You had a last meal didn't you? That was me being generous."

Pierre wiggled the gun from side to side. "Get inside now. No funny business or I will shoot you."

The frigidity of the room engulfed them as they stepped over the threshold. Goosebumps rose over every inch of Jasmine's skin. One glance confirmed it was a small walk-in freezer. Ice coated the walls, the floors. It glistened white in the artificial light above them.

"Enjoy your last moments together, *mon ami*. I doubt you will last long. Your friend Mr. Smith did not," Marcel's voice told them from behind.

The door closed with an ominous click. Pivoting on the spot they found themselves trapped.

"Fuck," Jasmine muttered. "You should have just attacked them or whatever you planned to do. I could have taken care of myself."

"I had no wish to risk your life, Jasmine," Eric snapped back. "I doubt you would have easily avoided a bullet in the brain. I could not chance it."

Shooting forwards, Eric placed his palms flat against the door. A breath hissed out between his teeth and Jasmine thought she heard him swear.

"Reinforced steel and warded with magic so deep, it is making my skin crawl," he muttered in disgust. He dropped his hands and stepped back beside her.

One stark light lit the space they stood in. Jasmine was thankful it remained on. She had a feeling it was the fat man's doing. No doubt he wanted them to be able to see each other in this freezing environment.

"What about Raoul? Can't you contact him?" She knew her tone was nervous.

Being trapped in a freezer made her a little on edge. Also knowing the powerful vamp with her couldn't bust out was more than worrying. Even now the chill of the room was working its way through the layers of her clothes. Her breath was coming out in tiny, white puffs.

Eric's eyes met her. "The magical wards prevent me from using my telepathy. They have done their homework well. Only certain ancient magic works."

Panic was doing a slow creep up her back. With a shudder, she began to rub her arms.

"Fucking fantastic. How are we supposed to get out of here now?"

Eric shrugged out of his leather jacket. Realising his intent, she quickly pulled off her woollen coat. The vampire gently, but quickly helped her into his coat. It was still deliciously warm from his body heat. The smell of snow and pine curled itself around her. Hastily she struggled back into her thick woollen coat over the top. It was a tight fit, but she managed to get everything on, buttoned, and zipped.

"We wait." His tone was snappy. "Raoul will come looking for us when he cannot contact me. He knows the address of this place and Marcel was stupid enough not to take us somewhere else."

Jasmine found this did not alleviate anxiety levels. It seemed to be getting colder by the minute. Were they lowering the temperature from outside?

"We might freeze to death first," she decided to point out. How long would that take? Hours? Minutes?

"The cold does not affect me," Eric replied in a low, deep voice. "I have mastery of it, but I cannot make it warmer in here for you."

She shot him a disbelieving look. "So I will fucking freeze to death alone?"

He flicked her an irritated look. "I will not allow that to happen, Jasmine."

Why was he being so harsh with her? It was not her fault they were in this mess. She had been following his bloody plan. Scowling at him, she realised he was not even looking at her any more.

The vampire's eyes were running over every inch of the little room. His facial features were tight. She could see a nerve twitching in his jaw. Tension was radiating off his strapping body in a way she could not ignore.

Was he nervous? No, this was more like fear.

"Are you alright?"

"Yes." The answer came out in a growl. His gaze dropped to hers.

With a sigh, he ran a hand through his tousled hair with agitation.

"I am not fond of enclosed spaces," he admitted softly. "This is quite a small room with no windows. I find it unsettling."

Jasmine stared at him incredulously. The vampire was scared of something. Was he for real?

"I didn't know vampires could have phobias." She couldn't keep the curiosity out of her voice.

Irritation flickered over his features. "It is not a phobia."

Apparently the vamp didn't like admitting to having a weakness. Then again, neither did she.

"I don't like spiders if that helps." She stamped her feet trying to keep them warm. The coats were keeping some heat in, but she knew that might not last.

Eric snorted. "That is not the same thing."

Jasmine tried not to roll her eyes. Just because they were different fears, did not mean hers was any less frightening. He probably did not like the fact she knew he was scared or something.

She glanced around the space. Nothing else was in it apart from them. Nothing they could use to help open the thick metal door. She moved to the door and pressed her hands against it. When the cold metal practically burnt her with its icy bite, she yanked them back.

"I'm starting to feel like I'm just stuck in a fucking Bond movie with an evil villain and everything."

Eric's deep rumbling chuckle filled the room. "I have never heard you swear so much."

"I'm fucking nervous, OK?"

Jasmine didn't know how long she could last trapped in the freezer. She really didn't want to find out. Hopefully Raoul would figure out something was wrong quickly and come to their rescue. She really did not want to think of the alternative—for her at least.

An arm coiled around her waist. The vampire pulled her against his chest. She went willingly, turning and pressing herself against him as much as she could. Body heat was essential in situations like this. Jasmine didn't know how long that would be able to last, though. The vampire might not die from freezing, but his body was still getting colder. The more the temperature dropped, the more heat they would lose.

She wrapped her arms around his waist and rested her cheek against his big chest.

"The main thing is not to panic, right?" she said, closing her eyes. The thud of his heart was reassuring. "Raoul will come and get us out soon."

"I agree. Panic would do us little good. It is best if you conserve body heat," he said quietly against her hair.

His big hands moved up and down her back briskly. The action warmed her a little through the layers of clothing. It wasn't sexual and she knew he was just trying to keep her warm, but that didn't stop desire from singing through her blood. Delicious tingles tightened her breasts.

With a sigh, she remembered Marcel's parting words.

"They killed Mr. Smith, didn't they?" Jasmine asked softly.

"Yes, I fear he is no more from what was said," Eric replied in a calm even tone.

She had a feeling he was trying to keep her calm. The fact someone they knew had died in here was not helping. Smith had seemed like a nice guy. How the hell had everyone's cover been blown? Had he spilled what he knew? What had they done to him to make him talk if they had?

Her breath came out in white puffs. Light shivers had begun to grip her body. Any lust she had been feeling was being frozen away.

"Who was he working for?" Rubbing her face against his polo T-shirt, she felt the firmness of the muscles beneath.

"CIA." The vampire's breath barely warmed her neck.

Not even her clothing now felt like it provided any warmth. The cold was working its way through the layers into her skin. It was almost painful.

"I'm sorry they murdered your friend," she said, rubbing herself further against the hard male body. Maybe if she made some friction it would help.

Eric arm's tightened around her. "This business is full of risks. Nothing is ever certain."

"Not for you though, right? Vampires are immortal."

The light flickered above them threateningly. Tilting her chin, she gazed at it, silently pleading with it to stay on. Total darkness was something they did not need.

Eric's eyes followed hers upwards. "Even we can die, kitten. Not so easily, I admit, but we are not indestructible."

Jasmine squeaked as her feet left the ground. Eric had scooped her up. With unnatural grace he sat down on the floor, his back to the wall. She found herself sitting on his lap. Muscled, firm thighs supported her bottom as he kept her from the cold, hard floor.

"You'll get frostbite this way," Jasmine warned. It was a strangely comforting position, one she didn't want to admit she enjoyed.

"I have already told you—the cold will not affect me." An amused smile tugged at the corners of his lips. Eric cuddled her close. Arms around her waist, he drew her nearer against him.

"Are you comfortable?" she asked settling her head against his chest.

His chin nuzzled her short, coppery red hair. "I am indeed. Are you?"

"Yes. You make a good pillow."

"I am glad this position pleases you." She could hear the smile in his voice as he spoke.

The shivers increased and she couldn't stop them. They rolled through her uncontrollably. She tugged down the coat sleeves over her hands and kept her hands balled into fists while gripping the material. It wasn't much protection, however. Jasmine was so cold now, everything throbbed and stung with the glacial temperature in the little space. Her legs and arms had started to go stiff. She had never felt so cold in her life.

They sat in silence for a while as Jasmine struggled to stay warm and awake.

Eric was leaning back against the icy white wall. He seemed completely unaffected by the freezing environment around them. His body felt as cold as hers, though. As cold as ice. The heat was being sucked right out of them.

With a soft moan of pain, Jasmine tried to snuggle impossibly closer to him. "I . . .I don't want to f-fucking d-die." Her teeth were chattering. She had no control.

The vampire's lips brushed her forehead. "Jasmine, I promise you will not."

Angrily she raised her head to glance at him. "H-how can y-you promise that?"

A raw and tender look graced his handsome face she had never seen before. He actually looked like he cared.

"I have yet to have my wicked way with you, so I refuse to let you slip through my grasp," he answered softly.

"W-icked w-way with m-me?" Her laugh trembled more with cold than anything else. Every muscle on her face was starting to go numb.

"Indeed." Eric stroked the curve of her cheek. "I confess, it is the only thing I have thought about since setting eyes upon you."

"I-I'll try n-not . . . to ex-expire any time s-soon then."

The corners of his lips twitched. "Are you making fun of me?"

She rolled her eyes. "Y-you do say some old f-fashioned words sometimes."

Eric tried to cuddle her up closer against him. They were already pressed body to body. The only way to get nearer was if she crawled inside him. Concern poured from his eyes. Jasmine gathered from his expression she was in a bad way. How long before hypothermia set in? Would she slip into unconsciousness first?

"W-why do I affect y-your control?" She wanted to know. If these were going to be her last moments, then she was pushing the embarrassment aside.

Eric hesitated, like he was picking his words. "Your mere presence seems to influence my moods. I do not know why."

"S-sorry I'm m-messing with your m-mojo."

The heaviness of her body becoming tired was weighing her down. It would be so easy just to close her eyes and let it take her. Maybe the coldness would end quickly.

Eric dropped his forehead to hers and exhaled. "Jasmine, I can place you in a state of suspended animation. Very much like hibernating animals do."

"Hu-humans can't h-h-hibernate."

Lips brushed against her cheek, distracting her. "With my help you will be able to achieve this."

Jasmine tried to keep focused. Her eyelids were starting to feel increasingly heavy. "H-how?"

"I will regulate your body temperature so that you do not die," the vampire explained.

The shivers were racking her body now. Even snuggled up again Eric's big body was not helping any more. What choice did she have? She would have to put her life in this vampire's hands. The energy was seeping from her body.

He took her chin in his forefinger and thumb. Gently, he tipped her head up so she could meet his gaze. His cold eyes were tender.

"Trust me, Jasmine." The words were soft and deep. No power of persuasion lay behind them. Eric, she realised, was leaving the choice up to her. Life or death, it was in her hands.

"F-first I w-want to know why y-you can go out in th-the sun." Tiredness was sweeping over her. Her teeth were rattling in her jaws now. It was painful.

Eric stared down at her in silence with a look of exasperation. His dark eyebrows inched up slightly in surprise.

She sighed wearily. "L-look I'm guessing I m-might come out of this dead. P-p-please just share with me a little h-here."

He raised his hand and ran a finger lightly down her cold, pale cheek. "You are a most stubborn woman. I am a vampiria."

Jasmine stared at him blankly. The word meant nothing to her.

It was his turn to sigh. "A born vampire. I have never been mortal."

"Oh. Th-thanks f-for telling me. L-let's do what n-needs to be f-fucking done then."

His expression did not change, apart from the slight crinkle at the corners of his smiling eyes. Jasmine recognised she had pleased him.

"Kiss me, Jasmine."

CHAPTER 20

ERIC COULD FEEL THE CONVULSIVE shivers rolling through the girl's body. Her face was pale. Those green eyes of hers held confusion and a growing drowsiness. All these were sure signs of increasing hypothermia. He had no wish to see her die. Definitely not in his arms while they waited for rescue.

He had not lied about the state of hibernation he could put her in. Other vampires with similar abilities to his had achieved this, even though Eric had never done it before. Jasmine was nervous enough and did not need this knowledge, however. He was concerned if he told her she would reject his offer. That was something he would not allow. Keeping her alive was now important to him, although he did not examine why.

The only regret he had was that this was going to be their first kiss. Something Jasmine would not enjoy.

Jasmine brushed her lips shyly against Eric's. She had dreamed of kissing him, of getting to know that sinfully sexy mouth. It was something she had started to crave badly. They were soft, warm and lush, just as she had imagined they would be. In fact, they were even better. His tongue traced her cold lips, teasing them until they parted. Jasmine did this willingly with no other thought in her head. She moaned as he thrust his tongue inside her mouth. Warm, moist, and oh so tempting.

Her heart started an excited pounding in her chest, beating like a drum against her ribs. One of Eric's hands slid up to cup her face. His tongue danced with hers, rubbing, sucking. Hungrily, he explored every crevice as he tasted her sweetness. The kiss went on and on, as if Eric craved the connection between them. He consumed her. Devoured her. He seemed to savour every little moan, every sweet sigh. It left her feeling dizzy, breathless. Craving more of what he could give her.

Jasmine placed her hands on his chest, where his heart thumped wildly. She could feel his excitement. When his breath blew into her mouth, Jasmine stilled. Frozen from the outside she was not prepared for it within. The frosty sting of ice surged down her vulnerable throat. It burned but not with heat. This was a cold so raw it felt like it was peeling away her insides.

Panic exploded in her head. Tensing like a board she tried to escape. Twisting, turning, she fought. As if he had been prepared for this, the vampire would not allow it. Eric's lips were fused firmly to her own. They no longer gave her pleasure but were now a source of torture.

One of his hands held her to his lap like a steel clamp. The other had slid under her jaw controlling her movements. His grip was almost bruising.

Jasmine clawed at his arms, his chest, but he was immovable. The beautiful eyes that stared into her own were remote and ruthless. Any trace of tenderness snuffed out. She whimpered, screwing her eyes shut. More of his wintry breath entered her body. It sliced through her. Back arching, every inch of her spasmed with the pain.

Eric breathed through his nose and exhaled through his mouth.

An arctic chill poured agonisingly into her lungs, like ice water pumped into her veins. Body convulsing, she was not sure how much more it could take. She was suffocating inside. Jasmine desperately tried to draw in oxygen, but everything was blocked. Solid.

Pain filled her chest, making her heart beat achingly behind her ribs. It was slowing. She could feel it with every frantic thud.

Eric's fingers caressed her jaw. His lips left hers and gently trailed down her cheek.

"Forgive me, Jasmine. I know it hurts, but it is part of the process."

She thought she could hear regret and sorrow in his words.

Her lips moved, but nothing came out. She couldn't make any sound. Jasmine's vocal cords felt like they were fused together. It was too hard to open her eyes now.

Gradually the pain began to change. An empty numbness took its place. She could feel it expanding through her system, shutting her body down. Was he really helping her? Or had he decided it was better to put her out of her misery?

She tried to struggle against it. Darkness threatened to drag her down to what she feared was nothingness. She didn't want to go there. Didn't want to die.

"Do not fight it. Trust me. Let yourself go." A pleading note was laced in Eric's tone. "Trust me, Jasmine."

The vampire was nuzzling her cheek, her neck. His lips were loving, gentle against her frozen skin. She heard soothing words and noises whispered in her ear. She knew she had already made the choice when they started this. Eric now had her trust. She just hoped he would not let her down.

Jasmine was too tired now to fight. Without a second thought, she let herself go to the coldness.

Eric didn't know how long he sat there with Jasmine on his lap, enfolded in his arms. The weak rhythm of her pulse beat in his ears. How long could her body endure something it was not meant to bear?

She was mortal after all. A fragile thing. Eric began to consider his options. If he left her like this for too long, he feared it would damage her brain. He could not wake her to watch her die of the cold, although if he withdrew his power now she could slip away in peace.

His arms tightened around her protectively. He knew in an instant he could never do that. The other avenue open to him was to turn her. Eric had never turned another living soul into a vampire before. It was something he had never considered doing up until now.

She would not be as strong as him or as powerful. Never again would she see the light of day. Being turned would force her to sleep during the daylight hours. She would not be like him. Not a vampiria. That was something she could never be.

Eric relaxed as he reached a decision. If he had to, he would make Jasmine into a human vampire to save her from death. It was the only solution.

The click of the door dragged him from his thoughts. Raoul stood in the doorway. One fine eyebrow rose as he regarded his friend with astonishment.

"What are you doing down there?"

"Trying to keep Jasmine alive," Eric snapped. "Help me! Quickly!"

As gently as he could, he placed the little female in the other vampire's arms. She did not stir. She was limp and deathly still. Her lips were blue, her face pale. A frosty covering of ice coated her skin. She felt frozen.

Raoul was staring down at her in alarm. "You managed to place her in hibernation?"

Eric rose gracefully to his feet and made his way to the door. The freezing temperature had done nothing but lower his body heat. This would quickly correct itself on its own. Apart from that, he was unaffected.

He wanted to be the one to carry Jasmine out, but knew Raoul would warm her better at this point. And she would need heat.

"Indeed, my first attempt and it was most successful. I fear we must take care to wake her." They moved out of the freezer. "She must be brought out of this in the correct manner or I fear we may lose her still."

They encountered no one on the way back up in the lift. Eric could sense there was no longer anyone in the building. Had Marcel given the staff the rest of the day off? It would make sense if he had not wanted them found. By the time the staff arrived tomorrow Jasmine would have been dead. Eric himself would have been stiff but mostly unaffected.

Rage rolled through him.

Marcel had a lot to answer for. Now, trying to hurt Jasmine had been added to the list. He would have great pleasure repaying it all tenfold.

He glanced at Jasmine's limp body in his companion's arms. They had to hurry. It was imperative he begin the process to raise her body temperature. If not she would likely die.

Raoul had left the car parked on the street right outside.

There is a blanket in the back of the car, Raoul's voice informed him quickly in his head.

Eric jerked open the back door and grabbed the blanket. As the other vampire drew closer, he wrapped it around Jasmine. At that moment, he would have given anything to see the flash of her lovely green eyes.

Once Raoul and Jasmine were safely installed in the back, Eric rushed to the front and slid behind the wheel of the car. He prayed the Paris traffic would not impede them too much to the hotel. If it was clear, the journey would not take long.

His gaze flicked to the back seat. Raoul had the little female on his lap. The blanket was swaddled around her. She still had not moved. The heartbeat he could hear was still thready and weak. He feared it might give out at any moment.

She was strong and stubborn, though. He was certain she would make it through this ordeal. He would not let her go.

Eric ran through several red lights in his battle to get back to the hotel. Like a racing driver, he vied for space. He drove aggressively, dominating the road. Twenty minutes and they were there. Eric was actually surprised they had not been stopped by the police.

Raoul remained silent. He did catch Eric's glance a few times in the rearview mirror. He seemed faintly surprised Eric was taking such risks. His friend was normally so careful.

After throwing his car keys at the valet, Eric helped Raoul, still holding Jasmine, from the car. As the trio hurried past, he could sense the looks of those in the lobby, but he ignored them. None of them mattered. The need to see to Jasmine was much more important. Raoul kept up with his fast pace knowing the urgency. They didn't speak.

Eric growled with impatience when the lift seemed to take forever. His normal discomfort at the small space inside the lift was forgotten. Running a hand through his tousled hair, he glanced at the girl. She looked the same. Blue lips, pale skin, fragile, and still unconscious. Not good.

We are almost there, Eric, Raoul told him quietly in his head. *Patience, my friend. Her heart still beats. We have time. Calm yourself.*

Eric spoke aloud instead of responding telepathically. "When Jasmine is the correct colour, we will wake her. And not before."

Eric strode into the suite and straight to the bedroom. He wasted no time thrusting open the door.

As Raoul made it to his side, Eric finally took Jasmine back into his arms. It felt strangely right to have her there. Calmness washed through him.

As quickly as he could, Eric began to strip off her clothes. Eric knew he would have to warm her slowly. If her body went into shock now it could kill her. She had placed her trust in his hands. He would not fail her.

"Raoul, I require hot water bottles and many more warm blankets."

Nodding and without a word, the other vampire sped from the room. It was moments like these Eric appreciated his friend. He obeyed now without question.

Eric hastily removed her underwear. She lay naked—pale and limp on the mattress. His body stirred at the sight of her, but he ruthlessly pushed the feelings aside.

Eric avoided the urge to rub her arms or legs. This could stress her body more than it already was. It was something he could not allow. Instead he covered her quickly and completely with the heavy duvet. No inch of her apart from her head was left bare.

Raoul returned swiftly with three, filled hot water bottles and two more blankets. They were quick to add the covers to the bed.

Eric took small towels from the bathroom and wrapped one around a hot water bottle. He tested it was not too hot with his hand. A grunt of satisfaction left his lips.

Her rushed to the bed, pushed back the duvet, and settled the prepared hot water bottle carefully on her chest. He wrapped the second one and placed it on her groin. The third he wrapped and put against her neck. He then flipped the duvet back over her and stacked the extra blankets on her, making sure she was warmly covered.

He knew he would have to make sure she did not knock them off. It was imperative they remained where they were. Nothing else mattered but the girl in the bed.

He stripped out of his wet clothing and left them in a pile on the floor. He was naked now, but it held no embarrassment for him.

Raoul tossed him a large fluffy towel. Drying himself quickly, he crawled into the bed beside her. Eric pressed his length against her cold side. She was still far too cold.

A faint shiver rippled through her. After a few minutes the chills had intensified, taking over her body and contorting her muscles.

Eric made sure the hot water bottles remained in place. With his body and hands, he tried to keep her calm. Jasmine's body was reacting violently to the change in temperature. He knew this was not going to be easy. Any slip up now and they would lose her.

Raoul stripped down to his underwear. Quickly as he could, he slipped into the bed on the other side of her. Eric sent his friend a grateful smile. All the body heat she could receive was most welcome.

Jasmine's teeth clenched and then began chattering uncontrollably. They rattled wildly in her mouth non-stop. Eric held her through the convulsive shaking. Hands caressing, he tried his best to soothe her. He knew she was in pain, groaning and breathing hard. She was also barely conscious. Still, this was all a good sign. Her body was awakening, striving to pull itself from the icy limbo the vamp had forced upon it.

Raoul was vigilant with the hot water bottle on her neck and her chest. Not once did he move to touch her body with his hands, though. He also kept his gaze averted from her breasts.

Eric knew his friend was doing this out of politeness. He also had a feeling Raoul suspected he might become jealous. It was something he did not waste time to think about.

He knew that if Jasmine were awake, her nakedness would embarrass her—her lovely, pert breasts bare along with the rest of her slender form. She would also be mortified to find both vampires in her bed. Those big green eyes would widen in shock and dismay. Eric liked it best when they flashed with green fire. Usually that was with annoyance or defiance.

He would give anything to see her pretty blush now.

Jasmine suddenly tried to curl into a ball, but he would not allow it. He needed to keep her against their heat, which meant keeping her horizontal.

Eric pushed himself more securely against her side. He was gentle but firm in restricting her movements. His hands continued their movements to relax her. Raoul also snuggled more solidly into her figure. He wisely still kept his hands to himself.

"It is alright, Jasmine. You are safe now," Eric whispered against her ear. "It is time to wake up now, kitten."

She did not respond. Her little body was racked with more frenzied shaking.

He frowned. No reaction was worrisome. Eric needed her conscious even if it was for but a moment. Then, finally, he could be certain she would live. Only then he could relax himself.

Anxiety shot through him. If it took everything in his power, he would see her through this.

"Jasmine, I told you to awaken. You will obey me." Eric laced his tone with authority and his power of persuasion, which tingled in his words.

Jasmine's eyelids cracked opened. Her eyes were unfocused and glazed. She blinked slowly, then her long lashes closed again. She turned agitatedly on her side, dislodging the hot water bottles.

Eric felt her arms slide slowly, clumsily around his waist. Then just as suddenly she was burrowing against him like a little animal. She desperately clung to his warmth.

A ripple of pleasure blazed through him. They were now pressed chest to chest. Jasmine's breasts were crushed against his chest. Her silken skin rubbed enticingly touching his own. A sigh left his lips. It did not matter that she trembled in his arms. He held her close, absorbing the sensation of her nearness. Dropping his chin, Eric nuzzled her red hair.

The girl's feminine scent assailed him. It was like sunshine, warm with a hint of something flowery. An aroma he doubted he would ever forget. He was pleased she had turned to him and not Raoul. She knew he would help her. Jasmine had trusted him.

Her body had become tense, shuddering against him. Running his hand down her side, Eric crooned softly. Raoul helped him remove the hot water bottles. They tucked them around her legs beneath the duvet. Wiggling closer, the mocha-skinned vampire pressed his front to the little female's back. His arms remained away from her body.

Jasmine suddenly moaned as if in pain. She moved herself restlessly. Eric pressed as close as he could and continued to talk softly to soothe her. He did not know how long they held her.

The shivering soon stopped. She was still breathing deeply, although she relaxed against them. He knew the worst had passed.

She felt warm now. Her skin was no longer pale, now a pretty pink. Her lips were no longer blue.

Trailing his fingers over her hip, Eric released a sigh of relief. He felt her body stir.

His legs were tangled with her own. Such an intimate position. One he wished they were experiencing in a more pleasurable situation.

The little female seemed to have dozed off. She had to be exhausted. So he decided to let her sleep.

"My contact has gone silent. I believe he has been discovered," Raoul whispered into the silence.

Eric raised his focus to his friend. This news was indeed bad. It could only mean that Marcel had discovered his lover was their informant.

"The mage was not where I was told," Raoul continued softly. "I believe we have been exposed."

"Marcel knows what I am. He proved that tonight," Eric replied grimly.

How the arms dealer had acquired this information was a burning question in his mind. It was not something easy to come by. The fat man's downfall was his lack of knowledge of Eric's mastery of the cold. Without that, the freezer would have rendered him helpless. He was more than sure Pierre would have been back in the morning to finish him off. Then, no doubt, he would also have been tasked with getting rid of their bodies.

Eric's fingers caressed Jasmine's hip once more. Her face was pressed into the hollow of his throat. The warmth of her breath whispered against his skin, sending delightful tingles through his body.

"That is impossible, Eric." Raoul looked worried. "How could he guess you are a vampiria?"

"You sensed the wards on that vault yourself, my friend. They are meant only to contain our kind."

This meant that Marcel had knowledge he should not have. Vampiria were always careful to keep themselves hidden. They could not afford to be discovered.

"What do you intend to do now?" Raoul asked, shifting uncomfortably.

Gently as he could, Eric pulled the girl more firmly against him. "We observe, then move when the time is right."

CHAPTER 21

JASMINE AWOKE TUCKED IN a delicious cocoon of warmth. A mattress was soft and comfortable beneath her. The smoothness of a duvet brushed against her skin.

A small sleepy sigh of contentment left her lips. If this was a dream, she was enjoying it. She felt so secure, so safe. Things, she realised, she hadn't experienced for quite a while.

A vague memory of feeling as if she had been frozen to her very core buzzed around inside her head. Ice had coated her insides with a thick, cold, burning layer. Then a numbing darkness had stolen every feeling, every sensation. She had drowned in it. The air had literally stopped in her lungs. Had she died? Maybe that had been the dream?

As her mind kicked into life slowly, she became aware of other sensations. A big naked body was pressed up against her back. She could feel hard, thick legs tucked up beneath her own. The chest behind her back was muscled and firm. Heat was radiating off the male in waves.

She was also, she realised, very naked herself.

Nipples pebbling into taut peaks beneath the blankets, she felt desire tighten in her stomach. The smell of snow and pine enfolded her, wrapping itself around her like a blanket.

Eric.

Her heart did a strange little flip flop in her chest.

Startled, she turned her head.

Bright cerulean blue eyes were watching her tenderly. With him so close, her body was thrumming with sudden arousal. It was as if now she was highly tuned to the vampire.

"You have slept for five hours since your temperature was raised," Eric told her softly. "I am very glad to see you awake."

Jasmine's mouth turned down. Five hours? In a rush the memories crowded her.

The frozen little room. Being trapped. The bitter glacial cold that had been killing her slowly. Their kiss.

Fuck, she was alive.

For someone who had practically been a popsicle, she felt pretty good.

Eyes wide, she peered around. They were alone and once more back in the hotel room. She realised she had a huge gap in her memory, though—she didn't remember how they had gotten back.

"You can thank Raoul later for eventually coming to our aid," Eric said as if reading her thoughts.

Meeting his watchful gaze, she smiled. Raoul was going to get more than thanks when she saw him. He was going to get a hug. Stretching her limbs beneath the blankets, she tried to ignore her nakedness. She didn't know why they were all rather naked in bed, but maybe it had something to do with her being warmed up. She wasn't about to complain though. Having Eric so close, so bare was a fantasy.

Flopping over onto her back, she kept the blankets up covering her chest. "What's been happening?"

She knew life would have carried on around her. The vampires would have continued on with the case. How much could have happened in five hours?

Eric sighed heavily. "Smith's body was discovered in the Seine two hours ago."

Jasmine felt her heart sink. So it was true the American agent was dead. She had been half-hoping it was a lie. She had really liked Smith. All that talk of retiring and he hadn't managed to do it. She didn't even know if he had any family.

"Marcel's building is a hive of activity according to Raoul," Eric continued. "We do not know what he has planned, and unfortunately, our informant had also been silenced. We fear he, too, is dead."

He had his head propped up on one arm. The blankets were draped over his lean hip as he continued to lie on his side facing her. A relaxed, carefree position. Eric's full pecs and well-defined muscles of his chest were on show. The skin looked smooth and flawless. He wasn't as pale as she had thought he would be.

Jasmine licked her dry lips. She was ogling her boss again, not that he seemed to mind. Her eyes strayed downwards. His stomach was flat and muscular, his abs were muscled, firm, and sharply contoured. The vampire definitely had a body any woman would pant over. Continuing down, she followed the slight hairy arrowing of black hair that dipped below the blankets. What lay beneath was hidden from her gaze. Disappointment curled through her.

Jasmine bit her lower lip almost painfully. The beat of her heart picked up. She had imagined Eric naked once or twice. Seeing him almost all on display was nothing how she had pictured. It was way better. From what she could see, he was sculpted to perfection.

A dull throb started between her legs. Squeezing her thighs together, she tried to ease it. Blinking, she tried to remember what they had been talking about. It seemed surreal having this conversation in bed with the vampire. Intimate. Unreal.

"Who was it?" She asked fairly sure he had said something about an informant.

"Claude, his lover." The vampire's voice had grown huskier, deeper. Did he like her looking at him? Did he know his nearness was turning her on?

Dragging her eyes away from his chest, Jasmine met his gaze. "Oh no! What happened to him?"

Those icy eyes were now burning with a dark, hungry look. One she had caught glimpses of before. But this time he did not try to bother to hide.

Jasmine suddenly forgot how to breathe.

"We do not know. His body is yet to be discovered," he replied, his voice thickening even further with desire.

She swallowed down her growing excitement. "You think he's dead?"

"It is a possibility."

A sense of guilt washed through her. Claude was someone she had promised herself to help. Not knowing he was the informant had not helped. These vampires and their damn secrets were driving her nuts.

Dropping her gaze, she glanced towards the windows. The curtains weren't drawn and it was dark outside. Paris was lit up with twinkling lights. The Eiffel Tower glimmered in the distance in all its beauty.

"Marcel has to know we escaped by now." It wasn't a question. If the fat man was like any other villain, she doubted he would have waited to make sure they were dead.

"Indeed he does." Eric's fingers brushed the curve of her hip in a small caress, making her jump. "We were sure to disrupt any cameras. He will also believe we were both carried out half-frozen to death."

The little gesture had Jasmine's heart rate increasing. Moisture damped between her thighs, as she pressed them together once again. One fucking touch and her body was ready for him. No, that was not true. She had been ready for him the moment she had woken up.

"You saved my life," she said softly. Eyes on his face again, she drank in his cold handsomeness. He had kept his promise.

The vampire smiled. It was a charming curving of his lips. "I told you I would not let anything happen to you, kitten. And I always keep my promises. I am sorry I caused you pain."

Jasmine began to fidget with the duvet. "It was the only way it would work. I understand that. I'm glad you didn't warn me, though. I'm not sure I would have let you do it."

His eyes seemed mesmerized by her mouth now. "My kisses are not usually so cold. I can assure you of that."

As if to prove it, Eric leaned over and let his lips brush hers. Jasmine flinched at first. It was an automatic reaction to the memory of the biting frozen pain.

He did not give up though. Instead he continued to tease her with soft butterfly kisses. Slow and sweet, gentle sweeps of his mouth against hers. They coaxed and comforted, drawing her out of any fear that she felt.

He didn't go further, didn't deepen the kiss—as if he were afraid it might shatter the sensual spell he was weaving. It felt like he had been kissing her forever by the time he drew back. Instantly she missed the press of his mouth.

Eric's face, holding a fierce passion, was inches above her own. The thickness of his erection pressed against the curve of her hip. He made no move to hide the evidence of his body's desire.

Jasmine's heart pounded excitedly in her chest at the unfamiliar pressure.

"Let me take you, kitten. Give us both the release we crave."

Jasmine shivered at the heat in his voice. She was vibrating with anticipation, but still a small part of her held back.

"I don't know if I can do that, Eric." Past pain flashed in the depths of her eyes for a moment. Could she really overcome the events from so long ago? Would it really be this easy?

He stilled beside her. Concern filtered through the blazing passion in his look. "I sense you have had a bad experience that has frightened you away from being intimate."

Jasmine felt her throat close up. He was right. And it was the same event that had triggered her gifts. She still remembered the burning red eyes boring into hers. A shudder of fear rolled through her. It was something she was never likely to forget. Even now it haunted her nightmares.

Taking a deep breath, Jasmine decided to tell him part of the truth. "I was raped two years ago. I was a virgin before that." She was amazed her voice kept so steady. "I haven't been with anyone since. It's never been easy for me to . . . well . . . be like this."

Eric swore under his breath. Something raw and tender flashed in his eyes. A moment later, Jasmine found herself cradled against his big chest.

"I am so sorry, Jasmine." His voice was incredibly gentle, nearly bringing tears to her eyes. "I never imagined it was such a thing."

His cheek rubbed against her short hair. His hands caressed her arms. Comfort and reassurance. She recognized them for what they were. The vampire was trying to ease her past pain.

She didn't want to talk about it. The only reason she had shared this was so he would understand her hesitation.

The vampire somehow made her forget to be afraid. He washed it all away. It was the only time in the last two years she felt like she could be close to a man.

Eric brushed his lips gently against her mouth in a feather light kiss. The things she said were still tumbling around inside his head. He could almost feel her pain, her fear. His little female had been violated. Someone had hurt her in one of the vilest ways. Anger and rage boiled inside of him, trying to force their way upwards.

Had she been avenged? Where was the perpetrator now? Had he been immersed in the pain and misery he so deserved? Did he now burn justly in the depths of hell? If not, Eric was willing to see to the task.

Reining in his control, he easily pressed the dark feelings back down. Now was not the time for such emotions. The girl needed comfort, understanding. He could give her this. He couldn't go back and change what had been done, but if he had such a power, he knew he would. Eric recognised it had taken her a lot to share such a thing. The pain he had seen once or twice now made sense. Obviously she had told him so he understood any faltering she might have. This just made his lust burn hotter.

Unable to help himself, he trailed kisses down her jawline. Jasmine moaned softly. Reaching her chin, he ventured lower down the curve of her neck. He could sense the racing of her blood beneath her fragile skin. The pulse point at her throat throbbed with the beat of her heart. He licked it, tasting the saltiness of her flesh.

A moan vibrated up from her chest.

Raising his head, he found her eyes glazed with desire. The scent of her arousal was thick and potent. No trace of fear lingered now. Ever so gently, Eric settled his mouth over hers again. Soft and welcoming, Jasmine lips clung eagerly to his. Her silken limbs rubbed enticingly against his own. A conscious gesture or not, it conveyed her need for fulfilment.

When she sighed against his mouth, he slipped his tongue into its moist depths. Just as sweet as he remembered. Their tongues danced together— gliding, sucking, sliding.

He wanted to overwhelm her senses. Rip away the trauma of the past and pleasure her beyond her wildest dreams.

Jasmine was pliant and yielding against him.

The urge to bury his cock inside her heat surged through him. He would make Jasmine his. Sate the hunger for physical connection, completion that he craved. He knew he would have to be careful with her. Show her there was nothing to fear.

"Will you trust me, Jasmine?" he whispered softly against her lips. "I shall not hurt you. All I wish is to give you unimaginable pleasure and wipe away your fears."

She replied without hesitation. "Yes, Eric. I will."

Eric tasted of warm, hungry male. It was addictive and delicious. Jasmine soaked him in—his scent, the feel of him against her. He was lying half on her. His hard, velvety cock was a pleasurable, unfamiliar pressure against her belly.

Her hands clutched the spread of his powerful shoulders. Desire spiralled through her, white hot and wild.

Eric's lips teased hers. One large hand covered her naked breast. His long fingers began to tease the taut nipple.

She moaned with pleasure.

Need roared through her like a raging storm. Any reservation, hesitation, or fear was carried away in its maelstrom. Jasmine wanted this badly. Up until now it had all been foreplay. All of the words, looks, and touches that had passed between them. Everything led up to this moment.

Eric nipped lightly at her lip. Then his head dipped lower towards her breast.

Anticipation gripped her. His sensual mouth was inches from her taut, aching peak. The slow swirl of his tongue began to tease it.

"Jazzy?"

Jasmine squeaked in surprised. Twitch's voice was loud and clear, purring in her left ear.

Eric stilled. Pulling back a few inches from her breast, he searched her face with concern. His features were stretched tight with desire. The look in his eyes was smouldering, sultry.

"I'm here, Twitch," she muttered.

Surprise lit Eric's eyes. Then a look of resignation settled over him.

Hands pressed to the vampire's hard, muscled chest, she pushed him away.

He went willingly. Rolling to the side smoothly, he sprawled gloriously naked on the mattress. A groan of pained annoyance left his lips. He draped an arm over his eyes for a moment in a gesture of male frustration.

Yanking up the blankets, she covered her own nakedness in embarrassment. A moan escaped her lips. The tips of her sensitive breasts chafed against the material. Her body was tight with its own frustration. Pressing her thighs together, she tried to alleviate the slightly painful ache.

Why now? Just when things were about to get oh so interesting, the mage had to interrupt? The universe had obviously decided to play a cruel joke.

"What's up, Twitch?" she said, managing not to growl out the words.

Eric still lulled on the bed. The duvet was no longer covering all of him. He had dropped his arm and was watching her expectantly.

Twitch was saying something urgently in her ear, but she didn't hear a word of it.

Jasmine's eyes instead feasted on the sight of the male perfection before her. Muscles, firm flesh, powerful chest and shoulders. He had the body of a god.

A small hum of appreciation left her lips.

With a knowing, teasing smile, Eric laced his hands behind his head. Stretching out, he seemed happy to let her look her fill.

Eyes dropping to his groin, her eyes widened with wariness. Holy shit, he was certainly well endowed. His cock was huge. Jasmine felt her mouth go dry.

Her eyes darted away with nervousness. How was all that supposed to fit? Surely something that big was going to hurt.

"He's attached it to the top of the Eiffel Tower. It goes off at midnight." The techno mage's words snapped her out of her perusal. Tearing her eyes away from temptation, she tried to focus on her friend's words.

Confusion slapped her in the face. "Sorry, attached what?"

Twitch gave an irritated sigh. "The bomb, Jazzy! The bomb!"

"Holy fuck." Eyes wide, she fixed them on the vampire. "Eric, there's a bomb on the Eiffel Tower, courtesy of Marcel. It goes off at midnight!"

Shock registered on his features. When he opened his mouth to speak, Jasmine shushed him.

"What else do you know, Twitchy?"

She felt the mattress moved as the vamp beside her sat up. The heat from his body warmed her back. A moment later, he pressed his naked chest against her. Her thoughts scattered before she dragged them back.

"I have managed to attach a little spell," Twitch was saying softly. "You should be able to sense. It's pretty undetectable otherwise. I don't think . . ."

Jasmine waited, but the mage never finished what he was saying. Brows drawing together, she pressed a finger against her ear.

"Twitch?"

Silence.

"Twitch, you there?"

Nothing. No answer. Tension snaked through her. Had they lost the range with the earpiece again? That had to be it. She couldn't think about the alternative. Marcel wanted Twitch alive. The fat man was not going to hurt him.

"We have three hours to stop the device from exploding," Eric said against her ear. The breath from his words tickled her skin.

Sighing, she pushed her worry for her friend away. Right now, stopping a bomb from exploding was their priority.

"Let's go."

Eric nuzzled the side of her neck. When his lips brushed the curve of her shoulder, she shivered. Tipping her head to the side, she granted him greater access to her neck. She couldn't seem to help it. Having Eric's lips on her anywhere was becoming addictive.

Something sharp grazed against her supply flesh. Holy crap. That had to be his fangs. A shudder of desire shot through her. Did he want to bite her again? It was something she had been unable to forget. Jasmine melted back against him.

"You are to remain here." His words were soft, but firm. "I do not relish the thought of you in any more danger and you are still recovering from almost freezing to death."

Biting her lips, she knew that was not going to be possible.

"Twitch says the bomb is really hard to find, but he's attached something I can sense." Turning her head, she met his glittering blue eyes. His fangs were nowhere in sight. "Eric, I have to come or you might not find it in time."

He looked torn for a moment. The concern he was feeling for her was clear. Then resolve darkened his gaze. "Very well. Come, we have not a moment to lose."

Eric sprung from the bed. One moment he was beside her—the next he was on his feet. Jasmine was left gaping after him.

Eric sprinted across the room naked and flung open the door. He didn't seem to care he was completely nude.

Jasmine admired his tight buttocks and muscled back for a whole thirty seconds. Then he disappeared into the sitting room.

She rolled off the bed and moved to the wardrobe. Surprisingly she wasn't suffering from any aches or pains. After being almost frozen to death, she had kind of expected them. She found some lacy white panties in one of the drawers and quickly pulled them on.

She could hear the vampires' voices in the other room but only caught snatches of conversation. Whatever was being said was low and urgent. Eric had to be filling Raoul in on what was happening.

She stabbed her legs into her jeans and buttoned them up. Yanking open some more drawers, she began to search through them for a top. She tugged things out along the way, discarding them messily on the floor.

Jasmine's stomach grumbled in a very unladylike fashion. She hadn't eaten in hours and her body was now demanding food. Unfortunately, it was still going to have to wait.

She scooped up a red bra and did up the fastening at the back. Her underwear was mismatched, but she didn't really care. She had to wonder what Eric was going to do with all these clothes. It had been nice of him to buy them for her. Maybe he could return . . .

A squeak left her lips. Her train of thought vanished in a second. The vampire was standing directly behind her. Still wonderfully naked. Eric held a plate of French pastries and pushed it into her hands.

Fingers curling around the plate, she held it in astonishment. She blinked in confusion while staring down at the food. Then she raised her eyes and stared at his bare, muscled chest.

"I had these sent up earlier for you," he explained with a flash of a seductive smile. "Eat quickly. You will need all your strength."

Jasmine was a little shocked by the sweet gesture. She couldn't stop staring at him. Why the heck was he still naked?

"Thanks." Her reply sounded husky.

Without a word the vampire moved away.

She snagged a *pain au chocolat* and bit into the puffy pastry. It was cold, but she still made a hum of pleasure when she reached the dark chocolate centre.

Eric was gathering his own clothes. He shrugged into a black jumper and a pair of black jeans. She noted he didn't bother with boxers. Did he always go commando?

She placed the plate down on the bedside table but not before grabbing a croissant and popping it into her mouth. Turning, she went in search of a jumper.

"Raoul is contacting the French police. The tower will be evacuated as quickly as possible," the vampire informed her from behind.

She glanced his way as she slid a green, woolly jumper over her head.

"Will it be open?"

He was sitting on the edge of the bed. A pair of black socks were already on his feet as he pulled on a pair of trainers.

"Yes. I believe it is open until eleven at night in the winter."

Jasmine grabbed her own trainers and shoved her feet into them. "Marcel is going to get suspicious if he sees what's happening."

Eric had a dark wooden trunk open now and was rummaging through the contents.

She was pretty certain it was something she had never seen before. When had they brought it in here and where was it from?

The clink of metal on metal met her ears. Curious and intrigued she moved closer.'

"If you planted a bomb, Jasmine, would you truly hang around waiting for it to explode?" the vampire asked over his shoulder.

Jasmine pulled a face at his back. "Point taken."

Standing right behind him, she peered eagerly over his shoulder. Weapons filled the inside of the trunk.

Not guns or grenades. Just knives, swords, maces, and crossbows. Positively medieval.

He turned to meet her gaze and flashed a gleeful grin—the kind of smile a small boy had with his favourite toys.

With almost feline grace, Eric rose to his feet. Two of the many weapons were gripped in his hands. He laid the daggers carefully on the bed.

"Why are you going armed if you don't think anyone is going to be up there?" Jasmine asked, watching as he collected a short, leather jacket from the wardrobe.

He flipped the jacket down on the mattress and opened up the inside. Two sheaths had been woven into the silky, black interior. Both were lying crossways so they would fall just above his lower back.

"Never underestimate an enemy." His voice was deep and smooth.

Eric tucked the two double-edged daggers in the coverings within his coat.

"What about me?"

One dark eyebrow rose slightly at her question. "I will protect you, Jasmine. You will have no need of a weapon."

Jasmine glanced longingly at the trunk. He could at least give her a knife or something. Maybe she wouldn't need it, but she would feel safer.

"Do not pout." Amusement was threaded in his words.

When she looked up to meet his eyes, he was smiling. Was this sexy vamp teasing her?

Jasmine stuck her bottom lip out a little further. Then she pinned him with big pleading eyes. Something that never failed on her boss, Mark.

"Just one little blade or something? Please, Eric." She raised her hand up and held two fingers a few inches apart.

The vampire's deep rumbling laughter rippled over like a velvety caress. "Very well, my lovely."

Turning swiftly, he knelt and began to rummage once again through the chest. He seemed to be considering every small piece of weaponry. After a moment Eric rocked back on his knees. A small, sheathed knife was in his hand.

"Here." He held it out towards her.

Jasmine carefully took hold of it. Taking it in both hands, she gently pulled the blade from its plain leather covering. The metal glinted lustrous silver in the light. It seemed much brighter than normal knives. This made her wonder if it was really coated in silver.

She couldn't help but grin. "Thank you."

He quickly showed her how to clip the scabbard to her jeans–on her hip, any easy place where she could access it if needed. The weight of it was strangely exciting.

"Seeing you armed, even in such a small way is quite arousing," Eric confessed huskily. Shrugging into his leather jacket, he was surveying her from head to toe. Approval was shining in his eyes.

Jasmine felt her heart skip a beat. Why she felt ridiculously proud and happy about his opinion, she wasn't sure. But it left a warm glow inside.

Hurrying to the wardrobe, she hooked out her own small, black leather jacket. It came to her waist and fit comfortably. She zipped it up and hurried back to Eric's side.

He dropped a swift, hard kiss on her parted lips. A moment later, his long legs were striding towards the bedroom door.

"Come, let us make haste." He threw the words over his shoulder.

After snatching two more croissants from the plate on the table, Jasmine jogged after him.

God knows what awaited them. At least she wasn't going to face it hungry.

CHAPTER 22

THE PORSCHE ROARED LIKE an untamed beast along the busy road. They were fighting with late evening traffic but making some headway. Jasmine sat, hands clenched tightly in her lap. She still couldn't get over the way they drove here. She doubted she would ever get used to it.

Eric had been right about it snowing. The air had turned crisper, lighter. A soft flurry was falling softly from the sky like a thousand unblemished white feathers. It did not seem to be melting when it reached the ground. Instead it was creating an ever-growing carpet of pure white.

Eric, seemingly preoccupied, hadn't said a word since leaving the hotel. Jasmine was feeling a little shy and awkward. They had been in bed naked less than half an hour ago. If Twitch hadn't interrupted them, they would still be there. An erotic image of their sweaty, sated, and tangled bodies swirled through her mind. She swallowed down a groan as her body clenched with need. Sexual frustration, she was learning, was a bitch. Her whole being was screaming for release. Was she ever going to get it?

The Eiffel Tower lit the darkness in a glow of golden lights shining in the darkness like little beacons beckoning them closer.

"I just realised it's Christmas Eve," Jasmine murmured to herself.

Being so swept up with everything that had happened, she had barely been aware of the days. It felt like she had lived whole weeks in such a short time.

"Were you planning something special?" Eric asked, glancing briefly in her direction.

The car had picked up speed now. They seemed to be leaving most of the choking traffic behind. The light flurry of snow continued to fall around them outside the car.

"Just lunch at a friend's house. That was all." She shifted a little in her seat. "What about you?"

Jasmine didn't even know if he celebrated Christmas. If he had never been human, did he do that sort of thing? She had so many questions she wanted to ask him. So much she wanted to know. Yet she was holding back. She had no idea if he would answer them. Up until now, he had been very secretive.

"I never have time to celebrate." His eyes were dark and fathomless when he looked her way once again.

A frown marred her brow. "Why not?"

The car growled throatily as they slowed when another car pulled out in front of them. Eric was quick to react to avoid an accident.

"I am usually on assignment," the vampire explained softly with a sigh. "It makes something like that very difficult."

Her eyes widened slightly at that. "I'm sorry."

Manoeuvring with precision, he made the car roar again as he sped up once more. The sound vibrated beneath her, making her body tighten with excitement.

His expression was suddenly perplexed. "For what?"

"That you don't get to celebrate."

An amused smile tilted his lips. "It is of no consequence to me."

So what he was saying was he didn't care. Like his job was more important to him.

Turning her head, she watched the snow drifting outside her window.

"Where did Raoul go?"

The other vampire had not been in the suite when they had emerged from the bedroom.

"He has gone with some of the French police to raid Marcel's premises. His house and the building we first met in."

That jerked her head around again with interest. "He might find Twitch."

The headlights of the car shone brightly, cutting through the blur of motion before them. Eric kept his eyes on the road when he answered her.

"Do not worry. His orders are to bring your friend back to the hotel. You will be reunited with your co-worker soon."

The landmark they were travelling towards was situated in the Parc du Champs de Mars, a large sprawling open public space.

Jasmine knew it was normally full of greenery, but tonight the snow coated everything in a pristine, white blanket.

The Porsche sped down the Avenue Anatole, the roar of his engine drawing attention.

Police cars were everywhere, their flashing lights bright in the darkness. They were holding people back with a cordon a good distance from the tower itself.

After swinging the car up onto the pavement, Eric was already leaping out as he killed the engine. The snow whirled around him as he moved.

A group of policemen dashed their way. They were pointing at the car, their voices raised angrily. A few of them had hands resting on the top of their holstered guns. They weren't happy. That was clear.

Jasmine slid out of the car but stayed beside it. She did not have to worry, though. A few curt words from the vampire and the men backed off. Their body language changed from aggressive to nervous.

Looking over his shoulder at her, Eric nudged his chin in the direction of another group of men. Realising he wanted her to follow, she moved around the car. The snow crunched under their feet as they hurried along.

A few flakes landed on Jasmine's eyelashes, making her blink. Using her hand she wiped them away. The night was cold, almost chilling to the bone. She couldn't help the shiver that rippled through her. She pulled the zipper on her jacket up as high as it would go and followed the vampire.

Eric was soon in a deep conversation with the man in charge. French flowed off his tongue smooth and flawless. A couple of times Jasmine felt the subtle tingle of persuasion leave the vampire's lips. Whatever he was saying, he was making sure he got what he wanted. With a power like Eric had, she doubted anyone ever denied him.

The man nodded at Eric.

"Come, Jasmine."

The vampire's deep, familiar baritone washed over her.

Startled, she raised her eyes. Standing before her, his features were grim and cold. A hand gripped her arm. Before she could even blink, Eric was steering her quickly forwards. Their legs ate up the distance as they crossed the open area. The sounds behind them began to lessen and dim. Jasmine was pretty sure she could feel the eyes of the policemen on her back. They had to be wondering who she was. It had to look strange with just the two of them. What cover story had the vampire used? What velvety lie?

Jasmine found she was too nervous to ask. Her tongue felt heavy in mouth. Heart thudding wildly in her chest, she tried to breathe through her fear.

Could they get to the bomb in time? What if they couldn't disarm it? Did they even have a fucking plan?

"What the fuck are we going to do with the bomb when we get it?" she said, unable to hide the hint of fear.

"Are you nervous again, kitten?" Eric asked with a laugh.

"We're about to face a bomb on the Eiffel Tower. What the fuck do you think?" Jasmine released a long breath through clenched teeth. "We are fucking insane."

A large, warm hand suddenly slid over hers. Eric laced her fingers with his until he was holding her hand.

"I have had some training with bomb disarming. If all else fails, we shall wing it."

That stopped her in her tracks. "Wing it?"

The vampire continued their progress by tugging her along.

"Yes, I believe that is the correct term."

Jasmine rolled her eyes. Wing it. Their doom sounded like it was already tolling somewhere in her head.

Eric glanced at his watch. "We have an hour until midnight. Plenty of time."

The magnificent wrought iron tower soared above them in its entire splendour.

"We cannot risk the lift," Eric muttered. "It shall have to be the stairs."

Jasmine's heart lurched in her chest. She knew the monument was almost the same height as an eighty-one storey building. Did he expect them to use the stairs the entire way up?

Eric seemed to sense her hesitation. He flashed a look of impatience. "We do not have time for second thoughts Jasmine. You are the only one who can sense the device."

Swallowing down her trepidation, she trailed him to the stairwell. Eric began a swift ascent, not looking back to see if she followed.

Closing a hand over the cold metal railing, Jasmine began to take the steps as quickly as she could. It was eerily silent and still. Everything seemed surreal. The snow seemed to mute everything around her.

Glancing up, she realised the vampire had already disappeared. She hadn't realised he could move so fast. Trying to hurry she found the stairs zigzagged back and forth. They seemed endless, but she tried to keep up an even pace. Her foot tread sounded ominously loud.

The tower's golden illuminations—their dazzling brilliance bright in the inky blackness of the night—that lit her way.

She stopped to try to catch her breath. Jasmine knew she was not in terrible shape. She ran every day and her boss made sure they were all physically fit. Obviously not as fit as she thought; Eric was no doubt already at the bloody top with his vampiric speed. Swearing under her breath, she began to climb again. She had to reach the top. People were depending on her.

The snow was falling in a steady, thicker flurry now. A bitter wind was blowing and nipping at her numbing face.

Something was buzzing against her sixth sense. Like a lazy bee trying to get her attention. It was faintly familiar magic and Jasmine was sure it was Twitch. The little crackle licked the inside of her brain. It had to be the spell he'd attached to the device so she could sense it. The bomb was somewhere here. Taking a breath she focused her senses.

Remembering Eric's lesson, she tried to centre herself as she climbed. It only took a second for the mage's magic to draw her higher. Tilting her chin, Jasmine gazed upwards. The bomb was up. Way up.

Maybe Eric had already found it? She could see no sign of the vamp.

Peeking down through the mesh fencing, she could see the darkness below. In the day, it would be filled with eager tourists waiting to make their way up. No sound could be heard apart from her footfall on each metal step. By the time she reached the first platform, her legs were burning. Pausing, she tried to steady her breathing. The stairs rose upwards into the open area. Cautiously Jasmine poked her head up and peered through the yellow railing around it.

Her eyes scanned the zone, which was bathed in the soft glow of the lights. A larger space than she had imagined. Half was sheltered, the other open. She caught a glimpse of photographs, posters, walkways, and staircases.

If Marcel had planted the bomb, would he have left it guard? Stealthily as she could, she eased around the wall.

Nothing moved. The snow fluttered down silently. It had started to cover the open space in a fine, white layer. Eric was nowhere to be seen.

Jasmine frowned. Where the hell was he? Weren't they supposed to be working together? Was he already at the top?

Glancing upwards, she could see the rest of the tower stretching ominously above. Its metal beams and girders eerily reminded her of a giant spider web. She knew she did not have time to search the whole expansive area. All her senses were calling her higher. Jasmine was thankful for that at least. The bomb was somewhere above.

A faint noise teased her ears. Everything was muffled, though, because of the snow. Cocking her head, she recognised the sound of footsteps. They were from somewhere behind.

Scurrying forwards, trying not to fall, she slid quickly behind a thick metal support beam.

Moments later three men made their way lightly up from the stairwell, from the way she had come. They must have been waiting hidden down below, she realised. Had they been waiting for them?

Jasmine instantly recognized Pierre, the arms dealer bodyguard. The other two were probably also his goons. Eyes dropping to their hands, she could see the guns they held.

She swore inwardly. Eric had disappeared and left her. All she had was the knife on her belt. Against guns, this was not an even match. How was she supposed to defend herself now?

The men were speaking in low hushed voices. Jasmine could not make out what they were saying as her French sucked. Still, she was pretty certain it was probably to kill them on sight if they were spotted.

The goons moved closer. Jasmine realised she had nowhere to go. If she moved now she was going to be seen. When that happened she was screwed. Flattening herself against the frigid metal, she prayed they would just move on. If she kept quiet enough, maybe they wouldn't do a search.

The temperature abruptly dropped a few more degrees. It was like the air suddenly became arctic. A shiver rolled through her.

Eric watched the dangerous males hasten nearer to where Jasmine was hiding. Snowflakes brushed against his face. They settled on his eyelashes and in his hair. He didn't mind the cold, and in fact, it was his very essence, his power. It lived deep within his immortal body as if it were a living breathing part of him.

He had the perfect vantage point from where he sat up high. Any moment now she would be spotted. He could never allow that. His protective instincts kicked into high gear.

Letting his powers rise, he let the coldness free. When the little female shivered, he knew she had felt it. A sea of translucent ice spread rapidly across the expansive floor, coating the surface like a frozen, glittering lake.

As the bitter wind whipped his coat around him, Eric drew upon it. The falling snow lashed sideways as it became a gale. He breathed it in, held it deep. The elements swayed, bending to the very force of his will.

Swearing, the men took its brunt. Temporarily blinded, they did not see the danger before them. Like newborn foals, their legs went in different directions when their feet hit the sheet of ice. It was almost amusing to watch them panic. Their arms flailed as they tried to regain balance. And still Eric kept the snow and the wind slicing into them. He let them taste its frigid power, its icy wrath.

He knew he could not keep it up forever. They would need to be dealt with. They still held guns tightly in their hands. One stray bullet was all it would take to hurt the girl.

Wide-eyed, Jasmine stared at the men as they slipped and slid across the floor. Pressing her lips together she tried not to laugh. It was comical. Their confusion was written across their faces. Pierre's eyes were practically bulging from his head. They didn't seem to know what was going on.

Eric was close. She could feel his power in the snarling arctic wind and driven snow as it beat down upon the men. The kiss of its icy touch caressed her numb cheeks and the tip of her nose. It was so distracting she found herself leaning into it, as if it were a physical stroke.

Pierre managed to find his feet. Eyes narrowed, he spotted her at the same moment.

"Come here, you little bitch," he roared, launching himself towards her. The sound snapped Jasmine's attention back.

He was already off the icy floor. Murder burned in his hard eyes. Pierre was going to kill her.

Racing away from the metal support beam, she bolted towards some stairs.

The loud crack of a gunshot rang out behind.

As Jasmine's heart nearly stopped in her chest, it took her a second to realised he had missed. Adrenaline was already pumping erratically through her veins. Breathing hard, she did not stop moving.

As she reached the stairs, something large and heavy smashed into her back. A shriek of surprise left her lips. The blow sent her tumbling forwards. Knees hitting the metal steps painfully hard, she grunted from the impact.

Without warning a hand grabbed the back of her head. Fingers sank cruelly into her short, red hair and a yank forced her back. She winced. The action brought tears of pain to her eyes.

"Did you really think you could get away, you little whore?" Pierre muttered harshly against her ear. His hot stinking breath burned against her cheek.

Her hand moved jerkily to the knife at her hip. Its hilt was a reassuring pressure against her palm. As Jasmine tensed to move, she felt the barrel of his gun press between her shoulder blades. She froze.

Pierre released his grip on her hair, and his hand moved down her shoulder. It slid over her leather jacket until he was cupping her breast, protected by the layers of her clothes. He squeezed hard, fingers digging as deep as they could.

Panic threatened to swallow her whole. A shudder of revulsion rocked through her. Her fingers curled around the knife hilt. She wasn't going to let Pierre have his way with her. She would rather chance a bullet.

A second later, she was free.

Swallowing hard, Jasmine crumpled forwards. Hands and knees resting on the coldness of the metal steps, she turned her head.

Eric had the bodyguard. One hand wrapped around his throat, he held Pierre dangling, his feet inches above the ground. The gun was nowhere to be seen. Eyes blazing with an unholy look, Eric was shaking him like a dog with a chew toy. The vampire looked lethal.

She was barely aware of planting her bottom on one of the steps. Her focus was on the two males.

Tongue snaking out to lick his lips, Eric's fangs extended.

Jasmine had felt their sting once but had never seen them. She was taken aback by how long they were – razor sharp canines that peeked out onto his bottom lip.

Pierre was clawing at the vampire's arm. He was struggling to breathe, choking on his own breath, which was still trapped in his lungs. The man was no match for the vampiric strength he withered against.

In one swift motion Eric forced the man's head to the side as he lowered him to his feet. With ease he subdued every frantic struggle.

Before she could blink, he had struck. Eric's fangs sank deep into Pierre's exposed neck. His icy blue eyes were fierce, savage as he fed.

Entranced, Jasmine could not look away. No hint of fear lay inside her. No repulsion. In fact, watching him feed was dangerously enticing.

Chest rising and falling quickly, her breathing quickened with a strange sense of dark excitement. She couldn't explain it. And she couldn't look away either. Her vision was trapped on the whole scene.

Almost as if he had sensed her excitement, Eric's eyes locked on to hers. A look of pleasured blood-thirstiness was etched on his face. A tinge of red lurked in their depths, diluting the cold brightness of the blue. He bit down harder into the supple flesh. His eyes looked almost glazed with bliss.

The entire time his gaze on hers, as if he were daring her to look away.

Jasmine felt a thrill rush through her. The whole time she remained in place on the cold, hard step.

Colour drained from Pierre's face.

His struggles had weakened, becoming slow and sluggish. The fight for survival was flowing out of him as his blood continued to fill the vampire's mouth. Lips blue and skin pale, the life began to ebb from his eyes.

Eric pulled back. With his lips pulled back in a snarl, his fangs glistened in the lights of the tower around them.

She had known he was a vampire, but it really hadn't hit home until this very moment seeing him feed.

Desire spiralled inside her.

He was so beautiful, in a dark and compelling kind of way. Maybe it was the danger that was a turn-on. Knowing that fangs and a cold, winters power lay beneath the layer of smooth sophistication.

He licked the traces of blood from his lips. The fangs retracted back into his mouth with a seamless quickness.

Jasmine shivered, biting the edge of her lower lip.

All the traces of the darker side of Eric had vanished again. It was now hidden beneath the veneer of an English gentleman.

"Did you kill him?"

Eric released the man from his hold. She watched as Pierre's body crumpled lifelessly to the floor.

"I did indeed." His brooding gaze searched her face for a moment, as if he were watching for her reaction. "He was in no way innocent, Jasmine. Never forget that."

She had no doubt. In fact, she didn't feel very much at all seeing the man dead at his feet.

Her cheeks felt frozen. A few stray snowflakes were clinging to her eyelashes and hair.

Eric offered her his hand. Jasmine took it without a second thought. His fingers were sure and warm as they closed around her own. With a gentle tug he pulled her to her feet.

Glancing around, she suddenly recalled the other two assailants and noticed them—motionless on the ice covered floor. Eric must have taken them out first, before coming after Pierre.

His eyes followed hers to the still forms. Snow had begun to settle over them.

At her questioning glance, he said, "They are merely unconscious. I told you I would protect you, Jasmine. You should know by now that I always keep my word."

CHAPTER 23

"Do you sense anything?"

They had secured the men with plastic hand ties that Eric had produced from the pocket of his jacket. The vampire had come prepared for everything.

"Yes, but it's not on this floor. It's higher." She glanced towards the stairs that led up to the top and grimaced. They were not something she was looking forward to.

Eric smiled. "It is merely three hundred more steps up to the second level, kitten."

Jasmine groaned, not sure she had really wanted to know. Just the thought of them had her legs aching.

Together they approached the stairs. The snow was swirling down harder now. It had thickened, whiting out anything else.

"Do you not find all this exhilarating?" His breath tickled her ear.

Biting at the plumpness of her lower lip, she shivered with awareness. "I wouldn't say that, no." She couldn't hide the huskiness in her voice.

A grin spread across his face and he moved forwards. "Come on, my lovely."

With boundless energy Eric, vanished up the rising stairwell, and with a sigh she followed.

Why the heck couldn't he carry her? It would have been a hell of a lot quicker. Maybe he was worried they would run into more trouble. It didn't make sense that Pierre had been here if there was a bomb. Would they really chance staying so close before it exploded? According to what Twitch said, it was supposed to be well hidden.

A sense of foreboding had crept up into the back of her skull. She could feel it thumping—slow and insistent like the ticking hands of a clock. Breath puffing against the crisp air, she swallowed down her dread. As she trudged onwards, her legs began throbbing with intensity. Her calves and thighs had begun a slow burn of exertion. Focusing on her breathing, she tried to move through the growing discomfort.

The higher she climbed, the more she got glimpses of the twinkling sight of Paris by night. The snow now was almost thick as soup, which kept most of the city hidden from view. Jasmine was thankful it was not the middle of the day. She was not sure how she would have felt with the height if she could see it more clearly. She knew she had to keep moving to keep her momentum going. If she stopped her jello legs would probably fail. Stopping now was not an option.

Jasmine's senses started to tingle with something new. Eric's familiar power was emanating from above, yet she could feel something else, too. It was another energy, which felt slightly different to his.

Her legs were on fire by the time she reached the second level. This seemed to be split into two sections. She could make out what looked like darkened shops. The whole place looked like more of a viewing area.

The sound of scuffling distracted her momentarily from her physical anguish. Blinking, she saw movement through the hard driven flurry of snow.

Eric was grappling with a bald man. Arms locked together above their heads, they were both fighting for dominance. She could see them straining together in vicious combat.

Sixth sense on full alert, it told her he was another vampire. That was why she had felt the difference, she realised. Their energy was slightly different. She was sure it had something to do with Eric being a vampiria, a born vampire.

Jasmine stood still, not quite sure what she should do. She glanced towards the darkened, empty shops. Should she help or carry on up to the last part of the tower? Time was ticking down. Maybe if she found the bomb first, it would save some minutes.

When the vampires pushed apart, they both bared their fangs. They were like feral things—hissing and snarling as they snapped their teeth together.

The bald man slid a hand from beneath his puffy jacket. Metal caught and glinted in the light. A knife. In the next instant, Eric had withdrawn his daggers from their hiding place in his jacket.

Mesmerised, Jasmine watched as they circled each other in the open space. Snow was pelting them in a vortex of swirling silvery-white.

The man's knife lunged out. The movement was so quick it was a blur to her eyes. Eric was faster. Dodging to the left, he avoided the blow. With a sweep of his arm, he thrust with a dagger. A hiss left the other vampire's lips. A long gash gaped open his puffy jacket.

Eric's mouth curved in a cold, merciless smile. It looked like he was enjoying himself. Enraged, the bald male charged forwards. They slammed sideways together, hitting the protective fencing with an incredible force. It shuddered, vibrating dangerously with the force of the blow. The vampires didn't seem to notice.

Slowly, Jasmine edged forwards. She had already decided she needed to find the next set of stairs up. When her scalp tingled perceiving a werewolf, she stopped. It prickled against her sixth sense. The breath she had been holding escaped her through the clench of her teeth.

Fuck. This was trouble.

A low, warning growl rumbled behind her. Every single hair on her body rose at the spine-chilling sound. She swung round swiftly and saw a man just below her. She recognised him instantly:

the werewolf from the boat. He was wearing jeans and a forest green polo neck. Wolves didn't feel the cold the same way humans did. They generated their own heat, which not even winter could suck away.

From the light of recognition in his look, he had remembered her, too. An evil grin spread over his rugged features. His eyes flashed yellow. She sensed his beast lurking just beneath the surface of his skin. Savage, ferocious, and straining for release.

Suddenly her aching legs were forgotten. Never taking her eyes of the male, she backed up nervously. She continued to go backwards, shaking slightly as the wolf moved forwards.

Peeling back his lips, he growled again low in his throat. The teeth he flashed were pointed and becoming sharper by the second.

"Fuck." Jasmine sent a panicked look towards the vampires.

They were still in a deadly dance. Blows were being traded with speed and grace. The metal of their blades gleamed like silver in the illuminations of the tower. Eric was too busy to help. She wasn't even sure if he was aware of the werewolf. This was the one he hadn't been able to sense before.

She had only one option. Turning, she dashed away down the long walkway. The snow hugged the uncovered ground and she tried not to slip.

The thud of footsteps followed. She didn't know where the hell she was going. Escape and hide. Those were what her instincts were screaming. If Eric could finish the other vamp quickly, he would soon come to her rescue.

Heart pounding in her chest, she could feel adrenaline kicking in. Skidding on the slippery surface, she smacked into the safety fencing at the end of the causeway. The hard mesh dug into her back. Fingers clinging to it for a moment, she caught sight of Paris once again.

Breathing hard, she immediately sprang to her left. The sound of ripping and rendering metal filled the air. Jasmine's head snapped back to look. The fearsome claws that now tipped the guy's hands had sliced through the metal mesh like butter.

Eyes large and round, she swallowed hard. He was so close she didn't have time to run.

Grabbing her arm, his claws bit into her bicep. A shriek left her lips. It had more to do with surprise than the slicing pain in her flesh. Without hesitation, Jasmine wrenched the knife from its sheath on her hip. She jammed it into the werewolf's side and pushed it in with all her might.

Shock widened his pitiless eyes. "You fucking bitch."

Shoving her sideways, he clawed at the knife. It was bedded deep, right to the hilt. A darkening stain had begun to spread through the material of his polo shirt.

Jasmine stumbled to her hands and knees. The snow was cold and stinging as it pressed into her bare, open palms. Its rawness seeped into her unprotected skin. She winced.

The dagger suddenly skidded across the floor. The movement registered in the corner of her eye.

Shifter magic rippled frenziedly over her and she knew he was about to change. The sound of clothes ripping filled the air. She didn't want to watch. Fergus, the wolf she worked with, had once shown her, so she knew it took only a handful of seconds to achieve.

A deep and menacing growl sounded right next to her head, sending a vibration through her body. Her eyes slid sideways. It was the only part of her she dared to move.

The beast was huge and scary as hell. She had seen Fergus in his fur before, but it was nothing like this. This werewolf had messy, sandy-coloured fur. The body was long, muscled and sinewy—and three times bigger than a timber wolf. The longest black curved claws she had ever seen tipped his paws. Snout long and lean, it bared rows of sharp, pointed teeth, which glistened with strings of saliva. When it snarled, it's lips peeled back, revealing even more terrifying teeth.

She could barely get her lungs to function. Her heart froze and her stomach turned to ice. The wolf held her immobilized, her mind blank of all else.

The beast stuck it's snout in her hair. She could feel its hot breath scorching the back of her neck. It inhaled deeply, as if drawing in her fear, tasting it, on it's now lulling tongue. Its teeth were so close to her vulnerable flesh.

Adrenaline was doing double time blazing through her veins. Preservation slapped her in the face the moment one massive paw was raised. Dodging to the left away, she avoided his blow by inches. Her sudden movement seemed to have taken him by surprise. Clambering to her feet, Jasmine fled. A snarl echoed from behind and she knew he was loping after her.

His hunting instincts were probably now in place. He had her scent, too. There would be no giving up. The only thing she could do now was put something between them. If he couldn't get to her, he wouldn't be able to tear her apart.

A disturbance in the air warned her when to move. Leaping out the way, she dodged the werewolf, who hit the fencing instead of its intended target, her back. She heard the barrier shudder with the force of the blow.

Sucking in frigid cold breaths, she dashed blindly forwards until she hit a wall that didn't seem to be there. She suddenly found herself standing on a glass viewing platform. Her hand was pressed flat against the glass partition. Beneath her was darkness, snow, and the twinkling lights from below. Vertigo hit her hard.

Propelling herself sideways, she headed inwards towards shelter. Taking a chance, she glanced over her shoulder. The beast was nowhere to be seen.

Breathing hard, her eyes whipped around her surroundings. A souvenir shop, locked up tight, lay in darkness. Unless she had something to get the door open, that was a no-go. She could see more walkways, a telescope bolted to the floor.

Her eyes, though, fastened on something against the wall.

Jasmine grabbed hold of the fire extinguisher. It felt heavy but reassuring in her hands. She had never used one before but prayed it was easy. It was the only option as a weapon she had left.

Her knife was still out in the open where the wolf had thrown it. Going back out was too exposed. It was also what he could be waiting for her to do.

Hands shaking, she checked the cylinder over. Pulling the pin at the top, she knew it was primed and ready.

Prickles danced over her skull. She knew the wolf was getting closer. Trying not to hyperventilate, she tried to calm her mind. Inhale, exhale. Jasmine breathed, as Eric had taught her. The fear, which had crowded her mind, began to ebb as a sense of calmness washed over her.

The prickling sensation had increased. It tightened her skin almost painfully beneath the hair on her head. He was stalking her.

The clicking of claws on metal met her ears.

Flattening herself against the wall of the shop, she waited. She wasn't about to go meet it head-on. If she could catch it at a disadvantage, she would.

Continuing to breathe slow and even, she slid her finger to the lever. Aiming the nozzle she squeezed as the monstrous shape emerged around the corner.

A stream of white exploded outwards with blinding force, hissing all the way. A howl of pained shock left the werewolf's lips. Jasmine directed it right at its eyes. White billowed around them in thick, heavy clouds. It was choking, making her eyes water. Holding her breath, she tried not to breathe it in. She was barely able to see.

Keeping her hand jammed down, she let the wolf have it all. The foam spluttered to quickly an end. As the discharge cleared, everything became clear.

Yellow eyes burning with rage rose to hers. Saliva was gushing from its mouth, as if the foam had managed to work its way down its throat.

Fuck. It looked like she had just enraged it.

A hoarse growl emanated from its hairy muzzle.

Holding the spent fire extinguisher aloft, she threw it at its head but missed and bounced off one of its fur-covered shoulders.

The werewolf snarled, peeling back its lips so far she could see the pinkness of its gums.

Jasmine turned and ran. Her heart was once more thundering agonizingly behind her ribs. She needed to get her arse back to Eric.

She slipped on the snow, sliding back out onto the open walkway before she could stop herself. It took her a second to right herself. The next thing she knew, the werewolf was up on its hind legs towering over. Its hot stinking breath panted against her cold, pale face.

He had shifted from full wolf to the form in-between—a mix of man and wolf.

His clawed hand closed around her neck. Before she had time to make a strangled scream, Jasmine found herself airborne. The platform spun in front of her eyes. In horror, she realised she was going to hit the broken protective barrier.

A scream burst from her lips. Something hard painfully ripped into her shoulder. The broken links of the fence. The barrier did not hold but instead fell outwards. Then she was falling. With flailing arms, she tried to grab onto something solid. Her hands found nothing but empty air.

When her fingers did seize something, she clung for dear life. Panic was trying to swallow her alive. She knew if she looked down, it would only get worse. Jasmine realised, she was hanging from the broken fencing. It now lay flat, jutting out away from the platform. Her feet were dangling with nothing below but air.

The falling snow had turned into a white, swirling blizzard. Jasmine was blinded, unable to see anything further than her broken latticework she clung to.

She wasn't sure how long it would hold her weight. If she fell, it would mean certain death when she hit the ground below.

Her heart was beating manically against her ribs. The harsh sound of her own frantic panting breaths was loud in the silence that enveloped her. Nails trying to dig into the metal, Jasmine knew she was not strong enough to pull herself up. Pain was shooting up her limb already. Her arm felt like it was being wrenched from the socket. If she could get a better hold, she could support herself better.

The cold night was biting painfully into her fingers. Her leather jacket was little protection against the sharp winter wind. The snow was harsh and stinging. Taking deep breaths, she tried with desperation to pull herself up. When that did not work, she reached up to grip the broken fence with both hands. Her fingers grazed the cold metal as she strained up.

The fencing shook ominously. She was positive it was about to give out. Once it ripped free, it would all go down, her included.

Jasmine felt her hand slip. Fuck. She was going to fall. Die.

Heart thudding excruciatingly swiftly, it drowned out the deafening silence.

Her numb fingers slid free. With a cry of shock, she fell.

A hand flew out of nowhere and locked forcefully around her wrist. Grimacing in pain, she hissed.

Jasmine's eyes clashed with Eric's, where he hung above her. Blue eyes burnt unblinking into hers.

Pulling her up effortlessly, he placed her hand on his firm shoulder.

"Take a hold of my neck and climb onto my back." It was a clipped order, which she readily obeyed. "Do not look down."

Clutching at his leather jacket in a desperate grip, Jasmine hauled herself up and over him.

Like a baby spider monkey, she wrapped her legs around his hips. Her arms hugged his neck. Jasmine could feel the fencing shaking beneath their combined weight.

"I'm too heavy for you," she gasped anxiously against his ear. "It's going to break."

"You will never be too heavy. Now hold on tight," the vampire replied.

With surprising graceful ease, he began to scale upwards with swift speed, as if he had done this many times before.

"What happened to the vampire and the werewolf?"

"The vampire is dust. As for the werewolf, we will see how quickly he can heal from a snapped spine." Eric's words were low and grim. "What possessed you to think you could take on one such as he?"

Advancing over the outside of the fencing, they were soon back on the second platform.

Jasmine slid carefully from Eric's back. "You were busy and he wouldn't take no for an answer." Her voice was wary and she could tell he was angry.

Her legs were shaking badly, but she managed to stay standing.

Turning instantly, his gaze raced over her. One big hand gently cupped the side of her face. Jasmine felt herself melt into the warmth. She wanted nothing more than to curl up into it and rest her aching body.

Reaching out a hand, she braced herself against the vampire's firm chest. She felt the muscles beneath bunch.

"Are you hurt?" The concern in his voice warmed her.

"Just sore and bruised. I think the metal gouged my back. That might be bleeding." Jasmine moved her shoulders then winced. "We still have to go higher though."

She could feel the buzz of Twitch's magic getting stronger. She could sense she was right below the bomb now.

"I indeed do smell your blood," Eric informed her gravely.

Cradling her head in his hands, he angled his mouth over hers. It was a gentle kiss that made her knees go weak. He nibbled delicately at her lips, sipping at her in a strange, heady way that made her ache.

Her stomach clenched and her pulse skittered. If she was not careful she was going to fall for this vamp. The problem was she felt like she was halfway there already.

His breath whispered against her mouth as he ended the kiss. With one gentle caress, he pulled his hands away.

Eric's breath had stilled in his lungs the moment he had seen Jasmine go flying. The sound of her panicked, terrified heart had filled his ears like a death toll. That she lived was a miracle. Yet again this little mortal had cheated death.

The pain of believing he had lost her had been unbearable. It was also something he could not explain. He barely knew her. Yet somehow she was now important to him.

Here she stood before him. Her large, jade green eyes, stared up at him with barely disguised discomfort. Snowflakes had settled in her short, coppery hair. Jasmine's face was pale, apart from her rosy cheeks, her lips slightly blue-tinged.

She had never looked as beautiful as she did right now.

The sight of her watching him feed earlier had been more potent than any aphrodisiac. The scent of her arousal and excitement had been headier than any expensive perfume. His body's response had been painfully instantaneous. His erection even now had only half abated. The thickness in his pants pressed uncomfortably against his zipper.

Jasmine had stared into his darkness. She had seen him for who he really was, what he really was. He had shown her something no other mortal had borne witness to. And she had, apparently, liked what she had seen. There had been no fear, only an innocent lust. His desire, his need for her had almost incinerated him on the spot.

Taking on the werewolf had been foolish of her but also incredibly brave. Eric could not resist giving her one last kiss. Leaning down he planted a hard, quick one on her lips. He bestowed it for luck.

CHAPTER 24

ERIC'S KISSES WERE SHORT and sweet. After a near death experience, she had expected a little more. They had no time though.

"Let us continue," he said inches from her lips.

Jasmine let out a soft groan. What she wanted to do was lie down. She was not sure she could face more stairs.

Eric seemed to read her mind. An amused smile curved his sensual mouth. "We take the lift from here."

As she looked around for the lift, she caught a glimpse of the wolf. His upper half was jutting out at a weird angle, half-hidden by the inside area. Blood covered his naked pale chest. She couldn't see his face as his head was pointed away from her. He was deathly still. It looked like Eric had done more than snap his spine.

The vampire stepped in front of her, blocking her view. "Come, Jasmine. We do not have time to waste."

Searching his suddenly remote expression, she nodded. It didn't look like he wanted to talk about what he had done. She also knew he was right. They had already wasted enough time getting all the way up here.

Following when he moved, she soon found herself in a tiny glass elevator. Unease uncoiled inside her. The sense of foreboding she had felt earlier was still pounding dully away in her head.

The vampire hit a button and the lift began to climb.

Jasmine pressed herself into one corner. This way she felt supported and less likely to fold into a heap on the floor. Adrenaline was still going strong, but she didn't know how long that was going to last. She hoped it was a little longer. Once it ran out, she would feel every ache and pain her body had endured. She was not looking forwards to it. Right now she needed to keep strong.

With no warning, the lift surged upwards with a burst of sudden speed. Gasping, Jasmine's wide eyes flew to Eric's.

"That is completely normal, kitten," he assured her with a tight smile. His glance was bouncing nervously around the small space, as he tried to hide his claustrophobia.

The vampire had left some space between them. She assumed he had done it in case they encountered anyone at the top. Spread out they were two targets rather than one large one standing together.

"How long have we got left?"

He glanced at his watch. "Fifteen minutes precisely."

She shifted nervously from foot to foot. Fifteen minutes to find the bomb and disarm it. Was that even possible? Releasing a long, stressed-filled sigh, she swallowed down her panic. They had to do this.

"Here," Eric said as he pressed the handle of one of daggers into her hand. He had pulled it, complete with its sheath, from the lining of his jacket.

Jasmine's fingers closed around the hilt. It still held his warmth. A little jolt of electricity shot up her arm at the contact. Her toes curled in her trainers. The beat of her heart thumped erratically for a moment.

"Thanks." She sank her teeth into the edge of her lower lip.

When she looked up, he was staring at her mouth. The pupils of his eyes dilated as his nostrils flared slightly. A second passed before he tore his gaze away.

Maybe it was all the adrenaline and the situation, but Jasmine felt extremely turned on. Her body was practically vibrating from the vampire's nearness. She fought down her arousal. They both needed to stay focused and clear-minded.

Fiddling with the dagger, she managed to clip the sheath to her jeans. Her hands were shaking and not all of it was to do with the cold.

The lift was still moving, taking them to the highest accessible point of the entire tower. It felt like forever before the door opened. In fact they had only been in the cramped space for a matter of minutes.

They found themselves in another covered level. It contained windows with maps and various information above each viewing area.

Jasmine didn't bother to look. A sense of urgency was now crawling through her. They searched around but came up short. Neither of them found any sign of a device of any kind.

Frustration was etched on Eric's face. "There is nothing here."

Jasmine watched as he shoved his hand through his tousled hair. It left it messy, in a just-been-fucked kind of way. She wet her dry lips with the tip of her tongue.

"I hate to say this," Jasmine said, "but everything inside me is screaming to go higher." Her eyes danced around the space. Twitch's magic was stronger now. She could practically taste it on the cold wind calling her upwards.

"Are you sure?"

Lifting her chin, she met his cold, blue gaze head on. "Yes."

He nodded, not saying a word. The fact that he trusted her abilities left a warm glow inside. She just hoped they weren't about to fail her now.

Eric guided her to a narrow staircase. He neither hesitated nor faltered. The vampire seemed to know exactly where he was going.

Jasmine kept her eyes on his back. She was more than happy to let him lead the way.

"This will be the highest point. If nothing is up here, we will need to search again," he told her over his shoulder.

Their footsteps echoed on the metal steps as they ascended. Ten minutes left to find the device. They both knew they didn't have the time. Jasmine knew she was right, though.

As they stepped out onto the open area, the wind began to buffet them. Jasmine swore. She thought she felt the entire structure sway beneath her feet. It was disorientating and unnerving.

The snowstorm had eased, so there was just a light flurry now. She could see the city more clearly through the latticework. Paris stretched out before them in an unparalleled view. The dizzying height made her catch her breath.

Eric's eye's rested on the champagne bar, which was closed up tight.

"What a pity," he mumbled. "We could have toasted your first time here."

Jasmine eyed the place longingly. "I could have done with a bottle right about now. With a nice, hot bath. I don't think I am ever going to feel warm again."

Everything felt numb. The tip of her nose was hurting with the raw bite of the cold air. Her lips felt chapped and her teeth had even began to chatter.

The vampire's eyes warmed as he regarded her. "Perhaps I shall buy you one when we are done here."

Jasmine felt her lips twitch. He spoke so casually—as if they were simply strolling around the place—when the reality was they were risking their lives to diffuse a bomb, which was meant to go off in a matter of minutes.

They moved further along. This level was much smaller than the rest. It wouldn't take them long to search.

Through the slower flurry of snow, she spotted movement. A figure stood huddled by the protective fencing in one corner. He was shivering even with the thick layers of an expensive-looking coat. Marcel.

The fat man eyed them. From the look on his face, he had been expecting their arrival. Jasmine's eyes fell to the gun in his hand pointed downwards. Following its trajectory with her eyes, she felt fear race through her when she saw its target.

Jasmine recognized Twitch's tall, slim form lying prone covered in snow. His eyes were closed. Cinnamon curls a mess around his head. Wrists bound behind his back.

"Twitch!"

She went to move forwards, but Eric's hand on her arm restrained her. He squeezed it gently in warning. Pushing down her panic, she stilled. She had to keep her head. If she did something stupid, she could get herself or her friend killed.

"Don't move," Marcel barked. "If you open your mouth, vampiria, I will shoot the mage. So don't even think to try any of your persuasion on me."

Marcel had said vampiria, not vampire. Jasmine felt Eric stiffen beside her in anger. Confusion crashed through her. She had gotten the distinct impression that this had to have been a secret.

"How do you know what Eric is?" she blurted out. It looked like she was going to have to do all the talking again.

"Dasyurus knows you've been looking for him." Marcel's beady eyes never left Eric's. "He was the one who told me what you are. You thought you were clever, didn't you? My partner is a genius. You can't compare to him."

"Where's Claude?" She couldn't help but ask the question. The guy should never have been mixed up in this mess. She just wanted to send him home.

"Claude thought I would forgive him." Marcel shook his head in disbelief. "Once he told me he was feeding you information, I had to get rid of him."

Shock reverberated around inside her though she tried to keep the emotion from her face. "What did you do with him? Where is he?"

"I sold him."

"You what?"

Marcel giggled. "It is what I do with all my discarded lovers. Don't worry, he won't last long."

At that moment, Twitch decided to moan and move slightly. It looked like he was coming around.

Marcel kept his gun trained on his captive. A strange manic glint was in his frog-like eyes. "Once this goes off and releases the toxin into the air, every shape-shifter within a hundred miles will lose control and revert to their beastly side for twenty-four hours."

She was still reeling from what he had done to Claude. It took the pressure of Eric's fingers on her arm to remember to keep talking.

"The world doesn't know about them."

A grin spread across the fat man's face. His eyes bounced to something on the latticework to the left of him.

"No, not yet, but it will. We will bring them howling into the spotlight."

Jasmine followed his eyes. A black box was attached to the fencing. Twitch's spell was spiralling off it in subtle waves. There seemed to be different coloured wiring coming out from one side and a digital screen was counting down the minutes.

She refrained from staring at how long they had left. More stress was something she didn't need right now.

"Just because they shift doesn't mean they're going to attack anyone. They can pretend it's a city-wide prank, not even real. That kind of shit is being done all the time and it looks realistic," Twitch mumbled.

He was still lying in the snow, but he raised his head. Annoyance was fluttering over his face. She could see him struggling with his tied hands.

"What's the point of all this? Most shifters live peacefully," Jasmine said. If she could keep his attention on her, maybe the mage could get free.

Marcel looked almost gleeful. "Not once the toxin gets in their system. They will go on a rampage. It's designed to keep them aggressive."

Feeling a little brave, she took a step closer. "I still don't see the point of this. You're just going to expose the world to something it's not ready for."

The snow had come to a stop. Even the wind had dropped now, too. The frigid air was stone still around them.

"Imagine my sales after this comes out!" The fat man waggled the gun in his hand from left to right. "People will want to protect themselves against the monsters. Weapons will be created just to destroy them. My business will boom."

Jasmine tried not to cringe at his use of that word. If they weren't careful there was going to be one quite literally.

"So it's all about money?" She was just trying to kill time now, waiting for the vampire to come up with a plan. He was going to have to hurry. She had a feeling he was fishing for more information, though.

"Of course it is, you stupid little bitch. What else would it be?" Marcel sneered. Swinging the gun around, he aimed it at her chest.

Eyes wide, she froze. A faint blue, eerie glow had started to pulse around Eric. Jasmine could see it from the corner of her eye. His hand dropped away from her arm, as he took a step away. She could see it growing stronger by the minute. Even through the numbing coldness of the night, she felt the brush of his power–practically glacial at this point. The kind of cold that cut you bone deep.

She shivered.

Would Marcel notice? No one else seemed to be aware the vampire was glowing. Jasmine was certain that her heightened senses allowed her to see it. She knew she needed to keep Marcel talking. Licking her chapped, dry lips, she kept her eyes on the gun. One squeeze of the trigger and she would be dead.

"I didn't think you would be stupid enough to be up here when it explodes."

"Explodes?" He giggled again like an excited school girl. "Who told you that?"

"That was me." Twitch replied in a tetchy purr. He had given up his battle with the rope that tied his hands. Now he kept blowing away the tumble of hair falling across his eyes.

"I thought you were supposed to be clever." Marcel slammed his foot into the mage's side. "The toxin will be released safely into the air. It won't explode."

Twitch groaned but kept right on talking. "That's not what's going to happen. It *is* going to explode."

"Shut up." The fat man kicked him harder this time. A whimper left the mage's lips.

"I would listen to Twitch. He knows what he's talking about," Jasmine snapped anxiously. She didn't like seeing her friend in pain. If he carried on, he was going to end up getting himself shot.

But Twitch wasn't done. Stubbornly he raised his chin and looked the arms dealer right in the eye. "The bits of instructions I was sent by your partner added up to a detonation device. Even lying down here, I recognise what it is. I can also feel it."

Marcel's eyes leapt nervously to the bomb. "You're lying."

"Dasyurus has deceived you." Jasmine edged closer. She was itching to get to Twitch. If she could free his bonds, he could help.

"Silence!" The fat man caught her movement. Raising the gun he had slightly lowered, he once more aimed at her chest.

Jasmine stilled. What the fuck was Eric waiting for? An invitation? She daren't glance back at him. One mistake and she was sure Marcel was going to shoot her. His movements were jerky. A slither of doubt was in his eyes now.

"Seriously, I am not making this shit up," Twitch said impatiently. He was eyeing the bomb now, still blowing the annoying piece of air out of his face.

"Why are you up here in the first place then?" Jasmine asked, bringing Marcel's attention back to her. She arched her eyebrows questioningly.

"Dasyurus knew you would probably try to stop us. That's why I had Pierre and the others on the other levels, but it seems you got past them."

"And he suggested you should do that? Wait up here alone with Twitch?" she persisted.

She recognized the moment the fat man decided to shoot her. Hardness appeared in his beady eyes and his lips flattened.

In that same split second Eric's icy power lashed out. A bitter wind picked up so fast it was blinding. She could sense the vampire's influence in the very air molecules.

Scrunching her stinging eyes shut, she lunged for Twitch. It was clumsy, but she knew she was headed in the right direction.

She landed on his back with an oomph.

A string of swear words was issued from below her. His messy hair brushed against her face. She buried her frostbitten cheek into the hollow of his shoulder, trying to escape the howling wind. The settled snow was swirling around them like a blizzard. Harsh and biting, it whipped around them.

The crack of a gun shot went off. In alarm, Jasmine unthinkingly raised her head. Had Eric been shot?

A hand suddenly clenched her short red hair. Gasping in pain, she was wrenched backwards. Stumbling, she found herself dragged to her feet. As she lifted her hands to grab the arm above her head she felt the barrel of a gun press the base of her neck. Releasing a breath, she lowered her arms.

The wind dropped just as quickly as it had started. Eric was standing two arms' lengths away from them. His face was focused with a cold intent. The blue iciness of his eyes was chilling.

"Back off, vamp, or I put a hole in her pretty little head." Marcel's words were chattered through his teeth.

Jasmine couldn't see him but was pretty sure he had taken the brunt of the vampire's frozen attack. She was certain Eric had not even used his full force. He had most likely done it in the fear of hurting her or Twitch.

Eric's eyes locked with hers. No reaction showed on his face. Something shifted through in his eyes–a quick, imperceptible movement of an unidentified emotion, but she caught it nonetheless.

"For fuck's sake, let her go, Marcel!" Twitch shouted from the floor. "We are all going to get blown up if we don't stop the bomb now."

Jasmine's hand, which was down by her side, reached slowly for the dagger at her hip. If she could take Marcel out, she would. If he shot her, then she was taken out of the equation and the vampire wouldn't hesitate.

Gaze never wavering from Eric's, her fingers closed around the hilt. It pressed reassuringly into the palm of her hand. Now or never.

"Shut up!" the fat man screamed hoarsely down at the mage. Panic was coursing off him in thick waves. He was freaking out.

In one fast, fluid motion, she yanked the dagger from its sheath. Gritting her teeth, Jasmine plunged it behind her back. The blade was so sharp it sliced through flesh without resistance. She thrust it deep.

Marcel was screaming. It was a high-pitched sound, almost ear-shattering. Instead of letting her go, his hand tightened in her hair. He clutched so hard, her scalp became agonizingly painful.

Tears of pain filled her eyes. A wail left her lips as she clawed at his wrist.

The next thing Jasmine knew she was on her knees. No longer was his hand gripping her head. The gun was in her face instead.

Skin almost white as the snow around them, the fat man snarled down at her. The dagger was still embedded in his side. Blood was staining his coat and the hand he had pressed near the wound was soaked in his own blood.

Jasmine's heart turned to ice. This was it. She was taking her last fucking breath in the world.

Everything seemed to be happening in slow-motion. Marcel's finger on the trigger of his gun tensed. His blue-tinged lips curled up over his gums in an evil sneer.

The air around them was suddenly drenched with Eric's power. One moment the fat man was about to shoot; the next the vampire's other dagger was buried in his chest. A direct hit. Straight to the heart.

A shocked gurgle leaked from Marcel's lips. Eyes bulging, he peered down in confusion at the protruding weapon for a second. Then his eyes lost their light and he crumpled sideways.

"Jasmine, are you alright?"

Eric's deep, concerned voice penetrated her daze. She was shaking from both the cold and the turn of events.

"Yes," she said rather calmly in light of what was happening. "It took you fucking long enough to jump in!"

She grasped the hand he offered her. His fingers gave a reassuring squeeze as he helped her up. He did not seem bothered by her harsh tone.

"You were doing admirably well, my dear. I had no wish to interfere," Eric explained. A hint of a smile touched his lips.

"If you two have a moment could you untie my hands?" Twitch's purring voice interrupted them. "I can't use my magic without them and I really think we are going to need it before the shit hits the fan."

He was peering up at them through a tumble of knotted cinnamon curls. Lips pursed in annoyance, peridot green eyes narrowed. Cold, wet flakes of snow were plastered all over him.

Jasmine fell to her knees again. Her numb fingers, feeling like fat, frozen sausages, fumbled with the knots of his bonds.

"Fuck, my fingers are frozen. I can't do it."

Eric pushed her hands away as he knelt beside her. Skilfully he undid the knots.

She glanced at the device on the latticework. The numbers on the digit screen were still moving backwards. Just the sight of the red changing numbers made her catch her breath as she willed herself not to hyperventilate. They were cutting this close.

"The bomb is still counting down," Jasmine muttered, biting hard on her lower lip, her teeth clamping down until it was stingingly painful.

They each grabbed one of the mage's arms and tugged him to his feet. Twitch grimaced, moaning in pain, as the blood once more flowed into his limbs. Shoving the messy hair from his face, he took a look at the bomb.

"Can you disarm it?" the vampire asked. No sign of anxiety on his face, he actually seemed calm and detached.

"Yes, I think so," Twitch replied, brushing clumps of snow from his hair and face.

"You *think* so?" Jasmine's voice suddenly sounded unnaturally high.

Twitch limped up to the fencing. Tipping his head to the side, he studied the black box carefully. "Remember I haven't seen the whole thing together. Give me a fucking minute."

"I do not think we have one," Eric said under his breath.

The mage carefully placed his hands on the device. His eyes skimmed the collection of coloured wiring that was visible. He clucked his tongue and frowned.

Jasmine didn't have a clue if this was good or bad. She was nibbling on her nails at this point. If Twitch couldn't disarm it, what the fuck were they going to do?

Her eyes fastened on the display. The minutes had already slipped away. They were almost down to seconds.

Magic danced over Twitch's skin like little electrical sparks. His lips were moving soundlessly with the spells he cast. It tickled her numb flesh, playing against her senses.

The counter, though, continued to tick, which she felt the need to tell him.

"Twitch, it's still counting down!" Panic filled her voice.

Eric's arm's whipped around her. Drawing her backwards, he held her close. She could feel him caging her protectively with his big, hard body.

"I KNOW!" Twitch snapped.

Hands flitting above the wires, he began to call on his magic again. This time, it leapt and crackled around him. Raw power was sparking off his skin, his hair, flashing like streaks of tiny lightning from his fingertips. The air felt charged with static electricity and raised every hair on their bodies.

"Twenty seconds to go," Eric said.

Jasmine found herself whirled around. The vampire's hand was on the back of her head. Forcefully yet gently, he pushed her face into his chest, as if he wanted to shield her from what was to come.

"TWITCH!" Jasmine's yell was muffled. Clinging to Eric, she kept her face buried against him. His arms bound her tightly to him. Her own held on to him just as tightly.

"10, 9, 8, 7 . . . " The vampire's voice was soft, calm and measured. "6, 5, 4, 3, 2 . . . "

Jasmine braced herself for the blast. Suddenly she regretted not getting to sleep with Eric. Wished she'd had more time in the job. Told friends how much they meant to her.

A whirr, sounded, then a click.

Nothing happened.

Jasmine peeked up from Eric's chest. The tower had been plunged into darkness. Then abruptly the illumination lights began to pulse and dance around them rhythmically.

Jasmine flinched.

Eric's deep, rumbling laughed rolled over her. "It is merely the light display Jasmine. It happens upon each hour for five minutes."

She let her shoulders sag with relief. "Fuck, Twitch, you didn't have to cut it that close."

The techno mage sent her a relieved grin. "There was nothing really to worry about. I had it all under control."

A squeak left his lips when she grabbed him by the arm and dragged him towards them. They found themselves in a three-way embrace. Jasmine squeezed them both tight.

They were alive. She couldn't keep the big stupid grin off her frozen face. Here they were standing in the freezing cold, in the snow, and it was the best fucking night of her life.

The two males stood awkwardly as she hugged them together.

"Eric, this is Twitch, my best friend. Twitch, this is Eric the vamp I mentioned." Jasmine beamed up at them both.

Meeting each other's eyes they nodded, neither saying a word.

Eric abruptly cleared his throat. "We should remove the bomb and the toxin."

"I can get the bomb down to the ground," Twitch said quickly, embarrassment colouring the tone of his voice. "But the toxin, I don't have a clue what to do with."

The vampire was first to move out of the hug. "Raoul, my associate, will deal with it once we are there."

Twitch didn't move. Instead he crushed Jasmine against him for a moment, his eyes alight with caring and relief.

"It's good to see you, Jazzy."

Jasmine hugged him back. "It's good to see you too, Twitchy, but I need you to do me a favour when we get home."

Eyes widening slightly, a small wary smile tilted his mouth. "What's that?"

Grabbing a handful of his long knotted curls, she tugged. "Get your fucking hair cut."

A raspy laugh left Twitch's lips. "Anything for you, Jazzy."

Stepping back out of his embrace, she leaned back against the fencing. "I am taking the lift all the way fucking down. You can forget the stairs."

Her energy levels were starting to crash. Already she could feel the adrenaline, which had kept her going draining away. The shakes had started in, moving through her body. If they were walking, someone was going to have to carry her. No way was she taking another step.

"You took the stairs the whole way up?" Twitch looked horrified as he moved towards the diffused bomb, which was still attached to the latticework. He began to detach it carefully.

"She did indeed," Eric replied smoothly. "And also fought a werewolf."

Eyes huge, Twitch glanced at her over his shoulder. "I always thought you were a little crazy."

Jasmine pulled a face. "Thanks. I think."

CHAPTER 25

WHEN THEY ARRIVED to the bottom of the Eiffel Tower, the French police wanted to know what had happened. Eric used a little of his persuasion to bend the truth. As far as the authorities knew, Marcel Coupe had set a bomb up there. Eric and Raoul erased any evidence of the supernatural, and, of course, the toxin was never mentioned.

Twitch, the story went, had to help take down the device and dispose of it. The vampires had both agreed this was safer rather than let the human bomb disposal unit tackle it.

Just as Eric had said, Raoul took the toxin. It was now safely out of human hands, but Jasmine had no idea what he had done with it.

Jasmine's energy had already been more than lagging by that point. The adrenaline rush had crashed hard, leaving her feeling achy, exhausted, and nauseated.

By the time they got into the suite sometime after three a.m., Jasmine was barely awake. She had vague memories of curling up fully clothed on the bed, but the next time she opened her eyes, she was naked under the covers. Eric was asleep beside her, naked as well, lying on his side. One of his hands was draped possessively across her stomach. As carefully as she could, she lifted his arm and wiggled out of the bed.

Now she lay relaxing in a hot bath full of fragrant bubbles. The aroma of lang lang and patchouli drifted in the moist air. The moment her body had hit the hot, soothing water it had washed away most of the aches. There were places, though, that still might need a few days in bed.

She was happy. Twitch was safe, but she really did not want him interrupting her relaxation. Knowing him, he would want to chat. Jasmine just wanted a few minutes of peace. She tipped her head to the side and stuck her finger in her ear. The moment her fingertip touched the magical ear piece, she heard a pop. The pink, gum-like substance fell discarded into her palm. It fizzed quietly as the magic burnt out. It was useless now. Once these things were out, they could never be reused.

Taking aim, she tossed it into the little wire bin under the sink. Jasmine smiled when it hit its target, making a satisfying ping against the metal. She released a long, relaxed sigh. Her head rested on the rim of the bathtub. Lying back, she closed her eyes and let the heat soak away the stress from her body.

Bruises marred her wrist where Eric had grabbed her. Where her shoulder had hit the fencing, a monster bruise had already started to form. Gashes marked her skin, but they had healed so well she suspected Eric had used drops of his blood to help them along. She was just glad to be alive. Three near-death experiences were her limit for one night.

Eric had rented Twitch his own room in the hotel. The vampire had insisted on paying for it and any room service Twitch might want. Obviously the vamp didn't know what he had let himself in for.

The mage had been more than happy about this. She had no doubt in her mind that Twitch was enjoying the free Wi-Fi and satellite TV. He also had a sweet tooth a mile wide and was probably indulging it with a vengeance. Eric would have a heart attack at the bill.

Raoul was still out consulting with the French police. They had raided Marcel's offices and rounded up a lot of his people.

Doctor Dasyurus was still a faceless ghost. According to the arms dealer's henchmen, Marcel was the only person who had ever spoken to and seen the Doctor—and it was hard to get answers when Marcel was dead.

They still had no word on Claude, Marcel's ex-lover. No one seemed to know what had happened to him. Jasmine felt a pang of regret. She had wanted to help him. He had been an innocent mixed up in this mess. The guy had only wanted to go home.

Awareness washed over her and sent a delightful rush over her wet skin. Suddenly she felt like she was being watched. Opening her eyes, she found she was no longer alone.

Eric stood in the doorway. A pair of jeans covered his long, thick legs, and his muscled chest was bare. He was leaning against the door, eyes watching her with a familiar, hungry, dark look. He held two flutes filled with a pale liquid.

"Merry Christmas." Sauntering forwards, he extended one glass towards her. "Dom Pèrignon. Champagne for my lady."

Jasmine realised then he was right. It was Christmas day and she had slept almost all the way through it. Oddly she didn't feel uncomfortable laying naked in the bath with Eric watching her. She took the offered glass and raised it to her lips. It was cold. The bubbles danced on her tongue and down her throat.

"Good?" He propped himself against the sink, seeming content just to watch her.

Heart doing a little flutter, Jasmine smiled. "It's very good, thank you."

"I thought it was appropriate for this evening." He lifted his own glass and took a sip. "I did promise you a drink back on the Eiffel Tower after all."

His cerulean blue eyes wandered lower to where her breasts were hidden by a fragrant mound of bubbles and sharpened with intensity. Seconds ticked by and still he remained staring at her concealed chest.

Jasmine licked her dry lips. The taste of the champagne lingered on their plumpness. He had seen her naked before, but this time it was different. She wasn't unconscious or hurt. This time she was fully aware of her nakedness.

The fragrant air grew sultry. An undercurrent of expectation seemed to hover between them. Did he intend to stand there all night or was he just waiting for all the bubbles to pop? Suddenly she was glad that she had used a generous amount of the expensive bubble bath. All Eric could see of her were shoulders, neck, and face.

An enticing, teasing smile danced across her lips. Taking another sip, she watched him over the rim of her glass. Jasmine didn't have a clue how to seduce a man. She was willing to give it a try, though.

Eric watched the siren's smile that touched her lips. It was beguiling. She looked like a mermaid in her sea of delicate, white bubbles. He was quite tempted to join her in the tub, which would accommodate two bodies perfectly.

Just the thought of their slick, wet skin sliding together had him painfully aroused. This seemed to be his permanent state around this little female. The water did look inviting. Unfortunately it was not what he had planned for this evening.

Reining in his thoughts from wet, bare flesh, he took a sip of champagne. Anticipation was buzzing through him like a drug. Just fucking her was something he was unwilling to do. This needed to be special for Jasmine and he intended to ensure this.

Tonight there would be no interruptions.

"I have taken the liberty of ordering dinner." Eric's deep baritone had a silky quality to it.

Jasmine frowned. "I thought we were going to eat with Twitch."

She had a vague memory of agreeing to have dinner with her friend. Everything was a little jumbled, though, after getting down from the tower. She had been dead on her feet.

"Tonight I thought we could spend together. It is, after all, your last night in Paris before you go home," he explained softly. "I acquired you and Twitch first-class tickets on the Eurostar. You will be going back to London tomorrow afternoon." He paused for a moment, his eyes caressing over her. "Twitch has told me he is content to amuse himself online this evening."

Had the vampire bribed the mage somehow? She tried to keep her expression neutral, but it was hard to keep the thrill from her face.

"If he's really OK with that," she said and took another sip of her drink.

"He is indeed."

Jasmine shifted her legs restlessly beneath the water. They slid deliciously together. She felt her nipples hardening. Excitement uncurled inside her. They both knew they had unfinished business between them. Something she knew that could no longer wait.

A knowing smile curved Eric's lips. "How are you feeling?"

"Feeling?" Her eyes widened slightly in surprise.

Did he know how excited she was already? That her body was practically sizzling from just his presence? She began to nibble nervously at the edge of her lower lip.

Eric watched, his eyes darkening slightly. "In just over twenty-four hours, you have almost frozen to death. You have been attacked twice, once by a particularly nasty werewolf. You have also walked the entire steps of the Eiffel Tower before dangling precariously off of said structure." Amusement was etched over his handsome features. "I thought such an experience for a mortal would be a little . . . tiring."

"Well, I have aches in a few places, if that's what you mean," she told him with a laugh.

Tingles that had nothing to do with the hot water had begun to shiver over her skin. A small sense of anticipation had started to grow.

After placing his glass on the sink, Eric turned to open a cupboard. She watched his broad back as he searched for something.

"Not too tired for dinner with me tonight then, I hope?"

"I want to have dinner with you, Eric," she replied in a quiet voice. There was nothing she wanted more in the world right now. Spending time with Eric felt precious.

Turning back, he smiled charmingly. A collection of white tea lights were gathered in his hands. The vampire began to light them and place them around the bathroom.

When he was done, his eyes met hers. "Why not enjoy your bath for a while then. When you are done, I shall be waiting for you."

Jasmine nodded. "OK."

With a flick of his finger, he switched off the main light. The room became bathed in the incandescent glow of soft, flickering candlelight. It made her bath all the more perfect.

Jasmine felt her heart expand. Eric was really going out of his way to spoil her tonight.

The vampire watched her for a moment. The look in his wintry eyes was fathomless, mysterious. And then he walked out without looking back.

Light from the candles stretched, swaying shadows over the walls. It made the room feel more intimate, cosy. Jasmine's body was strumming with arousal. Tonight she was going to let Eric have his wicked way with her. A smile spread across her lips. Her heart did a flip flop in her chest.

She was pretty sure under his sexy mouth and caressing hands, she was going to find heaven. Taking another sip of champagne, she sank down further into the hot water. She felt almost desperate for him at this stage, hungry for his touch. Her body had been on a low, simmering burn of arousal since she had first set eyes on him. It had never stopped once.

It was crazy how different she had become in a few short days. She was usually shy and wary around men. There had never been an attraction. No, that wasn't true. She had never allowed herself to feel attracted to them.

With Eric it was like a fuse had been lit and was burning away at an incredible rate—getting closer and closer to detonation.

The soft, straining notes of Mozart drifted through the open door of the bathroom. She wasn't sure which piece it was, but she recognized the music.

Leaning back, Jasmine rested her head back on the rim of the bath.

Tonight the explosion was going to happen and there was no doubt in her mind they were going to make fireworks.

CHAPTER 26

WRAPPED IN A BIG, LONG, fluffy white robe, she entered the sitting room and found a food cart waiting. Silver metal domes covered the plates hiding what Eric had ordered. The vampire was standing by the window admiring the night-time view. His hands were clasped behind his back. A snowy white shirt now covered his torso. The music was still playing softly in the background.

Confusion bounced through her. It looked like Eric had laid the small table for two. Yet hadn't he said Twitch wasn't joining them? Then it hit her.

Surprise lit her face. "You can eat?"

He had been watching her reflection intently, she realised, as he turned.

One dark eyebrow rose ever so slightly. "I can digest food although it is blood I survive on and need. I can go without eating, but tonight I wish to join you."

Why did this suddenly feel like a date? The vampire seemed to have gone for romance this evening. On the table there was even a tapered red candle sitting in a frosted glass vase, the little flame flickering.

A thickness formed in her throat. It had been a very long time since she had been on a date.

Jasmine placed her half-empty flute of champagne on the table. Touching the lapels of her robe, she fidgeted with them self-consciously. She felt under-dressed.

"I should go put something on." Curling her toes in the plush carpet, she made a move to go.

286

Eric stalked swiftly from the window, coming to stop before her. "No. You look perfect as you are."

His eyes did a slow perusal of her from head to toe. A wicked gleam glinted in his eyes. Did he like knowing she was completely naked beneath? From his expression it seemed he did.

Jasmine swallowed hard. When he looked at her that way, it was hard to say no. She let her hands fall slowly from the robe.

Eric's eyes warmed at her compliance. A ghost of a smile tilted his lips. Moving round the table he held out a chair for her. Smiling her thanks, she slid onto the seat. Nervousness was coursing through her, but she was trying hard not to show it.

"I hope you are hungry." Eric lifted one of the covered domes with a flourish.

Two broiled red lobsters lay on the plate below. A small white pot of what looked like garlic butter accompanied them along with lemon slices.

The smell was tantalising and made her stomach growl.

"I've never had lobster before," Jasmine admitted with an excited grin. "I heard it can get a bit messy."

Eric smoothly took his seat across the table from her. "Indeed it can."

"How do you even open it?"

The vampire shook out his linen napkin and placed it neatly on his lap. "I shall do such things for you."

Jasmine took her own napkin and draped it over her thighs. This all felt so decadent and indulgent. Something she had dreamed about but never had the opportunity to try.

Raising another dome, Eric exposed some more plates. A large mixed bowl of cucumber, tomatoes, and lettuce. Then a dish with a creamy coleslaw. A basket of fluffy white rolls also sat on the cart.

"Please, Jasmine, help yourself." The vampire gestured towards the food. "I shall make a start on opening your lobster."

Reaching over, she helped herself to some of the salad. She was starving and couldn't wait to get tucked in. It looked like he had order a feast.

Eric used a lobster cracker, which looked very much like a nutcracker on the tough shell of the lobster. He was both efficient and quick with an air of practised ease. Soon he had both open and they were digging in.

Jasmine used the fork to dig and scoop out the fleshy meat. She had never had lobster before, but she found she enjoyed the taste. She found the rolls were still warm and the coleslaw was just how she liked it. The salad was fresh and crisp. She was tearing through everything.

Eric used a bowl for bones and shell so she did the same.

They didn't speak. The silence between them was comfortable, a companionable kind of quiet. Mozart continued to serenade them, floating throughout the room.

The vampire retrieved a bottle of champagne from an ice bucket, which sat beside him. Leaning forwards he refilled their glasses.

Jasmine watched at the pale liquid filled her flute. Lifting it up, she took sips to wash the food down.

"This is amazing," she enthused, breaking the quiet.

An indulgent smile crossed Eric's face. "I am very glad it pleases you, my lovely."

He twisted off the lobster claw with graceful ease. Using his fork he began to dig out the meat.

"What are your plans now?" Jasmine asked, as she forked some salad into her mouth.

Curiosity was getting the better of her. Now that their mission was over, she knew the vampires would be moving on. Did they have another case lined up?

She ignored the heavy ache in her chest. Tonight was special and she wasn't going to let her emotions take over. Missing Eric was something she knew she was going to do. Maybe there was a chance they might still see each other?

"There are things yet to be cleared up here before I can head home." Eric said softly in reply. He was idly swirling the contents of his glass around.

Shifting nervously in her seat, she pulled a roll apart. "Where do you live? Here in France?"

"England." Eric's deep baritone voice hesitated for a moment. "Tell me, Jasmine, do you enjoy your job? Do you live in London?"

Jasmine felt a small flicker of disappointment. She knew instantly he was drawing the conversation away from himself. He was always so secretive. After everything they had been through, she had thought he might share a little more with her. Then it dawned on her. Eric wasn't planning anything more than this one night. Why would he share things when he wouldn't be seeing her again?

They were strangers—proverbial ships passing in the night. All that was between them was this raw, primal lust.

Foolishly she had been hoping for more. Eric was exciting like no other male she had ever met. A small sense of desolation settled over her.

She forced out a smile that didn't quite meet her eyes. "Yes, I like using my gift to help people. I have my own flat in London."

"It is usually a traumatic event that awakens such abilities in a sensitive," Eric said. He was probing for answers. Curiosity and a thirst for knowledge, she knew, were in his nature.

Jasmine felt herself pale. She really did not want to talk about what had happened to her. What still haunted her sometimes in her nightmares. Only one other person in her life knew about it and he had promised never to say a word.

Placing her fork down on the table, she could not meet the vampire's penetrating eyes. "Please, Eric. I don't want to talk about it." Her appetite had now fled. Dropping her gaze, she stared blindly at her plate.

Extending his big hand, he covered her own that was resting on the surface. Its warmth was soothing, reassuring. "Very well. I have no wish to make you feel uncomfortable."

Looking up, she found genuine concern shadowing the vampire's gaze.

Jasmine smiled sadly. "Thank you."

His fingers squeezed hers affectionately before he drew his hand away. "Will you be going straight back to work?"

Collecting her champagne once more, she cradled it in her hands. "Probably yes, knowing my boss. I don't mind though."

Eric had also stopped eating. Elbow leaning on the table, he had his chin cupped in one palm. His other hand was fiddling with the stem of his glass.

"So what's it like being a born vampire?" Jasmine asked.

She hadn't forgotten his confession in the freezer. She would likely never forget it. Would he share though?

The thickness of his eyelashes flicked down to hid the emotions in his eyes. "I was hoping you had forgotten I had said such a thing."

She blinked with surprise. "Why?"

The vampire sighed heavily. "This knowledge, my lovely, is not widely known and we like it this way. You caught me in a moment of weakness."

"Do you regret telling me?"

"No," he said without hesitation. His eyelashes fluttered up and he fastened the mesmerizing brightness of his blue eyes on her face. "I believe the information is safe with you. But please do not ask me any more."

Disappointment tumbled through her again. This was not exactly going as she had imagined. Eric had given the evening all the trappings of romance, yet he didn't want to talk personally.

"I guess we both have secrets we want to keep." Tipping up her glass, she took a long gulp. If he wouldn't share, why should she?

"It appears so." He balled up the napkin on his lap and discarded it on the table.

They both sat awkwardly for a moment. Eric seemed just as nervous as she was now. What did you talk about when neither person wanted to give up their secrets? This was all leading to one conclusion. Sex. The vampire had been sweet setting this all up, but they both seemed to be dancing around saying it.

"I keep forgetting to ask, what are you going to do with all the clothes?" Jasmine asked quietly as she placed her glass on the table.

"Clothes?" Confusion tightened his features.

"The ones you bought me."

Dark eyebrows rose with astonishment. "They are yours, Jasmine, to do with as you please."

Jasmine stared at him for a moment. Something like that was way too much. She hadn't missed all the expensive brand tags. He had probably spent a small fortune.

"Eric . . . I . . . That's generous of you, but can't you take them back?"

It did not look like he understood her reluctance to keep them. His lips pursed in slight annoyance. "If you do not want them, then leave them. The staff here at the hotel may have them."

Jasmine blinked at him in bewilderment. "You're not that bothered about it?"

He shrugged one large shoulder. "Taking them back is something I have no time for. Why not accept them as a Christmas gift from me? Would that not make you feel better about keeping them?"

Biting at her lower lip, she considered his words. "I guess. Thank you. You didn't have to treat me to dinner, as well you know."

Gracefully he rose from his chair. Moving around the table he helped her to her feet. He was standing so close. She could feel the heat of his body. The smell of snow and pine trees washed over her.

"After what you have endured the last few days, it is the least I can do."

Jasmine tilted her head so she could look up into his handsome face. Their lips were only inches apart. "But it's not just going to be dinner, is it Eric?"

Lowering his head, he brushed the softness of his cheek against hers. "No. We have unfinished business—you and I."

She licked her suddenly dry lips nervously. "Yes, we do."

"I am offering you one night of pleasure, Jasmine." Eric's breath warmed her skin, his words whispered against her ear. "All it requires is that you submit to me completely in that time."

She shivered at his nearness. She wanted to. Oh God, how she wanted to. Maybe with this darkly handsome vampire, she could finally overcome her fears. Excitement raced through her.

If nothing else, he was offering her pleasure she had never experienced before. She might never seem him again, but she would have the memory of this one night to cherish. It would be one night in Eric's arms.

Desire and fear warred inside her. Could she really give up control to this dominant vampire?

Eric seemed to sense her hesitation. "Trust me to take care of you, kitten. Follow my commands and I shall see to your pleasure. There is nothing for you to fear. In my hands you shall be safe."

The words tickled her ear. No power of persuasion laced them, just heat and longing in there.

Jasmine nodded, surrendering to her desire.

It was one night after all. What harm could come from giving herself over to Eric until the sun rose again? Then he would probably be gone. Jasmine didn't want to live with regret. Life was too short.

"Yes," she said with a shaky voice. "One night."

CHAPTER 27

HE HAD CRAVED HER like no other and now tonight she was to be his. The plan was to pleasure her within an inch of her life. Eric had hated the awkwardness between them. Giving up secrets and knowledge regarding himself was something he found hard to do—probably from centuries of being guarded. The fact he found himself longing to tell her secrets was most disturbing. He could not do that. By tomorrow he would be gone and she would be returning to her life in London. Their paths were unlikely to cross again.

He had already given her more than any other woman in his life so far. Romance was something he never did with the women he fucked. Dinner and talking were too personal, too connecting. Women tended to expect more.

If she had been any other female, she would have already been flat on her back with his cock buried deep. But Jasmine wasn't just another warm, willing body to bed. Eric didn't dare examine why. He pushed the feeling to the back of his mind.

Excitement and a savage need were thumping through his body now. The dinner had been merely another form of foreplay. Since they had met it had all been leading up to this.

Tonight he would show her how much he desired her. He wanted to savour her tight little body wrapped around his cock. It felt like he had waited an eternity to have her.

Eric did not waste any time. Scooping her up, he carried her to the bedroom. Gently he placed her on the large mattress.

She lay still, looking up at him. Wariness and excitement sparkled in her big green eyes. Jasmine was more than desirable. He burned for her.

He dropped his gaze to the knotted belt of her robe then reached down. His hands were shaking and a strange sense of nervousness gripped him. It was something he had never experienced before.

Still, easily and efficiently he undid the belt. Flipping open the sides of the material, he bared her to his hungry eyes. She was just as beautiful as he remembered.

Jasmine was slender with pale limbs, her body young and nubile. Her little breasts were perky firm. Her areolas were dusky rose coloured, tipped with a slightly darker shade for her nipples.

Eric's mouth began to water for a taste of them. He wanted to suck them into his mouth, nip them, bite them.

"Beautiful," he said as he looked down at her.

Jasmine's arms came up to cover her breasts self-consciously. A pretty blush was staining her cheeks.

"No." Gently, he tugged her hands away. "I wish to see your breasts, my lovely."

Keeping her arms at her sides, she lay nervously under his scrutiny. Already the little female's breathing had increased with excitement. Her chest quivered with each quick breath.

Eric crawled onto the bed beside her, still fully dressed. Gently he helped her out of the open robe before tossing it aside. His eyes ran over every inch of her. Reaching out, he ran the tip of his finger over one of her taut nipples. She shuddered in reaction. Her musky arousal was already enticingly pungent in the air.

Eric wanted to take his time enjoying her. He wanted her so wet and ready for him that when he finally fucked her, it would hold no fear. Intense pleasure was what he had promised and he intended to deliver. This little female deserved all he could give her. He would give her everything.

Bending down, he flicked the tip of the other nipple with his tongue.

Jasmine moaned softly. Her body squirmed against his touch. Idly he played in turn with each breast. Letting his fangs descend, he grazed them against her supple skin. Normally he never let a lover see his vampire teeth. Jasmine had already seen them, though, and he knew they excited her.

The need to drink her sweet blood surged through him. An impulse so strong it was almost blinding but still he resisted. When the moment was right, only then would he sink his fangs once more into this lovely girl.

A small gasp left her at the sensation. Her aroused scent grew thicker by the moment. Eric savoured it.

Eyes never leaving her face, he blew gently on one rigid peak. "Tell me want you want, Jasmine."

Her legs were moving restlessly on the duvet. He could sense her building need, her excitement. Languidly he fondled the other tit.

"I-I want you to suck them . . . suck my breasts." Her voice was small and breathy.

She was feeling uncertain, vulnerable—he could understand this, sense it. But he intended to show her there was nothing to fear from his touch.

With one hard lick, he suckled a nipple in between his lips. Whirling his tongue around the tip in his warm, wet mouth, he grazed it with his teeth, his fangs. He was careful not to break her skin with their sharpness.

Jasmine moaned in response and wiggled against him. She grabbed his head, tugging at his hair hard.

Eric relished the bit of pain. Chuckling against her breast, he resumed his pleasuring. Eric began to feast on her ripe, little tits. Her small nipples enchanted him. He teased them back and forth, licking, nipping, and suckling.

Eventually he was forced to put his fangs away. Biting her was becoming too much of a growing temptation. It was something he was drawing out.

Soon she was withering in earnest against the mattress. Her legs entwined with his as she rubbed her lower half against his hip.

The zipper of his jeans was already painfully pressing into his erection. It strained against the denim. Eric ignored it, fully focused on the woman before him. He gave Jasmine no mercy as he continued to pleasure her with his mouth and his touch. She seemed almost mindless—a slave to sensation.

One of his hands skimmed down her stomach to her navel. He could feel her muscles quivering. Leaning up, he teased her mouth with light kisses.

She was still a little nervous. He could sense it the moment his hand had moved lower. Tenseness had invaded her limbs. He soothed her with caresses, stoking her need. Little mewls and noises were escaping her throat. Soon, he would have her relaxed once more. There would be nothing in her mind to scare her. Instead she would only feel.

"I intend to taste you now, my lovely." Eric said the words against her parted lips. Champagne still flavoured their fullness.

He nibbled gently on her lower lip. Taking it between his teeth, he nipped at it as he had seen her do a hundred times before briefly sucking it into his mouth.

Her eyes were clouded with desire. They widened in surprise when he ventured slowly down her body.

Placing a kiss on each nipple, he ran his tongue down between her breasts. Reaching her navel, he circled it teasingly. He loved tasting her skin with his tongue. Before the night was out, he would lick every inch of her.

His fingers traced the crescent moon-shaped birthmark on her hip. It thrilled him to find it. He placed a kiss there and then traced it with his tongue.

Jasmine was watching him through half-closed eyes. Her breathing was shallow with growing excitement. She knew what he intended to do and he could see she wanted it. A tiger-like smile curved Eric's lips.

Parting her thighs gently, he hooked them over his shoulders. The folds of her little cunt were pink, wet, and glistening. It just begged to be tasted.

The muscles in her legs and thighs trembled and jerked. He knew this was an involuntary reaction. It pleased him to see her body's innocent response to his attentions. This reminded him to take it slowly.

Eric nipped playfully at her inner thighs then trailed kisses from her knee downwards to her womanhood. Her nervousness and excitement were a heady concoction to his senses.

Bending forwards he inhaled her enticing scent. "Such an alluring smell."

His big hands curved over the cheeks of her bottom. Kneading them gently, he rubbed his cheek against her mound. "I am going to fuck you with my mouth, Jasmine, and then I shall fuck you with my cock."

She began to shake. Eric raised his gaze from her cunt. The pulse in her neck fluttered with excitement. Her little breasts quivered with each of her erratic breaths.

The girl seemed lost for words. Anticipation and anxiety glittered in her green eyes. Locking his own onto hers, he lowered his head.

He trailed his tongue up the inside of her trembling thigh. Nuzzling the curls at the juncture, he licked her slit in one long swipe. Her honey taste hit his tongue. Eric groaned.

Jasmine gasped and her hips rose slightly from the bed in surprise.

Seeking her clit, he circled it eagerly with the tip of his tongue.

Her hips rose again to meet his mouth, hands desperately clutched the sheets beneath her. The increased beat of her heart filled his ears. He could hear it thumping away crazily in her chest.

A half-gasp, half-moan left her lips. Holding her down, he mercilessly teased and pleasured her. Lapping at her slick folds of her opening, Eric thrust his tongue inside. Already she was soaking for him.

Slowly he inserted a finger. Her channel was slick, hot, and wet. He pushed his finger forwards, until he buried it to the hilt. It felt divine. Her little sheath tightened around it. He tongued her clit at the same time before rolling it with his tongue.

She went wild. A small, keening sound escaped Jasmine's throat. Her hips writhed against the bed.

Eric began to suck on her clit while at the same time easing another finger inside her. She was so fucking tight–almost virginal. It made him crave her even more.

This time a small wail left her lips. Her fingers tunnelled through his tousled hair. Holding on tensely, she held him against her.

He made a muffled sound of approval.

Slowly he began to move his fingers within her. Steadily he built a rhythm that had her pumping her hips frantically in the air. It was all the encouragement Eric needed.

He suckled harder, thrusting his fingers deeper. When her inner muscles started the clench around his finger, he tongued her clit.

Every muscle in her body tightened, as her release began to crash over her. Nuzzling her inner thigh, Eric sank his fangs deep.

Jasmine screamed as she orgasmed. Holding her hips down and still, he drank her potent blood. Its sweetness coursed down his eager throat.

A sob left her and Eric knew he had heightened her pleasure with his bite.

Lapping at the puncture marks, he gently lowered her leg to the bed. Stroking her sides and stomach, he waited for her to recover.

"My Jasmine, you are so beautiful when you come, so exquisite in your pleasure." He nuzzled her with his lips, brushing the corners of her mouth.

Eric knew she would be able to taste herself on them. Darting his tongue into her parting lips, he couldn't resist letting her sample her honeyed flavour.

She moaned, sucking on his tongue. Mouth clinging to his, the kiss became a lazy tangle of lips. Pulling back he surveyed her face. Her lovely green eyes were closed. She lay limply on the bed, her chest heaving as she tried to catch her breath.

Her lips were swollen from his kisses. A pretty pink flush had washed through her skin. Her nipples were reddened and distended and still wet from his attention.

Eric's cock was painfully hard. He wanted to flip her over, sink himself into her heat and pound her into the mattress. It was a testament to his restraint that he did not. Even now, he did not have full grasp of his emotions. He needed to fuck her now, though. Eric knew he could no longer wait.

CHAPTER 28

JASMINE'S LEGS WERE SPRAWLED wide open. She felt Eric lazily nuzzling the curls on her mound again. Her whole body was vibrating from her mind-blowing climax.

She felt sleepy and sated. Snow and pine, Eric's scent, wove itself around her dazed senses. Jasmine was still floating on a cloud of contentment.

The mattress moved and she knew Eric had climbed from the bed. The sound of clothes rustling reached her ear. Then a belt being undone followed by a zipper being lowered.

"I am not done with you yet, Jasmine." The vampire's sexy voice curled down her spine. "That was only a taste of what is to come."

Opening dazed eyes she surveyed him. "Only a taste?"

Eric's eyes roved greedily over her with lust. He stood gloriously naked. Cock jutting proudly from a nest of dark curls. It was long and thick. The tip already glistened with clear liquid.

His hair was mussed, in a just rolled out of bed way. A pair of high black heels hung from his fingers.

"The moment I first saw you in your heels, I wanted to fuck you in them." His voice was a deep, seductive caress. "I have desired little else."

Jasmine laughed breathlessly. "Seriously?"

He knew she hated the damn things. Being fucked in them was the last thing she had imagined.

"Please." Eric waggled his eyebrows at her. It was such a funny thing to see him do, she laughed. It seemed this vamp had a playful side.

"OK," she told him, still laughing. This was one night. Jasmine could bear them just for him.

He prowled towards to the bed and sat on the edge. When he patted the spot beside him encouragingly, she stretched out her feet. If he wanted her to wear them, he was going to have to put them on.

Her actions didn't seem to perturb him. Taking hold of her feet one by one, the vampire caressed them with his hands. Then gently he slid on the shoes.

"Not on the bed." He offered his hand as he stood. "Near the window, kitten."

Wariness rippled through her.

"B-but won't people see us?" she asked as he tugged her to her feet. It felt strange being completely naked in a pair of heels. Jasmine felt both sexy and embarrassed.

Being nude in front of a man for the first time was also making her feel awkward. Even after what Eric had just done to her, she felt the urge to cover up and hide. Jasmine felt shy and couldn't meet his eyes.

"The windows are tinted," the vampire assured her soothingly. "No one can see in, but we can see out. Trust me. I would not lie about this to you."

He enclosed his arms around her. Jasmine found herself hugged up against his delicious, naked, hard length. The large erection he was sporting pressed against her belly.

Her taut, sensitive nipples rubbed his chest. A jolt of desire shot through her groin. Biting her lip, she tried not to groan.

"I trust you."

With a finger under her chin, he nudged it up to bestow a hot and hungry kiss on her lips. Their tongues duelled, entwined. She clung to his shoulders for support as all shyness slipped away.

He was the first to break away. The intensity of his bright, icy blue eyes searched her face for a moment. Then a smile of satisfaction touched his lips.

Taking her hand, Eric guided her to the window. It was ceiling to floor, with a glass door leading out onto a small balcony she hadn't noticed before.

The lights of Paris shone in the darkness. White sheets of sparkling snow covered everything as far as they eye could see.

Jasmine felt self-conscious standing directly in front of it. Even though he had said no one could look in, she felt nervous—and yet a small thrill of exhilaration was fizzing through her blood.

The vampire stood behind her. He nuzzled the side of her neck teasingly. "Are the lights not beautiful, Jasmine?"

"Y-yes." She tilted her head, granting him better access. The soft grazing points of his fangs dragged lightly across her skin.

Jasmine couldn't help but moan. Every time she felt his fangs touch her flesh, it felt incredible.

"Bend over, my lovely."

At his quiet, commanding words, she met his gaze in their reflection in the glass. Eric was watching her patiently. The intensity of his icy blue eyes was almost spellbinding.

When she didn't move, he raised his hands. Starting at the tops of her shoulders, his fingertips caressed slowly down her arms.

Her breath quickened. She found she was unable to tear her gaze away.

The vampire stroked light patterns over her wrists and the backs of her hands. Somehow he had moved, closing the gap between them. His cock was now nestled against her back.

Excitement was spiralling out of control inside her. Squeezing her thighs together, she tried to elevate a throb that had started deep within her womanhood.

Eric placed her hands flat against the glass in front of her. The coolness of the window eased her heated skin. She was doing her best trying to keep her heart in her chest. It was suddenly beating too fast.

Taking hold of her hips, he towed them back, until she was bent at the waist. The vampire's hands caressed her back. He petted, stroked, and soothed her. All the while he never said a word.

Jasmine stared out into the darkness. The Eiffel Tower was lit up in the distance like a Christmas tree, the lights twinkling in the night sky.

"Part your legs."

Without a word she obeyed Eric's order. She widened her stance, bracing herself against the window. This helped stop her falling with the high heels on.

"Hmm. Good girl." His deep, baritone had deepened even further. "I love your delectable little derrière." Large, firm hands began to massage each globe.

Jasmine sank her teeth into her lower lips. A shiver of desire quaked through her. She still couldn't believe she was doing this.

Eric wanted to fuck her until nothing else mattered. He needed to claim her.

She was naked apart from those black high heels. Her little arse up in the air, body stretched out as she bent over hands braced against the glass.

He had never seen a more beautiful or captivating sight. Eric wanted to mark her as his own. The urge to wipe away her first and only sexual experience rocked through him. He wanted to teach her the intimacies between a man and a woman. Initiate her properly into the pleasures of the flesh.

"I'm going to fuck you now, Jasmine," he said softly.

Gently he ran a finger between her legs. The slickness coated his fingers. She was sopping wet. Finally she was ready to receive him.

Taking his shaft in hand, he moved up behind her. Eric gritted his teeth as the urge to plunge into her overwhelmed him. He resisted. Jasmine deserved gentleness the first time they fucked.

She tensed when he pushed his rock-hard cock inside her. He knew he was big and had no wish to hurt or frighten her. Finally now she was going to be his.

Jasmine felt Eric rock himself slowly in and out of her. He had hold of her hips, controlling their movements. When she slowly began to relax, he slid himself deeper.

"Yes, that is it," he crooned softly. "You will take all of me. Relax, kitten."

He carried on rocking into her, a little more each time. She knew she was tight and he was trying to be gentle.

She could see his reflection mirrored in the glass of the window. His face was taut with desire and restraint. He looked large, dangerous, and sexy as hell. She revelled in the knowledge that this vamp wanted her. The feeling of his slow penetration was making her needy. Inch by inch was becoming torture.

Jasmine wanted to feel him stretching her, filling her completely. She now craved it, needed it. Moaning, she thrust her hips back against him wanting more.

His grip on her hips tightened.

"Be still," he growled through clenched teeth. "I have no wish to hurt you."

Jasmine found suddenly she did not want to go slowly. Now that her initial fear was not ruling her, she wanted him badly. She desired, no needed it all.

"Please, Eric," she whined.

Thrusting her hips back again silently, she dared him to go deeper. It was all the invitation he needed.

With a strangled groan, Eric thrust forwards, burying himself balls deep.

A long, throaty moan left Jasmine's lips. The whole, hard length of him was inside her now. She could feel it pulsing, twitching, in the tightness of her sheath. It was a little uncomfortable, but her body adjusted to the intrusion.

Eric was not moving. He stood his groin flush against her bottom and held himself within her. His fingers were clenching and unclenching where he grasped her hips.

She could sense he was holding himself in check. Knew he did not want to hurt her.

"You're so tight, it is almost indescribable." Eric's voice was a thick growl. It was almost unrecognisable. "Tonight I will show you the pleasures of the flesh."

Jasmine felt him gently caress her sides.

"The only thing you will remember is my cock buried deep. My hands, mouth, lips pleasuring you. It will blot out the painful past. This is my gift to you." Persuasion beat in every word.

His hands settled back on her hips. Slowly at first, he began to thrust in and out of her. The glide of his cock tore a small mewl of pleasure from her throat.

She curled her fingers against the glass. Every time he drove into her, it pushed her forwards. She had to brace her arms straight to stop herself from being shoved up against the window.

Eric kept to slow, measured movements, ruthlessly controlling the rhythm. The whole time his gaze never wavered from watching her reflection.

All she could do was stare lustfully back. It was all such a turn-on. Eric fucking her felt amazing.

The vampire's icy power rose around her, like a growing frost. Its coldness swept over her heated skin.

Jasmine could feel her body tightening. Her inner muscles clamped down hard on his thrusting cock. Eric moaned and began to thrust harder.

"Yes." His voice was uneven. "Feel me taking you, fucking you."

She withered back against him. Her hips moved to meet each movement of his hips. The slap of his flesh against her own just drove her excitement higher.

Ice crystals began to form and spread across the window glass before her. It glistened like tiny, bejewelled, crystalline kisses. The chill pressed against her palms.

The tension inside her was building. She felt Eric's chest brush her back. Then his mouth landed on her neck. The sting of his fangs pierced her supple flesh.

An explosion came from deep within her. Jasmine screamed as her body contracted around his.

Eric began to plunge harder and faster. Any control he had desperately been clinging to had now slipped away.

With a snarl he released her neck. She felt the rough lick of his tongue on her skin. He did not lessen his pace. The grip on her hips became almost bruising, as he continued to pound into her. His movements were now wild, frantic.

Jasmine's legs had gone weak. His strong hands were the only thing keeping her up now.

The air became frosty, electric. The sharpness of a frigid wind soared around them and nipped at her naked flesh with a wintry sting.

Eric suddenly roared as he came in one long, hard shudder. Chest heaving, he struggled for control, collapsing half over her. His hot chest pressed to her chilled back.

A shiver of delight tingled through her. She was still afloat in the bliss of her own release.

One of the vampire's arms was around her waist, the other he had placed on the window next to one of hers. The brush of his lips teased her shoulder blades.

His power fell away. The chill in the room faded and the warmth was restored.

A small moan left Jasmine's lips as his spent member slipped from her body. The evidence of their joining was wet and sticky between her thighs.

Gently Eric lowered her onto the floor. The plush carpet met her naked back.

"You are so exquisite." His voice was deep and thickened. Lying beside her, he used the tips of his fingers to swirl patterns on her collar bone.

Dazedly she basked in the afterglow. Her eyes were closed and coloured lights were awash dancing behind her eyelids. Never in her wildest dreams, had she thought it was going to be like that. A sense of contentment engulfed her.

The smell of sex and their combined scent was heavy in the air. It stirred an ember of desire. Jasmine felt her body tighten with an eager, primal need.

Eyelashes fluttering up, she met the vampire's tender look. "Eric."

The length of his body was tucked into her side. She could already feel his cock hardening against her thigh.

"I have not yet finished with you, kitten." A seductive smile curved his lips. "I promised you the whole night, did I not? And we are merely getting started."

CHAPTER 29

ERIC WATCHED THE GIRL AS she slept an exhausted sated sleep. She was more than he had ever dreamed. The lust that had been burning inside him for her had not been extinguished. It had only grown hotter. Why this was, he could not explain.

The fact that his powers had slipped from his control while he had been taking her also excited him. That had never happened before.

His bite mark was apparent on her neck. Eric felt a surge of savage pleasure when he saw it. It had been almost a primal need to mark her as his. The thought of the other mark on her left inner thigh beneath the thick duvet excited him even more.

One night, he now knew, would never be enough. His body was again hardened and ready to take her. He wanted to sink his cock into the welcoming heat of her tight little cunt again.

He had already fucked her in so many positions, he had no doubt she would awaken sore. Eric knew there were, though, so many more and pleasurable ones yet to try.

He wanted to possess Jasmine with a strange feral urge he had never encountered before. Not even once with the many women he had bedded throughout his long existence.

Eric knew he could not linger, however. Much still was left to do now that Marcel had been taken out of the picture. He and his team had loose ends to tie up.

But when all was neatly wrapped up to a satisfying conclusion, he would seek the girl out. A smile curved his mouth. For now he would leave her with memories of this night.

Jasmine awoke with a sly smile of contentment on her face. Her body was still heavy with fulfilment. A pleasurable ache tugged deep inside. Eric had fucked her thoroughly so many times she had lost count. He had been insatiable—as if he hadn't been able to get enough of her.

They had never even made it to the bed. He had given her so many mind-blowing orgasms, her voice became hoarse from her screams and cries.

The only time she had laid down was out of pure exhaustion. Even then, the vampire had crawled under the blankets with her. His big, muscled chest pressed to her back as he spooned her. It had been strangely comforting.

She had fallen asleep to the gentle caress of his hands over her skin. He had wiped the last of her fear from her mind. She knew she would not let the past haunt her any more. Thanks to him she felt lighter, suddenly freer.

Jasmine rolled over and discovered she was alone. The other side of the bed had long been empty judging from the coolness of the sheets.

She was not surprised. Eric had told it would be one night of passion.

A heaviness settled in her chest. A lump formed in her throat as she felt the sting of tears behind her eyes. She had thought as least he would have said good-bye. Even maybe shared breakfast with her.

But then he had shared so little of himself. She barely knew anything about him at all. He was a cold, handsome ghost. For all she knew, Eric wasn't his real name.

A long sigh left her lips. Like it or not, he had taken a little piece of her heart.

Just then, her eyes focused on the beautiful red rose that was laying against his pillow. Reaching out she brushed one of the soft petals. A note sat beside it.

Forgive me for leaving you Jasmine, but I have business to attend to. Last night you were more than any fantasy I could have imagined.
Until we meet again,
Eric

Jasmine traced the boldly handwritten words with her fingertip. A watery smile curved her lips. A gentleman until the last minute.

Just with a glance, she knew all his clothes were gone. The trunk with all the medieval weapons had vanished. Several open suitcases stood awaiting her.

Eric, it seemed, had been considerate enough to leave her something in which to carry the clothes he had bought her.

The place was so quiet. She knew both vampires had disappeared. There hadn't even been a chance to say good-bye to Raoul.

Eric had mentioned sorting out loose ends. Did they mean to go after the doctor who had evaded them? Would they pick apart Marcel's empire now that he was gone?

She hoped there was a way Claude aka Kevin could be found. Maybe Eric would let her team know if he did. Twitch was finally safe. Marcel and Pierre were dead.

It was time to go home.

The End

Thank you for reading **FROSTBITE by Claire Marta**

If you enjoyed this book please consider letting me know in a way of a review. Writing them means more to an author than you know and helps other readers hear about the series. Below are links to my fan pages and other social media if you wish to follow me.

I took great pleasure in starting Jasmine's story and I can promise you there are more things to look forwards to ahead in the series!

Claire Marta

Find me at:

Facebook
http://m.facebook.com/Clairemartbooks/
Twitter
@ClaireMBooks
Instagram
@clairemartawritesbooks

ABOUT THE AUTHOR

CLAIRE MARTA HAS A PASSION for writing and finally took the plunge getting published with her first book Frostbite.

A native Brit, she lives in Italy with her husband and daughter. When she is not writing and drinking copious amounts of tea, she enjoys taking photos of her adoptive country, trying to stay fit with running, reading amazing books and being a stay at home mother.

37645957R00188

Printed in Great Britain
by Amazon